Boyfriend

Makeover

River Jaymes

The Boyfriend Makeover
The Boyfriend Chronicles Book 3

Cover art by the Killion Group

ISBN-13: 978-0-9912807-5-9

Chapter One

Noah knew he was in trouble the moment his reason for attending tonight's fundraiser, namely one Walter McKinney, smiled. Yes, *smiled.*

Unfortunately, his expression matched the cold, vacant-eyed vibe of the sand shark lazily swimming past in the aquarium behind the portable yet fully stocked bar.

"I don't know if I can swing a donation this year, Noah." The sixty-three-year-old CEO of McKinney Industries leaned against the counter. White LED lights lit the inside of the ultra-modern, large acrylic-block furniture arranged to form the bar, the otherworldly glow reflecting off the blue waters of the massive shark exhibit beyond. "I'd love to, but..."

"But?"

"Times are tough."

The twenty-thousand-dollar Kiton tuxedo the man wore suggested otherwise.

"Walter," Noah said, forcing a smile as he carefully waded through their subtext-fueled conversation, "I know your girlfriend has a special place in her heart for the Front Street Clinic."

Translation: Her cousin is gay and everyone knows you treat him like shit. Your annual contribution is one of the reasons she keeps letting you back in her pants.

"Glenda once told me," Noah went on, "that her dream was to ensure every homeless person in San Francisco had access to proper medical care."

"My girlfriend is a bleeding heart for vagrants."

"Including those who have HIV."

"Which wouldn't be a problem if you people kept it in your pants."

You people.

Noah bit his lip against a sharp retort, ignoring the insult. "Your donation will help Glenda's dream come true."

Walter's salt-and-pepper eyebrows of monstrous proportions rose a fraction of an inch. Noah checked the urge to whip out a pair of tweezers and divide the unibrow in two.

"Glenda also dreams of a day when every stray dog has an owner who treats their pet as well as she treats Coco." As Walter spoke the pampered Pomeranian's name, his lips twisted in distaste. "The reality is, that will never happen," he said with a look that spoke volumes.

In other words: *Nice try, but no hand-rolled Cuban cigar, Noah Tanner.*

"Coco is lovely," Noah lied.

"Coco is a menace."

"She's known for being very...affectionate."

"She's *known* for humping every leg within a twenty-mile radius."

"And *you* are known for your generosity," Noah returned smoothly. He ignored the murmur of conversations around him as he went on. "Case in point..." He gestured at the Bay Aquarium—the venue of choice for this year's Humane Society Pawpawpalooza—and the designer-clad guests milling about. "As usual, you've outdone yourself putting on the gala."

He employed a dramatic pause, hoping to bring home a win. Because, holy deity on a stick, the clinic needed him to close this deal.

As he held his breath, Noah focused on the dimly lit, beautifully decorated cavernous room in an attempt to appear adequately impressed. The garlicky scent of sizzling shrimp scampi filled the air.

After a non-response from Walter, Noah tried again. "And we both know the Front Street Clinic offers vital services—"

"Vital?"

"*Vital*," he replied, "just like the Humane Society."

Because homeless people deserved to be treated as humanely as, Lord, please, maybe even a little better than, homeless animals.

"Maybe." Walter's smile grew wider, an act that somehow managed to increase the creepy vibe. "I heard you and your little band of queer doctor friends didn't qualify for the People First grant this year."

Translation: *Admit it, you asshole, you're desperate. Now lick my shoes and repent of your fagotty ways.*

"Is that true?" Walter went on.

"That's true," he murmured.

"Too bad." His expression suggested otherwise. The older man's smile seemed almost gleeful now. "Losing those funds must have been a low...*blow*."

Noah resisted the urge to roll his eyes.

Seriously, the abuse of clichés he put up with in the name of his favorite charity. Thing was, for the most part, he loved his not-job. He loved attending upscale events where the beautiful people socialized and the alcohol flowed freely. He lived for the challenge of smooth-talking the rich and powerful into giving for the greater good.

But people like Walter?

Noah sighed and watched the sand shark swim past again.

Maybe he should get an actual paid position instead of donating all his time schmoozing the wealthy in order to keep the clinic's doors open. If he had to put up with the occasional homo-slanderous comments, condescension, and passive-aggressive bullshit, he should at least be putting his degree to work and getting benefits in return. Benefits like better health insurance, a fat 401(k), and disability.

If he could write off the occasional bar tab as a business expense, all the better.

But...he couldn't.

"We'll manage," Noah finally said. "We always do." He wouldn't rest until he'd succeeded. "Especially with the help of our benevolent regular sponsors." He sent the man a winning smile. "Benevolent sponsors like McKinney Industries."

The sound that escaped Walter's lips could only be described as a *you'll have to try harder* harrumph.

The bartender handed Noah his drink and turned to take Mr. McKinney's order. Noah considered his next move as he eyed the crowd in suits and dresses critically and took a sip from his glass. The sea breeze contained too much cranberry and grapefruit juice in relation to the vodka, especially in light of the asshole-y nature of his current company.

"As I said," McKinney continued as the bartender handed him his whiskey sour and moved on, "times are tough."

"Even tougher for those living on the streets."

"The Lord helps those who help themselves."

Ohmygod, really? Well, he could quote ancient texts of debatable authorship, too.

"He who gives to the poor will never want," Noah recited. "But he who shuts his eyes will have many curses."

And Noah Tanner, badass, queenly son of a not-bitch was known for his creative cursing.

Walter frowned, clearly expecting Noah to burst into flames for daring to quote the verse. But Noah already knew what hell was like, and this?

This didn't even come close.

"Are you sure you're properly armed for a theological debate?" Walter asked.

"That's not the debate I came to have."

"Yes, your little clinic," he said, an empty smile on his face. "It would be a shame if you had to shut it down."

A cold sweat broke out along Noah's back. The clinic closing wouldn't be a *shame*, it would be a horrendous tragedy. An epic tragedy, just like Rick's death.

Rick.

Noah's stomach lurched, and the surge of grief threatened to make him hurl. Noah's definition of hell? Going to bed every night knowing that treatment had been available but not *accessible* to a down-on-his-luck, HIV-positive young adult.

Close, yet so far away.

Just like the McKinney donation.

With renewed determination, Noah turned to his opponent. "Mr. McKinney—"

"Yes, Mr. Tanner?" he said drolly.

Noah cranked up the wattage of his smile, only to be interrupted by a female voice calling from a good distance behind.

"Noah!"

Swiveling on his barstool, he spied the couple threading their way through the crowd.

Well...damn.

When Noah had given his event coordinator two tickets to tonight's gala, he hadn't counted on

Savannah bringing her *brother*—half brother, to be specific. Her tall, dark, and unfairly-blessed-by-the-gods brother.

A man who made Noah want to thank deities he didn't believe in.

Ky's dark brown hair reached his collar and managed to look adorably rugged and damn sexy at the same time. He'd defied the crowd's designer preferences and donned black jeans, which were good, and a sleek, black leather jacket, which was beautiful. Unfortunately, both pieces had been paired with a shirt that was...less than fabulous.

Not quite an epic tragedy, but a fashion tragedy nonetheless.

The man's expression, however, left no doubt. He wasn't clueless as much as he just didn't *care*.

"Savannah"—as the petite blonde drew closer, Noah adopted his first real smile of the night—"you look lovely, as usual."

He shifted his gaze to her brother, hoping to muster a suitable greeting beyond an embarrassing dribble of drool. He settled on a cautious nod.

"I've been looking all over for you." She came to a stop in front of him. "Do you have a minute?"

"Uhm." How was Noah supposed to work his magic on Walter with Kyland Davis standing around with a guarded expression, looking so...so...unhappy to be here and in need of a makeover and a blow job? Not necessarily in that order. Noah wasn't picky.

Except for when he was.

"I need to discuss something with you." Her earnest green eyes settled on Noah. "It's really important."

He mentally sighed. Saying no to her sweet face was impossible.

Noah turned back to the man to his left. "Do you mind, Walter?"

"Not at all."

"I'd like to continue our little chat later." Because he had every intention of getting into the man's wallet, in the name of justice and health care for all.

Rick's memory deserved nothing less than his best efforts.

The shark grin returned. "I'm looking forward to it."

I bet you are.

"Me, too." Noah faked a pleasant expression.

He watched the head of the McKinney family fortunes saunter off before facing the brother-and-sister team again.

"Thanks again for the tickets to the gala." Savannah's pixie cut framed her delicate face. Her cocktail dress had zero cleavage and showed less leg on her youthful frame than the one covering the seventy-year-old treasurer of the local Humane Society. "And you were right, as always." She slid onto the barstool next to him. "Seeing the aquarium all decked out is giving me lots of ideas for this year's Bachelor Bid."

"You and your sister did a fabulous job on last year's."

"But Sierra couldn't come out from Texas to help me this time." Worry flickered through her green eyes. "So this is the first one I'm doing alone."

"Savannah"—Noah briefly touched her arm in reassurance—"this is the third event we've worked on together. I trust you."

The bartender appeared, and Noah waited while the siblings decided on their order.

He hadn't been lying about trusting her. Hiring the fresh-faced recent college grad to help plan the upcoming Bachelor Bid—the annual fundraiser for the Front Street Clinic's housing fund—had been a given. Last year's failure to raise enough money during the event hadn't been due to her considerable efforts. And this year, Noah planned to fix the failure.

Well, just as soon as his libido recovered from the presence of Savannah's brother. The bartender handed the man a mug of beer.

"Dr. Davis," Noah said to the surgeon hovering just beyond his sister's shoulder. "It's a pleasure to see you again."

Did the man's mouth just twitch? And if so, was that supposed to be a greeting?

Either way, Savannah didn't give him time to respond. "I had to drag Ky along tonight."

"Really?" Noah said, faking surprise.

She slanted a look at her brother. "He doesn't like getting dressed up."

Against his will, Noah's gaze dropped to Ky's cowboy boots, the tips peeking from beneath the hem of his jeans. Noah had only been around the surgeon twice before, but both times he'd worn the scuffed leather as though carrying a piece of Texas along for the ride. And, seriously, the indecent things the footwear brought to Noah's mind...

How had he reached thirty years of age without realizing he had a secret cowboy fixation?

"In the interest of full disclosure," Noah said to the surgeon, "I have to tell you that I'm forming an illicit attachment to your boots."

As predicted, a look of disapproval appeared on Ky's face, and his sister's lips quirked in amusement.

"Sounds like a personal problem," Ky murmured.

Noah laughed. "I have plenty of personal problems," he said, stupidly thrilled the surgeon had finally joined the conversation. "My obsession with footwear, however, doesn't rank high on the list."

"You have a list?" he asked.

"Doesn't everybody?"

Ky's answer came in the form of an unimpressed stare—what color were his eyes, anyway? Brown? Hazel?—that lasted two beats.

Although their interactions had been very limited, Noah liked to think they'd established a working relationship. A relatively simple working relationship where Noah continued to toss his admittedly ridiculous comments in the man's direction and Ky continued to pretend he didn't find his outrageous ways amusing.

Either that or the surgeon wasn't pretending. Noah wasn't sure.

"Hard to believe, I know," Savannah said. "But those Stetson boots aren't the only shoes he owns. They're the only shoes he *wears*. Outside the OR, of course. I'm lucky I convinced him to put on the jacket."

"Nice choice," Noah said. The black leather coat was simple yet ultra-sleek—not a word he'd normally apply to the surgeon.

"Doesn't it look good on him?" she said.

Noah bit back an inappropriate reply of an overtly sexual nature. In the presence of a jawline crafted by the gods and covered with attractive scruff, he should be commended for his restraint.

"I suspect everything looks good on him." Noah smiled at the deliberately blank look on Ky's face before turning to Savannah. "Was the jacket a gift from you?"

"Me and Sierra."

"Ah, Sierra," Noah said with a smile. "Your delightfully evil twin."

Savannah was sweet and earnest. Sierra, on the other hand, was sharp-tongued, opinionated, and endearingly devious. If Noah had been straight and into monogamy, he would have married her instantly.

"My sister is definitely..." Savannah gave a magnanimous shrug.

"Intriguing?" Noah suggested. "My sister from another mother?"

Ky's lips twitched—in amusement, perhaps? "A handful," he said above the rim of his mug.

"A *delightful* handful," Noah added.

A soft huff from the surgeon managed to convey disagreement, resignation, and a hefty dose of affection, all at the same time. He clearly had the maximum expression with the minimum of effort down pat.

"Delightful on a *good* day, with a penchant for trouble on the rest." Ky propped his foot on the bottom rung of Savannah's barstool.

Noah was inconveniently hit with the urge to dress him up like a mannequin in a window. Against his will, his gaze returned to the leather toes of the cowboy boots. Perhaps the window of Abercrombie and Fitch—

Ky leaned an elbow against the bar and his jacket shifted, revealing a truly awful belt buckle worthy of any rodeo star.

Noah suppressed a grimace. Maybe Tex's Farm and Feed store window would be more appropriate.

"There's something I wanted to talk to you about," Savannah said. "Essentially, this." She waved her hand along the length of her brother's frame, the vision sending a frisson of excitement up Noah's spine. "We need your help."

Ky shot his sister a warning look. "Savannah—"

"Please," she went on, ignoring her brother.

Noah's eyes got caught on shoulders so broad a man could get lost licking his way from one side to the other.

"My help," Noah repeated dumbly.

The help *he* wanted to provide would entail tongue. Lots and lots of tongue. On various and sundry naked body parts. Although that probably wasn't what Savannah had in mind for her brother.

"After blackmailing him into participating in the Bachelor Bid, now I have to convince him to get ready," she said.

"I am ready," her brother grunted out.

Noah couldn't get past the sexy speed bump created by the first part of Savannah's statement. "Blackmail?"

A wary look crossed Ky's face.

Savannah's eyes lit up with humor. "Yes."

Before he could stop the words, Noah leaned forward and stage whispered, "Did the blackmail involve pictures?"

Video would be better. And if there *was* a God, the video would involve the dude in various states of undress and would be accessible on the wonderful World Wide Web. Preferably YouTube, but a Tumblr gif or two would suffice.

"They're *childhood* photos," Ky said wryly.

Noah's shoulders deflated. That was it, then. Definitive proof there was no God.

"*Unique* childhood photos," Savannah added with a smile. "Anyway, I was hoping you could help my brother get ready to be auctioned off for a date."

"Ready how?"

"Haircut, new clothes, that sort of thing."

"You're talking about a makeover." Noah's heart did a joyful cartwheel in celebration.

Over the years, he'd logged a lot of hours on his knees—and the *God please* on repeat in his head had been of the pornographic variety, not that of penance. Apparently all those prayers he hadn't actually uttered were now being answered anyway.

Except...

The look on Ky's face brought Noah's thoughts to a halt. As much as he'd love the chance to take Ky and up the hotness factor, he wasn't into torturing people. Unless they begged for it, and then he was all in.

Noah cleared his throat, crushed he felt obligated to turn this chance of a lifetime down. "I don't think that's a very good plan."

The disappointment in Savannah's eyes almost made Noah change his mind.

And then she turned to her brother and sent him a pleading look, holding up her empty plate. "Will you fetch me a few more stuffed mushrooms?"

Ky ticked his gaze to the crowd of people around the appetizer table and then back to his sister's face before blowing out a breath in defeat.

"Fine," the man drawled, taking her plate. "I'll be right back."

Savannah smiled in thanks and waited until he was out of earshot before turning back to Noah.

"Please," she said clutching his arm. "This is really important."

"Uh..." He glanced down at the fingers squeezing his bicep. As much as he agreed that Ky's belt buckle and choice of shirt were a disappointment, the serious tone of her voice seemed way out of proportion to the request. "We aren't exactly brokering a peace talk here, you know," he said gently.

"Ky has no idea how much he needs this."

He inhaled slowly, fortifying his will.

"As much as it pains me to say this," he said, "I'm not into tying people down and doing a makeover against their will." Damn, he shouldn't have used the bondage words, because now his nervous system was buzzing with electric energy. "Your brother seems, well, *reluctant.*"

He silently congratulated himself on the restrained choice of word.

"He'll cooperate. And it's not just about the clothes." Savannah's gaze settled on Ky across the room, worry lighting her eyes. "He works too hard, Noah," she said softly, and dammit, his heart gave a painful catch at the look on her face. "All he *does* is work," she went on. "He rarely goes out. I can't remember the last time he had a date. He doesn't hang out with friends. I don't think he's even *made* any friends since he moved to San Francisco."

One beat passed and Noah couldn't help himself.

"Why did he?" His curiosity regarding the surgeon-slash-cowboy knew no bounds. "Move, that is."

"It's my fault he left home," Savannah said with a guilty wince. "Sierra has ranching in her blood, but I wanted something different. Ky grumbled a bit when I accepted the scholarship at UC Davis, but he let me move away from Texas without kicking up too much of a fuss." She blew a wayward, feathery strand of hair from her eyes. "And then I met this guy who seemed great. At first." Her gaze drifted to the left and went unfocused. "And when I broke up with him, things turned kind of ugly..."

Her cheeks flushed pink even as her words died out. Noah had imagination enough to fill in the blanks with a crazy ex morphing into a scary stalker. The subtle change in her wardrobe over time, much more subdued than the first time they'd met, suddenly made sense. He'd also noticed she seemed a bit off. Not her usual decisive self.

"How could I have been so *stupid*?" Savannah smoothed a hand down the dress that covered her knees and seemed to gather her composure. "Anyway, Ky quit his job in Dallas and accepted one here just to help me out. I've tried to convince him I'm okay now, but he's being stubborn, as usual." She didn't look quite convinced of her okay-ness herself. "I think if he didn't look like he just fell off a hay truck from Texas—fit in a bit better, you know?—he might relax some and enjoy life a little more." She gave a small shrug. "Meet someone special, maybe? So he wouldn't be so alone."

Noah felt his resolve crumbling in the face of all the sisterly concern, and he was so busy reminding himself of the reasons he should be saying no he missed Ky's return.

"Here." The former Texan held the plate of stuffed mushrooms out to his sister. "Your turn." He tipped his head in the direction of the dessert table along the far wall. "You know how much I love cheesecake."

An awkward moment slid by during which some kind of unspoken communication took place between the two siblings. Savannah's wide-eyed *are you serious?* expression met with Ky cocking his head in what appeared to be a *hell yes* response.

With a sigh, she set her untouched plate of mushrooms on the bar counter and picked up her glass of wine. "Fine," she said to her brother. And then she headed off in the direction of the dessert table, casting Ky a look over her shoulder. "Don't think you've won this round."

Round? What round?

Noah blinked, scrambling to keep up with the silent sibling conversations, vague statements, and the brother-sister tag-team thing that seemed to be going down. "Why do I get the feeling I'm being dragged into the middle of a family feud?"

Ky kept an anxious eye on his sister's retreating back, and Noah's heart melted more. Seriously, he was turning into a total softie. Two heart-tugging looks of concern from a single family were one too many for Noah to stomach and stay strong.

The man finally pivoted to face him head on. "Let me explain how this makeover thing is going to go down."

Noah's eyes went wide. "You're agreeing to it? You don't strike me as the type to care what other people think of your appearance."

"I *don't* give two jack shits."

"So," he said, confused, "you're going to say *no* to your sister's plan?"

Noah felt a manly sob or two coming on.

"Nope. Instead," the doctor replied in that drawl that did unspeakable things to Noah's insides, "I'm gonna let her talk me into it."

"Erm...hunh?" he said eloquently.

"Just what I said."

Noah squinted in confusion. "Why not just say yes?"

The surgeon's gaze drifted back to his sister. "I'm hoping that winnin' this argument with me will help her gain some of her confidence back."

Oh.

So the shift in Savannah's behavior hadn't been his imagination. Even Dylan, Noah's best friend, had remarked about the change when the twins had organized his charity poker run earlier this year.

"Also, she needs to focus on organizing her first event without Sierra's help," Ky said. "I don't want her stressing about me trying to prepare for the Bachelor Bid between shifts. She already thinks I work too hard, so she *will* worry."

As if on cue, a deep V of worry appeared between Ky's brows, and Noah was struck with an urge to smooth the wrinkles from his forehead.

And because he was the ultimate philanthropist, he'd toss in kissing the concerned frown away for free.

"She didn't used to be so unsure of herself, but the last couple of years have been rough on her," Ky went on, and the fiercely protective glance he shot in the direction of his sister nearly knocked Noah over.

Who'd have guessed that the growly, protective vibe would be such a turn-on?

"In short, you want her to rechannel her inner fire," Noah said.

"Right. Eventually I'll let her win this hard-fought argument. But"—his gaze scanned Noah's favorite Tom Ford suit and Prada dress shoes—"I have no intention of winding up looking like you." And then his expression softened a fraction, as though realizing the harshness of his words. "Nothing personal. I'm just not a *GQ* kind of guy."

Noah bit back a smile and studied the gift horse he'd been offered. Ky didn't really want to go through with his sister's plan, and there was definitely some underlying tension between the two. But who cared that he was only agreeing to make his sister happy?

He was *agreeing*.

And when the universe handed you something as epic as this, you seized the opportunity.

"Savannah is headed this way," Ky said in a low voice, interrupting Noah's thoughts. "So, convince me."

Wait, what?

The murmur of the surrounding crowd and the tinkle of cutlery filled the air as Noah waited for the surgeon to use more words and less frowning to communicate.

"I'm not following," Noah finally said.

"Convince me that you're the man for the job."

"You want me to *try out* for this gig?" Noah asked. "The one you've already decided to agree to?"

"Yep."

For chrissake. Why did he always wind up with jobs that didn't come with paychecks? Not that he needed the money, but still. And now he was being asked to *apply* for a makeover gig by a man who paired generic plaid with designer leather jackets?

Ky's voice went low and rumbly, doing decadent things to Noah's body. "In order for this to work," the surgeon said, "it has to look like you and Savannah convinced me—"

Savannah appeared at her brother's side and smiled up at him as she stuffed a plate in his hand. "They didn't have cheesecake, so I made an executive decision and grabbed you the tiramisu. So..." Concern clouded her eyes as they flitted between Noah and Ky. "What's the verdict?"

Noah met Ky's gaze for two seconds, the silence filled with a *just play along* loaded stare from Ky and finally a *fine, fine, you big, ridiculously handsome guy* eye roll from Noah.

Or something like that.

He turned to Ky's sister. "The verdict is," Noah said slowly, "I've been given the opportunity to apply for the privilege of taking your brother shopping."

Somehow, he managed not to choke on the words.

"Keep in mind, purple is his signature color." Savannah tossed a knowing grin at Ky, and then the smile faded away. "Wait, did you say *apply*?"

Noah used a deliberately flat tone. "You have to convince him to agree. And I have to prove I'm the man for the job." He turned to the dude who wore a belt buckle that could double as a weapon. "First off?" Noah gave him a critical look from head to toe, resolving not to hold his tongue. The man wanted him to pretend to apply for the job? Then he would bloody well go all out. "The best part of your outfit came from your sisters."

If Ky's expression was anything to go by, not only did he not give two jack shits, he also had exactly zero fucks to give.

"Your siblings should be commended," Noah continued. "This beautiful jacket is a quality product."

"Thank you," Savannah said.

"You're welcome." Noah stepped closer to her brother and went on, rubbing the smooth leather between his fingers. "And the fit is excellent. So it's a definite keeper"—he smoothed a palm across the endless expanse of hard shoulder and, *shit*, just managed not to cream his pants—"as are your shoulders. My God, one could build a temple worthy of worship on something so broad."

Ky sent him his standard, barely subdued bland look, the look that screamed *I'm willing to put up with your nonsense, up to a point.* The ominous dot-dot-dot following that statement was easily inferred.

"The comments aren't necessary," Ky said with a dry tone.

Noah's mouth twitched as he patted the man on the shoulder. "Of course not, my little soon-to-be-discovered Abercrombie and Fitch model."

"Are you done?" Ky asked wryly, glancing down at Noah's hand.

"Actually..." He suppressed a laugh and released the boner-worthy shoulder. "I'm just getting warmed up."

"No need to put yourself out," he drawled.

"Trust me, Dr. Davis. You're worth the effort."

Noah sent him a bigger smile to temper whatever came next. His brain-to-mouth filter was minimal on a good day. The sexy surgeon broke down the process even more.

"The dress jeans are good." Noah studied the denim with a critical eye. "I would have chosen a pair with a little more detail," he said as he went to lift the back of Ky's jacket for a better view. "Perhaps a little something on the pockets—"

As the magnificent ass came into view, Noah's brain began firing way too many signals to his vocal cords, all of them coalescing into a squawk sounding like a dying pterodactyl that Ky probably didn't deserve to be on the receiving end of.

Resisting the urge to touch was difficult. Noah deserved an award for his restraint—multiple, *multiple* awards.

Or at least some sort of certificate.

"Denim definitely has a place in the casual, dressy look," Noah said, voice hoarse as he tried to keep a straight face. "Especially if the pockets had a little embroidered—"

"No embroidering," Ky said firmly.

Savannah appeared to be smothering a laugh—a sight that warmed Noah's heart. If nothing else, this crazy conversation was making her happy.

Noah struggled for an innocent tone. "Rhinestones?"

A flash of terrified horror crossed Ky's face, and Savannah definitely seemed closer to laughing out loud.

"Fine." Noah dropped the leather and stepped back. "Ix-nay on the inestones-rhay." The doctor appeared unimpressed with the pig Latin, so Noah sent him another look. "Although that ass cries out for some sort of embellishment."

Ky's judgy expression returned with a vengeance.

Noah couldn't help himself. "How about some understated bead work along the waistline?"

"No."

"A little fancy stitching along the seams?"

"Absolutely not," Ky replied.

Seriously, the surgeon's bitch face was too cute, as endearing as the brotherly concern and the ability to rock the boots like a cowboy Adonis.

Hunh.

The pay might be nonexistent, but the benefits of this new job were definitely going to be worth the effort.

"So," Noah continued with a twinge of guilt

for enjoying himself way too much and for his

flirtatious tone, "are there any *other* preferences I

should be aware of, Dr. Davis?"

Chapter Two

"Preferences?" Ky Davis asked.

His *preference* at the moment was to be somewhere less *disturbing*.

Under the cover of a frown, he studied Noah. His black suit fit his trim physique well. Since their first encounter months ago, his brown hair had grown out enough to be artfully mussed. In addition to the attractive mouth—frequently accompanied by outrageous words—and the square-cut jaw, there was an intriguing vitality in his dark eyes and constantly gesturing hands.

Looking like everything Ky had ever wanted but could never have...

And the humorous light in Noah's gaze was now inviting him to play along with his wacky way of fulfilling Ky's request. Even more worrisome? Flirt mode seemed to be the guy's *only* mode.

Jesus.

"Preferences about what?" Ky asked Noah.

"Your clothing options."

"Depends on my choices," he drawled.

"Fur?" Noah asked with an engaging grin.

"Hate it."

"Leopard print?"

"Despise it."

"Cropped pants that show off your mankles?"

Ky refused to dignify the question with a response.

Two ominous beats passed before Noah went on. "Leather collars?"

The blood cells in Ky's body couldn't decide whether to flood his face or fill his dick. He had a feeling they were doing both. Before he could reply, a loud laugh escaped Savannah. A *laugh*.

Sweet mother Mary, he'd missed that sound.

He stared at his sister, the one who'd been far too pensive of late, as the amused noises continued to roll from her mouth. All but melting his urge to bolt from Noah's distracting presence.

Ky almost smiled. "What's so funny?"

"You—" she wheezed out, "in a leather collar."

Savannah collapsed against the LED-lit bar counter and laughed even harder.

"Careful, kiddo," Ky said, a grin making a brief appearance, "or you'll sprain somethin' important."

But the sight eased the ever-present knot of anxiety that had been living in his chest for months.

The knot first formed when, during one of Sierra's many visits to see her twin at UC Davis, she'd placed a frantic call to Ky about the ex-boyfriend. He could practically feel Sierra's panic over the phone— a young woman who, much to Ky's distress, didn't fear much of anything. When he'd arrived in town and stepped into her apartment, Savannah had looked fragile and broken, her self-confidence shot to hell. Her attempts at rallying a brave face would've fooled most people, but not a brother who knew her well. So Ky had shoved aside any doubts he had about moving to San Francisco to make sure the ex *stayed* gone.

Which turned out to be more difficult than he'd first assumed.

Unfortunately, the ex was smart, his behavior just skirting the edges of restraining-order levels and making the situation all the more frightening for it. Many months later, after multiple heated conversations and several bodily threats—with maybe a mention or two of his skill with a scalpel— Ky had finally set the narcissistic ex-boyfriend turned stalker straight. Unfortunately, much as she tried to pretend, Savannah still hadn't fully recovered from the experience.

Which meant sticking around to keep an eye on her.

Nurturing didn't come naturally to Ky. But the day his mom had handed him a two-day-old Savannah, pink and helpless and tiny, so she could deal with a screaming Sierra, well...ever since then, it had been a trial by fire.

He liked to believe his hard-won skills had been his mother's influence, that part of her he carried with him as he did his damnedest to honor the memory of the most selfless and kindhearted person he'd ever known.

The familiar pang of sadness hit, so Ky focused on the sister who was clearly enjoying herself.

"Yeah, I'm pretty sure leather collars aren't your brother's thing," Noah said.

"Maybe not." Sheer delight infused Savannah's gaze. "But he could exchange the style depending on his mood."

"One for each of the many subtle flavors of Ky's unhappy eyebrows?" Noah asked.

The man looked at him expectantly and...good God.

An unwanted surge of awareness filled Ky's gut.

"The answer is no," Ky said to himself as much as anyone else. "No to the fur. No to the leopard print." He tipped his head and met the gaze of the guy who wore his suit like a fashion model. "And an unequivocal *hell no* to mankles and a leather collar."

Noah's eyes crinkled in amusement. "An artist needs the proper equipment to create a masterpiece."

"It's a charity bid," Ky said with a skeptical twist of his lips. "Not an art auction."

Noah shrugged, as if to say *same difference*. "The body is our canvas. Clothes provide the paint."

Shit, there must be something seriously wrong with me.

Because despite everything, the only word Ky could come up with to describe his current feelings was *charmed*. He found Noah *charming*.

And Noah's mouth, man, it was somethin' else.

"Speaking of your choice of paint..." Noah said.

Ky tore his gaze from the full lips. "The only thing left to discuss are the boots," he said, fishing for a response. Two could play at this game. "And the shirt and the buckle."

Noah's eyelids flared wider at the mention of the buckle, and Ky knew he'd hit the jackpot. He worked hard to subdue a grin while shamelessly goading the man into a reaction.

"'Course," he drawled, ratcheting up his accent, "there's not much to say about the buckle 'cause it's perfect."

Noah crossed his arms in protest. "Perfect for baking pizza over a campfire."

"Perfect for a dressy occasion."

"Or subduing an attacker," the man replied.

Ky almost chuckled out loud. "Maybe it has sentimental value." It didn't, but it could have. He could declare it had some now just to see what the man would say in reply. "Like a family heirloom."

"Then it should be melted down and turned into a cameo pendant," Noah said with an energetic gesture of his hand. "I'm willing to compromise. The boots stay. We lose the belt."

Ky hoped his expression looked stubborn. "How is that a compromise? You admitted you have an illicit attachment to my boots."

And how the heck that was possible, Ky had no idea. Although Noah definitely seemed to dance to his own tune, a song he seemed the only one capable of hearing. Which was probably a good thing, given his idiosyncratic ways and all.

Case in point: the first time they'd met. Memphis Haines—Ky's patient and Noah's friend— had just been diagnosed with cancer. Noah had shaved his head in solidarity even though he'd only known the man about a month.

That kind of loyalty and sacrifice deserved respect, despite the irreverent mouth that came with the package.

"Yes, I'm definitely attached to those Stetson boots," Noah said, glancing at said footwear. "But I also have a weakness for trashy reality TV." He cocked his head and met Ky's gaze. "That doesn't mean I approve of all of my choices."

Ky pursed his lips to keep them from twitching in amusement. "Okay," he said, "anything else?"

"Your shirt."

"What about it?"

"For an event like this," Noah said, "to pull off the casual look right, you needed a dress shirt with the jacket."

Ky glanced down and this time his frown of confusion was genuine. "And this one isn't?"

"Just because there are buttons doesn't make it a dress shirt," Noah said patiently.

Ky blinked, stumped, and decided to keep his mouth shut.

"And now you're wondering about the criteria for a dress shirt, aren't you?" Noah said.

No way was Ky gonna say yes.

"And that," the man said as he gently poked Ky in the chest, "is why you need my help." As he dropped his hand, he lightly ran his fingers along the sleeve of Ky's coat, goose bumps popping up beneath the path as Noah went on. "I have so much to teach you, my young apprentice."

Ky wondered if the man's penchant for touching things, including people—especially *him*—was going to be a problem.

And the answer was a hearty *hell yeah*.

"Come on, Ky," Savannah said. "Let Noah help."

She seemed to sense his hesitation.

"Besides, I'll be too busy organizing the fundraiser," she went on. "I won't have time to give you the attention you need. And you could use a little fashion advice."

Ky bit back a sigh. "My clothes aren't *that* bad."

"I know," she said softly.

Ky's frown felt set in stone, and his sister looped her arm through his.

"Let Noah help you," she said again as she gave him a gentle squeeze. "Think of how great you'll feel after. It'll still be you, only the San Francisco version."

Savannah looked up at Ky with their mother's sage-green eyes, a sight that never failed to crush a little of the breath from his lungs.

"Just say yes, Dr. Davis." The wannabe makeover man sent him a knowing gaze currently lit with delight. "How can you say no to such a sweet face?"

Ky blew out a breath. "Fine," he said. "I'll let Noah help."

Savannah's triumphant grin cheered Ky's heart, as did her fierce hug. He returned the embrace, gratefully pulling her close, and his gaze met Noah's over her shoulder in a silent *thank you*. He received a *you're welcome* wink in return. When Ky let his sister go, he took a step back and faced his fashion consultant.

"As long as you understand one thing," Ky said. "I retain the right of veto power." He skimmed his gaze down Noah, the lithe form with just enough muscle definition to be intriguing. During Ky's rare, anonymous hookups, he'd always favored the type. "No exceptions."

"Noah, just out of curiosity," Savannah asked, "what would *you* have worn with this jacket?"

"Skinny black jeans—not boot cut, like your brother's—a skinny tie and a tailored shirt."

"I don't do skinny ties," Ky said.

Noah nodded solemnly and, for the first time, his expression looked completely sincere. "I wouldn't put you in one," he said. "It wouldn't look right."

"I don't do that flipped-up collar thing, either."

"I promise," Noah said. "No collar erections."

Ky let out a sarcastic snort—was *everything* a sex joke to this man?—and his sister laughed again.

"Are you going to bid on someone this year, Noah?" she asked.

"Me? I would but I have to MC the event. Which means," he went on with a small smile, "my job is to focus on the cause, not finding a date."

"Well, you deserve a good man, Noah," Savannah went on. "I'd set you up on a date myself if I knew any men worthy enough." A cloud of sadness passed through her eyes, and then she glanced at Ky and smiled. "Present company excepted, of course. Very inconsiderate of you, big bro, to be so straight."

A confused *really?* expression briefly flitted across Noah's face, and Ky's stomach took a sharp turn toward his toes.

"Yes, his straightness is a terrible shame," Noah murmured with a questioning look that strung Ky's nerves tighter than barbed wire. "If I were a lesser man, I'd be tempted to show him the error of his ways."

Jesus.

Growing up in Oak Hollows, Texas—a buckle on the Bible Belt tightened to near lethal degrees—meant Ky Davis could be no kind of "queer," a word most of the town uttered with disdain. Years ago he'd stopped caring what other people thought. Unfortunately, his stepdad...

Fuck.

He rubbed his eyes and shoved the unwelcome memories aside. He wasn't that fifteen-year-old kid anymore. Nevertheless, if Savannah felt betrayed by her dirtbag of an ex, how would she feel if she learned the true extent of her father's homo-hatin' ways?

Hell, Ky would sooner surgically remove one of his kidneys using a plastic picnic knife than cause Savannah pain.

Neither would he disappoint her by backing out of his promise now. But one look at the amused question in Noah's eyes had Ky stifling a groan.

What the ever-lovin' hell had he signed on for?

~~~***~~~

"Savannah"—from the comfort of his couch, Noah gripped his cell phone, his stomach sinking—"you might want to rethink your latest plan. I mean, last Saturday I helped you convince your adorably scruffy, socially reclusive brother to agree to a makeover, for god's sake."

"I know."

"And you *already* blackmailed him into participating in the Bachelor Bid," he said.

"I know."

"So don't you think setting him up on a blind date now will kind of blow his mind?"

And not in a fun, dirty sort of way.

"That's why I'm not telling him. He'll think he's meeting *me* for lunch," Savannah said, and Noah bit back a groan. "Lisa's a friend of mine," she continued. "And...well, Ky's hard to read, I know, but he's always nice to her. That must mean something, right? Plus, for the last year, she's had a huge crush on him."

She. *She.*

Noah covered his eyes with his palm. How had he let himself get pulled deeper into this tug-of-war of sibling concern? A makeover was one thing, but a stealth setup? The blindest of the blind dates?

Noah was king of the iffy ideas but this seemed like the *worst.*

"If I make reservations at that new restaurant on Nob Hill," Savannah went on, clearly thinking out loud, "he'll *have* to wear something decent. Ky agreeing to let you take him shopping will be beneficial in so many ways."

"I tried to spare him the ordeal," he said.

In an effort to save the busy surgeon some time, Noah had asked for his measurements, selected several appropriate suits—*beautiful* ones, actually— from Noah's favorite high-end stores, and had them delivered to Ky's apartment so he could choose one in private. But the guy had rejected all three, so the issue of how to dress him for the Bachelor Bid had suddenly grown more complicated.

"So when you take him shopping to find something he's willing to wear," she said with a *good luck with that* tone of voice, "can you help him pick out several nice casual outfits as well?"

"Of course I can."

"Perfect. That way he'll have something nice for the date, too," she went on, and the excitement in her tone made him cringe. "Thanks for everything, Noah."

Christ. After signing off, he tossed his phone onto the coffee table, feeling torn.

Savannah was right. Ky Davis was a hard man to read. But falling for anyone named Lisa seemed unlikely. At some point Ky would have to list his preference for the fundraiser. All evidence pointed to him claiming to be strictly straight.

But Noah had tons of experience with men who looked at him *that way.* He was seventy percent certain Ky was into men—

Okay, maybe sixty-five percent.

Perhaps he'd been wishing so hard he'd imagined the moment Ky's gaze had lingered on his mouth? More importantly, the reserved doctor would hate anyone sticking their nose into his personal life. And rightly so. Which meant Noah should keep his mouth shut and ignore the impending train wreck of a lunch.

He drummed his fingers against his thigh, objectively weighing his options.

Until a visual of the worst-case scenario crossed his mind: Ky arriving at the restaurant to an upsetting surprise that triggered an unhappy scowl, inadvertently upsetting Lisa, leading to crippling awkwardness for all and emotional devastation for some. Of course, this would likely leave Savannah sad, which would make *Ky* sad—and Good Lord, hadn't the world reached its quota of sadness and then some?

Not to mention Noah's part in all the unpleasantry, remaining silent while knowingly helping Ky select the clothes for the sneak-attack blind date.

Noah chewed on his bottom lip, thoughts churning.

He still felt guilty for taking advantage of the surgeon's dedication to his sister by agreeing to this job as fashion consultant—not guilty enough to resist a little good-natured teasing along the way, of course. All of which would probably earn Noah a special place in hell. But he'd resigned himself to that fate years ago, especially after the way things had ended with Rick.

The familiar toxic cocktail of guilt and *loss* twisted in his stomach, and Noah squeezed his eyes shut.

Toward the end, when Rick's condition had looked hopeless, the doctor had offered him a Hail Mary option. The odds of success had been abysmal, but Noah had talked Rick into the experimental treatment anyway, extending his life a bit. The decision had bought Noah about six more months with his boyfriend. Which had been good for Noah. Kind of.

Not so much for Rick.

Those six months had been full of mostly pain and suffering. What kind of person did that? What kind of person put their terror of losing someone they loved ahead of said loved one's well-being and happiness?

"Shit." He flopped onto his back on the couch and stared up at his ceiling.

Warning Ky and perhaps averting a very uncomfortable date, and the subsequent sibling sadness, might help Noah earn one of the more desirable circles of hell instead of the worst.

Yes, he should definitely warn Ky.

After all, he'd never *promised* Savannah he wouldn't say anything. And he wouldn't, as long as Ky was into women. If not, then providing a heads-up seemed the humane thing to do.

Today, when the surgeon dropped off the rejected suits to Noah so he could return them, covertly determining the truth about his sort-of client's orientation shouldn't be too difficult. Maybe. Hopefully. Besides, Noah had skills.

He also had an *in*, so to speak—namely, his good friend who was currently honing his culinary techniques in the next room.

"Hey, Memphis," Noah called out as he pushed up off the couch. He entered the kitchen, where the man was currently cutting asparagus into one-inch pieces. "Ky Davis is your surgeon—"

"No offense to the dude, but I'm hoping I won't need his services again."

"All right, so Dr. Davis *was* your surgeon." For a moment, he watched his friend attempt to cut the vegetables without losing a hunk of his finger in the process, another iffy scenario. "One would assume a successful stuntman like yourself, a man who jumps off buildings and dodges explosions for a living, would be able to handle a knife."

"Ha," he said with a twist of his lips.

"Especially a little *paring* knife."

"Size isn't everything."

"I disagree, but that's a discussion for another day." Noah watched as Memphis pressed the utensil too hard and a piece of asparagus shot across the counter. "Perhaps if you were using a dangerous weapon, like a scimitar, you'd look"—*like you knew what you were doing*, he didn't say—"a little less awkward?"

Only a grunt came in response.

"Okay, so how much do you know about our boot-wearing Scalpel Man?" Noah asked.

"Other than his ability to save my life by cutting out my cancerous thyroid?" he replied. "Not much."

In a simple T-shirt and frayed jeans, Memphis continued with his task. Noah would offer to help, but he'd bought the condo for the view and the built-in bar in the living room, not its high-end kitchen. He appreciated the beauty of the stainless steel refrigerator and dark wood cabinets but had zero plans to use the restaurant-quality appliances.

Noah leaned his hip against the counter. "You must know *something* about him."

"Man of few words. Workaholic. Great with a scalpel." He shrugged as if the rest wasn't important, strong shoulders stretching the fabric of his shirt.

"Any guesses as to which way he swings?" Noah leaned his elbows on the center island. "Straight? Gay? Bi? Experimental? Demisexual?" he asked. When no reply was forthcoming, he went on. "Open to the power of suggestion and lots and lots of alcohol?"

"I don't know, man," Memphis said with a distracted tone. "The general anesthesia they hit me with kind of prevented a heartfelt chat while he was, you know, *slicing my neck open*."

"He did a nice job." He stared at the faint horizontal line beneath his friend's Adam's apple. "The scar is hardly noticeable anymore."

"Yeah." Memphis's lips curled into a smile. "Which is great except now I can't keep claiming my boyfriend tried to slit my throat in my sleep."

"As if Tyler would," he replied with a roll of his eyes.

Noah's two friends appeared firmly committed to one another. Ever since Memphis and Tyler had finally worked through their tangled web of a past and moved in together, they also seemed hell-bent on making up for the ten-year gap in their relationship: Tyler by constantly grinning like a love-sick fool, Memphis by seeking out new ways to do special things for his significant other. In turn, Noah risked overdosing on their ridiculous love fest. Despite that fact, he'd volunteered his kitchen in support of Memphis's latest quest to do something nice for his partner.

"Why would Tyler want to slit your throat, anyway?" Noah popped a raw piece of asparagus into his mouth. "Especially on the days he makes his rounds." As one of the physicians on staff at the Front Street Clinic, Tyler often spent time walking the streets of San Francisco, bringing health care to the homeless. Noah's mouth crooked into a teasing grin. "I've heard you occasionally massage his feet after a long day at work, like a devoted little wifey."

Memphis squawked in protest and his hand slipped on the knife. He cursed and put his finger in his mouth. The pink tint to his cheeks left Noah fairly certain his source—God bless his best friend and informant, Dylan, and his blunt mouth—had accurate insider knowledge of the goings-on in the Tyler-Memphis household. "What is this birthday surprise you're working on for Tyler, anyway? I mean"—Noah waved his hand in the general direction of his disaster of a kitchen—"other than trying to impress him with your ability to use every dish in my condo and crack twenty eggs just to get five that aren't mostly shell?"

"It's a soufflé," he said defensively, looking more wounded than he had the day after his neck had been filleted open. "It has a lot of eggs. I'll clean up the mess."

Noah felt his expression soften. "I know you will." He watched the stuntman with the paring knife a minute more, the awkward movements painful to watch. "Maybe you should try for something easier, though," he went on, striving to be gentle.

This was the guy's fourth attempt at the soufflé in as many weeks, and he didn't seem to be getting more proficient in the kitchen. If anything, he seemed to be getting worse.

"I can figure this out," Memphis said.

"I'm sure you could."

"This knife is dull."

"I sharpened it yesterday."

"My skills are just a little rusty."

Noah pursed his mouth. "A little?" He stared down at one of the abandoned bowls, five yolks and at least thirty pieces of shell floating on top. "I'm beginning to suspect you've never cooked in your life."

"I just—" Memphis scratched the back of his head, the golden-brown hair now boyishly tousled, a frustrated expression on his face. "Asparagus soufflé is one of Tyler's favorites and I want to do something he'll remember. Something *worth* remembering."

A small catch in Noah's chest left him speechless, because he couldn't *forget*. All those little details, like Rick's love for Thai food, his easy laugh at Noah's ridiculous statements, the way his eyes would light up when Noah entered the room.

Noah shut down the memories.

"Listen," he tried again, leaning closer to emphasize his point. "I, more than anyone, know that Ty burned through more boyfriends than a Victoria's Secret supermodel. But he *chose* to put his heart on hold for you for ten years, Memphis," he said. "The past is the past and you can't undo what happened. Besides, things have changed. Without the choke-hold the grim reaper had on your balls—" Noah grimaced at the man who'd already suffered through two rounds of testicular cancer. "Sorry, no offense."

"None taken," Memphis said, clearly amused.

"Good. But the point is…" He straightened and braced his arms against the center island. "You literally had death nipping at your heels for years, which had a profound effect on the choices you made. I think Ty understood that better than most."

"I just want to make him happy."

"Being with *you* makes him happy."

"And doing things for him," he said, the stubborn tone returning, "things I probably would have done during those missing ten years, makes *me* happy."

God, what would it be like to have someone so gone on him again? But that line of thinking would get him nowhere.

"I gave you a key to my condo so you could use my kitchen to practice your birthday surprise for your boyfriend," Noah said. "I'm keeping secrets from one of my *oldest friends* for you. Surely you can share your guess as to Ky's orientation. For example, are there any clues in his office?" Noah asked, because maybe Savannah had exaggerated her brother's bleak social life.

"What kind of clues?" Memphis tipped his head in question, and the knife slowed as he reached the end of the asparagus.

"Photographs," Noah explained. "Pictures of gorgeous women on his walls. Or maybe gay pornographic shots with him and his dom. I don't know, anything that could help?"

Memphis looked at Noah like he'd lost his mind. "How about I just ask him?"

Noah's every muscle went tense. "No."

Backing the man into a corner wouldn't go well.

"Why not?" Memphis asked. "You said yourself he'll be here soon. Besides, I can be subtle."

Subtle?

Noah stared at him in disbelief. "You did an illegal BASE jump off the top of a downtown San Francisco building just to get Tyler's undivided attention." He slowly shook his head. "You are about as subtle as a cocaine-snorting bull in a china shop. No," he went on, resigned to his fate, "don't ask him a thing. I've got this."

"Yeah, sure," he said. But his expression didn't mesh with his agreement. "The dude clearly thinks you're crazy."

"We forged a friendly alliance at the Humane Society fundraiser," he said with a defensive lift of his chin.

Memphis chuckled, clearly unconvinced.

"Okay, maybe I'm exaggerating a bit," Noah went on. "But I did manage to stand within a five-foot radius of him and he let me breathe the air without too much of an incredulous *oh no you didn't* face."

"Like he had when you guys first met and you asked if he spelled his name *K-Y like the lubricant*?"

"I was flustered!"

"You were blabbering."

"He made me nervous!"

The stuntman laughed again, and heat flushed up Noah's cheeks. The knock at his front door sent his heart rate soaring, his face more heated than ever as he headed toward the foyer. Even after several encounters with the doctor, Noah still wasn't completely prepared for the reality of having him in his home.

"Enter at your own risk," Noah said as he pulled open the front door.

Ky said nothing, but his expression already looked guarded, the garment bag containing the rejected suits hanging over his arm.

As usual, the tall man had an athlete-slash-model-cum-rugged-cowboy thing happening that shouldn't be allowed outside of old spaghetti westerns and porn. Or spaghetti western porn, if there was such a thing. And if not, that should be remedied immediately.

Jesus, he needed a drink.

"Welcome to my home." Noah stepped back so the guy could enter.

"Thanks," he said, handing over the suits.

"Surely one of these looked decent on you?"

"I didn't try them on."

Noah gaped at him, heavy bag hanging from his hand. "Why not?"

"I don't wear suits."

"Fine," he said with a defeated sigh, hanging the bag in his front closet. "I assume you realize our job just got harder. So...we need to discuss our new makeover plan of attack."

The surgeon adopted a cautious expression, as though tensed and ready to bolt should Noah chase after him with a razor or a pair of scissors. How would he look after a carefully worded question about his orientation?

"I promise to try and keep the process as painless as possible," Noah said.

"Just the thought of a shopping expedition is painful enough."

Noah surveyed the man's faded denim and the tips of the cowboy boots that were rapidly beginning to qualify as a fetish. Both items of clothing were expected, but the football jersey hugging his biceps was definitely a surprise—

Holy shit.

The idea hit Noah like a lightning bolt.

Maybe he could accomplish both of today's goals by asking *just the right questions*. Why hadn't he thought of this before? Because how could he help find clothes that fit Ky's wants and needs—and possibly divert a blind-date disaster—without learning as *much* about him as he possibly could? Anything less and Noah wasn't doing his job *properly.*

Really, he should receive the fucking not-employee of the year award.

"Are you a closet football fan?" Noah asked.

Way to sneak in the word closet, *Noah.*

Ky warily studied the living room done in russet and gold and overstuffed furniture, Texas A&M emblem stretched across his chest. "In Texas, football is a religion."

"Great," he muttered. "Another reason to go atheist."

"Do you know much about the sport?"

Noah pretended to give the question some thought. "I got tossed into a dumpster by the quarterback of my high school team once—wait...no, actually it was twice." He sent him a smile. "Does that count?"

Ky studied him with a hint of alarm and a slightly *open mouth*—dear God, the things Noah could do with such a vision—as though struggling for an appropriate phrase of sympathy.

Looking that delicious and concerned about Noah's well-being should be illegal, a crime punishable by a hefty fine. Or serving time handcuffed to Noah's bedpost for a day or so. Maybe three.

Oh, for chrissake, Noah. Yet another example of why you deserve the worst circle of hell.

"Don't hurt yourself trying to come up with an appropriate response." Noah waved a hand as if the high school event had been no big deal. "It's probably just karma biting me in the ass. I've propositioned more football players than I can remember. But enough about my shortcomings, let's get back to your makeover..."

A cute snort shot from Ky's mouth.

"Don't worry," Noah went on. "Today will be easy. Shall I make you a cocktail before we start?"

"No, thanks. And I returned the clothes, as requested," he said with a frown. "What else do we need to do today?"

"You rejected three *amazing* suits." He crossed to the bar, pulled a paring knife from the drawer, and sliced a lime for a much-needed gin and tonic. "Which leads me to conclude that, in order for me to help you without us driving each other crazy, we need to get to know one another better." Noah finished preparing his drink and turned to face Ky. "I need a little more information about your likes and dislikes, your fashion preferences. And, just as importantly"—the dramatic pause, he'd learned long ago, should be reserved for maximum emphasis. He employed one now—"your *lifestyle*, uhm, preferences."

Noah could tell the man was struggling to keep his expression blank, but his lips shifted in...amusement. Surprise. And frustration, too, maybe? Yes, his reaction was always evident, if one looked hard enough.

And Noah was always looking.

He also held his breath while waiting for a response.

"Lifestyle preferences," Ky finally repeated, his tone flat.

A loaded staring contest ensued, their visual standoff lasting seemingly forever until a crash followed by a loud *goddammit* came from the kitchen. Ky cocked his head in question.

Noah sighed and picked up his cocktail. "Welcome to my culinary hell. Memphis is abusing my kitchen in an attempt to learn how to cook." Setting aside his *very important* research for a moment, he turned and headed out of the living room. "Follow me."

They found the stuntman cleaning up what looked like raw egg from the floor.

Ky leaned a shoulder against the doorjamb and addressed his former patient. "What are you trying to cook?"

The next few minutes passed amicably by as the surgeon listened to Memphis explain his efforts with the same kind of patience Noah imagined the man listened to his sisters make horrible life choices.

"Tyler has two favorite dishes, and I went with the one with the easiest list of ingredients," Memphis finished.

Ky rubbed his jaw, fingers scratching the facial hair too long to be called stubble but not long enough to qualify as a beard.

"Soufflés are hard to make because they have a tendency to collapse," the surgeon said, valiantly, Noah thought, ignoring the fact the stuntman couldn't crack an egg to save his life. "What's his other favorite dish?"

"Vegan eggplant lasagna with tofu."

"That one will be easier," Ky said.

At the man's confident tone, Noah's lids widened in surprise. "You sound like an expert," he said, taking a nonchalant sip of his gin and tonic. "Do you normally wear the apron in your relationships?"

The surgeon's eyes flickered with amusement but he didn't take the bait. Although there was definitely a hint of an *I'm on to you* in his expression.

"Or are you more of a grill master?" Noah studied him over the rim of his glass.

The muscles around Ky's mouth ticked briefly in humor as he met his gaze, but his expression didn't provide Noah with the answer he wanted.

After another two-second stare-a-thon, the doctor took a seat on one of the barstools at the center island and addressed Memphis. "Don't let the ingredients scare you. Tofu is easy to work with."

Noah shot him a confused look, because Dr. Davis and tofu in the same sentence didn't compute.

"Sierra went through a vegan phase when she was a preteen," Ky explained. "Longest six months of my life."

"You cooked for your sisters?" Noah set his drink down with a *plink* of glass against marble, grappling with this new information.

"I've helped raise them since they were born." He hesitated for a moment before going on.

"Especially after our mom was killed in a car accident."

"How old were the twins when she died?" Noah asked.

"Four."

"How old were *you*?"

"Fourteen."

Good God.

Noah's chest ached so hard that, for once, he couldn't think of a thing to say. Fortunately, Memphis murmured an appropriate condolence as he slid the completed soufflé dish into the oven, giving Noah a moment to recover without having to speak.

Thirty minutes later, Noah had learned that Ky occasionally wore cargo pants for their convenient pockets, loathed neckties, preferred leather footwear, and was opposed to alligator-skin boots out of deference to his animal-rights activist sister. All of which was helpful but, unfortunately, led to a discussion about an upcoming football game between the Florida Gators and Texas A&M. Noah had nothing to add to the conversation, except for tossing out the occasional sexually suggestive comment and leading questions that went unanswered by Ky.

Noah was almost relieved when the kitchen timer beeped.

A delighted look overtook Memphis's face as he carefully pulled the appropriately puffy dish from the oven, but when the soufflé deflated like a slow-leak balloon, his expression slipped into one of defeat.

They all stared down at the flattened mess, and Noah allowed his friend three seconds to mourn before speaking.

"Cheer up, hot shot," Noah said as he consoled the man with a pat on the shoulder. "Maybe they make Viagra for soufflés."

"Is there any situation that doesn't warrant a sex joke?" Ky asked dryly.

Noah tried to look offended. "I certainly hope not."

"Word of warning," Memphis said to Ky, "don't ever agree to a drinking game where you have to down a shot of whiskey every time he makes a sex joke. Everyone will be trashed within the first hour."

"I'll keep that in mind," the surgeon drawled. "And as much fun as this has been, I've got to get goin'."

"Already?" Noah paused in the process of helping Memphis load the dishwasher, heart pounding. He hoped the desperation in his voice wasn't too obvious. "But I haven't learned everything I need to know."

Not that he needed to know for himself, mind you. But how could he justify betraying Savannah's confidence about hearts-in-her-eyes Lisa without just cause? Wasn't he *obligated* to save Ky from a potentially embarrassing situation and the subsequent family drama?

Really, Noah was only doing the siblings a huge favor.

"Can't you stay a little longer?" he went on.

"'Fraid not," Ky said. "I've got clinic this afternoon and the start of a long call shift tomorrow night."

Noah's mind scrambled to revise his plan. "Okay...well, we'll just finish this at your place when you have time."

"Finish this," the doctor said with a skeptical tone. "At my place." The air seemed to grow thicker during the pause. "Why?"

Noah couldn't tell if all the words were supposed to form a complete sentence or not.

"To assess your current wardrobe, of course. That way," he said with a smile, warming up to his brilliant, spur-of-the-moment idea, "I can also help pick out the most appropriate pieces to pair with the clothes you already own." His grin grew as he continued to strengthen his argument. "We want to get the most bang for your buck, don't we?"

There must be something he could glean from the man's living space. Some sort of clue about his orientation. The intensely guarded look on the surgeon's face right now didn't bode well should Noah grow a pair, as Memphis liked to joke, and ask Ky directly. "All right," Ky said, clearly reluctant. "I'll call you when I have some free time."

Noah escorted him toward the front door. "Perfect."

It wasn't until after Ky left, off to save lives like the good little broad-shouldered doctor he was, that the guilt hit full force. Noah dropped his head to the front door with a *thunk*.

"I *am* trying to divert a disaster here," he muttered to no one, failing to convince even himself.

Because, altruism be damned, he wanted to know the truth about Ky. He wanted to know with the intensity of a thousand screaming orgasms, but mostly for personal reasons. *Selfish* reasons. Self-serving reasons that involved fantasies requiring several bottles of lube, nakedness, and debauchery of the highest order.

Shit, his not-employee of the year award needed to be permanently revoked.

Chapter Three

Four days later Ky heard the distant knock at his front door and hesitated, still wholly unprepared for today.

During their last encounter Noah's attempts to suss out his orientation had been less than subtle. Ky should lie and claim he was straight, just to put an end to the unspoken conversation the man kept trying to have. But their game of cat and mouse had become far too...amusing.

Dammit, he shouldn't find it *amusing*.

Ultimately, though, he couldn't give Noah the information he sought.

A massive knot formed in Ky's gut.

The day his stepfather discovered Ky's secret stash of gay porn, the resulting backhand across the face had been enough to knock him on his ass. Head throbbing, world spinning, nose bleeding, Ky had struggled to his feet with half a mind to fight back, despite only being a scrawny fifteen-year-old at the time.

But Ray's verbal threats had proven to be much worse.

So much worse.

Ky scrubbed a hand down his face and pushed the thought of those untenable threats aside. Unfortunately his stepdad also held all the cards, having inherited the ranch when Ky's mother's life had been cut short by a drunk driver. He had no memories of his father, he'd died when Ky was a toddler, but every room in the house was filled with reminders of his mom—like the living room and her words the day she'd handed Savannah to Ky, trusting him to take care of his then two-day-old baby sister.

Remember, family comes before everything, Ky.

Every day he tried to honor that mantra.

Not only would going public about his sexual orientation get Ky banned from the only real home he'd ever known, the ranch, it would also put his sisters in the position of choosing between the father they *thought* they knew, and loved, and the half brother they adored. He knew how it felt to lose both parents, and the girls had already lost their mama, so Ky couldn't do that to them, even figuratively.

He just *couldn't.*

A second knock finally spurred Ky toward the front entrance, and he braced for the interaction. Maintaining a bland expression around Noah was getting harder and harder. Which meant Ky needed to get this task done as quick as possible.

"Thanks for stopping by," he said as he opened the door.

"I'm thrilled to be here."

"I'll try not to take too much of your time."

"No trouble at all," he replied as he swept into the room with the kind of energy Ky had come to expect.

Ky had gotten used to the man's animated personality, but right now Noah practically vibrated with anticipation. Which meant hustling him through this task might prove more difficult than Ky had hoped.

Great.

"The doorman in your building is adorable." Noah met his gaze, brown eyes full of mischief. "Don't you think he's adorable?"

Despite his promise to himself, Ky had to work to suppress a smile. "Adorable is a relative term," he said in non-answer to the not-spoken question.

Noah laughed. "Too true."

In a denim jacket, the hem of his red shirt visible beneath, Noah looked as though he'd walked off a runway for the casual collection of some fancy designer the girls would drool over. His jeans fit him well.

Perhaps too well. An uncomfortable heat built low in his gut, and Ky shifted on his feet. "Okay, then," he said, suddenly feeling awkward. "Let's get started sorting through my clothes." He stepped in the direction of his bedroom, anxious to hurry things along because, *Jesus*, Noah's denim-clad ass was distracting.

Noah followed alongside him down the hall.

"As much as I've refused to live my life in a closet," Noah said as they walked, "I really shouldn't be this excited about combing through yours." He slanted Ky a sideways look. "I'm not going to find anything too personal, am I?"

An amused huff escaped before Ky could contain it. "I'm not sure why you care."

"As the saying goes, you are an enigma. A fascinating conundrum," he said as they passed the entrance to the living room. "You are a mystery that I intend to—" Noah stopped short, the sentence ending in a squeak as he stared through the doorway.

Hunh.

This wasn't his usual flair for the dramatic. This was genuine dismay on Noah's face.

The guy tried again. "Djuh..."

Heat slowly filled Ky's cheeks. Although the view of the bay was nice, his place was just a space to crash between on-call nights, a retreat to hole himself away from the noise and the lights and the people of a city that Ky still hadn't gotten used to. The view of the water helped ease his longing for home.

Anything more than functional furniture wasn't necessary.

Noah's mouth opened and closed several times before forming coherent words, albeit linked in an incoherent way. "You've... I've... How?" He swept his gaze across the admittedly Spartan room containing the utilitarian ugly couch, as of yet unpacked cardboard boxes, and a plastic orange tote doubling as a coffee table. "I can't even."

"Is there a point you're tryin' to make?" Ky said dryly.

"This is a really nice apartment building," he said slowly, as if choosing his words carefully.

"Yep."

"In a primo location."

"I know."

"You must pay a fortune in rent for this little piece of—" He splayed his hand in the general direction of the vaulted ceilings with bare wires hanging, awaiting a decision about light fixtures, the exposed brick a beautiful yet bleak blank canvas just waiting for someone to do...something. "There are no words," he finished, his arm dropping back to his side.

"It's a place to crash between shifts," he said, turning toward the hallway and hoping the guy would follow.

Noah didn't budge. "Shouldn't that space be more, uhm, appealing?"

Ky pivoted to face him. "Why does everything have to be pretty?"

"Because so much in life *isn't*."

The words shot from Noah's mouth with such force he looked as though he'd surprised even himself.

Two awkward seconds ticked by as twin spots of color appeared on Noah's cheeks. After all the blatant come-ons and ridiculous statements he'd uttered, *now* he was embarrassed?

"It's...it's"—Noah gave a halfhearted gesture toward the space—"a disappointment, that's all."

Ky lifted a sardonic brow. "It's just a living room."

"Yes," he replied. "With emphasis on the word *live*. How can you stand a room where the prevailing scheme is simplicity to the point of austerity?"

Realizing there was no escaping this discussion, Ky sighed and shoved up the sleeves of his plaid shirt. "Not all of us require beautiful surroundings," he said. "A little austerity never hurt anyone."

The breath that broke from Noah's throat sounded a hell of a lot like sarcasm. "I've spent enough time in crappy surroundings. So, no thank you. I'll never willingly make that choice again."

Confused, Ky frowned. "I thought you came from money."

"Inherited from my father when he died five years ago."

"So...by crappy surroundings, you mean something as humdrum as middle-class suburbs?"

"No." He pressed his lips together. "County hospital."

Ky froze, the response not at all what he'd been expecting.

"My boyfriend spent his last months in a crappy county hospital. An ugly, 1950s monolithic building fashioned out of concrete, cement, and utter despair," Noah said with a tight smile. "Austerity and simplicity at its finest. I didn't have the money to move him somewhere better, not back then."

Unsure how to respond, Ky hooked his thumbs through the belt loops of his jeans, the surge of sympathy making him uncomfortable. Savannah had mentioned the boyfriend who'd died of HIV.

But Ky was still confused as hell.

Noah glanced at him and must have read his expression. "Oh, I had plenty of *things*," he went on. "Except all that I had at the time—my fancy car, my beautiful apartment, *everything*—was owned by my dad." He fingered the button of his denim jacket. "My mother never went against my father's wishes. Ever. And my father didn't think a homeless dude turning tricks on the street could care about his son for anything more than his future inheritance potential."

Jesus, Mary, and Joseph.

"Can't really blame dear old Dad for that." Noah's laugh sounded hollow.

"That must have been rough."

"Rick suffered," Noah said, "and I was powerless to help him. It was the ugliest damn thing I've ever experienced." He met Ky's gaze again and then rolled his shoulders, as if trying to rid himself of the heavy moment. And, just like that, his demeanor changed. "But your apartment," he said with a smile, "is a tragedy that can be fixed."

Clearly the man wanted to move on from the uncomfortable subject.

Ky blinked, shaking off the effects of the topic. "My place is a work in progress."

"You mean you've actually put some thought into this?" he said, back to an easygoing tone. "What was the theme you were going for?" He gestured

toward the stacks of cardboard boxes lining the far
wall. "Early American U-Haul?"

Ky caught himself before he laughed. "I haven't
gotten around to unpacking completely."

"Really?" he asked. "And how long have you
lived here?"

Ky hesitated before answering. "About a year
and a half."

The silence that followed said more than Noah's
many, many words usually did.

"I've been busy," Ky added.

Busy working and worrying about his sisters.
And, dammit, he was supposed to be hurrying this
task along. Unfortunately, his too-attractive guest
ventured farther into the living room.

"Is your favorite color beige?" Noah asked.
"Because I've never seen so many variations of the
same bland shade. I wouldn't have thought it
possible."

Ky leaned against the doorjamb. "It's not that
bad."

"The only splash of color," he went on, turning
a slow circle to take it all in, "is the god-awful orange
of the beat-up plastic tote you're using for a coffee
table."

"It was convenient."

"It's hideous."

"I don't spend a lot of time here."

"Who would want to? This is like...like..." Noah
threw his hands up in the air. "Like the worst case of
bachelor chic meets penitentiary vibe I've ever seen.
Seriously. *Bleak*." He slipped his palms into his back
pockets. "This is what I imagine an Eastern Bloc
country's bus depot looked like during the '70s
economic depression."

"The kitchen is good."

"For storing root vegetables?" he asked.

Ky's mouth quirked. "I do make a pretty mean bowl of borscht."

Noah tipped his head back and laughed, his neck a long, lean line that shouldn't have been so entrancing. And, heaven help him, Ky couldn't stop the sigh of relief. The man had a beautiful smile. Seeing it again—the real one, not the forced one—eased the last lingering traces of the heavy conversation.

Unfortunately, as Noah finally followed him out of the living room and down the hallway, the closer they drew to the bedroom the higher Ky's anxiety climbed. He wanted this over, sure, but this space was personal. They were entering the only place in the apartment that contained traces of Ky, facts even his sisters didn't know.

He felt as though he were about to be split open.

"After the living room, I'm almost afraid to see what the bedroom looks like," Noah said as he shot him an amused look. "And that was the first—and *last*—time I'll ever utter those words. Regardless, once we take inventory of what you already have, we'll have to decide on a time to go shopping." Clearly oblivious to Ky's change in mood, Noah passed him by and stepped into the room, abruptly changing topics. "Okay, this is not so bad."

He stopped to stare at the medical school diploma hanging over the dresser, and Ky wondered what the man was thinking. In truth, he shouldn't *care*.

Ky had gotten accepted to Johns Hopkins but had chosen a lesser-known school in Dallas so he could commute from home. At the time the girls had only been twelve and leaving them was an unacceptable option. The age-old disappointment had grown less sharp over the years, but Ky *never* regretted his choice to stay.

The girls favored their mother—Sierra had inherited her love of the ranch, Savannah her artistic flair and gentle soul—and being with them was like having little pieces of his mom around.

Noah picked up the photo of the girls at Sierra's graduation on the dresser. "I heard Sierra is working for your stepdad now."

"Yep. She finished her degree in Rangeland Ecology and Management at Texas A&M and then moved back to the ranch to help Ray."

"No wonder she isn't visiting San Francisco as often as she used to."

"She still manages to get away from time to time," Ky said. "Right now she's visiting one of her friends in Seattle."

"Good for her."

Ky grunted in disagreement. "Maybe. She was supposed to head home yesterday but she didn't. Unfortunately, the only contact we've had is the occasional text message. A sure sign she's up to somethin'."

And sleeping at night wasn't easy with a sister who thought sit-ins and attending protests that sometimes turned violent were a fun way to spend a weekend away.

"I think she's deliberately ignoring my text messages," Ky muttered.

Noah set the frame back on the dresser. "That must put a serious crimp in your role of protective older brother."

"You have no idea," he murmured.

"Definitely less depressing," Noah said as he looked around the bedroom.

"Less depressing?" Except for the diploma on the wall and a photo of the girls, this room was a blank slate, too. "How so?"

"For one, the lack of cardboard is a definite improvement," Noah said with a nod. "And the bed is beautiful and big enough for a game of tennis."

Yeah, he'd gotten a little out of hand when he'd purchased the extra-long king-sized mattress when he'd moved to town.

Noah shrugged out of his denim jacket, tossed it aside, and sat on the bed. "This sucker is amazing. You take your indoor sports seriously, don't you?" He gently bounced up and down a couple of times like a small child. "And I'm curious. Are these games co-ed?"

An amused sound broke from Ky's mouth at the most direct line of questioning the man had used since first trying to ask—without really asking, of course—if he was gay.

"Lame attempt," Ky said dryly.

"Lame is part of my charm."

Ky nodded down to where Noah still bounced a bit on the bed. "That and the five-year-old mindset?"

"Of course." He flopped onto his back and stared up at the ceiling, arms splayed outward, his shirt riding up his trunk a touch. "This really is a decadent piece of furniture, though." A thoughtful frown spread across his face. "It almost makes up for the disastrous living room. *Almost.*"

Ky studied the lithe form and the strip of exposed skin above his waistband, the faint dusting of a happy trail that heated Ky's gut.

And made his jeans uncomfortably tight.

With Noah half sprawled on the bed, their question-and-non-answer game had morphed from entertaining to serious—complete with serious visions of how good he'd look naked. Writhing beneath Ky. And what kind of noises would come from his mouth?

Fuck.

"The closet is over here," Ky said, trying to keep the strain from his voice. He crossed the room and opened the heavy wooden double doors. He waited for a comment about the sparse contents, but none came until...

"Oh, my god."

Noah's voice came from farther away than expected, and Ky turned to discover that he was nowhere to be seen. Along the far wall, the bathroom door stood open.

Oh, shit.

Noah's voice reeked of awe. "This is beautiful. And your *bathtub*. This is definitely the mother of all masturbation paradises."

Would Noah find the expensive bottle of lube he kept next to the tub, within handy reach? The one sitting next to his favorite porn magazine...

"You have the good stuff, too," the man continued.

The good stuff?

The heat that had infused Ky earlier was nothing compared to the inferno blazing up his face now. He strode around the bed and headed for the open door.

"Noah," he said in warning, "our agreement didn't include you commenting on my brand of"—Ky entered the bathroom and caught the focus of the man's attention—"soap," he finished weakly.

"Why, Dr. Davis. You are a closet bubble-bath taker." Soap dispenser in hand, Noah eyed the decadent two-person tub. "Who would've guessed?" He brought the pump container up to his nose and sniffed before reading the description. "*An addictive blend with a hint of bourbon vanilla, mahogany, and almonds*."

He paused and sent Ky a smile. "I didn't hear anything after the word bourbon," he said. "And that explains why you smell good enough to eat. I wholeheartedly approve." He set the bottle back by the tub, and Ky thought he saw the beginnings of a teasing smile. "And don't get me started on the mention of mahogany *wood*—"

"Noah."

Ky took a deep breath and leaned against the doorjamb, trying to maintain a casual posture despite his budding boner. "I thought you were here to take stock of my wardrobe. Last I looked," he said with a droll tone, "normal people don't keep their clothes in the bathroom."

"*Normal people*," Noah said as if he had little use for the words, "don't use cardboard boxes and gaudy-colored totes to make a statement, either." He glanced at the medicine cabinet over the sink. "What other secrets are you keeping?"

Ky refused to reply.

Noah sighed. "Fine," he said, heading back into the bedroom. "But you're sucking all the fun out of this nonpaying job of mine." He stopped in front of Ky, his proximity disturbing. "Speaking of the words sucking and fun—"

"Yeah, yeah." He stifled a smile, but *sweet baby Jesus*, he couldn't take much more. "I get it."

Ky grabbed him by the arm and led him back into the bedroom. His biceps were better-defined than one would have guessed, and the lean frame wasn't as delicate as Noah's self-effacing words had implied.

"Time to focus." *And that goes for you, too, Ky.* He hustled him past the bed and faced Noah in front of the open closet. "Knock yourself out."

Fortunately, the man complied. Which was helpful in some ways, not so much in others. It took concerted effort to ignore the mesmerizing shift of lean hips as Noah worked. Twenty minutes later, every shirt Ky owned, including the ones from his dresser, lay piled on the center of his bed.

"It's worse than I thought." Noah studied the mound of fabric like something had died on the pile and left an awful stench and a trail of entrails behind.

"I like comfort," he said defensively.

"Flannel," Noah said, picking up two of Ky's shirts—granted, he did own a fair amount of the accused style—and waving the plaid fabric as if to solidify his point, "is meant for lumberjacks and pajamas. And pajamas aren't as preferable as sleeping in the nude." He tossed the two shirts back onto the pile. "However, this trip has been informative."

"In what way?"

"Because, one"—Noah held up a finger, counting out his points—"now I know you have little that's useful and we'll be starting from scratch. And two"—he added a second finger with a grin— "the big, surly surgeon likes bubble baths."

Ky employed a sardonic tone. "And that's helpful how?"

"Now I know what to buy you for Christmas if I get your name in our secret Santa pool."

Ky slowly shook his head, losing the thread of the conversation. In fact, from the moment Noah had swept into the apartment, Ky felt as though he'd lost his grip on reality.

"Every year I get together with my friends," Noah explained. "Namely Dylan, Alec, Tyler—with the recent addition of Memphis and Julissa—and we do secret Santa gifts."

"Julissa?"

"We always include Memphis's ex-wife. She's lovely. And now," he said, sending Ky a brilliant smile, "there's you."

Ky paused and forgot to blink. "Me."

"Of course," he said, as though everything was just that simple.

Something in Ky's chest shifted.

He'd be the first to admit moving to San Francisco had left him totally out of his element. Not that he'd had a bustling social life in Texas, but despite the hundreds of thousands of people he could never escape, he felt a little, well...*lost*. Amazing how a bursting-at-the-seams population could make one feel more alone, not less.

"So"—Noah turned and began to rehang Ky's shirts—"when are you available for a fun-filled day of shopping?"

This afternoon hadn't been the easiest, what with Noah's skinny jeans, the arousing sex jokes, and the...arousing sex jokes.

Ky sighed, dreading the event in more ways than one. "I have office hours on Thursday and I work the graveyard shift Friday night," he said. "But I have Saturday off. We can go then."

And, yeah, a full day in Noah's company while in various half-dressed states just might do the rest of Ky's resistance in.

~~~***~~~

Several days later, Noah led Ky up the bustling sidewalk of the Financial District—towering skyscrapers shrouded in an ethereal, heaven-like fog—convinced he had died and gone to his own custom-tailored paradise. The time had come to take the surgeon shopping. Ky Davis, a makeover, and Noah's favorite boutique store...

The stuff hard-ons were made of.

People and vehicles streamed by, car horns muted by the blanket of moisture. The smell of wet concrete sat heavy in the air. A shiver slid up Noah's arms that had nothing to do with the day's cool mist and everything to do with the day's mission.

He hoped he wouldn't embarrass himself. If history was anything to go by, he most likely would. Everything *seemed* perfect.

Perfect except for the fact that Ky clearly didn't want to be here.

"Aren't you excited?" From the corner of his eye, Noah peeked at the doctor keeping pace beside him, the set of the cut, scruff-covered jaw bringing to mind condemned prisoners walking that last mile. "*I'm* excited," he went on. "Won't this be fun?" He winced, belatedly realizing the stupidity of phrasing that in the form of a question. "We're going to have *fun.*"

Maybe the exclamation-point voice had been overkill.

"Fun." Ky stopped in front of the display window, where several mannequins sported suits, neckties wrapped around expressionless heads and used as blindfolds, gags, and restraints for their wrists. He frowned at the Wall Street bondage scene. "I doubt that."

Noah opened his mouth to say something about the surgeon clinging to his Texas roots tighter than Noah clung to his dildo...only to be kneecapped by the look on Ky's face.

Crap.

Fatigue creased the corners of Ky's eyes. Tension lined his shoulders. He looked beat after his shift last night, and as though one ill-timed remark might cause him to crack.

Noah slowly exhaled. "Don't worry, cowboy."

"Easy for you to say."

"It's just a window display. An outlet for the clerk's creative side."

"Wouldn't go over well in my hometown," he said dryly.

An amused breath broke from Noah's throat. "Probably not." He closed the gap between them. "But this store's clothes are excellent and mostly meant for everyday wear, not a night at your friendly neighborhood BDSM club."

Noah had no doubt the man was perfectly capable of getting his frisky on. And the more time they spent together the more convinced he was that Ky was attracted to those of the male persuasion. *Men.* Proud carriers of the XY chromosome combination.

Maybe even guys like Noah.

Regardless, Ky apparently didn't feel free to express his preferences out loud. Oh, he'd handled the suggestive comments in his apartment well enough. But toss in a crowd and he shut down tighter than Noah's skinniest jeans. The *whys*—small-town Texas roots, family issues, or shame, *whatever*—didn't matter.

Especially when the man looked tired and braced for badness, triggering a sharp twinge of sympathy in Noah.

A delivery truck rumbled by on the street behind them as Ky continued to frown at the window display. But Noah was on to him now. The glowering expression always appeared when the man felt out of his element.

Or backed into a corner.

"Seriously," Noah said. "There's no need to be so concerned. My original leather-collar idea was just a joke, obviously."

"What about *that*?" Ky nodded at, of all things, a mannequin's scarf arranged not in a bondage-y way but in a perfectly normal, fashionable-choice-against-the-damp-chill kind of way.

"I promise," he said to the surgeon as he resisted the urge to pat him on the shoulder, "I won't dress you in a similar fashion. No ties. No high-finance bondage. No jaunty scarves."

And no more flirting, Noah.

The time had come to give the overworked surgeon a break. Ky had spent all night helping sick people, working at the county hospital that ensured the neediest of patients received quality health care, too. Fortunately, the hospital had built a beautiful new state-of-the-art trauma center.

Which was nothing like the facility where Rick had died.

Noah braced himself as the memory surfaced...

The morphine pump whirred softly next to the hospital bed, and Noah stared at the ugly gray walls, the white sheets, and the harsh fluorescent lighting that sapped what little color his boyfriend had left.

"You should go," Rick said without opening his eyes, lids pale, the spidery blue veins visible beneath. He tried to shift his position and then sucked in an agonized breath. "You need to get some rest."

They both needed sleep, but sleeping in a hard visitor's chair—or lying in an uncomfortable bed, body racked with pain—wasn't happening. Not for either one of them. Not today.

Not tomorrow, either.

"Rest?" Noah's grin felt tight as he waved away the request. "I'm a man of leisure. I told you when we first met—"

"You mean when your car ran out of gas and you thought it was broken?" Rick said with a tired smile.

Despite the bleak surroundings, Noah laughed. He remembered that day in vivid detail. The new vehicle his dad had leased for him sputtering to a halt in a questionable part of town. Noah, confused by the unfamiliar dashboard, sitting there like a complete idiot.

"I got lucky," Noah said. "A kind, mechanically inclined stranger stopped to help and gave me a lesson about my car."

"You looked pretty clueless."

"I kept waiting for you to tell me I had more money than sense."

"The Porsche should have been a huge freaking sign. Now...go home and get some rest, Noah."

"I can sleep later. As I've said before," he went on, "I'm a man of leisure."

Inexplicably, his boyfriend's smile was filled with fondness. "You're completely crazy."

"Crazy is the word you're going with, huh?" He gave a careful squeeze of Rick's hand, the skin and bone feeling too fragile to withstand much. "We both know you're just being kind."

Despite the crap life had heaped upon him, Rick had always been kind. And now, making a concerted effort to follow in his footsteps was the least Noah could do. Today provided a chance for him to try, *yet again*, to push himself harder to pass that kindness forward. To honor the boyfriend who'd loved him.

Noah was perfectly capable of engaging in a conversation that didn't put Ky further on edge. No suggestive comments or oblique references to sex. He could do this.

Jesus, surely he could do this?

Noah took a deep breath. "And while I'll happily give the scarves a pass, you won't find any scrubs inside, either."

Ky's scowl of reluctance morphed into a defensive frown. "I don't have to think about them," he said. "I just throw 'em on and go to work. This"— he waved his arm encompassing all of downtown San Francisco, and Noah got the feeling clothes weren't the only subject they were discussing— "isn't my thing."

The faint Texas twang made *thing* sound almost like *thang* and, for no reason Noah could identify, had a currently-not-allowed effect on his libido.

"What is your 'thing'?" Noah asked.

Ky's mouth quirked. "Cattle drives. Fixing windmills," he said with a hint of nostalgia in those fascinating, multicolored eyes—a blue-green that faded to a brownish gold in the center. "And fixing abdominal gunshot wounds while a patient tries to bleed out on me."

"No cows here, I'm afraid." He sent a sympathetic smile. "But, hey, maybe you'll get lucky and someone will get gunned down in front of us. This *is* San Francisco. Anything could happen."

Ky shot him a sideways look. "That's what I'm afraid of."

"Look." He gripped the sleeve of the man's flannel shirt, careful not to touch skin. "I have faith that you're capable of graduating past the Garanimals phase of mix and matching coordinates that scrubs provide. I believe that line of clothing stops at the five-year-old size. So come on." He vainly tugged Ky toward the door and then tried again. "Think how happy you'll make Savannah."

As usual, the mention of Ky's sister did the trick, and his immovable form loosened and finally took a step toward the store door. Seriously? Noah was almost embarrassed he held such knowledge and power in his hands.

"Fine." Ky blew out a breath and trailed behind him toward the entrance to the store. "Let's just get this over with."

"There's the half-assed spirit."

"What's the plan?" Ky said as he opened the door for him.

Noah opened his mouth to share the KISS rule as it applied in this case—as in Keep It Sexy, Surgeon—and then pressed his lips together. Because, dammit, he couldn't say that now.

No flirting. Absolutely no flirting, Noah.

"Make you as biddable as possible," he said instead.

A single eyebrow rose in response.

"Remember this is for a bachelor auction," Noah said.

"So?"

"So where's that predictable surgeon's God complex? That cutthroat, competitive nature?" He sent him a firm look. "You don't want to be the man who ends the evening left on the sales rack, do you?"

Ky didn't appear concerned.

"Marked down for any bidder with a checkbook," Noah continued as he passed Ky to enter the store, ignoring the scent of almonds and well-worn leather. "With the appropriate clothes"—*and all the pretty you bring*, he didn't say—"you'll fetch a high-end price and thereby help fulfill my fundraising fantasies."

Sadly, all other fantasies had been permanently shelved—all in the name of being a better man. Sometimes altruism sucked.

The door closed behind them with a tinkle of a bell announcing their arrival. The upscale shop was well lit, with oak floors, slate-gray walls, and chrome track lights shining on the meticulously arranged merchandise.

A muscle-bound blond-haired clerk approached and began to fuss over Ky. But two queens using him as their personal dress-up Ken doll might be too much for the poor man to contend with. His gorgeous head might explode, and not from a wave of orgasmic pleasure.

Which Noah should definitely not be thinking about, either.

The blond eyed Ky closely. "So, how can I help you today?"

The doctor glanced longingly at the exit.

"No need," Noah answered for him.

"Just part of the service we provide, gentlemen."

"That's okay." Noah smiled. "I've got this."

The employee gazed at Ky with hearts and bottles of lube in his eyes. "Let me know if you change your mind."

"*We* won't," Noah said dryly.

When the salesman headed back behind the counter, Noah turned to Ky and mentally recited his list of goals: hands off, no overt ogling. And no smut talk. They were just two guys shopping for clothes.

"Okay," he said with a serious tone. "We'll have to find you something casual yet classy. Last year, most of the men wore suits," Noah said. "One even wore a very nice tux that I would have made fabulous by forgoing the bat-wing collar."

"Bat-wing collar?"

"Yes, and I prefer my collars mostly straight, like I prefer my m—"

He caught himself before saying *men*. Shit, when had *not* mentioning sex become such a massive problem?

"—my whiskey," he finished.

Ky's mouth twitched in amusement before his gaze swept across the rows and rows of merchandise, and the amusement died as he swiped a hand down his face.

"As a reward, when we're done," Noah said, heart pinging at his weary expression, "I'll buy you a cup of coffee."

"It won't get complicated, will it? Because coffee orders shouldn't take ten minutes to recite."

"Oh, God," he said. "You are so small-town it hurts."

Faint humor briefly eased the tired crinkles around Ky's eyes again, and a thrum of pleasure hummed along Noah's veins. Props to himself. He could totally tease the man in a non-suggestive way.

"So," Noah said, forcing himself to focus. "Let's get started."

After convincing Ky to use this time to expand his wardrobe—Noah *had* promised Savannah, after all—they spent a mostly silent hour as he selected three pairs of pants, several casual shirts, and a nice pair of dress jeans that would do wonderful things to Ky's wonderful ass.

Which Noah absolutely did not ogle.

Over the next thirty minutes, the doctor emerged from the dressing room long enough to be carefully poked and prodded, Noah testing the fit of the casual shirts and the dress jeans. Ky, bless him, didn't complain. Even more impressive, Noah managed to resist the urge to skim his hands over broad shoulders or his palms down the man's arms. However, he did check the jeans by tugging on the waistband. He silently congratulated himself for his restraint until he caught a glimpse of the waistband of plain white BVDs beneath.

Unfortunately, that sent Noah's mind wandering into designer underwear territory and licking the happy trail leading to Ky's...

God, he needed a diversion.

"Shoes." Noah turned and headed for the footwear section, knowing he sounded a little scattered. Ky hadn't even tried on the rest of the pants hanging in the dressing room. "We definitely need shoes."

He sized up the selection and made his choices quickly. Years of practice had honed his ability to make split-second decisions without sacrificing good taste.

"These are just the basics," Noah said, piling the appropriately sized items into Ky's arms. "Two pairs of dress shoes, one black—"

"I don't need—"

"And one brown," he plowed on, proud of his ability to keep his lust to himself despite the urge to attack the man with his tongue. "And two pairs of casual shoes with the same color choices."

"Who needs four pairs of shoes?"

"Are you kidding me?" Noah said, risking a scandalized look at the man. "Everyone, Ky. Everyone. And—" His gaze landed on a gorgeous gray suit, and he let out an undignified squawk that, okay, was probably more a squeal of delight.

Ky's eyes drifted to the target of Noah's focus. "No."

"Please."

"I told you, I don't do ties."

"This beautiful thing doesn't need one."

And would look *amazing* plastered across Ky's physique. Noah couldn't help himself as he turned and employed his best pleading look. If he wasn't allowed to flirt or touch or taste the man, the least he deserved was the sight of Ky in a suit.

Just this once. Even if only for a minute.

"You don't have to buy it. All I'm asking is for you to try it on before we leave," Noah said. He waited two beats. And then three more. "I'll take a picture for your sisters." He used another deliberate pause for the maximum effect. "Think about how happy that will make them."

The man studied him for a second before grunting out an *okay*, the agreement accompanied by a frowny gesture that lacked heat but contained plenty of exhaustion, the accompanying eye roll calling attention to the faint bruise-y smudges beneath.

Even in the face of his exhaustion, and a clear loathing for suits, one mention of his sisters and the man caved.

Suddenly the knowledge of how pliable the man was in deference to his sisters no longer made Noah feel powerful. It made him feel, well, sad. Clearly the man reflexively sacrificed his own wishes at the mere thought of making his sisters happy.

Which was noble and all...but. Suddenly Noah's heart was doing more than pinging. His heart *hurt*. Noah was struck with the urge to take the man home and put him to bed, and *not* for sex, because clearly Noah had a problem.

A huge fucking problem, if the previous thought was anything to go by.

The last time he'd tried to take care of someone, his failure had reached tragic proportions. Rick had suffered longer, had died anyway, and then the world had the nerve to cruelly keep turning.

Ky returned to the dressing room, and Noah inhaled a breath.

Crap.

He silently pressed his forehead to the doorjamb. The sound of rustling fabric drifted from the two-foot spaces above and below the door blocking Noah's view.

"I get that you are a very busy, important surgeon, Ky," he said. He stared at the mahogany just inches from his eyes. "But you should take better care of yourself. For your sisters' sakes at least." He bit his lip and considered how to phrase his next statement. "They seem incredibly fond of their big brother."

And worried. And determined to subject him to a sneak-attack setup with a woman.

"After our mom died, they got pretty attached to me," Ky said.

"And what was your father doing?"

The sound of shifting fabric came to a stop.

"My *step*dad"—his voice took on a harsh quality that didn't encourage further questioning— "was working the ranch and, fortunately, rarely around."

Rarely around. *Rarely around.*

No wonder Ky gave off the fiercely protective vibe that Noah found so endearing. The guy went all papa bear, mama bear, and brother bear rolled into one.

That was a powerful lot of bear.

Noah straightened and glared at a row of meticulously folded shirts as though they were personally responsible for robbing Ky of a normal teenager-hood. The upside to the uncomfortable turn in the conversation? The man almost sounded relieved when he asked Noah to hand him the suit to try next.

After Noah complied with the request, his victory felt hollow, and he wandered away to wait for Ky to change and wound up in the underwear section. A subconscious decision, no doubt. He sorted through the selection until he found the perfect style and returned to the dressing room.

"What do you think?" Two pairs of designer boxer briefs clutched in his hand, Noah bent over low enough to display them beneath Ky's door, eyes firmly fixed on the doorknob. "Your former patient, Memphis, is the model and spokesman for this particular brand. I can speak from experience that they are incredibly comfortable. Do you prefer understated black?" he asked, wiggling the appropriate pair. "Or racy red? Which one..."

...screams *here there be ass cheeks of gloriously manly proportion?*

Noah cleared his throat. "Which do you prefer?"

Without warning, Ky opened the door, catching Noah still crouched in underwear-display position. The perfect lip level to be doing dirty, dirty things.

Holy shit.

His thumping heart reached heretofore unattained intensities, and Noah swallowed, every molecule of moisture in his mouth gone.

Ky, in the slim-fitting Versace suit with a classic two-button jacket, had left the silk shirt open at the collar. His expression radiated doubt and distrust. Strangely enough, his heaven-sent body looked completely comfortable, as though oozing sex appeal almost against his will.

That level of hotness should be declared an anomaly of nature.

"When did underwear become part of the makeover?" Ky finally asked.

"Uhm..." He slowly straightened, voice hoarse as though he'd just been deep-throated. "Since the only payment I'm receiving for my services is the joy I'm reaping knowing you'll be cradled in quality?"

God, would that be considered suggestive? That would probably be considered suggestive. Unfortunately, without the freedom to wield his usual smutty words, he felt mute. Stripped bare. The sensation forced him to take a step back.

The time had come to snap the agreed-upon photo, but he couldn't breathe, much less operate his phone.

"Guh, I'll just—" Noah flailed an arm in the general direction behind him and hoped the *wait from a safer distance* was understood. If humiliation were contagious, everyone within a ten-foot radius would probably keel over dead.

After a tense two-second pause, Ky turned and disappeared back into the dressing room.

Noah closed the door with a firm *thunk*, electrified nervous system still trying to recover. He pivoted on his heel and forced himself to head somewhere, anywhere, away from this spot. His buzzing brain kept returning to the image of him on his knees in front of Ky...

No such luck on the lethal secondhand-humiliation thing, though, because a familiar male voice broke his thoughts.

"Lots of eye-banging going on between you two."

Noah looked up to where the clerk stood, smirking at him.

"No." Chest tight, Noah kept his voice low. "Absolutely not. There is no eye-banging going on here."

The employee propped a hand on his hip as though judgment were a part of the services he provided.

"He's... We're..." Noah helplessly waved a pair of boxer briefs in the direction of the dressing room. "Shopping for underwear."

Fuck.

"All he needs now is a couple of dress shirts," Noah went on.

"Are you through helping the gentleman?"

"He doesn't need help," he lied. Because he'd made a promise to himself, dammit, to not visually accost the man who looked like he was ready to drop on his feet.

Maybe they should call themselves done—

No, they still needed those dress shirts to complete their selection.

They should reschedule—

Wrong. Because then they'd have to go through this painful process all over again.

Noah pressed his eyes closed and slowly sucked in a breath. He just needed to hurry this along—he hadn't been this wound up and ready for sex in *ages*. And Ky hadn't even touched him. He hadn't even *looked* like he was going to touch him. Worse, the longer Noah spent in the man's company the more he realized the sexy touching would likely never be an option.

Nobody had the right to tell another person when, or even *if*, to come out. That was an intensely personal decision. Clearly Ky remained in the closet for reasons he'd deemed important, which left him vulnerable. No doubt he was exceedingly discreet about his hookups.

And no one had ever accused Noah of being discreet.

"Well, if you're finished," the clerk said, eyelids flaring in blatant excitement, "I'd be happy to assist him."

I just bet you would.

Ky's earlier expression had left no doubt he wouldn't appreciate the clerk's help. So when the blond stepped in the direction of the dressing room, Noah reluctantly held up his hand.

"No," he said. "That won't be necessary." He'd failed to keep his own libido in check, but he couldn't subject Ky to an even more awkward situation. "I'll do it."

How hard could it be? He'd choose a few dress shirts, throw them on the man to ensure they fit, and then drag him out the door and drop him off in front of his apartment building. Alone. Unmolested, both visually and physically.

Noah eyed the dressing room door with trepidation.

God, he was definitely going to embarrass himself again today.

Chapter Four

Ky stared, unseeing, into the dressing-room mirror as his heart banged against his ribs from a hellish combination of sleep deprivation, the constricting suit, and a surprising attraction to a man who was too beautiful for his own good.

And that *mouth*.

When Ky had opened the door to find Noah's lips at the level of his cock, the sight struck like a thunderbolt. His body—already fried from an OR case involving an unstable gunshot victim who kept trying to die—had *completely* fizzled out. Yesterday's crazy twenty-four hours of call meant he hadn't gotten more than two hours of sleep, max. He didn't trust his exhausted state.

Right now he was all raw nerve endings exposed at the root.

A dangerous combination when paired with a mind flooded with fantasies. Nothing concrete, mind you, mostly just half-formed snippets, vague impressions of pretty, pretty lips against hot, hot skin on well-targeted body parts.

He'd risk Ray permanently banning him from the ranch just for a chance to have Noah's mouth on his cock.

Except Ky's life wasn't the only one the truth would affect.

He fisted his hand at his side, pushing that thought away as he battled the heat licking along his groin. And then Ky inhaled deeply and proceeded to carefully undress and hang up the overpriced suit.

Before taking off the silk dress shirt, however, in a pitiful act of defiance, he pulled on his old jeans and stomped his feet back into his scuffed boots, letting out a satisfied sigh.

Thank God for broken-in leather.

He was almost done unbuttoning the black shirt when a sharp rap came on the door, and he groaned in protest. "Yeah?"

"First things first." Loaded down with a pile of shirts, Noah entered and closed the door behind him.

What the ever-lovin' hell?

"I absolutely insist on natural fabrics," the guy plowed on.

Body braced for the next few minutes, Ky watched as Noah began to hang up his supply of goods—including, of all things, the designer underwear—with barely restrained energy. Seemed as though the more nervous the man was, the more he cranked up his exuberant demeanor. Almost as though he wore it like a protective cloak of invisibility.

Except totally the opposite.

Noah avoided his gaze. "Natural fabrics are a nonnegotiable criteria."

"Nonnegotiable," he repeated dumbly.

"No polyester anywhere near that"—without looking, he waved a hand in Ky's general direction— "that...body."

Ky got the impression he'd meant to say something else. Or maybe include a few choice adjectives. Normally the man tossed out sexual innuendos and bold observations like confetti at Times Square on New Year's Eve.

Today, for some reason, he seemed different.

"Silk, linen, or cotton only," Noah went on, eyes fixed on his clothing selection.

Ky sighed and leaned against the wall. "I guess the wash-and-wear ones are a no-go."

"Absolutely," he said. "Use a laundry service. Or buy an iron and learn how to work it. It's what earns us a higher rung on the evolutionary ladder."

"Irons?" He struggled to hold back a smile. "Not opposable thumbs?"

"Opposable thumbs were an adaptive trait *specifically designed* for grasping irons," he said, the ludicrous statement uttered without cracking a smile. "So. Like high-quality bedsheets, the higher the thread content the softer the fabric." He finally faced him, and his eyes got caught on the strip of Ky's chest bared beneath the unbuttoned black shirt. "And the softer the fabric," Noah went on with a distracted, husky tone, "the more decadent they feel against your skin."

Sweet merciful heaven above.

Ky could almost feel the remainder of his coherent thought processes leaking out his ears. He did his damnedest not to stare at Noah's smooth skin, the thickly fringed eyes. Yep, he had a thing for eyes. He was a sucker for a nice set of lips and a toned body, too, but the thing he noticed most about a person was their eyes.

He'd witnessed enough pain and loss to know that they were indeed little windows into the soul. The first time he'd met Noah, the man's had been wide, roving up and down Ky's body with a glib, gleeful air. But something in the dark gaze hinted at a depth that his flippant mouth seemed determined to deflect.

Ky should be protesting the tiny quarters. Maybe it was the sleep deprivation talking, but now that the dude was here, he kinda liked having him close. And how long had it been since he'd had a man's hands on his skin?

Not helping, Ky.

"Are you gonna stay while I try the shirts on?" he asked dryly.

"Yes, because I can see your patience for shopping is running out."

"A blind person could see it."

"If I stay, it'll save time." His gaze briefly met Ky's before flitting away. "And the overly eager clerk out there is starting to hover. I think he wants in on"—he waved a hand down Ky's torso, clearly holding back the more detailed words again—"dressing this."

"Fine." He pulled off the black silk shirt and held it out.

Several loaded seconds passed by, Noah staring at Ky's naked chest as though his pecs had mind-control powers. Brown eyes traveled over every inch before the man swallowed, Adam's apple rising and falling.

Jesus. They definitely needed to get this done.

"Stay focused." Ky snapped his fingers in front of Noah's face.

Noah's mouth slapped shut. "Sorry." He took the shirt and hung it up before handing him a navy blue one. "I'm usually more subtle than that."

"Subtle?" he said with an amused huff. "You certainly don't know how to be borin'."

"I make it a *point* never to be boring."

"So I gathered." Ky threaded his arms through the sleeves. "Anything else you avoid?"

"Dry towns that ban alcohol."

"I'm not surprised."

"And being mistaken as straight," Noah went on.

"You've got that down pat, too."

Noah dropped his eyes and adjusted the front of Ky's shirt, the expression on his face deliberately casual. "It took me a long time to learn to embrace who I am."

Ky's gut took a nosedive. He didn't know if the statement was indirectly aimed at him and his situation or not. But he didn't sense any judgment. And for that, he was more than a mite grateful.

"How long did it take for you to 'embrace yourself'?" Ky asked.

"I was five years old at least."

"That long, huh?" he said, lips quirked.

Noah adopted the fake innocent look he seemed to favor. "What?" he said. "Kindergarten was a pivotal year for me."

Hunh.

"Rough?" Ky asked.

"For about twenty minutes."

Despite his bone-deep fatigue and the charged atmosphere, Ky cocked his head in curiosity. "What happened?"

Noah stepped back and leaned against the wall, placing about a foot of space between them. The distance helped Ky focus, and he wondered if the man needed the buffer, too.

"The first day of school, my teacher took roll call," Noah began, "and the moment I opened my mouth and said *here,* another kid called me a queen. Which, honestly, as insults go, I don't mind at all. Who wouldn't want to be royalty?" he said with a lift of his shoulder. "Anyway, everyone looked at me and laughed." The tips of his ears grew red, as though reliving the moment. "Well, the ones who knew what the kid was referring to, anyway. Most of them were confused, wondering if I'd hailed from some Disney movie."

Ky remained silent and simply waited for him to go on.

"Regardless," Noah said, a faint flush on his cheeks. "Despite the risk to my Armani Polo and Little Marc Jacobs jeans—I even had a leather varsity jacket, because I was totally *rocking* the school look—I wanted to crawl under my desk and suck my thumb."

Ky blinked, sorting through all the information before landing on the one piece that brought the most vivid imagery. "You were a thumb-sucker?"

"My mother is convinced my fixation for sticking cock-like objects into my mouth began in the womb."

"She—" He coughed, choking on his tongue, due both to the blunt words and the visual they provided. "She said that?"

"Well, she uses the phrase 'phallic-like objects.'"

Ky stared at him, his expression likely approaching one of disbelief.

"I'm completely serious." Noah stepped forward and began to button Ky's shirt. "Hanging on her living room wall is an ultrasound photo of me in the womb, sucking my thumb." He rolled his eyes. "She says it supports the claim that homosexuality begins before birth."

A chuckle tried to rumble out of Ky, but he managed to contain most of the sound. That Noah's mother was eccentric and threw out shocking statements surprised probably no one.

"What happened at school?" Ky asked.

"While the classroom continued to laugh at me, and my teacher did nothing"—he studied Ky's buttons as though slipping them through the holes required the concentration of dismantling a car bomb—"I climbed up onto my desk and promptly told them all to go fuck themselves."

For a moment, Ky forgot how to breathe. For some reason he felt proud of the man he barely knew and horrified for him at the same time.

"I imagine your response didn't go over too well," Ky said.

"The teacher took me to the principal's office, and they called my mother, who proceeded to show up and ream both of them a new one," he said. "And then she pulled me from the school. From that town, even."

"Y'all moved?"

"We moved," he said. "She packed up our house and relocated us to San Francisco, where my father already lived, mostly because she wanted me to grow up in an environment where I would 'be accepted for what I am.' Her words, not mine." Noah winced, his hands slowing on Ky's shirt. "The phrase makes me sound like I suffer from some sort of incurable affliction, and I know she doesn't mean it that way."

Ky tried to keep his voice even. "That must have been rough."

"It was," he said. "But I got over it."

"Like you got over the dumpster incidents?"

Silence stretched between them while Ky waited for the guy to respond to the implied suggestion that he *hadn't* recovered. Because something seemed to be driving the man, something more than the fact his boyfriend had died.

"I know I'm occasionally over-the-top and loud and..." Noah gripped the edges of Ky's shirt as he blinked up at him, and good God almighty, the eyes were too much, too close, far too honest and open. "And sometimes swishy."

Ky had to smile now. "Swishy?"

"In a tastefully delightful way, of course."

"Of course."

Noah tipped his head curiously. "You say that as though you mean it."

"I do," he said firmly.

The guy continued to stare up at him, fingers clutching the shirt and mere millimeters away from bare skin. Ky suppressed the urge to groan as the proximity turned the previous snippets of fantasies into full-fledged graphic ones.

"This is nice," Noah said.

Of course, his statement could have been in regards to anything: the navy-colored shirt, their frank conversation, or the two of them—gazes locked—packed into a small space that felt smaller with every passing second.

"I have several shirts in this size and style, but I think the periwinkle one will really bring out the color of your eyes." Noah gave a brisk, businesslike nod that broke the moment. He stepped back and pulled the bluish-purple shirt from the hanger. "Try this on next."

What, that was it? That's all he had to say?

Lordy, he missed Noah's amusing, flirty comments. Actually *missed* them. Clearly he was a glutton for punishment of the inappropriate kind.

Ky sighed, took off the current shirt, and reached for the new one, threading his arms through the sleeves while trying to decide exactly how this shopping expedition would end.

"Your sister is right, you know," Noah said.

"About what?"

"Two things, actually. Purple is *definitely* your color—"

"I don't wear purple."

"—and you work too hard," he went on, undaunted by Ky's declaration as he hung up the navy-colored shirt. "You also look tired."

Except the guy was back to looking everywhere but at him.

A tense expectation lingered in the air, an odd mix of pointedly ignored sexual frustration, exhaustion, and the man's concern for his well-being.

"Not just fatigued. You look tightly wound," Noah went on with a worried frown, finally studying Ky's face, "like you need a massage or a really good blo—"

Noah froze, and every one of Ky's red blood cells turned into hot concrete blocks, plummeting southward and filling his cock. Strangely enough, the unfinished statement had been delivered without a suggestive tone.

As though making a simple observation about getting sucked off.

Ky held his gaze. "A blow job, huh?"

"I didn't say that."

"The word was implied."

"Okay, fine. Whatever." Noah crossed his arms as though in defense. "But what do you have to say for yourself?"

"In regards to what?" he asked, although he knew the reference was to his workaholic ways. "In regards to the offer of a blow job, it depends on who's offerin'."

Noah briefly looked as though he'd choked on air.

After several blinks, he shut his expression down and attended to Ky's way-too-purple shirt with not a mention of the leading statement. Just a focused concentration on buttoning a couple of the buttons.

When had the atmosphere morphed from teasing to serious? When had this shifted from an amusing game of cat and mouse to one that left Ky ready to confess everything? Confess everything for a chance to have those pretty, pretty lips on his skin...

The heat from Noah's breath on Ky's chest muddled his already sleep-deprived brain.

Noah began to examine the fit of the fabric, and Ky's skin felt as though he'd been out in the sun too long, sensitive and hot and prickly. Forehead furrowed in concentration, Noah simply checked the shoulder seams and the length of the sleeves. He studied the way the fabric hung on Ky's body with a determined look and the slow sweep of dark lashes against cheekbones as he avoided a direct gaze.

In fact, the man hadn't even noticed that, as he tugged on the bottom of the shirt, his fingers were mere inches from Ky's hard-on...which was currently as big as hell and half of Texas.

And why, when Noah *wasn't* playfully coming on to Ky at every turn, couldn't he get his mind off of the possibility of having that mouth wrapped around him?

Noah's eyes landed on the bulge beneath the jeans, and his fingers went still. He also appeared to stop breathing.

Blood pounded in Ky's ears, broken only by a sharp rap on the door.

"You boys need any help in there?" the clerk asked from outside of the dressing room.

A stunned pause filled the air before Noah's dark gaze flew up to meet Ky's.

"Just let me know if you need another opinion," the employee went on. "Three heads are better than two, I always say."

Body humming with awareness, Ky briefly pressed his lids closed. "We, uh," he rasped out, fighting to keep his voice even. He tried again, the words louder and, unfortunately, a lot rougher. "We need...we need a minute."

Jesus. He sounded like he was already engaged in something completely debauched instead of a little eye-fucking of the most arousin' kind.

The four key elements in Ky's every sexual encounter to date were quick and dirty—which definitely fit here—and private and discreet, *neither* of which applied to the current situation. But Ky wanted this. Lord, how he wanted this. The cumulative effects of a prolonged dry spell, bone-deep fatigue, and the beautiful man in front of him were too much.

Not like he could hide the truth now.

"Anything I can do to help?" the employee called with a gleeful tone.

The dude wasn't gonna go away. Goddammit, time to make an executive decision.

Face flushed, Noah said, "No, we..."

His voice died out as Ky reached into his back pocket, flipped open his wallet, and pulled out three one-hundred-dollar bills. Noah watched, obviously baffled.

"Should I leave you two alone?" The clerk's tone was clearly amused. "I could check back in five minutes." A loaded pause followed. "Ten?"

Ky stuffed his hand through the opening above the door and dropped the money. Noah's face made a glacially paced transition from confusion to stunned understanding before finally landing on intensely aroused.

Without breaking Noah's gaze, Ky spoke to the clerk. "We're gonna need another fifteen minutes, at least."

~~~***~~~

A squawk came from the other side of the door, whether in dismay at the lack of invite or in delight at the three hundred dollars scattered at the clerk's feet, Ky wasn't sure.

A hand began to snatch the bills from the floor. "Fifteen minutes, boys."

Noah pressed a palm to his eyes. "I was trying so hard to be good," he muttered, and then Ky watched, stunned, as the guy pulled out his own wallet and another two hundred bucks.

Revving Ky's libido like an electrically charged fence.

"A bribe to ensure your silence," Noah called through the door as he dropped the money, "and, to allow for a peaceful afterglow, an extra five to the originally agreed upon fifteen minutes."

At this rate Ky wouldn't last two, much less twenty.

As the sound of the clerk's footsteps headed away from the dressing room, Noah faced Ky with an expression three parts *game on* and one part *what the hell?*

The latter left Ky with an acute need to explain. "Uh, yeah..." He rubbed his neck. "My sisters don't know." The last thing he wanted was to give the impression his silence on the subject meant shame. And he had no interest in trying to explain the complicated set of circumstances the situation entailed. "It's just...simpler that way."

"I understand," he said solemnly. "And for the record," Noah went on, his smile strained, "I'm painfully aware of the risks. So I'm always careful and I get checked regularly. I assure you, I'm clean."

"So am I."

"Oh, and one more thing before I get phenomenally distracted. Savannah has plans to invite you to lunch and send a friend instead."

Huh?

The pause that followed was clearly meant to be significant. Distracted by the too-tight state of his jeans, Ky couldn't respond, his mind unable to connect the dots Noah had shared.

"A bait and switch," Noah explained. "A secret blind date with her friend, Lisa."

Oh, great.

Ky groaned and rubbed his eyes. "Thanks for the warning."

"You're welcome. So," he said, studying his face before tilting his head in curiosity. "Gay, bi, or something more complicated?"

"Plain, straight gay."

Instead of commenting on the absurd combo of words, Noah paused, a fleeting look of concern fluttering across his face, then disappearing. Several seconds ticked by. And shouldn't somebody be doing something now?

Because Ky's boner hadn't abated and the clock was ticking...

Two more tense heartbeats thudded by, and he began to worry he'd signed on to be some version of himself he'd never met before: self-possessed, with all the right moves. Or, hell, with at least a *few* right moves.

An *adult*.

Sadly, he simply felt awkward, as though he'd been shoved back to the gawky adolescent years that, due to responsibility and circumstance, he'd skipped right over. Sure, he'd mastered the art of the occasional five-minute blow-n-go in med school and residency. But that was with random strangers at random clubs and nothing remotely resemblin' intimacy.

And if he'd never engaged in anything more emotionally charged than a figurative—or literal— back-alley hookup, what made him think he was ready now? Unsure what to do with his hands, he jammed his thumbs through his belt loops.

Noah raised both eyebrows. "You look like you want to change your mind."

"I don't."

"But...?"

"We just invested five-hundred dollars."

"Which bought us time," Noah said.

"And unreasonable expectations?"

Fuck, now was not the moment for brutal honesty. But what if Ky came too fast? What if he couldn't come at all? Except, given the current state of his hard-on, that hardly seemed likely. In response to the concerned look on Noah's face, Ky gave an awkward shrug.

"Nope," Noah said. "Just no." He skimmed warm hands up Ky's chest, undoing the few fastened buttons and spreading the edges of his shirt wider, leaving a trail of goose bumps behind. "None of that."

Noah leaned in and pressed a kiss to the center of his chest.

Christ.

The gesture was so soft and so sweet and so simple, for a moment Ky was confused. He gripped the man's elbows, hoping the contact would ground him in reality.

Noah rested his chin on Ky's chest. "All kinds of no to the performance anxiety pressures." Hands cupping his torso, he looked up at him, eyes warm and bright. "If it's any consolation, it's been so long that I've forgotten what this is like."

"What do you mean?"

And, good Lord, Noah had dropped his hands to the front of Ky's jeans, briefly short-circuiting the nerve endings connecting mouth and mind. The guy had the button open, the soft rasp of the zipper lowering before Ky managed to pull his thoughts together.

"A long time since what?" Ky prompted again. Because he couldn't imagine a sexual situation that Noah hadn't already participated in numerous times. Hell, he could probably give lectures on the subject. "Since you had sex in a dressing room?"

"No."

"Since an encounter involved a five-hundred-dollar bribe?"

"Nope. Since an encounter involved a one-hundred percent, bona fide confirmed gay."

Those distracting fingers now reached down the front of Ky's jeans, beneath his briefs, and...

Shit.

Ky bit his tongue against a moan.

A soft hand closed around Ky's very hard dick, and Noah let out a happy-sounding sigh and ran his nose around a nipple, sending fiery sparks radiating outward.

A ridiculously hot turn-on for such a simple act.

Noah stroked Ky, fist sliding insistently along the shaft, while his mouth got busy on his chest. A rub of his nose here. A flick of wet tongue there. A damp, open-mouthed press of lips. Slowly he teased the two flat buds until they grew stiff.

And then he pulled a nipple into his mouth with a greedy sound that shot straight to Ky's cock, leaving every hair standing on end, his voice hoarse.

"*Noah.*"

And this? This part didn't surprise Ky in the least.

All of the man's measured looks, all those knowing smiles had to have meant something— probably sizing Ky up and determining the best way to make him lose his mind. And despite their surroundings, or maybe because of them, Noah seemed determined to take his time.

As though cataloging the reaction of Ky's body to every move.

Ky was used to dark and dirty, hurried and harried—every encounter to date a heated rush of lips and tongues and cocks and hands. Satisfying, sure, but he'd never achieved a state where he could *completely* relax and enjoy the moment.

Noah pushed the shirt off Ky's shoulders, the fabric dropping to the floor with a quiet *shush.* "You're thinking too much."

"I'm impressed I can think at all," he drawled.

"Clearly I'm failing at my job."

His job?

Before he could ponder that further, his jeans and boxer briefs were shoved to his thighs.

"Jesus, Noah. I—"

The man dropped to his knees and pressed his nose to the base of his dick, and Ky sucked in an unsteady breath, the rest of the words dying in his throat.

"This is my favorite part," Noah said in a low voice.

Ky's thighs tensed, anticipation humming in his veins.

"The musky smell," Noah murmured. He dragged his tongue up the sensitive shaft and finished with a teasing flick at the precum collecting at the tip. "The taste. And the feel," he went on, hand stroking Ky's dick without pause. "The spectacular view."

Without so much as a warning, the man swallowed his cock deep.

"Nyuh," Ky's voice broke on a groan.

He stared down at the bobbing head, the flushed cheeks hollowing out with every pull.

Noah's mouth stretched wide, lips sliding along Ky's shaft as pleasure coiled low and tight in his back. The hot rasp of tongue circling the head on the way up slowly took him apart, only to be repeated again.

Ky's muscles trembled with the tension.

His balls felt tight.

He bit his lip, struggling to keep the noises to a minimum.

But God, he needed...something. He threaded his fingers through the guy's hair, gently scraping his fingers along the scalp. The action pulled a satisfied groan from Noah that shook Ky all the way to his boots, leaving him super-heated.

Skin too hot.

Noah began to bob his head faster, and all Ky could do was close his eyes to try and keep from coming. But the warm, wet suction continued to drag him relentlessly toward the finish line.

"Noah," he gritted out, "*please*."

Which could have meant *slow down* or *hurry up*, and all Ky could think was yes and *yes*.

Every once in a while he peeked down, storing away images to pull out later in the privacy of his own bedroom. Or the bathtub. Or wherever the hell, heaven help him, Ky could relive this fucking glorious moment. Noah going down on him was everything he'd imagined—

The man gripped Ky's ass and shifted them both until the back of Noah's head hit the wall, pulling hard.

Ky's cock hit the back of the guy's throat. "Fuck." The word belted out with a thick twang.

From somewhere in the store, the clerk laughed.

A confusing mix of emotions hit, two parts illicit thrill and one part toe-curling arousal, all tinged with a trace of anxiety. He clenched his jaw, thighs shaking from the effort to rein his movements in.

"Fuck," Ky whispered again.

He received a reassuring hum in response, so he clutched Noah's hair and rocked his hips. The tighter he gripped his head, the more Noah moaned and dug his fingers into Ky's ass, encouraging him to dig deeper.

Gradually the act shifted from something Noah languidly gave into something Ky *took*.

Apparently the guy enjoyed a little manhandling, as evidenced by the vision he presented: eyes almost rolled back in his head, enthusiastic whimpers of encouragement as Ky's length disappeared deep inside over and over again. Not to mention the telltale bulge beneath Noah's pants...

Sweet Jesus, he was done.

"Noah, I'm—"

Ky fucked into his mouth once, twice, cock straining. One more thrust and every muscle in his body clenched, his too-hot blood rushing through his veins as he released his load, hitting the back of Noah's throat as he came.

For a moment all Ky could see were white stars flickering against the black backdrop of his lids.

Eventually he managed to open his eyes and stare stupidly down at Noah. Lips spit-slick and rough-red, he ran his tongue up the length of Ky's cock and paused at the tip to suck the last drop from the slit with an appreciative sound. As though the flavor was meant to be savored.

Skin overly sensitive, Ky whined in protest, too come-dumb to speak.

"Sorry." Noah looked up at him with disheveled hair and a debauched expression, his breath heavy, dick tenting his pants. Clearly something needed to be done.

And Ky, thank God, got to be the one to do it.

"Come here," Ky said.

He cupped the man's face and urged him up until his chin leaned against Ky's collarbone, their bodies pressed together from waist to toe.

"Jesus christamighty." Noah arched his hips, erection rubbing against a thigh, and his eyelashes fluttered closed. On the second thrust, a desperate sound broke from his mouth.

With a hard cock wedged between them, suddenly it didn't matter that Ky had technically finished. The need to touch, to taste everything, was overwhelming.

He dipped his head for an open-mouthed kiss, the man panting as though he were the one who'd just seen stars. A hint of salt lingered on his tongue.

Seeking *more*, Ky slid his hand between them in search of Noah's dick, frustrated by the awkward angle and the barrier of clothes. He needed to feel skin. The heat of his hard-on. But first things first. He upped the urgency of the kiss and palmed the fabric covering the erection, pressing hard.

A surprised noise slipped from the back of Noah's throat, the sound rumbling into Ky's mouth, and with two jerks of Noah's hips, the fabric grew damp beneath Ky's hand...

Hunh.

He gave the man a moment to recover before he smiled, lips still pressed against his mouth.

"Well," Ky murmured. "That was easy."

"Easy is my middle name," he murmured back.

"I thought it was princess?"

At the nickname, Noah laughed and pulled his head back to meet his gaze. "A guy wears a bandanna with the word princess *one time* and gets labeled forever."

"Typically only five-year-old girls consider it a legitimate fashion choice."

"Didn't your sisters ever make you play dress-up?" Noah asked.

"They did."

"Ballerina tutu?"

"Tiaras."

The moment the word tumbled out, Ky regretted being so honest. Heat infiltrated his face as Noah's eyes grew wider in comprehension. The man looked on the verge of creaming his pants a second time.

"Holy mother of..." Noah stepped back, a blatant wet spot at his crotch. "Is that the blackmail picture that Savannah mentioned? And please tell me that somewhere there's an online picture of you sporting a tiara and a scowl."

Ky's lips twisted in a cross between an embarrassed frown and an amused quirk, and he folded his arms in front of his chest. Despite the humiliating discussion, the delighted look on Noah's face was as addictive as the one he wore when he came. And that wasn't the kind of thought Ky should be having right now.

Or ever.

"I can neither confirm or deny the existence of such a picture," Ky said.

Noah unfastened his waistband, shifting Ky's heart rate higher again.

Did he want to go another round? Here? He was definitely up for another round, but this time he wanted privacy and time. His cock twitched the moment the man pulled off his pants and Ky caught sight of his dick, flushed red, semi-hard, and still glistening at the tip.

Damn, all he wanted was a taste...

Noah threaded his toned legs into the red boxer briefs and pulled them up, the mesmerizin' sight of his cock disappearing beneath the fabric. Ky struggled to keep the disappointment from his face.

"They're not my size, but these will definitely be worth the cost of purchase," Noah said, snapping the waistband in place. "At least my underwear won't be wet on the way home." He pulled his pants back on, pulling a face as he stared down at the wet spot on display. "But I'm afraid I'll have to buy you that coffee another time."

Oh, they were done for the day. Of course they were done.

Why had he thought otherwise?

Ky mentally chastised himself for being an idiot as he dressed and Noah sorted through the shirts and pants he'd chosen, rambling on about various combinations that would work for the bachelor auction. Items in hand, they made their way to the front of the store to pay. Ky decided it was best just to avoid the clerk's gaze. Noah didn't appear fazed at all as he set the articles of clothing onto the counter.

"And I'm currently wearing a red pair of these," Noah said, tossing the black designer underwear onto Ky's small pile of goods. "But you can charge them both to my account."

"No," Ky drawled. "I'll pay for them."

The clerk's smirk grew bigger. "Matching boxer briefs, how cute," he said. "Will there be anything else?"

"Yes." Noah held up the rejected periwinkle shirt that had been the prelude to the best blow job ever. "My friend here refuses to wear purple, but since we won't be doing this again, I'd like to buy this one for myself." He sent Ky a loaded look infused with nervous energy before letting out a mock, wistful sigh. "As a memento."

A memento.

Memento?

Mind churning on the phrases *we won't be doing this again* and the accompanying tone, Ky paid and gathered the shopping bags. There certainly wouldn't be a repeat shopping expedition, but the expression on Noah's face implied the blow job was a one-shot deal as well.

And why couldn't Ky decide if that was a good thing...or bad?

Chapter Five

From his super-comfy couch, Noah clutched his empty shot glass and stared up at his living room ceiling, wondering where his day had gone so tragically wrong.

After two shots of tequila, he'd just jerked off twice, *twice*, and still felt too keyed up to relax. Like his body expected more. As though after years of a beautiful relationship, his right hand had suddenly become a piss-poor adjunct to his sexual repertoire. Clearly the hot moment in the dressing room was no different from any of the other countless hookups he'd had over the years.

Except for the fact that it was.

Specifically, his choice of partner...

Noah slung his arm across his face, shielding his eyes from the bright, harsh light of reality.

In the beginning, he'd briefly held out hope that beneath Ky's disapproving expressions and occasional frowny face lurked the heart of a closet asshole. Granted, the evidence had been near nonexistent, at best. Sadly, Noah was now forced to accept the truth.

The man had sacrificed a good portion of his life taking care of his sisters, forever disqualifying him from asshole status. And somewhere out in the universe was a picture of Ky Davis in a tiara—and no doubt a scowl on his face—posing with at least one, possibly both, of the twins.

Just the knowledge of its existence did melty things to Noah's heart.

Even worse, Ky was gay. Not even a little bit of a confused bi. Which meant there'd be no last-minute self-doubt propelling him out the door before Noah lost his freaking mind and grew tempted to try for a repeat. In fact, Noah was starting to like Ky so much he now felt the first stirrings of...attraction.

And not in the beautifully buff, *I make you come in your pants* kind of way.

Sympathy for the man's plight was one thing. Respect for his character another. But real attraction? The kind that went beyond cut physiques, rugged masculinity, and amazing eyes?

This violated his personal KISS rule: Keep It Shallow, Stupid.

Only once since Rick had Noah made the mistake of considering more than simple sex.

One week after the first anniversary of his boyfriend's death, Noah had spent time with a man who treated him well, liked him back, and was pretty good in the sack. And every time they'd had sex, not only had Noah's skin broken out in splotches, a prickly itch that wouldn't go away, afterward he'd gone home and puked in the toilet.

Puked.

Eventually he'd decided that the ugly rash and vomiting weren't some heretofore undiscovered and horribly inconvenient STD but his body's way of reminding him he sucked at relationships—the mere *suggestion* of one and his skin and stomach had revolted en masse.

Which was good to remember, really, because only a truly selfish person sentenced their loved one to spending their last few months in pain, their life a living hell.

Except, unfortunately, that wasn't even the worst of Noah's crimes...

Oh, God.

The song "Midnight Rider" split the air, and Noah answered his phone, grateful for the interruption by his best friend, "What's up, handsome?"

"You coming tomorrow?" Dylan asked in lieu of a greeting.

Tomorrow.

Noah sat up on the couch. Shit. He'd almost forgotten about the meeting to discuss the Bachelor Bid preparations, a meeting he was required to attend...as was Savannah, seeing how she was the event planner and all. Would she drag her brother along?

His stomach twisted tight at the thought.

A loud, staccato *bap, bap, bap* belted over the phone followed by a grating whine, buying him some time and a distraction.

"Who the hell is that?" Noah asked over the noise.

"I hired some part-time help in the garage."

"What's he using? An Uzi and a bone saw?"

"Impact wrench."

Noah didn't ask more. Through the years, he'd shared a lot of things with his closest friend, but a love for the mechanic's job restoring vintage motorcycles wasn't one of them. Noah preferred bikers to bikes.

When the echoing noises in his garage died away, Dylan said, "Dude, you have to come tomorrow. You know my idea of organizing a fundraiser taps out at barbecue and beer."

"That's why we work so well together," he said with a smile.

"How do you figure that?"

"I broaden your cultural horizons—"

"Not even on a good day," Dylan said dryly.

"—and your caveman qualities make you a fascinating subject of study," he went on, ignoring his friend's remark.

A skeptical sound escaped Dylan, the verbal equivalent of an eye roll. "You'd be lost without me."

The teasing words cut so close to the truth Noah couldn't come up with a response. They'd met through Rick and forged a lasting friendship during his illness, the relationship solidifying into brothers-in-arms while dealing with his death. Dylan had fallen apart as his friend's body had wasted away. Noah never would have survived the aftermath without Dylan. And that wasn't his usual drama-queen exaggeration.

He'd very probably be dead.

Noah had come to, after a week of imbibing, to Dylan yelling at him, fear in his gaze and anger in his tone. In search of an alternate form of pain control, Noah had then hit on his best friend. But Dylan had simply hauled him home, spending the next several days hovering and nursing him back to health and in general telling him to get a grip.

"If you don't show up for the meeting, the Bachelor Bid will fail for a second year in a row." Dylan didn't mention the man whose memory had motivated the fundraiser, or how much he missed him, too. "I suck at planning these fancy things."

"Alec is perfectly capable."

"He's a little distracted right now."

"That's right, your surrogate is getting closer to delivery." Noah's tone turned amused. "I assume Alec's busy nesting before the arrival of the baby."

"Like a flock of nervous mother hens," he said. "And you're avoiding my question about the meeting." The silence stretched, as though the man was just now paying close attention. "Why are you avoiding my question?"

Noah rolled his top lip between his teeth, mind scrambling to come up with an appropriate response. His too-perceptive—but only when inconvenient—friend plowed on before he could respond.

"Memphis mentioned Ky Davis was at your condo the other day," Dylan said with a guarded tone. "You're not chasing another straight dude, are you?"

"Of course not," he said too quickly, the words a half an octave higher than usual. "What makes you think that?"

"Uh, because I know you?"

Too true.

After the interlude with Mr. Nice Guy, Dylan had witnessed Noah's ongoing quest for the vomit-free, hive-free big O...and the tragic, dark months that had followed.

Shame swamped him, hot and heavy, the air too thick in his lungs.

But he was quite capable of learning from his mistakes—good thing, too, since he made so many of them. Eventually, he also made an invaluable discovery. If he limited himself to men looking for a little sexual experimentation, their behavior after the fact was refreshingly predictable, awkwardly bolting as soon as the last man came.

Problem solved.

Feel-good sex for the win, minus the shame and ugly splotches, of course.

"I'm just fulfilling a makeover fantasy," Noah said.

A sharp, disbelieving grunt filled his ear.

"I recognize that tone of voice," his friend said. Silence followed, leaving Noah squirming against the couch as Dylan went on. "What did you do?"

"I didn't do anything."

"Noah, what did you *do*?"

Ugh, his least favorite Dylan setting was the incredibly rare, inconveniently wise and observant one.

"I...I sucked Ky off in the dressing room."

The man's dismayed groan put the previous grunt to shame.

Crap.

"You can't—don't—" Noah slapped a palm to his head, feeling like a lowlife. Ky had trusted him to keep his secret and...*dammit*. Unfortunately, Dylan's blunt mouth mixed with an unconfirmed suspicion were a bigger threat. "Don't tell anyone, okay? His family doesn't know. He doesn't want anyone to know."

"Relax, dude," he said, his voice soft. "I won't even tell Alec."

He wouldn't, either. Dylan's steadfast, loyal ways had pulled Noah through more shitty times than he could remember—literally, because a lot of those involved too much alcohol.

"This was a good thing, actually." Noah forced an optimistic tone. "I mean, it's better that Ky and I got the moment over with."

"Yeah, right."

Noah ignored his friend's wry tone. "Now we can both put the incident behind us and focus on preparing for the fundraiser."

He ignored the disappointed, pathetic whines taking place in his head. But if Noah felt this conflicted after the glorious time blowing the man, imagine how awful he'd feel after a full night of amazing sex? Amazingly, deliciously awful.

Blotchy hives, puke breath, and all.

"You're sure it's over?" Dylan asked.

"You know me," he said. "The queen of one and done."

His friend sighed and Noah pictured him plowing his hand through his hair.

"Noah, you know I take my job seriously—"

"Which job?"

"The one where I point out all your bullshit," he said. "But Tyler and Memphis are still busy making moon eyes at one another, and my boyfriend can't concentrate on anything other than the upcoming addition to our family."

Normally his friend wouldn't give a rat's ass—Dylan's expression, not Noah's—about the details of an upscale fundraiser. Obviously, he was feeling the pressure.

"I need you focused," Dylan said. "So just...just keep it in your pants and concentrate on the Bachelor Bid, okay?"

"Okay."

"And by that I don't mean *Ky* the bachelor, but the event itself."

"*Okay.*"

"And I don't want to be dealing with any awkwardness, either."

"Uh..."

Noah remembered glancing up at Ky's flushed cheeks and sex-stupid expression—the doctor with broad shoulders, a Texas twang, and a cowboy complex—and after a single push of the man's palm against his cock, Noah had come. Awkward moments *ahoy.*

He covered his eyes with his hand and waited for the anxious rush of blood to calm down.

"Don't worry," Noah said, telling himself the same. "Ky and I are adults. We would have gone for coffee afterward if I hadn't—"

Shit.

He held his breath, hoping he wouldn't have to go on.

"If you hadn't *what*?" Dylan asked.

"Jizzed in my pants," he mumbled, face growing hot.

"Jesus." The laugh that came held no sympathy. "When did you get so eighth grade?"

Noah frowned and briefly considered re-prioritizing his best friend designation, switching Dylan to second behind Alec.

Dylan sighed again. "This is definitely gonna get awkward."

"Not true." It wasn't like he didn't know how to handle the usual predicaments. "This is me you're talking to. I've never met a morning after I couldn't handle. Now," he said, smoothing his fingers down his favorite pair of skinny jeans, "I'll let you get back to your decrepit motorcycle du jour."

"I'll have you know I only work on *classics*."

Affection surged, and Noah smiled. He made a teasing, kissy-face sound, disconnected the phone, and flopped back to his original position staring up at the ceiling. Without the friendly, familiar ribbing from Dylan, Noah's confidence began to wane.

Then again, he hadn't lied. He *was* an expert at handling awkward post-orgasmic moments.

One time, he'd agreed to go down on a guy who'd been divorced for two years. After the man had screamed in pleasure, he'd broken down and confessed he still loved his ex-wife. The tears had been a bit of a buzzkill, yes, but Noah liked to think his life-altering sexual skills and the brief heart-to-heart he'd had with the man afterward were the reason the couple had reconciled. They'd even proceeded with a second, ill-advised walk down the aisle.

Because that's how Noah rolled: Model philanthropist. Giver of good head.

Saver of marriages.

He blew out a breath and stared at his ceiling, trying not to picture Ky's mid-orgasm scrunch face, which was *worlds* better than a worried frown.

If nothing else, tomorrow wouldn't be boring.

~~~***~~~

Shading green eyes against the noontime sun, Savannah said, "I'm so glad you're here."

I wish I was.

Ky held both his tongue and the driver's-side door open for his sister as he attempted to *not* look distracted. With any luck, Noah wouldn't show up today. Given his involvement in planning the fundraiser so far, things weren't looking too hopeful. Ky wasn't afraid the man would give anything away.

His lips twisted in a humorless smile.

Because, strangely enough, *Ky* represented the bigger danger.

Mind still blown from the dressing room, try as he might, he couldn't figure out how to arrange his facial muscles into a bland expression. Just days ago, he'd missed Noah's amusing, flirty comments. Actually *missed* them. But how the heck would Ky handle them now that he'd had the guy's mouth on his dick?

Heat swamped his body, and Ky bit back a groan.

"I know I mentioned this before," Savannah said as she climbed out of her car and into the brisk air, closing the door, "but thanks again for coming with."

"I don't mind."

"You sure?"

"It's not a problem," he lied.

"You must have better things to do on a Saturday."

She'd delivered the words with a genuinely hopeful expression and a trace of worry in her gaze.

Truthfully, his life outside of work wouldn't fill half an episode of a lame reality show.

As a kid, he'd never been the sociable sort, the situation made worse during his teens. He'd spent most afternoons doing chores and helping his sisters with their homework, countless nights after their mama's death waking to Savannah's screams, brushing her hair from a forehead sticky with sweat from yet another nightmare. He should be glad they didn't need him like that anymore, glad the dirtbag of an ex no longer created an immediate threat. And Ky was, even as he struggled to let them go.

Apart from his career, the girls were all he had.

In retrospect, he realized he'd chosen his profession for two reasons—a love for the OR *and* to provide an escape. As the twins had slowly grown more independent, burying himself in years of school and in his job had always been the easiest route to take. Being busy, throwing himself into his work beat thinking about the future.

"Hold out your hands," Savannah said.

"What?" Standing beside her vehicle, Ky pushed the unhelpful thoughts aside and did as instructed. "Why?"

She stared down at his splayed fingers as if checking for dirt. "Good," she said with a decisive nod. "I wasn't sure if you'd develop tremors."

"Tremors?"

"Yes, withdrawal from spending several hours away from the operating room."

"Ha," he drawled, dropping his arms to his sides. "Not funny."

She smiled up at him, her teasing tone lacking the sharp, sarcastic barbs her twin always tossed out. "Do they have a workaholics anonymous support group at your hospital?"

"You know what they say," he said, reaching for the familiar. "The problem with taking call every other night is that—"

"Is that you miss half the surgical cases," she finished for him. She lifted her gaze in a *spare me* expression, clearly unimpressed, and tugged open the trunk of her Honda Civic. "You've told me that a million times before," she said. "Amazingly enough, that stupid quip is less funny now than when you were a resident."

"That's the job I chose."

"*Your job* shouldn't define your entire life." She looked at him with disappointment in her eyes. "I think you and Lisa could have been good together."

He groaned. "No more secret blind dates." Thank God Noah had warned him, allowing him to prepare and deliver a gently worded *thanks but no thanks* yesterday at the restaurant. "Lisa's nice. But like I told her, I'm not looking for a relationship right now."

"You always say that."

"Savannah—" He didn't go on. What was left to say?

She groaned and reached into her car, pulling out an oversized box and holding it in his direction. "Here, make yourself useful and put those muscles to work."

As she piled smaller containers of fabric samples on top of the bigger one in Ky's arms, her short, blond hair made her look young and carefree. The stiffness in her shoulders suggested otherwise. That and the grim set to her usually very tranquil face were a testament to the mass of nerves teeming inside.

God, he should have noticed that expression sooner.

"Hey," he said softly. He shifted the boxes, securing the stack higher against his hip with one arm. "You've got this, kiddo." He ruffled her pixie-cut hair in a gesture of, he hoped, reassurance. "You've already got the job, and they're gonna love your ideas."

"I hope so."

She gnawed on her lower lip, staring up at Dylan and Alec's Mediterranean-style house with massive bay windows, well-kept yard, and two motorcycles parked in the brick driveway.

"Because this is shaping up to be the biggest event I've done yet," she said. "Not to mention the first time Sierra couldn't come to San Francisco for an extended visit to help me out."

"She's focused on the ranch now."

"I know. After a lot of rocky years, I'm thrilled things are going so well between her and Daddy now."

"Me, too," he said, his tone sincere.

For a while, Ky had toyed with the idea of coming out once the girls had started college. Once Sierra announced her plans to work with her dad, he'd nixed that idea. Because in no universe would the twins' father *not* cause a problem, a rift too big to be hidden, no matter how hard Ky might try. His mother had always counted on Ky to help take care of the twins. And, dammit, he'd honor his mother's memory by continuing to protect his sisters, no matter what.

Anything less would be letting his mama down.

Savannah went on. "It's just..."

He waited patiently for her to continue.

"The ticket sales are already twice that of last year's. Which means two times the crowd," she said, voice shifting up an octave in panic. "Some of the biggest movers and shakers in San Francisco are expected to be there. And..." For a moment, her face crumpled a little before she continued. "I hate the thought of letting Dylan and Alec and Noah down."

Ky sighed. From the moment Dylan Booth had hired Savannah for her first event—a motorcycle rally to raise money for AIDS research—both his sisters had thought the moon and stars orbited around the man. That had been two years ago, and Dylan had told Savannah the job was hers for as long as she wanted to organize the annual event.

Ky suspected that she'd fallen for the mechanic, just a bit. But Dylan looked incredibly content with his boyfriend. Ky had listened to his sisters go on and on about how cute the two men were together, until the need to escape almost overwhelmed him. His silence about his own orientation had weighed heavier with every comment.

"You're not gonna let anybody down," he said.

She pulled a face, probably in an attempt to hide her nerves, and Ky's heart pinched in sympathy. He hated the lingering self-confidence issues that continued to plague his sister. Made him want to hunt down the crazy ex of hers again and follow through on his threats.

"You can't guarantee I won't disappoint them." Savannah closed the trunk and pushed the key fob, the *click* of the locks punctuating her statement. "I'm not the little girl you used to yell at when she forgot her bicycle helmet. Or threatened ex-boyfriends for." She stared down the quiet street lined with beautifully restored homes and smelling of freshly mowed grass, a pensive look on her face. "You can't keep trying to protect me from the world."

Ky sent his sister a mock scowl. "Watch me."

Savannah laughed, and some of her tension evaporated. "You've got a one-track mind," she said as they made their way up the walk to the house.

Dylan Booth didn't seem the type to settle in such a nice suburb of San Francisco. His partner, on the other hand...

Blue eyes crinkling as he smiled, Alec opened the door and led them into the living room, offering them a drink from their impressively well-stocked bar. The oxford-shirt-wearing doctor had a bottle of water in his hand. Dylan, motorcycle enthusiast and lover of well-worn jeans, held a bottle of beer and didn't look the type to care for much else. Ky suspected their wide array of liquor choices was more in honor of their friend, Noah, than for a love of all things alcohol.

God, *Noah*...

Ky settled into a leather chair by the window, content to let the three engage in conversation while he lived in dread of the moment the man showed up. Maybe he wouldn't. Maybe Ky would get lucky. Maybe—

A knock sounded at the front door, and Ky's stomach plummeted.

Savannah popped off the couch like she'd been expecting someone. "I ordered pizza for lunch."

His sister crossed to the foyer, her hand twisting the bracelet Ky had given her as a graduation gift. It was another one of her tells. Her *nervous* tell. And as she disappeared into the hallway, Ky wondered why the hell ordering pizza would make her look so out of sorts.

Seconds later, Savannah reappeared with Sierra at her side, the long-blond-haired twin holding four pizza boxes and the biggest *got you* grin on her face.

Two beats passed before the sight fully registered. And then his heart surged and instantly grew lighter.

"Jesus, Sierra," Ky said.

He shot up, crossed the room in three long strides, and pulled his sister into a fierce hug. Fortunately, Savannah rescued the pizzas from her sister before they toppled to the carpet. Sierra wrapped both arms around his middle, squeezed hard, and didn't let go.

And Ky's world, off-kilter since the day the three of them no longer lived under the same roof, seemed to right itself again.

"You're here," he said, voice rough with emotion. "God..."

Ky closed his eyes. Right now the girls—*both* of them—were by his side, safe and sound, looking healthy and relatively happy. Given how hard they'd all fought to reach this point, Ky refused to feel guilty about his display of brotherly affection.

"Why didn't you tell me you were coming?" he asked, chin resting on her head.

Her voice was muffled against his chest. "I wanted it to be a surprise."

"Missed you," he said.

"I know," she said, the smile evident in her tone. "Couldn't wait to see you, either."

Sierra pressed her forehead against his chest, like she'd always done as a kid. The strawberry scent of her shampoo hit his nose, and he discreetly inhaled a contented breath.

"I get the feeling my being here today was planned," Ky said.

"You have no idea how hard I had to work to get him to come along," Savannah said to her sister.

"I wouldn't have been so subtle," Sierra said.

A wave of affection had him tugging on a strand of her hair like she was twelve and not twenty-four.

She leaned back, arms linked around his waist, and looked up at him. "On my drive back to Texas, I decided to swing by San Francisco and surprise you."

The smell of tomato sauce and the presence of the other men finally registered, and Ky cleared his throat and stepped back. Sierra greeted Alec and Dylan with a big grin and took the pizzas back from her sister.

"I got a meat lovers for Dylan." Sierra crossed into the living room, passing out the boxes as she continued on. "Alec, you get the feta cheese with spinach. And my brother, with his appalling lack of imagination," she said dryly, "gets pepperoni."

"It's a classic," he said, accepting the box.

"It's boring," his sister insisted. "And I got Noah—" Sierra paused and looked around the room even as Ky's gut tightened. "Where's Noah?"

"Not here yet," Dylan said around a bite of pizza. *Yet.*

Ky's hopes got dashed with the single word. Savannah was less likely to read anything into his interactions with Noah. But Sierra? Sierra had been born suspicious. Her sharp eyes wouldn't miss a thing. She'd probably see things that *weren't* there.

"So, you never told me why you stayed in Seattle longer than you'd planned," Savannah said to her twin.

Sierra's gaze flicked to Ky before skittering away. "Something kind of came up."

Shit, he knew that look. Tension settled between Ky's shoulders, and he broke out in a cold sweat. Damn, Noah hadn't even shown up yet and he was already perspiring.

"Sierra," he said in a cautious tone. "What—?"

"Dylan. Alec," she called out, her face lighting up as she shifted her attention to the couple. "Any news from your surrogate?"

A loaded pause passed as the room adjusted to the whiplash change in subject.

"The surrogate is doing well," Alec said evenly. "According to her last ultrasound, so is the baby." His smile put the sun to shame. "Could be any day now."

But Ky refused to let his sister's diversionary tactics stand.

"Sierra." Ky slowly set his unopened box of pizza back on the coffee table. "Not that I'm *not* happy to see you. You know I am. But why were you ignoring my texts?" he asked, muscles tensed in preparation. "What are you trying to avoid telling me?"

She studied the purse in her lap, her fingers twisting in the strap. "I might have had a run-in with the police."

Shit, not again...

The words drifted around the room with varying degrees of effect. Dylan looked impressed, Alec appeared to be withholding judgment until he'd heard more information. And Savannah?

Savannah had closed her eyes. Ky felt as though the day was crumbling in front of him and there wasn't a damn thing he could do. Time seemed to stand still, until the *beep, beep, beep* of the keyless lock on the front door interrupted the silence. As if specifically timed to make an entrance, Noah entered the room.

Sweet mother of Mary.

"Sorry I'm late," Noah said. "Did I miss anything?"

Ky stared. Hard. The man looked as though he'd stumbled out of a limo en route to a Hollywood event. Skinny jeans, navy pea coat, and dark sunglasses. Artfully tousled hair that looked perfect for grabbing during—

"You missed a lot!" Sierra perked up, most likely simply grateful for the interruption. "You missed the announcement of my recent arrest for disorderly conduct."

Noah removed his sunglasses, thick eyelashes blinking once, and then seemed to recover from the announcement sooner than anyone else in the room. "Well, whatever you did, sweetie"—he headed toward Sierra and gave her a quick hug—"I hope you at least had fun." He sent Ky a smile and a nod and then...nothing, before turning back to his sister.

Ky struggled to ignore the big brown eyes and full mouth stretched into a welcoming grin for Sierra. Ky couldn't make it past how those lips had looked stretched around him even as the word *arrest, arrest, arrest* kept rumbling through his mind until it finally gained traction.

He stood and reached for Sierra's arm, gently pulling her aside, away from the "meeting" that was rapidly deteriorating into the reunion-slash-pizza-party-from-hell.

Ky lowered his voice. "You had to share this now?"

Her overt expression of innocence made him grit his teeth in frustration. And, Jesus, he needed to decide how to address the dressing-room happenings with Noah, a man who had no trouble behaving as though the blow job incident had been just a typical day in the life of Noah Tanner.

Which, in his defense, might be true.

But Sierra was doing that thing she did, the one that had driven Ky crazy growing up. She looked up at him as though he were the one with a problem, not her.

"I thought you'd handle the news better, maybe listen to reason, if you had to at least *pretend* to be rational." She gestured around the room at the group of people watching them closely.

"Listen to reason?" he repeated dumbly as he guided her a few steps farther from the audience.

Ky couldn't wrap his head around the many issues he had going on his life. Tying off a life-threatening bleeder in a multiple gunshot victim seemed easy in comparison.

"Listen to reason when my sister has now racked up her second disorderly conduct charge"—concern for his sister had him shoving a hand through his hair—"in the name of...what?"

"In the name of a totally worthy cause," Sierra supplied.

Ky struggled to keep his words low. "Pardon me if I'm a little skeptical of your idea of a worthy cause," he said. "In the fourth grade, you won the right to represent our county in the regional spelling bee. Where, if you remember, you proceeded to use your position to stage a one-student protest against the complexity of the English language and its confusing spelling rules."

"If something is a rule, there shouldn't be any exceptions!"

"You mailed light bulbs to NBC in support of a TV show."

"And the fans earned themselves three more seasons of Friday Night Lights," she said, poking his chest with a finger. "A great lesson in people power."

"Because the Occupy Wall Street mishap of 2011, spending a night in *jail* at the tender age of nineteen, wasn't enough of a lesson?"

Ky swore he lost a year of his life just *thinking* about what could have gone wrong.

Sierra tipped her delicate chin higher. "Income inequality is a travesty."

A tired sigh escaped Ky's mouth. "Yes, but you shouldn't take an arrest record so lightly. It'll follow you around..." he said, pausing for emphasis, "for *life*." Aware that every eye in the room was on him and his sister, he reined it in an octave. "We'll talk about this later."

Savannah crept up to him and put an arm around his waist. Unfortunately, he wasn't sure if it was in sibling solidarity with his pain or an attempt to calm him down for her twin.

Knowing Savannah, probably a bit of both.

"There isn't anything left to discuss." Sierra shrugged but refused to meet his gaze. "Minor arrest records are what make people interesting."

Interesting?

"And exactly what did you risk a record for this time?" he asked, crossing his arms. "The Justice for Animals movement?"

"No." Sierra paused before she answered. "Family rights for same-sex couples."

Aw...fuck.

For a moment, every breath was a struggle and the room felt oppressive.

"Wow," Noah said to Savannah in a stage whisper, "your sister has *skills*." He studied Sierra as if recognizing brilliance. "She waited for him to get all worked up and then *pow*"—he smacked a fist against his palm—"hit him with the very worthy social-issue news." Noah glanced at Dylan and Alec, who were paying way too much attention to the pizza in their hands. "In front of the very people who are the most affected by her cause."

"She's had a lot of practice honing her bad-news delivery techniques," Savannah whispered back.

Reproductive rights for same-sex couples. *Same-sex couples.*

Ky dropped onto the couch, mind spinning as he tried to make sense of the news, a familiar apprehension digging a deeper hole in his gut.

Savannah often talked about finding him a girlfriend, but Sierra...

These last few years he'd begun to think Sierra's silence on the subject reflected more than just a desire to stay out of his personal life—especially as she seemed genetically incapable of keeping her opinions to herself. And every once in a while he'd catch Sierra looking at him as though she had something important to say.

Had Sierra guessed the truth about his sexual orientation? Did she have a bigger goal today? Is that why she'd shown up here, sharing her news in front of a group of gay friends?

Frowning, Ky tugged on the hem of the flannel button-up he'd tossed on over his T-shirt.

'Course, Sierra would have gone to great lengths just to protect the reproductive rights of the North

American Spotted Moth, if such an insect even existed. And it was a hell of a lot easier justifying his response when he found the consequences out of proportion to the importance of the cause.

And justifying an *arrest*?

Suddenly, the years of worry reached epic levels, tempting him to go home and bury his exhausted head under a pillow and not resurface for another century or so.

"I guess I should be grateful," he said, a wry weariness evident in his tone even as he strived to lighten the mood in the room. "At least you didn't drop out of high school to have a baby at sixteen."

"Well," she drawled, hedging her words as though to buy some time, "speaking of pregnancy..."

Ky sucked in a sharp breath as one of his oldest fears seemed about to materialize.

"I donated the egg for Dylan and Alec's baby." A smile lit up her face, as though she'd arranged world peace on her afternoon off. "Does that count?"

Chapter Six

Understanding struck Ky like a mule kick to the head as he gaped at his sister. All the questioning glances he'd ignored through the years suddenly morphed into one monstrous-sized knowing look on Sierra's face.

Yep, Sierra had guessed the truth about her brother. And she no longer appeared willing to ignore the issue. Savannah, thankfully, seemed blissfully unaware of the tense undertones.

Stomach churning, he shot Sierra a *what the hell are you up to?* expression and received a *now would be a good time to speak up* look in response.

God, she definitely had an agenda.

He'd always admired the twins' unfailing compassion for others—not so much Sierra's zeal for taking risks. She loved him too much to out him against his will. But she clearly wanted him to say something, *do* something himself.

Unfortunately, she'd decided that forcing the issue by taking a stand *herself* was an acceptable alternative.

Shit. He supposed he only had himself to blame for her naiveté.

"Ky!" Sierra squealed as she burst through the front door, dropping her book bag to the foyer floor with a loud bang. "You're never gonna guess who threw up at school today."

As per her usual, she jumped into his arms to give him a bear hug. He held her close for a moment, heart still pounding in anger from his earlier run-in with Ray. Dammit, he'd managed two weeks avoiding the man, no small feat while living in the same house. But running into him was one thing. Stupidly standing up to his derogatory comments another...

Scrawny legs wrapped around Ky's waist, Sierra pulled back to look at him, and her gap-toothed smile fell. "What happened to your mouth?" She gently touched the corner of his lip.

The sting left him inhaling sharply.

"You're bleeding." Sierra's face scrunched up with worry.

"It's no big deal, squirt. I was grooming Scout when she tried to defend herself from a horsefly. Her nose bopped me in the mouth by accident." By now the lies rolled off his tongue with ease. "Now tell me," he said, sending her a smile despite his tight, aching lip, "who threw up at school?"

He half listened as she began to gleefully chatter about the vomiting incident in that morbid way only a seven-year-old could muster, mostly tuning her out. Thank God the girls were easily distracted. But they were growing up. Getting savvier. From here on out, he needed to be more careful around Ray.

Ky shot to his feet and began to pace, ignoring the sound of Noah, Alec, and Dylan quietly making their way into the kitchen, graciously giving Ky space to adjust to Sierra's news.

Adjust? He'd spent a lifetime adjusting.

And a woman who'd risked an arrest for income inequality would likely risk everything in support of her brother...

"Jesus, Sierra," Ky said, his voice hoarse with alarm. "You can't tell Ray what you did."

Her hesitation spoke volumes. "Daddy won't care."

Ky stopped pacing and barely contained his *are you fucking kidding me?* response because, heaven help her, she was going to tell her dad.

Their gazes clashed, and for a moment his lungs ceased to function. He ignored the many, many ways her plan would go wrong as the previous niggle of foreboding blossomed to all-consuming levels.

She tucked her long blond hair behind an ear. "I'm telling you, he won't give me a hard time."

"Is your memory really that short?"

"Okay, so Daddy and I clashed a lot when I was young."

Ky's sigh communicated his *no shit* response. "And why do you expect this time to be any different?"

She bit her lip. "Our problem back then was that I was headstrong and he didn't have much patience with kids. Well," she went on with a wistful smile, "other than helping me with my 4-H projects." Sierra stepped closer. "Look, I know things between you and Daddy were always a little tense."

He barely maintained a straight face. A *little* tense? At least he'd managed to shelter them from the worst of the truth.

"But he's better now," she went on. "After graduation, I approached him about changing the ranch to a grass-fed operation, going organic." She laughed. "Who'd have guessed Ray Urban would say yes to something considered so progressive?"

Money being the likely answer to that particular riddle. Running a ranch meant keeping a sharp eye on the bottom line, and that was the one thing Ray did well.

"Daddy is getting physical therapy for a shoulder injury. And he's letting me do more of the work. We're actually having fun managing the ranch together, which is all I've ever really wanted," Sierra said, genuine joy lighting her eyes. "This last year has been *the best*."

Her excitement only made his heart twist harder. Of all of them, she had the most to lose if their faux peaceful-family atmosphere got shot to hell. And now she wanted to fix the underlying tension between Ray and Ky.

Goddammit.

"The only thing missing is the occasional visit from you," she said with a pointed look.

Ky ignored the gentle chastisement and struggled for a diplomatic response. "He won't be happy with you."

"He'll get over it."

"You donating an egg to two gay guys? Ray's made his feelings about homosexuality pretty clear."

Sierra rolled her eyes. "Don't put so much stock in the occasional bigoted comment."

"I'd put *more* stock in it if I were you."

"That's just how he was raised to talk, Ky." Her voice grew soft. "You should come back for a visit."

Ky groaned.

Sierra frowned. "If you did, you could see for yourself how much he's mellowed."

Christ, his smart, savvy, strong-willed sister really believed what she was saying. He could understand Savannah being optimistic about the situation. But Sierra? Should he have told them the truth about their dad?

"Daddy never meant much of what he said," Sierra went on.

"I think he did."

"He'll come around."

"I'm pretty sure he won't."

Yep, in regards to telling the entire truth about their dad, a better question would be: Would you like your shit storm now? Or later? What constituted the best time to obliterate the last vestiges of the twins' happy-family illusions?

He could still hear his mama's voice: *Nothing is more important than family, Ky.*

Nothing.

He briefly pressed his lids closed, torn between the need to tell the whole truth and the need to protect his sisters—the only family he had left. Besides, why risk Sierra's newfound happiness now that she was finally working the ranch with her father? Savannah leaned against his side in a comforting gesture. "Let's give this a rest, okay? Sierra," she said, turning to her twin, "we can finish this discussion another time."

"Sure," she said. She kissed Ky's cheek and hiked the strap of her purse higher on her shoulder. "I'll let y'all get to your meeting."

He watched her head toward the front door with an ache in his chest.

As an adolescent, if losing the ranch that lived in his blood had been the only issue, he would have left and become another statistic. Unfortunately, Ray's ultimatum had come with an unacceptably cruel *second* condition.

And after all these years, he couldn't let his mom down now.

~~~***~~~

"Alrighty, then," Noah said as he came to a stop in the living room doorway. He ignored the sound of Savannah now chatting with Alec and Dylan in their kitchen. When she'd joined the men seated around the center island, Noah had felt compelled to leave and go in search of Ky.

And found him looking like he'd been hit by a runaway bus.

"Sierra's news certainly classifies as a Surprising Revelation," Noah said.

And then some.

He watched Ky's failed attempt at a smile at the capitalization implied in the previous words. A strangely heart-tugging sight.

"I imagine you're feeling a little..." At a loss, Noah flailed a hand in the direction of the front door Sierra had exited through, and then gave up.

Alec and Dylan had, unsurprisingly, decided that their breakfast nook was the perfect place to discuss the plans for the upcoming fundraiser. Noah had followed them both there to give Ky a moment alone with his sisters—and time for *him* to ask his friends about the unexpected news about their baby. Savannah had appeared about ten minutes later, boxes of fabric samples in hand. Apparently her sister had decided to skip the meeting. A smart move, really, given the dumbfounded expression still plastered on their brother's face.

Sierra's exit, however, hadn't eased the edgy atmosphere.

On the plus side?

Now he and Ky had something to talk about besides their recent sexual adventure. The downside? The discussion would take place in the awkward shadow of the aforementioned sexual adventure.

Noah leaned against the doorjamb and watched the surgeon pace the length of the living room, eyeing him with concern. "You're worried."

"There's an understatement." His words came out thicker than usual. "What the hell am I supposed to do next?"

Noah took a deep breath and used a soothing tone. "What's done is done. You can't *un*do any of it. She's not the first person to have a run-in with the law or help a gay couple have a baby."

"This isn't just about her affinity for protests that lead to arrests." Ky grimaced as he kept walking. "Or even egg donations without a thought to the long-term ramifications."

Noah pressed his lips together, clueless as to how to help.

Ky plowed his hand through his hair, achieving a scruffy bed-head style—and, damn, even that looked adorable. But his expression reeked of anxiety and worry, clearly at his wit's end. He appeared to need...relief? Support? Friendly words of wisdom?

Wisdom.

Noah stifled a self-directed scoff. He didn't do wisdom well *at all.*

"Look on the bright side, Ky," he replied with forced cheerfulness. "Sierra got busted by the police several times. At least she only did the egg thing once." And then he thought better of his words, lips pursed in contemplation. "Unless you think she's plotting to become the human equivalent of a genetic PEZ dispenser."

"Jesus, Noah..." he groaned with a heavy drawl. He reached the far wall, pivoted, and paced back. "I thought things would get easier as the girls got older." He shot Noah a frustrated look as he passed by. "Weren't they supposed to get easier?"

"I wouldn't know." He settled onto the arm of the couch. "Maybe time eventually wears parents down until they don't have the energy to worry anymore?"

"She's never had children." He picked up his pace, and Noah watched, feeling helpless as Ky went on. "Sierra has no idea what that means, especially as a donor. Hell, I'm not even sure I understand."

"She's beautifully altruistic."

"Not to mention stubborn and idealistic. She hasn't thought through the long-term implications of her decision."

Noah blew out a breath. "She's a twenty-four-year-old woman who seems to know her own mind pretty well."

"I know. It's just..." A little of Ky's righteous determination drained out of him, and he flopped down onto the overstuffed couch. "I understand you bein' happy for your friends, Noah," Ky said. "I really do. But..."

Silence settled between them, as though the man couldn't think of a way to explain his concerns.

"I spoke to Alec." Noah kept his voice low, a lame attempt at protecting the tenuous peace between them. "Sierra approached them a long time ago about being a donor. They said no. But she kept bringing it up, telling them she would eventually wear them down," he said, and Ky made an *I'm not surprised* snort. Noah's smile felt way too fond. "You know how persistent and charming she can be."

"Oh, she can be charmin', all right."

"Eventually she told them she'd find another gay couple to donate to if they weren't interested," he said. "And they figured it would be better all around if it was them." He picked at an imaginary piece of lint on his pants. "They got her to agree to a psychological evaluation, just to be sure. I guess that's routine in these sorts of situations," he said with a shrug. "Anyway, the psychologist who did the evaluation felt Sierra was—" He bit his lip.

"Hell-bent on following through?" he said dryly.

"Strong-willed were the words Alec said the guy had used."

Ky let out a long-suffering groan. "The psychologist doesn't know the half of it," he said. "The situation is so complicated I can't make sense of it all, the *hello, I'm now a mother, but not really* angle."

"A mind boggler for sure."

Ky slumped deeper into the couch. "Honestly, though, that's not my main concern."

"What is?"

The pause went on so long he wondered if he'd get an answer to the question.

Ky stared up at the ceiling. "About a year after our mama died, Ray discovered my secret stash of gay porn and he—" He hesitated and then rolled his head to meet Noah's gaze. "He told me faggots had no place on the ranch."

Noah's breath turned to concrete in his throat. "How old were you?"

"Fifteen."

"He threatened to kick a fifteen-year-old out?"

"That wasn't the worst of it."

Noah forced himself to unclench his fists, his palms slick. What could be worse than booting a minor out of their home for being gay? Rick had suffered the same fate, the event triggering a tragic series of cause-and-effects that eventually ended in his death. In a way, Noah had played a part, too. To this day, he still couldn't remember his boyfriend's last few months without feeling conflicted.

Sweet Deity above, Noah longed for a simple, awkward morning-after conversation. At least then he wouldn't be hurting for Ky and dwelling on his own crippling self-doubt.

Torturing himself over what he should have done differently.

He brushed a damp palm down his pants, studying Ky's expression for a minute while grappling with his own memories before giving a sharp nod. "We need alcohol," he said. "I don't do my best thinking when completely sober."

Noah headed to the bar in the corner, poured a generous hit of brandy into two tumblers, and crossed back.

He held one of the drinks out. "Sorry about the simple presentation."

Ky accepted the offer, and Noah dropped onto the sofa next to him, his body humming at the proximity and welcoming the more pleasant memories and...okay, maybe he should shift a little farther away.

"No one cares about presentation," Ky said.

"Normally I'd argue with you about that."

Despite the tension, Ky huffed out an amused breath. "I know."

"But I think the current situation calls for expediency instead of one of my amazing cocktails."

Ky gripped his glass, knuckles white with tension. Noah tossed his entire drink back, savoring the burn in his throat, the heated hit to his muscles that helped keep his memories and conflicted feelings at bay.

Instead, he focused on the warm press of Ky's thigh against his...

Christ, he should definitely shift farther away.

He'd failed at his attempt to achieve nice-guy status during the shopping expedition. Sure, he'd managed to contain his smutty comments—covert eye-fucking aside—but he didn't think he'd win any awards for holding his tongue when said tongue had wound up wrapped around the man's dick.

More heat flooded Noah's gut, and he glared down at his perking-up-in-interest cock.

Goddammit, everything isn't about you.

Ky still looked like he was freaking the fuck out, a wiener shrinker of an expression if there ever was one. The frown that had taken up residence on Ky's face since he'd first learned the news grew deeper. He downed his drink in one gulp.

"So, go on," Noah prompted. "What was worse than just threatening to kick you out?"

"He told me he'd never let me see the girls again."

Noah's whole body went cold. "The *bastard*."

While he struggled to recover, he watched Ky stand and head for the bar, splashing more brandy into his glass before tossing the whole thing back.

The man shifted his gaze to Noah's. "Ray owns the ranch and if he learns that I'm still"—tumbler in hand, he made clumsy air quotes with his fingers—"'living out my faggoty ways,' I won't be allowed back. And if *Sierra* learns what her father did when I was a teen, that he threatened to block me from seeing them..."

Ky studied his mostly empty glass, swirling the dribbles left in the bottom. When he went on, his voice came out low.

"Taking over the ranch is Sierra's dream. Unfortunately, Ray can make things difficult for her should it come to a showdown. And you know my sister," he said with an exasperated grunt that managed to convey a goodly dose of fondness. "She won't be able to keep her opinions to herself."

Noah stared at the surgeon as the truth expanded uncomfortably in his chest. "Without you

around, the girls would have been raised on a
relentless diet of anti-homo propaganda."

And how would that have felt? Cut off from the
little sisters he loved, their minds slowly filled with
hate as their daddy attempted to turn them against
their brother. Good God, no wonder Ky chose to
remain in the closet. How different would the twins'
lives have been? How would they have turned out
without Ky's steady, protective presence?

Noah's words were rough with emotion.
"They're lucky you stayed."

"I never considered it a sacrifice."

Noah kept his disagreement to himself.

"But I figured things couldn't get worse than
Sierra's moody, angsty adolescent stage," Ky said.
"Now I'm beginning to look back on those years with
fondness." Expression still both weary and worried,
he groaned, his lips twisting wryly. "Even though
Sierra got a real kick out of sending me to buy her
monthly feminine products."

"I can't imagine how you dealt with all
those...those...*female* things."

"I started reaching out to other parents online,"
he replied absently, his blank stare trained out the
living room window. As though still too caught up in
the pending showdown to concentrate on the
change in topic.

"Support groups?" Noah asked.

"Bloggers, actually."

Two beats passed as the words sank in, and
Noah's eyes slowly grew wider. "You used to surf
mommy blogs?"

Ky turned to face him, color filling his cheeks.
"Some of them are a good source of information. I
followed several on Twitter."

"But—" Noah couldn't wrap his mind around the news, his jaw still slack. "Did they know that they were chatting with...with..." He waved his hand to indicate Ky's body. "The mother of all manliness?"

"I gave myself a female handle," he mumbled.

Wait, *what*?

Each millisecond felt like an eternity.

"My God," Noah finally said, voice hoarse. "You pretended to be a woman." He leaned forward on the couch, entirely too enthralled with the current conversation. "What was your handle?"

The color in Ky's cheeks intensified, and he rolled his eyes. "@TiaraTime."

Every one of Noah's facial muscles spasmed, his mind exploding in delight. "Wait, don't..." He buried his head in his palms as his shoulders shook in silent laughter, the effort bringing tears. "Please just"— face still covered, he held up one hand in a silent plea for more time, because he was *supposed* to be earning Nice Guy status here—"just give me a minute while I try not to succumb to the sheer beauty of this moment."

"Don't hurt yourself trying," he said dryly.

"Sorry." He wiped his eyes, cleared his throat, and sent him an apologetic look. "I'm glad you found support," he said. "Seriously."

Ky studied him, and the faint stirrings of a familiar sexual tension seeped into the room, sending a hot flush up Noah's back.

Ky's gaze shifted back to the view beyond the window. "If Sierra tells her dad what she's done—if they learn the truth about Ray and things go the way I suspect they will..." He groaned and rubbed his eyes. "Suffice it to say, Sierra will probably have to leave the ranch. Her *home*. And if Savannah felt betrayed by her emotionally abusive ex-boyfriend, how will she feel about her dad? And about *me* once she learns I've been lying by omission? Jesus, she'll probably need counseling."

Oh, God. *Counseling.*

Legs unsteady, Noah rose and crossed to the bar, pouring himself another splash of brandy. "I've gone down the counselor route before."

Ky stared at him. "Did the sessions help?"

"'Fraid not," he said, his lips in a rueful twist. "On the plus side, I learned to accept my baggage as part of my charm." Noah downed his false courage and forced a smile. "I guess you could say counseling taught me how to embrace my dysfunction with enthusiasm."

A sharp breath of humor escaped Ky.

"And I'm curious," Noah went on. "How would you feel about coming out if your stepdad weren't an issue?"

A perplexed look crossed Ky's face, as though the potential scenario just didn't compute, and two seconds ticked by before Noah decided to abandon the line of questioning.

"Listen"—Noah set his empty glass down and turned to face Ky—"life is messy." He looked up at the riot of emotions on his friend's face, and his heart suffered a pang of sympathy. "Messy and random and rarely black or white."

Because black and white made things too easy. And Noah had learned long ago that life was rarely easy.

"I know," the surgeon said. "I just—"

Ky's voice died out as he stared down at his half-full glass, and he looked...lost.

"For chrissake, cowboy." With the pointer finger of each hand, Noah gently pushed up on Ky's temples. "No Eyebrows of Doom," he said softly.

"Sometimes the best we can do is trust that everything will work out. So let's put our big, manly-momma panties on." He smoothed his thumbs across Ky's forehead and focused on everything *but* the memories of how the man tasted, valiantly ignoring the twitch of interest in his cock.

Because, dammit, that's right. Everything isn't about you.

"No scowls, either," Noah went on. "The only facial lines that are attractive are the little crinkles you get around your eyes when you smile. Which you don't do often enough, by the way."

He met the too-close gaze, unintentionally inhaling the scent of almonds. Several seconds ticked by as the amazing Technicolor eyes grew darker.

Fuck.

That hadn't been his intention. The man had a lot on his plate, and this wasn't what Ky needed right now. Time to prove that Noah Tanner could do the Noble Thing for once. And this time he wouldn't let himself get distracted, goddammit.

Noah dropped his hands, mind scrambling for a diversion. "You know what we need?"

Ky's voice sounded rough. "What do we need?"

Gazes still locked, the man slowly took a sip of his brandy with a knowing look, clearly thinking a smutty suggestion was coming his way.

Noah forced a grin. "We need an afternoon at the spa."

~~~***~~~

"Welcome to Veronika's Beauty and Vodka Bar."

The receptionist greeted them with a plastic smile that did nothing to ease Ky's nerves, nor did the subtle Russian accent he wasn't convinced was real. Her platinum hair and breast size appeared highly suspect as well.

How the heck had he wound up at the ritzy salon?

Oh, yeah, he'd been so surprised by Noah's suggestion, he hadn't been able to formulate a coherent *no* fast enough.

Before he knew it, they were on their way here.

"You're in for a treat, gentlemen," the woman continued.

Ky stifled a derisive reply. From beside him, Noah waved him forward with an *after you* gesture and a look of such enthusiasm that Ky groaned.

Because no way was he escaping with his dignity intact.

After Sierra's announcements, he still ached between his shoulders, the tension tight. The upscale salon-slash-vodka bar had hardwood floors, endless stretches of gray marble, and smelled faintly of lavender, the atmosphere probably meant to soothe. But Ky longed for something real. Something *familiar*.

Like the smell of antiseptic solution. Or blood. Heck, even cow shit would be an improvement at this point.

To his left, Noah was chatting with the maybe-fake Russian blonde, his mouth arranged in that mesmerizing smile that did funky things to Ky's chest.

And God...

Savannah still concerned him, and he was worried sick about Sierra—in the twenty years since his mother's death, he'd never felt her loss so acutely. And, yeah, he'd given up a lot in life. But, dammit, did that have to include another chance with Noah?

Because, while having the man's lips wrapped around him would definitely go down as one of his all-time favorite moments, the guy had come so quickly there'd been no time to appreciate his expression.

Or the kind of sounds he made.

For once, Ky longed to go after what he wanted, which included more time. More than his usual five-minute blow'n go. More than the fifteen they'd had in the dressing room for sure.

He wanted the man spread out beneath him. He wanted to taste him. He wanted Noah's legs tight around Ky's waist, his fingers desperate and leaving marks on his back.

Heat curled low in his gut, and Ky's gaze met Noah's.

For two beats, brown eyes simply stared at him with a look that left him wondering what kind of cogs were churning in Noah's brain now.

All Ky needed was to escape this place with some semblance of self-respect while figuring out if something more than their clothing-store escapade was possible. At least the services there hadn't sounded like an oxymoron, like the confusing sign on the salon counter proclaiming *back facials offered here*, or...

His gaze landed on the words *Hot Wax*, and his stomach dropped.

"Jesus," Ky muttered. "I should've never left Texas."

Noah sighed and stepped closer to take his arm. "Come on, you know you owe me," he said, gently pulling him farther inside. "Because that Gucci shirt I had on earlier at Dylan and Alec's?"

"What about it?"

"It *used* to be one of my favorites."

Ky studied the man's replacement shirt, borrowed from Alec's closet. "I'll pay to have it dry-cleaned," he said, struggling with the leftover guilt. His mouth screwed up, three quarters grimace and one quarter amusement. "But next time, maybe you should warn a guy before you suggest an afternoon at the spa."

Noah gently squeezed his elbow. "Getting showered in brandy—even when coughed from a mouth as gorgeous as yours—isn't the kind of facial I typically go for. Besides," he said, letting Ky's arm go and sending him a sideways glance, his voice low, "you had your chance at giving me *that* kind of facial in the dressing room."

Ky ignored the thrum of heat in his gut, wondering if the words were yet another not-so-subtle hint that there'd be no more chances. Regardless, the mention of the sexual act seemed the perfect lead-in to asking the blunt question.

The question dogging him all day.

"At some point," he drawled quietly as he came to a halt, "do I get to touch you again?"

Noah stared at him blankly, and Ky's heart sagged closer to his toes. He suspected the frown of concentration on his own face paired with the impatient-sounding words amounted to one miserable come-on.

Ky struggled to unfurrow his forehead and tried again. "Because, uh, I know you're capable of more than just one-off encounters." His tongue tripped over his words as he rushed on in an attempt to explain. "I mean, in the past you had a boyfriend—"

Who'd *died*.

Well...fuck. What a mood killer.

Noah froze, the muscles around his eyes twitching as though unable to decide on an appropriate expression. The discomfort reached mammoth proportions.

Real smooth, Ky.

He scratched his scruff, amazing even himself by just how much he sucked at seduction. "Hell and damnation," he said. "I'm sorry. I just—"

"Noah!"

A beautiful, raven-haired lady of Asian descent approached in skintight leather pants, pen stuck in her elegant coil of hair, her pointy heels clicking on the hardwood floor.

"Veronika." Noah plastered on a smile that rivaled the fake blonde's fake accent from before. "Thanks for working us in on such short notice," he said, kissing the salon owner's cheek. By the end of the process, he appeared to have recovered from his emotional turmoil. "This is the friend I was telling you about, Dr. Davis." He gestured at Ky. "Who, despite the gladiator body and dashing good looks, could benefit from your services."

False, gold-colored feather eyelashes shifted as Veronika eyed Ky up and down. "You said it was a rare opportunity, Noah." Neither her appearance nor her accent supported a stereotypical Slavic heritage. "And just look at all this wonderful potential."

Potential?

Yep, here came the beginning of the end of his dignity.

She pulled the pen from her hair, tapping it against her mouth as she slowly circled Ky. Her sharp gaze skimmed his scruff, his head, and his flannel-covered chest before spending far more time on his butt than necessary for someone about to give him a haircut.

Sweat broke out along Ky's neck as he wondered what his ass could possibly need that required the services of a salon. Then again, the sign *did* mention hot wax—

His thoughts screeched to a halt. "Beggin' your pardon, ma'am," he said, his hand adopting a *stop right there* gesture. "My ass is not a part of this deal."

Veronika laughed, a delicate sound that matched her salon. "Of course not, Dr. Davis." She shot Noah a look, eyes twinkling with humor. "And what, *exactly,* does this deal of yours consist of?"

Ky made a skeptical noise, because he was beginning to wonder that himself. How the hell had things gotten so muddled? They'd gone from Noah flirting and chasing to *not* flirting and chasing, ending with an awesome blow job. And now Ky's pathetic attempts at seduction—

"This deal," Noah said firmly to Ky before turning to Veronika, "consists of refining his appearance. Nothing more."

Well, shit. That sounded ominous.

"What *fun*," she said.

"I know, right?" Noah's smile lit his face and somehow left Ky strangely jealous of his own makeover.

Ky hooked his thumbs through the empty belt loops of his jeans. "I agreed to a haircut and to discuss—*discuss*—the possibility of getting rid of the scruff."

Long, feathery eyelashes widened a fraction before she sent him a reassuring smile. "Come," she said, sticking the pen back in her hair before taking Ky's hand. "Follow me."

Oh, great.

Veronika led him toward a leather styling chair that Fred, the barber Ky used in Texas, wouldn't be caught near. Then again, the dude was eighty at least. Still, when Ky used to visit home, he always dropped by the shop. Unfortunately, Fred always asked if he needed a cut, and Ky never had the heart to say no. And then he'd proceed to get a terrible haircut he'd spend months growing out in exchange for stories about his father bringing Ky by as a toddler.

"Sit," she said.

Ky did as instructed, and Veronika began to discuss their style options at length, combing blood-red fingertips through his hair as she tossed out her ideas. Ky tuned her out and resisted the urge to shift out of her reach, acutely aware of Noah's proximity and his cologne—a surprising mix of spicy and sweet—and fixed his gaze on the toes of his boots.

"Noah, your thoughts?" Veronika asked, pulling Ky's head back into the game.

The guy ran his hands through Ky's hair, much like feather-eyelashes lady. Except Noah's touch sent a skitter of goose bumps up his neck.

Oh, Lord.

He squirmed in the chair, trying not to lean into those mesmerizing fingers as they threaded through long strands, gently scraping his scalp. His mind pictured how those hands had looked wrapped around him in the dressing room—

"Any preferences, Ky?" Noah asked.

"Uh, yeah...about what, again?"

The man adopted an overly patient tone. "Your haircut."

Well, hair grew back, and the desire twisting in his gut was growing pretty persistent. Further discussion meant more delays...

"Don't care," he answered.

"You...*what*?"

"Don't. Care."

Noah responded with an *oh, really?* stare.

"Any other time I'd trim the layers and leave his hair just above his shoulders," Veronika said to Noah. "Because the scruffy cowboy look is the perfect accessory to that lovely southern drawl."

"Texan," Ky corrected automatically. "Not southern."

"But for the Bachelor Bid," she went on, undeterred, "I think we should go a little shorter, a touch past his collar." She waved her hand in an expressive gesture encompassing Ky's form. "More hot, young oil baron and a little less hired hand."

Veronika addressed Noah. "Would fetch more in bids, don't you think?"

Noah pursed his lips in contemplation, a vision that sent Ky's thoughts straight down another sexual rabbit hole, remembering that full mouth on his dick. The heat. The *friction*. And what about how Noah's cock would taste? How it would feel?

Would he ever get to experience that?

"I think so," Noah said.

Ky almost choked at the ill-timed words.

"What are your thoughts on the scruff?" Noah asked the beautician.

"Normally I'm not a fan of any kind of beard," she said, her smile fading and sadness filling her eyes. "Whether in the form of facial hair or...the other kind."

Noah silently placed a sympathetic hand on her shoulder, and Ky suddenly felt like he was intruding. The friendship between the two clearly extended beyond a simple client-customer relationship.

"Your last boyfriend was an asshole for using you like that," Noah murmured.

"I know," she said. After a beat, she turned to Ky. "What do you think?"

"Well..." He rubbed his neck uncomfortably and briefly shoved his goals aside, because hurrying past this question seemed wrong. "No one should use a lady to try and pass as straight. At least, not without her consent," he said. "It ain't right."

Veronika blinked, and then patted him gently on the cheek. "Thank you. Although that wasn't what I was asking you, it's certainly reassuring to hear your opinion on the other matter," she said with a smile. "If you keep this up, I might consider relocating to Texas for the gentlemanly manners alone." She turned her gaze back to Noah. "About the facial hair, you know me. I prefer the clean-shaven look."

Noah nodded, clearly focused. "It does have its advantages. But I'm partial to the perfect five-o'clock shadow."

Because he liked the sensation on his skin? The burn? And since when had Ky become so fixated on sex?

Man, he was so screwed.

"I know you're partial to stubble, Noah," she said, her eyes lit with mischief. "But I want to know if the doctor feels strongly about keeping his longer?"

The doctor felt strongly about getting this over with and fixing his lame attempt at seduction. And the longer this debate took, the longer he had to wait.

Ky made an executive decision. "No, ma'am. I can live without the scruff."

"Since when?" Noah asked.

"Since now."

Veronika ignored them and tilted his chin to the right to get a better side view, as if considering her approach.

Jesus, his jaw wasn't exactly a tickin' bomb needing to be dismantled.

"A nice compromise would be to leave it a touch longer than Noah's preference and shape it up a bit," she said. "I do adore his rough-cut looks, though." Her smile grew bigger. "Not to mention the Texan chivalry. Noah"—she turned to her friend—"you should find yourself such a boyfriend."

A noncommittal hum came in reply, and he was definitely avoiding Ky's gaze. In fact, he was avoiding Veronika's gaze as well.

"Your mother would be absolutely giddy if you did," she went on, unfolding a cape with a snap of her hands.

An expectant pause followed, and Ky got the feeling the two were rehashing a familiar argument.

"Every time she comes in," Veronika said, "she mentions how much she wants you to find a nice man and settle down."

Ky shifted uncomfortably in his seat.

Noah's snort managed to sound classy. "You know I'm allergic to anything beyond a one-night stand."

"Really, Noah," she said with a skeptical tone. "Allergic?"

"Break out in hives and everything."

A scoff escaped Ky, although his didn't come out nearly as classy. Besides, he hadn't thought much beyond getting his mouth on Noah. Was a reciprocal blow job really asking that much?

Several seconds ticked by, and then she sighed in defeat. "You always were prone to hyperbole, darling."

"No, it's totally true," he replied in protest.

With a disappointed frown, Veronika fastened the cape around Ky's neck. Noah took a seat in the leather recliner beside them, and the fake blonde brought him a drink in a frosty copper mug. Something alcoholic, no doubt.

"You don't believe my claim," Noah said, dark gaze meeting his.

Ky tried, he really did, but he lost the war with his restraint, rolling his eyes. "What you're claiming is medically impossible."

"So you say."

"So I *know*."

Noah held Ky's gaze over the rim of his mug, and everything that had gone *un*said ratcheted up the tension another hundred newtons. All the mood lighting and lavender scents and feathery eyelashes in the world couldn't overcome the sexual-tension-laden atmosphere.

"The last guy I attempted more than a one-night stand with," Noah said, addressing Veronika, "I woke up in his bed the next morning itching like crazy, my skin all blotchy."

"More than likely due to the laundry detergent he used," she suggested.

"Nope," he replied. "We used the same kind."

"Probably the shellfish at dinner," Ky muttered.

"We didn't eat shellfish." He crossed his legs and sipped his drink, long, distracting fingers drumming on his mug. "We had beef."

"I'm bettin' it was something else you ate."

"I'm sure that it wasn't."

Several seconds passed during which they engaged in a silent argument, Ky sending him a *you are so full of shit* frown. Noah responded with a wide-eyed, stubborn *I have no idea what you're talking about* expression.

Veronika reached over to touch Noah's hand. "You deserve to move on. Rick's been gone a long time, honey," she said quietly. The air around them grew miserably thin as she continued. "At least his passing was peaceful."

The gutted look on Noah's face paraded through a stream of emotions: pain, grief, heartbreak, and, finally...guilt?

No, definitely guilt.

"I'll be right back." She patted Ky's shoulder. "I'm going to get the hot wax."

With the tense atmosphere, the words took a moment to sink in...

"What? No—" Ky whipped his head around but she simply kept walking.

She disappeared through another door, and Ky turned the full force of his gaze on Noah.

"Hot wax?" Ky asked.

"Don't worry, big guy," he said, his expression close to shedding the last dregs of its previous emotional weight. "During my manicure, I have you scheduled for a massage to release all that...you know, tension."

"*Hot wax?*" He frowned hard in attempt to play up his response, relieved when the last shred of melancholy in Noah's expression vanished—which Ky would definitely count as a win.

"That's right." The man's smile grew bigger. "Gotta whip those judgmental eyebrows into shape."

Chapter Seven

Three hours later Ky exited the salon with a haircut, the perfect five-o'clock shadow—he'd lobbied for the nearly clean-shaven look in lieu of the hot-wax nonsense, 'cause...*damn*—and a thoroughly toasted Noah.

Getting the man home without incident wasn't gonna be easy.

"You look *amazing*," Noah said, words slightly slurred as he beamed up at him. "After a very rough start to our afternoon at the spa, now I *feel* amazing. Their Moscow Mule cocktails are amazing, too."

Ky bit back a smile and steered him down the sidewalk toward the waiting limousine, suddenly understanding a) why Noah preferred using a limo service on spa days and b) that manicures were preferred to massages as drinkin' vodka could be done at the same time. More importantly, he realized that c) Ky's lousy seduction technique was responsible for the quantity of alcohol consumed.

Well, more accurately, his and Veronika's references to the boyfriend who'd died.

Damn.

In the history of horrible come-ons, Ky's could be considered legendary. Regret gnawed a new hole in his stomach.

One thing he didn't regret? The hour-long relaxing massage during Noah's manicure. The man's hands looked no different, nails short, clean, and neat. But something was responsible for the smooth touch.

Heat sparked in Ky's gut, but Noah listed dangerously to the left, requiring a firmer grip to prevent a sidewalk face-plant.

"Anastasia"—Noah swayed a bit as he glanced back at Ky and reached for the limo door handle, missing by a mile—"I don't think that's her real name, by the way."

"You think?"

"Which is fitting," he plowed on, ignoring the playful reply, "because the blond coloring definitely came from a bottle and her boobs courtesy of a scalpel." He squinted up at Ky as the chauffeur discreetly opened the door behind them. "Do you do breast implants? Would you even *want* to be trained in that sort of thing?"

Amused, Ky opened his mouth to educate him about the difference between general surgery and plastic surgery but lost his chance.

"Anyway," Noah said with an *I'm boring myself* wave of his hand, "her counterfeit rack and almost-passable accent complemented her knockoff look like a fake set of 'designer' luggage." His clumsy attempt at air quotes almost put the driver's eye out, the elderly man ducking gracefully.

Ky pressed his lips together, a laugh trying to surface. At least Noah was an adorable drunk, swaying a bit as he attempted to climb into the car.

He watched Noah crawl inside and flop onto the backseat, limbs in an awkward sprawl, hair charmingly tousled, eyes bright. But the effort Noah put into his smile made Ky's chest ache as he ducked to enter the vehicle. The driver closed the door, rounded the limo, and started the engine.

"Now we get to take a magic carpet ride home," Noah said as they pulled out into traffic. "First stop, your place. Hey"—he struggled to sit up higher—"is your cute doorman working today?"

"I think," Ky replied mildly, "I need to make sure you get up to your condo okay."

Noah's eyes lit up even further. "Oooh," he said in a singsong voice, "are you going to take advantage of me?"

A surge of lust hit, and Ky's lips flattened in self-condemnation. "Nope."

"Why not?"

"'Cause it wouldn't be right."

"Damn that cowboy complex." He finally pulled himself into a sitting position. "When I first met you, I had no idea that behind the Scowly McScowly dude lurked such a mushy-hearted guy," he said, blinking slowly, lashes thick and heavy. "Tell me. Do all you men-of-honor types feel naked without a frown? Because your smile is *amazing*."

"Amazing, huh?" Ky's mouth twitched in humor. "I think you need a new word."

"That I do." He leaned forward and patted Ky's face, and everything went still.

Shit...the man wasn't going to make this easy, was he?

Ky took note of the heat from the hand cupping his jaw, the soft skin, and a whiff of something he didn't recognize. Whatever the scent was, it smelled good. Like *hold him down and lick it off* good.

Oranges maybe, with some sort of exotic spice?

A thumb stroked the cheekbone beneath Ky's eye, and his throat felt too tight as he tried to breathe in, taking care of that arousin' scent problem nicely. He waited through one, two, three anxious upticks of his heartbeat, all the while staring at the mouth that now made an appearance in his dreams every night.

"One of my favorite pornos is a backseat-limo blow job," Noah murmured, which, yeah, didn't help Ky's attempt at breathin' at all.

"Noah—"

"You asked about touching me again—"

"An event that needs to be postponed."

"—and I just wanted you to know," he went on without pause, "I think I'm ready to be convinced." He patted Ky's cheek a touch too hard this time. "Right now I'm totally up for 'nother round. Word of warning, though," he muttered. "I might throw up."

Ky chuckled. "I'll pass."

Hurt flashed through the brown eyes, almost too quick to catch. The forced smile that followed left Ky feeling a need to explain. As much as he'd wanted "another round" with Noah, he couldn't. Not now. Not in the man's current condition.

Once the alcohol was out of his system, though...

"I prefer my partners be of sound mind and body," Ky said.

"And I'm not?"

"Uh, you're *definitely* of right body." Pleasure hummed through Ky at the way the man seemed pleased by the words. "It's the consent part I'm havin' issues with."

"I *am* consenting."

"You're drunk."

"Like," Noah went on with a sloppy grin, "this is me, givin' you all my consent."

"You're too intoxicated to make informed decisions."

"Who cares?"

"I do."

"Your loss," he replied easily. After two more overly enthusiastic pats of Ky's cheek, the guy curled up against his chest like a loose-limbed, contented kitten.

What the heck?

Ky stared down at Noah's rich dark hair, acutely aware of the driver a few feet away, and fought the knee-jerk response to pull back. A quiet conversation, inaudible due to the hum of the limo engine, was one thing. An open display of affection? Quite another.

He'd never done anything like this before.

And he hated how the arrangement couldn't be the simple, casual gesture it was intended to be. He hated the urge to scan his surroundings, tensed for potential threats, instead of just enjoying the comforting position. Mostly he hated how he couldn't decide how to respond. Leave his arm along the back of the seat? Gently push him away? Pull him closer...?

Jesus, he shouldn't feel this conflicted.

Why did he feel so conflicted?

"I can almost hear your mind rejecting the sneak-attack snuggle," Noah said. "But you know I can't resist broad shoulders," he rambled on, shifting closer. "'S like you could carry my weight forever and ever and never get tired." He ticked his dark gaze up to Ky and sent him a lazy smile. "Which, FYI, I 'spect you'll have to do when we finally reach my condo 'cause I'm thinking my legs won't be working by then. Too much vodka on an empty stomach. Not exactly the sexy ending that you asked for today."

Ky sighed. "Noah..."

"I get it. Things are a little... compl'cated," he went on, ignoring the interruption. He shifted, burying his face closer as he continued on with a snort, his tone light. "What with your walk-in family closet problem and my dead-boyfriend issues and all."

Damn.

The words had come out far too easily for the emotional punch they packed. The limo slowed, downtown traffic building, the sound of the engine idling highlighting the break in conversation.

"Aren't we an interesting threesome?" Noah said, wry humor in his tone.

"Who?"

"You, me, and the whole heap of man-pain b'tween us."

"The *what*?" He pulled his head back to look down at the guy draped across his chest. He was beginning to find he liked the comforting heat, the closeness, more than he worried about potential repercussions, his years in Oak Hollows, Texas, be damned. Hunh. "Man-pain," Ky repeated. "Where in the fiery hell do you get this crap from, Noah?"

"I'll have you know, it is not crap." Cheeks still flushed—although how much was due to the alcohol and how much to the topic, Ky didn't know—Noah struggled to push up on his arms. "It's—" His hand slipped and he face-planted back against Ky's chest.

An *oof* escaped Ky's mouth, the sudden, unexpected weight shoving the air from his lungs and scattering stars behind his lids. He waited, dizzy from the topic and the lack of oxygen.

"Mmm." Nose smushed against Ky, Noah inhaled. "You smell even better close up," he murmured, snuggling closer.

Ky's lips tugged upward at the edges, and he shook his head as he finally succumbed to instinct and curled an arm around the man's shoulders. The casual embrace felt good—no, the simple description didn't do the feeling justice. The casual embrace felt *deeply satisfying* in a way that had little to do with sex and everything to do with the truth.

And Ky worked hard to ignore just how much he'd lost out on through the years. All the potential relationships—both the emotionally significant and the superficial one-night stands—he'd missed along the way.

Apparently the face-plant had sidetracked the conversation, which suited him just fine. Family secrets were one thing. He'd made his choices and learned to live with them. Mostly. In comparison, Noah's history was like a walk in the park, specifically *Jurassic* park.

The hope for a change in topic died a few moments later.

"Like Veronika, I s'ppose most people think I should have gotten over Rick's death by now."

Ky let the words settle into the deep crevice left when a hit-and-run accident had ruptured his mother's aorta, leaving her hemorrhaging internally. No amount of surgery could have saved her in time.

He'd learned long ago that grieving was a process, a ball and chain you got up and learned to deal with every day. One year, five years—or twenty—wouldn't make the feeling go away.

"This ain't about a carton of milk that's gone bad," Ky said, wincing at the country creeping into his voice, like it always did when hitting the hurting spots. "There's no expiration date on grief."

"I know, right?" He looked up at him, obviously pleased someone understood. "And all the *at least he was surrounded by loved ones* and *thank god he went peacefully* stuff only makes it worse." He tucked his face against Ky's neck and exhaled sharply. "'Cause I know better," he went on. "There was nothing, and I mean *nothing*, peaceful about Rick's death."

The dead man's story wasn't unique: a teen living on the streets and selling sex to survive, HIV being the tragic consequence. Not an *unusual* tale, unfortunately, but no less ugly in its familiarity.

"You did everything you could for him," Ky murmured.

"That's the problem."

"How can that be a problem?"

"You..." he said with a dismissive shake of his head. "You can't understand."

Ky squeezed the man's shoulder in a pitiful attempt to show support. "Noah—"

"Don't." The man fisted his hands in Ky's shirt, and Ky froze, the mumbled rush of blurred words continuing. "I don't deserve you being so nice. Quit being s' nice to me."

"I'm not—"

"I helped him do it." The fabric twisted and grew taut beneath Noah's fingers, his body tense, breath hot against Ky's neck. "I helped him."

Helped him...do *what*?

The ominous pause filled with the muted rumble of a passing truck. Noah was clearly workin' toward saying something he didn't want to say but felt he had to. Or something he wanted to say but didn't know how.

"I couldn't stand to see him hurting anymore," Noah went on, "so I...so I did what he wanted."

I did what he wanted.

The quietly slurred words and the ever-tightening grip on his shirt raised the hairs on the back of Ky's neck, a chill settling across his skin. He knew what came next wouldn't be pretty, had a general idea about what had happened, actually.

But he owed it to the man to listen.

He pressed a reassuring hand to the back of Noah's head and waited until his voice would sound steady. "Tell me."

For a moment, he thought the man wouldn't comply.

"Toward the end, they had 'im on a morphine drip, but he was still in so much pain," Noah mumbled against him. "And they refused to give him any more 'cause all prostitutes must be druggies, right?" His laugh sounded devoid of humor. "So he begged me to bring his leftover prescription from home. And I did." He blew out a slow breath. "Later, when I left to pick up Dylan for his turn at the hospital," he continued, a mountain of misery housed in a hushed tone, "Rick went to sleep and never woke up."

Ky closed his eyes, inhaling an unsteady breath. "Still, you can't be sure that—"

"When they gave me his bag of belongings, I found the 'scription bottle, empty."

Shit, he hated being right.

No way could Noah miss Ky's pounding heart beneath his hands and cheek. Without even thinking, he smoothed his thumb across the man's shoulder blade, not sure who the motion was meant to comfort more.

"If the nurse knew," Noah continued, "she didn't say anything. I never said anything. I never even told *Dylan*." He went on, the words coming out in an agonizing muffle. "I never told him."

"He'd understand."

"How can he when *I* don't understand? And I was *there*. I just—" He inhaled a sharp breath, his fingers increasing their grip on Ky's shirt. "Ugh, please go away and leave me to my humiliation."

A small sigh escaped Ky's lips. "We're in a moving car."

"I know."

"And you have an impressive death grip on my shirt."

"I know." He sniffed but didn't let go. "This is what you get for bein' too nice. Me, vomiting my feels all over you."

Ky hated his tone, part mocking self-deprecation and a whole heap of hopelessness. Noah finally loosened his grip on the shirt, slowly melting back against his chest, face buried in the crook of Ky's neck. The comforting weight and shared body heat helped ease the chill that had settled in his veins.

"No need to apologize," Ky said in a low voice.

"Let's hope the vomiting is just in a figur'tive sense."

"Fingers crossed."

"Otherwise that'll be two ruined shirts in one day." Two seconds later, Noah yawned. "Not that this plaid flannel would be missed." He rubbed his chin against the fabric, his breath warm against the skin beneath. "'S nice and soft, though. What's your laundry secret?"

"Uhm, wearin' and washin' them a thousand times over?"

"Devilishly crafty," he murmured through another yawn. "And effective."

Noah's lashes gradually began to sink lower, the flutter of eyelashes against Ky's throat slowing until they closed.

The limo came to an idling stop, a second traffic jam that looked worse than the first. No way would they be getting out of here anytime soon. Ky shifted Noah a little closer and, after the tense preceding minutes, he enjoyed the feel of his lax body sprawled half on top of his.

This cuddling thing was definitely new. And kinda nice.

Very nice.

The last of the tension leaked out of Ky's posture as Noah's breaths slowed and became sleepy little puffs against his neck. Hopefully getting him up to his condo and into his bed wouldn't be a problem. If Ky had to, he could carry him, no problem.

But then what?

Ky's gaze shifted to the tinted window, and he watched the pedestrians stream by on the sidewalk. Would Noah want him around when he woke up and realized what he'd confessed? Should he simply tuck him in bed and then go home? Let him sleep it off by himself?

Damn.

The last option didn't sit right. Ky couldn't leave. No way would he let Noah wake up alone, not after this. Not after sharing such a gut-wrenching truth.

Ky couldn't let the confession change how he treated the man, either.

If he pulled back now and tried to put some distance between them, Noah would assume his news had changed Ky's mind about him. That he was repulsed by Noah's confession and didn't want to be around him anymore.

And nothing could be further from the truth.

No, he clearly had to carry on as though his feelings hadn't changed, which wouldn't be hard because they *hadn't*. He also wanted to disprove the notion that Noah was, in some way, allergic to anything beyond a one-nighter.

The memory brought another eye roll from Ky.
The man clearly bought into his own unique brand
of wackadoodle bullshit. Ky definitely needed to talk
him into a repeat, in some fashion or another, of the
dressing room—at the very least to prove him
wrong.

He could practically hear Noah's voice saying
sure, it's for science, and Ky sighed.

Sadly, he just might be full of shit himself.

~~~***~~~

The sound of someone moving around his
bedroom woke Noah, and, with a nagging sense of
foreboding, he reluctantly cracked open an eye.

Ky, sporting ass-hugging jeans and a deliciously
tight T-shirt with the words *Everything's Bigger in
Texas*, whisked away an empty bottle of water from
the nightstand and plunked down a fresh one.
Noah's tongue felt fuzzy, his clothes bunched
uncomfortably, and that ominous feeling still
lingered in his gut.

"You're awake," Ky said.

"I...am?"

"Yep," he drawled.

"Um, okay."

But what the hell had happened?

He had hazy memories of stumbling out onto
the sidewalk after a successful afternoon at the spa.
Noah glanced at the dark window and the bedside
digital clock. Apparently he'd now been asleep for
five hours.

"How do you feel?" Ky said.

"I'm not sure." Still nestled in his cozy comforter
nest, Noah stared up at the man. "I need a second to
figure the answer out."

He remembered partaking of the refreshing
drinks made with *high-quality* vodka, obviously, if

the lack of a headache was any indication. In addition, he remembered Ky waking him up twice and making him down an entire container of water. All of which meant he felt well enough to contemplate how Ky would look in the designer underwear he'd bought.

A clear indication Noah's condition approached *status quo*.

Except his bladder was about to burst, which seemed like an emergency until he remembered mumbling the truth about Rick into Ky's chest—

Merciful motherfucker. What had he done?

Noah froze, trying to keep the choppy breaths and the racing heart rate from showing on his face. "I'm sorry," he finally croaked out.

"What for?" Ky said curiously, empty plastic bottle in his hand.

"For unloading my"—he cleared his throat—"ugly baggage on you."

The weight of which could sink an ocean liner.

"I didn't mind." Ky shrugged as though Noah's terrible secret were no big deal and tossed the container into the trash can with a muted *clink*. "The follow-up was kinda anticlimactic though."

"Wait...*what*?"

Follow-up? Damn, he couldn't remember. Did they do something dirty in the backseat of the limo? And he *couldn't remember?*

Noah propped himself up on his elbows, heart thumping. "How so?"

"We got caught in traffic."

"Did I take off my clothes?"

"You fell asleep."

"Oh..." he said as he flopped back, "I'm kinda disappointed in Drunk Noah. But I suppose it could have been worse."

"You drooled on me. Does that count as worse?"

"I—" He blinked up at him, feeling stupid. "I do not drool!"

Ky plucked at the hem of his T-shirt, the words and the outline of his home state stretching across pectorals that made Noah mentally whimper. "Why do you think I ditched the outer layer of plaid?"

"Uhm," he said, squinting up at the man, "because you finally took my fashion advice to heart?"

"No," he answered patiently. "Because I didn't want to walk around with a wet spot."

"Oh." He lifted his chin defensively. "At least it took care of that pesky flannel problem. I guess I should have tried drooling on you earlier."

"You did," Ky said with a level look.

Noah opened his mouth to disagree, and then the hot, dressing-room happenings hit him with all the subtlety of a high-speed bullet to the head.

"A favor I'd still like to return," Ky went on evenly.

Shit.

For a full five seconds Noah considered taking him up on the offer because—sweet, godless heaven above—he wanted Ky. He wanted him in so many ways he couldn't possibly list them all. The man was the protective older brother, the benevolent keeper of soul-destroying secrets, and the red-hot, real-life personification of Noah's ultimate fantasy.

"Excuse me for a moment." Noah threw back the covers and crawled out of his bed, grateful he was still fully clothed. "I need to take a shower."

A long one.

Full of nothing but cold water.

With a masturbation chaser.

He squeezed the bridge of his nose as he stumbled into his bathroom and then proceeded to relieve himself, shuck his clothing, and climb into the shower. Hot water hit his face, a poor attempt at scrubbing away the memories of emotionally shitting all over the poor doctor.

No more Moscow Mules, ever.

The Moscow Mule was *evil.*

An evil, delicious drink that should be banned for being named after a city located in a country known for its homophobic propaganda. Usually Noah was all about cultural diversity, but exceptions sometimes had to be made.

Sadly, this was one of those times.

And how was it that, after hearing the terrible truth—and what a fucked-up, train wreck Noah was because of it—Ky *still* wanted a go at him? Another surge of want baked his brain, and the soap slipped through his fingers as he reconsidered giving in to temptation.

But.

But.

Then he remembered one of his ugliest memories, second only to Rick's death. The last time Noah had gone home with a man before he'd finally decided to take a good, hard look at his horrible life choices. And by horrible choices he meant his selection of sexual partners *after* Mr. Hive-Inducing Nice Guy.

Ugh.

What had followed the vomiting and hives incident had been nine months of stupidity and mental self-flogging. Nine months of sexual escapades with men who treated him like shit. So, yay, no throwing up. But the encounters had gradually escalated until he experienced the most humiliating moment of his life—and he *excelled* at embarrassing himself.

He'd happily agreed to go home with a guy and, as soon as the dude had shoved him face first against the apartment wall, cheek now throbbing, Noah had started to question his decision.

Therein began a slippery mental slope that started with an *okay, a little pain can be sexy* before shifting into *isn't this supposed to be mutually enjoyable?* and finally ending on an *ohmygod, he's trying to fucking kill me*.

Two seconds after the guy came, he'd shoved Noah's naked body out the door—tossed out like yesterday's trash—followed by his clothes. Stunned, Noah had simply stood there, his favorite clubbing outfit clutched in his hand.

Cheek smarting.

Head reeling.

Even now the memory felt surreal, as though the incident had happened to someone else. Someone stupider than Noah, if such a thing were possible.

Fortunately, even he could learn from his mistakes. He'd finally come to accept that something needed to change and had carefully crafted his one-offs from then on. But what if he did a repeat with Ky and the blotches and vomiting happened again? Would he start up those horrible, masochistic choices once more?

Noah pressed his forehead against the cool tile wall and pushed the thought aside, steam enveloping him. If nothing else, he wouldn't, *couldn't* slip back into those self-destructive behaviors again. Not after taking so long to dig himself out.

Not after working so hard to overcome the shame.

Fingers fumbling, Noah shut off the water, dried off, and wrapped the towel around his waist as he made his way back to the bedroom. Propped in the doorway leading to the living room, Ky waited, arms crossed. A patient expression graced his well-groomed face, the faint shadow of stubble accentuating his cheekbones and amazing bone structure.

Fuck.

Acutely aware of the potential for embarrassing boner issues, Noah did a U-turn and entered his massive walk-in closet. He pulled on underwear and a pair of baggy khakis he never wore—because every ass deserved to be hugged, including his own—and a Ralph Lauren military-inspired sport shirt in crisp cotton that made him feel badass and ready to do battle.

As he reentered the bedroom, he fastened buttons and shot the handsome figure in his doorway an easy smile he didn't feel.

"Sorry," Noah said, and *no one* was sorrier than him, "I haven't changed my mind about us."

The man's expression didn't change, and Noah felt pressured to go on. "No can do."

And then...nothing.

Dammit, the guy excelled at working the silent expressions to his advantage.

"I told you before"—Noah sent the surgeon a winning grin—"I'm more of a one-trick wonder."

His MO of choice—random blow jobs for random men questioning their sexual identity—had been established as safe. Maintaining those ground rules was necessary lest he trigger another self-destructive spiral.

Ky tilted his head, broad frame leaning against the threshold, and studied him as if he could read all the chaotic thoughts swirling in Noah's head and was about to call him out on his bullshit.

"One-trick wonder meaning...?" Ky asked.

"I never sleep with the same guy twice."

"Sounds like a cop-out."

"Cops? I've blown a few of those, too."

"But never more than once?"

"Not anymore."

Silence followed, and Noah refused to budge, vowing to remain calm and focused despite the pounding of his heart and the vision of masculinity before him. And he wouldn't let this conversation drift back to...to the topic in the limo.

"Okay, so if you must know," Noah explained, "I get bored easily." Not a blatant lie, per se, but nothing about Kyland Davis was boring. And just the thought of getting his mouth back on him had his heart doing those stupid little cartwheels that the surgeon always triggered. "So..." he said, struggling to keep his composure as he gave an *oh well* shrug. "No repeats."

With minimal shift in his expression, Ky shot him a droll look.

"I gave you my reasons before, remember?" Noah said.

"I remember."

"Then why are we having this conversation?"

"As I said before, it is medically impossible to be allergic to repeat sexual encounters."

Well, Noah had felt the intense, prickly itch and the overwhelming need to claw at the blotches covering his body, not to mention the nauseating swell before upchucking. And where in the hell had the reaction come from? Was it a sign of a bigger problem, like being more messed up than he thought?

Holy crap, surely such a thing was impossible.

"And just so we're clear, monogamy isn't at all what I'm suggesting here," the doctor went on.

"So what are you suggesting?" How could he craft his argument without knowing the terms? "A once more with feeling?"

"A do-over."

"I... You..." His mouth hung open as his brain struggled to function. "A do-over suggests the first time went badly. The dressing-room blow job was *spectacular.*"

Eighth-grade coming in his pants notwithstanding.

Okay, a drink was definitely in order, so Noah headed for the built-in bar spanning the far wall of his living room. Ky trailed behind, bringing his patient expression and his delicious hotness along.

"Don't you think you've had enough for one day?" Ky asked.

"Is there such a thing?"

"Yes, there is."

"What difference does it make?" he said, focusing on the bar ahead.

"'Cause I don't want your senses dulled when I suck you off."

Noah stumbled. "Actually, I'm feeling in need of rehydration." He poured himself a club soda and turned to face the man, leaning his back against the bar.

Ky studied him for a moment and then reached past Noah, bringing their faces too close.

Too close.

Behind him, the tinkle of ice dropping into a tumbler was followed by the pop of a cork and a pouring sound from the Jack Daniel's Single Barrel, if the scent was anything to go by.

Noah struggled to concentrate.

"If I'd known the dressing room was all I was gonna get," Ky drawled, whiskey on the rocks now gripped in his fingers, "I would have planned the moment better."

Intrigued, Noah made a fatal error in judgment: he kept talking. "How so?"

"First," he said, taking a step in Noah's direction and bringing a whiff of whiskey, "I would've given the clerk more money so I would've had more time."

"How much more?"

"Two hundred, at least."

"I don't think the muscles around my mouth would've lasted long enough to give you your money's worth."

"Yeah, except"—Ky rested his free palm on Noah's neck, and the pulse beneath his thumb began to thump at an embarrassing rate—"you wouldn't have been doing all the work."

Noah swallowed hard. "Well, audience participation is always appreciated." He waited until he didn't sound so hoarse. "Anything else?"

"Second," he went on, shifting closer, "I would've gotten you naked to improve the view."

Oh, God.

"How can anyone argue with that kind of logic?" Noah said.

"They wouldn't."

"Anything else?"

"Third," Ky went on, his voice dropping an octave. "I never would've come in your mouth."

Noah groaned, a barely audible sound. His tongue licked his lower lip once, automatically seeking out the memory of that bitter, salty tang.

"At least not without tasting you first," the doctor murmured.

"I..." This time his voice ended on a squeak.

Every objection continued to drain away under the force of his arousal. Noah made a last valiant attempt, retreating for the familiar. He adopted a teasing look paired with a slow *it really is a shame* shake of his head.

"Unfortunately, Dr. Davis," Noah said, "unless you can bring something unique to the table, I'm going to have to stick with my original *no*."

He spent the tense pause counting out his harsh breaths as regret took hold. He'd engaged in a lot of sexual acts over the course of his life. Coming up with something unique would be next to impossible.

Christ, why had he proposed such an unobtainable goal?

"Something unique, huh?" Ky leaned in, lips so close to Noah's ear the words fanned across his neck, triggering goose bumps. "How about this? I can get you out of your clothes without touching a single button on that weird-ass shirt of yours."

"That's impossible."

"I'll bet you I can."

"I'll bet you you *can't*. And just how do you propose to win this wager?" Despite himself, Noah grinned, planting his hands on his hips. "Do your Eyebrows of Doom have powers I'm not aware of?" he said, and Ky straightened to meet his gaze. "Other than being completely ridiculous and totally hot?"

"Granted," he went on, ignoring Noah completely, "to even the odds, I'll need a few tools."

"What?" he croaked out.

A two-beat pause passed during which Noah might have had a stroke, because suddenly his tongue refused to work right.

"What kind of tools?" Noah finally asked, the words thick.

"I grew up on a ranch. Plus, I'm a surgeon," he replied. His mischievous smile sent a shiver up Noah's spine. "I'm good with tools."

Whoa, the guy could be totally charming when he tried. Noah hated to bring this ill-fated seduction attempt to an end; he was enjoying himself far too much. He sifted through potential responses, hoping to find one that would keep Ky thinking he had a chance but still allowed Noah to win.

"Okay, Tex. Whatever tools you can find in my well-stocked bar." He gestured in the direction of the drawers and dark wood cabinets behind him, no sex tools-slash-toys outside of possibly the spatula. "And just to be fair," Noah said because, despite everything, he absolutely adored the focused look on Ky's face right now. "In addition to the tools, I'll even allow you to touch me with one body part."

"One?"

Noah's grin grew bigger. "But I get to choose which one."

Because, dammit, this was a bet and his reputation was at stake. Losing wasn't an option.

Ky straightened to get a better look at Noah's face, and thank heaven, too, because now he could breathe a little easier.

Although the color of the man's eyes shouldn't be so distracting...

"Okay," Ky drawled slowly, bringing Noah's focus back to the man's mouth, which hardly helped. "Which body part am I allowed?"

"The most important one, of course." He felt positively giddy with amusement. "The tongue." Ky simply stared, and Noah couldn't restrain the triumphant look. "No teeth or lips or hands or fingers can touch me. *Just* tools and your tongue."

The knowledge the task would be impossible almost crippled Noah.

Somewhere in the distance Noah's phone rang, playing the tune of "Midnight Rider," but he ignored the sound of Dylan's ringtone. Instead, he watched in mesmerized fascination as Ky pulled open the drawer to his right. He couldn't remember what he kept there until Ky reached inside and pulled out a—

Jesus.

"That's the ceramic paring knife I use to slice limes and—hey!" Noah blinked, watching Ky slowly slide the kitchen utensil from its protective sleeve. "That really shouldn't be such a turn-on," he murmured to himself.

"This is you you're talking about," Ky said dryly.

"True. But *you* shouldn't look so comfortable."

"Well...I'm really feeling in my element right now."

"As opposed to the salon?"

The sexy half grin that came in response almost collapsed Noah's knees.

For the love of all that's unholy.

Ky stepped so close he towered over Noah. "Last time to amend the rules."

"Right." He struggled to focus. "The rules. So no"—he swallowed, eying the knife—"no loss of any appendages."

"Not a problem. Anything else?"

"No blood," he said. "Specifically *mine*."

"That's it?"

Noah blinked. "No pain, dismemberment, bloodletting," he listed out. "Yep, that pretty much covers the list."

"Agreed. Now, first," Ky said, his voice matter-of-fact, "we have to deal with all of these buttons."

While Noah's brain tried to catch up, Ky slipped the blade of the paring knife between Noah's top button and the fabric.

A distressed squeak caught in Noah's throat. "How are you—?"

With a little bit of pressure, the sharp instrument cut through the thread. A *pop* came, followed by a *ping* as the button hit the wood floor below—and a *thud* as Noah's heart had a seizure beneath his ribs.

"You can't..." Noah watched in fascinated horror as the knife slipped behind the second mother-of-pearl button, and it followed the first to the floor. "You have to..." His mind spun, trying to gain traction. "This is a Ralph Lauren and—"

The press of a knife and the third popped off and joined its fallen comrades below.

"Wait." Noah gripped Ky's wrist. "Are you really going to destroy all my clothes?"

"That wasn't on the list of things not allowed."

"I just assumed."

Ky leaned back a touch, allowing Noah to breathe and much-needed oxygen to return to his brain, before the guy went on. "So you're saying the destruction of clothing should've automatically been considered a no-go—"

"Yes."

"—but bodily injury needed to be clarified up front?" He cocked his head, crinkles of concern appearing around those amazing Technicolor eyes. "What kind of people have you been sleepin' with?"

A familiar shame swamped Noah's gut, and he released Ky's wrist, shifting his gaze to the couch. "The wrong types, apparently."

The response was slow in coming. "Apparently."

For the first time, Noah missed the judgmental expression, which was preferable to the one Ky wore now: unsettled, worried, and full of uncertainty. Concentrating on the counter edge digging into his back, Noah struggled to regain control.

"You want me to stop?" Ky asked, his voice sincere.

"No."

"You're sure?"

"For the love of all that's unholy, *yes*. I'm sure." The response sounded strained. He refused to allow pity or shame to play any part in this beautifully fucked-up, sexy scenario. "A bet's a bet."

Ky resumed his task, and, one by one, the buttons dropped to the floor, cranking Noah's heart rate higher. With each success, he panted for breath a little harder. Somehow the surgeon managed to slide the tip of the knife just a whisper away from Noah's skin.

A hairbreadth from touching.

The air grew hotter between them. The anticipation and the nerves and the slide of ceramic were the single most erotic moment of Noah's life.

And, technically, the guy hadn't even *touched* him yet.

Shit.

"Fear boner," he muttered to himself.

"Huh?" Ky said, sounding distracted, hopefully because he was too busy concentrating on the no-bloodletting aspect of their deal.

The knife tip passed close to a nipple.

Sweat popped up along the back of Noah's neck. "Fear boner," he squeaked out. "I thought it was a myth, but apparently, it is—"

A light scrape of a ceramic blade against skin, and Noah sucked in a breath.

"—it is a thing," he finished on a hushed breath.

Finally, *thankfully*, the deed had been completed and the shirt hung open.

Noah leaned back against the bar and gripped the marble edge, hoping to keep himself from reaching for the man.

"Now what are you going to do, cowboy?" He couldn't help but smile. "There's no way the knife is going to help with my pants. Because, you know"—he made a *voila* gesture at his groin—"zippers."

Ky chuckled. The sound warmed Noah's heart and sent a sizzle down his gut, heat settling in his hard-on. And then Ky lowered the knife in the direction of Noah's waistband—

"Cock!" Noah gasped, sucking in a breath in an attempt to make himself smaller. "I have one. Remember, you promised no loss of any appendages."

"That usually pertains to limbs."

"Well, my dick counts, too."

"Fine," he said with another chuckle.

It took several attempts before Ky seemed satisfied with the angle of his blade.

The man bit his delectable lower lip as he focused on his task, and it took everything Noah had not to smooth his fingers across the furrow of concentration on his forehead and lick the corner of his downturned mouth.

Another determined press of the paring knife and the khakis' button gave way. And if the boner beneath his almost-ruined trousers was any indication, maybe Noah should put up a little resistance more often.

Because making Ky work to get into his pants was, undeniably, the most fun he'd ever had with most of his clothes still on.

But the knife would only go so far.

"Foiled by the zipper," Noah said with an amused grin. "That must be aggravating."

Ky's gaze shifted from Noah to something beyond his shoulder, and his lids briefly flared, as though he'd seen something that ensured his success. Noah's smile slipped from his face as the moment of clarity hit.

Fuck.

I'm totally screwed.

And in the most pleasant of ways, too.

"I think"—Ky reached around Noah before holding up a pair tongs—"this will work."

"*Ohmygod*," Noah said, followed by a pornographic groan that should have been humiliating. "Now I won't be able to make a cocktail without developing a raging boner."

He'd also have to write Tyler a second thank you note for the Chef Craft stainless steel ice cube tongs with their smaller tip and life-saving teeth for easy gripping.

Best. Christmas present. Ever.

The scrape of said gift down the length of Noah's hard, fabric-covered cock sent a shiver down his abdomen and another shudder up his spine, the sight hotter than any utensil had the right to be—especially one that hadn't received approved sex-toy status.

Zipper undone, the loose-fitting pants fell to his knees faster than Noah usually did and then pooled around his feet. Effectively trapping him should he come to his senses and attempt to run.

Naked but for his boxer briefs, Noah stared up at Ky, goose bumps covering exposed skin both from the cool air and Ky's hot gaze.

Ky ran the tongs along the waistband of Noah's boxer briefs, as though searching for a way inside. "I figured you for more of a thong guy."

"Memphis promised me a lifetime supply of the designer boxer briefs he models," Noah said. "And, please." He rolled his eyes. "Thongs are hideous."

"At least they don't cover as much." He traced the tongs down and just to the left of Noah's erection, sending heated sparks through his dick.

Damn. Why couldn't the man just touch him already? Oh, right, only one officially approved body part...

Noah managed to croak out, "Promise me you'll never wear any."

For once, Ky looked as distracted as Noah. "Any what?"

"Thongs."

"Way ahead of you there." The tongs traveled beneath Noah's balls and up the other side of his still-covered—*dammit*—harder-than-diamonds cock.

Noah closed his eyes to cut off the arousing view and slowly counted to twenty. The metal touching his underwear went still, the only sound in the room their harsh breaths.

An intermission, of sorts.

"Any tools not on the counter?" Ky asked.

Noah considered keeping the knowledge to himself. "There are scissors in the drawer directly behind me." He opened his eyes and grinned. "Too bad for you I'm blocking the cabinet."

"I reckon I'll just have to get you to move," he drawled.

"*You reckon?*" The phrase was too adorable for words, and Noah did his best not to smirk. "You forget, I have no intention of losing this bet."

And if he *was* going to lose, he wanted to make the dude work for every blessed exposed inch of Noah's skin.

The corners of Ky's eyes crinkled. "Fine," he said. "Time to whip out the authorized body part."

Noah's lids stretched wide, and he held his breath. Against his better judgment, he dropped his gaze to the surgeon's crotch. The bulge beneath the man's jeans made Noah whine.

"Not that body part," Ky said with a wry tone.

Noah blinked, trying to keep up with the situation that had traveled so far beyond his control he had no hope of retaining his dignity.

"I'm only allowed the tongue," the doctor said. "Remember?"

"Uh..."

Right now he couldn't remember his favorite alcoholic beverage much less the conversation that had instigated a seduction scene ten times better than any porno flick Noah had ever seen.

And he'd seen more than most.

Ky leaned forward and traced his tongue along his collarbone, and Noah closed his eyes again, biting back a moan. The surgeon moved down, mere millimeters from the flat nipple, breath ghosting across sensitized skin. Lower, his tongue followed the happy trail that led from where the abdomen ends and the fun begins...

Noah's stomach muscles clenched.

Seriously, he was in big-time trouble.

Now kneeling, Ky paused along the edge of Noah's erection, and his heart thudded so hard he wondered if his whole body shook with the force. The man licked up the stretch of cotton just to the left of Noah's cock, so close Noah need only shift a bit to have the approved body part right where he needed it to be.

Jesus God, he wanted to thrust into Ky's mouth, feel his tongue on his dick.

But...but that was Ky's evil, diabolical plan to win this bet, because moving would allow him access to the scissors.

Sweat pooled low on Noah's back, and his thigh muscles clenched from the urge to arch closer.

"You're gonna have to move if you want my mouth on you," Ky said, and every syllable skittered down Noah's spine like a delicious promise.

"And if you succeed in getting me naked?"

"*When*," Ky said. "Not if."

"Okay, *if* you win, I shall hang a medal around your neck, but then what are you—?"

"Medal?" He frowned thoughtfully. "You know, sex isn't an Olympic event. There's no bringing home the gold for first place. No winners or losers."

"I disagree." Because Noah had *definitely* lost before. "Nevertheless, big guy, what's your plan if you succeed?"

Ky's cheek hovered near Noah's hip, his lips just a whisper away from the cotton stretched across Noah's hard-on, hot breath warming the fabric.

"My plan is to taste you from head to toe." The smile on Ky's face was slight but wicked. "And by that I mean *everywhere*."

"Everywhere..." Noah panted and clutched Ky's shoulders. Without the support, he'd collapse into a thoroughly seduced heap on the floor.

He wanted...

He *wanted.*

Noah swore viciously in his head and gave in, shifting toward that enticing mouth. He couldn't breathe as Ky, maintaining his crouched position, opened the now-exposed drawer and pulled out the kitchen scissors.

As though in reward for good behavior, Ky licked the damp spot of precum on Noah's underwear, his tongue a delicious drag across the sensitive tip.

"Shit." Noah's single word came out a whimper, the remainder of his good intentions caving.

Who could blame him? The paring knife technique definitely qualified as unique. And that kind of ingenuity should always be rewarded.

Preferably with a tongue and a hard dick.

"I think I'm about to achieve my goals," Ky murmured.

"I don't care," Noah groaned as Ky tasted him again. "Whatever it takes for you to win. Whatever destruction needs to be wrought. Whatever civilizations need to crumble. I can buy a new shirt. I can buy new pants. I can even replace the rug if there's a little accidental bloodshed but please, *ohmygod*"—another drag of Ky's tongue left Noah hissing—"please get this underwear off of me."

The cold metal scissors slid up his hip and began to cut, the fabric growing slack as Ky worked his way up, freeing one side. Cool air touched Noah's thigh as his cock strained beneath what remained of the briefs.

Close to completing his task, Ky touched his tongue to Noah's nipple.

"Fuck." Noah arched his back, chest seeking contact with Ky's mouth.

His hips shifted forward to make the movement easier, and, with one last snip, the boxer briefs slipped to the floor.

"You win," Noah whispered.

"Come here," he growled as he gripped Noah's ass and lifted him onto the counter.

Eyes dark, Ky took a sip of whiskey and then ran his tongue up Noah's throat.

The rasp of well-groomed, five-o'clock stubble burned his neck, and Noah sucked in a breath. "Is this a kind of body shot?" he asked, back pressed against the cabinet behind.

Instead of answering, that beautiful, beautiful mouth landed on Noah's shoulder. Large hands skimmed up the exposed torso beneath the ruined shirt, slipping the fabric from his shoulders. Noah longed to help, but right now he didn't want to break Ky's concentration. He seemed fixated on tasting the skin on his chest, his nipples. Little, sizzling kitten licks at odds with the frown of concentration and the sheer size of the man.

The careful consumption of his body left Noah's skin tight with anticipation. The cold marble cooled his ass and kept him from overheating as he was thoroughly and deliberately consumed.

A hand pushed up on Noah's knee until one foot rested on the counter, leaving all his important parts very nicely exposed.

"Coming to an orifice near you..." Noah murmured, gaze slipping between his own erection and the doctor's mouth.

"Eventually." Ky took another sip of his drink and leaned down to suck a bruise at Noah's hip before tracing his tongue along his balls.

Noah slowly relaxed, the building buzz lulling him into a sexual haze of complacency. Until the man spread his cheeks and licked his hole, sending a hot surge of need deep inside.

"*Ky—*" He arched his back with a broken sound, frustrated with his inability to communicate his happiness with the choice of body part.

Especially when applied to his asshole.

With continued attention, the small muscle slowly unfurling in welcome, every shocky rasp of warm tongue left Noah gasping.

An image of Ky's cock in his ass materialized in Noah's head in full IMAX glorious resolution. Over time, that kind of entrance had been reserved for VIPs only—Very Important Penises.

Now, it seemed, Ky definitely qualified.

Noah shoved the thought aside in favor of more urgent issues, like the mouth at his hole. "After claiming this wasn't a contest," he choked out, feeling closer to that bright, blinding orgasm in the sky, "you're clearly going for the gold."

"Maybe," he murmured before taking another sip of his drink and, without warning, swallowing Noah's cock.

"*Yes.*"

Noah whined and clutched the back of the guy's neck. The smell of whiskey wafted higher. The warm, wet suction of Ky's mouth was maddening, tongue swirling around the tip every other head bob as though they had all the time in the world.

Yeah, well, Noah begged to differ.

When every sensation grew sharp, muscles tight with tension and restrained energy, Noah dropped his head back against a cabinet door with a loud *thwack*.

"I— You—" Noah clutched the man harder, the *holy shit, I'm gonna come* tangled up in an epic five-word pileup.

Two seconds later he was making noises he hadn't known existed, calling out Ky's name as he spilled down his throat.

Chapter Eight

Heart hammering, body aching for release, Ky shucked his clothes and lifted Noah, but the guy's loose-limbed, lax state made hauling him across the room difficult. "You're supposed to wrap your legs around my waist."

"'Kay, 'n I will," he slurred out, "as soon's they start workin' again."

Hunh.

Post-Orgasm Noah sounded a lot like Drunk Noah.

The man attempted to hike a leg to help out, dragging a lean thigh with coarse hair up Ky's hard—and sensitive—cock.

"Wait," Ky hissed out.

He reached the bed, gently tossed him onto the mattress, and stretched out on top. Noah wiggled as though to accentuate the contact, writhing beneath him and...*goddamn.*

"Wait," Ky murmured again, slower this time, eyes closing as the sweat-slicked, skin-on-skin contact from hips to toe hit him full force.

Nothing but an exquisite pressure.

And *heat.*

Christ, that felt so good. How could something so beginner level—so minor league—feel so fucking *good*?

"What do you want?" Noah spread his legs, slotting them together, Ky's boner now wedged along the crease of Noah's groin.

Focusing the pressure in a breath-stealing manner.

Ky's mind spun and came up with the only answer possible. "You."

"Good to know," he said with a small smile. "But what else?"

"Haven't decided yet."

Noah squirmed again, eliciting shock waves everywhere they touched. "How about—?"

Ky ground his hips down in an urgent search for friction, and Noah groaned and pushed back. The simple sensation was so satisfying, so intense, something inside Ky broke, baser instincts taking over.

Who cared if he looked like a rookie?

He let his hips do what they wanted. No worrying about being in a hurry or finishing quickly. No worrying about excuses or expectations or explanations.

No worrying about...hell, *anything*.

Frank need ratcheted higher as time slipped by in a sexual haze of rocking hips. Noah wrapped his legs around Ky, his fingers desperate and, no doubt, leaving marks on his back.

When those fingers gripped his ass and pulled, a million tiny explosions of pleasure rocketed through Ky's body and propelled him over the edge.

"Fuck," Ky groaned out, thrusting hard through the pulsing of his dick, muscles now humming, skin tingling from the heated rush.

Eventually his arms threatened to collapse, but he kept rocking his hips anyway, Noah's lean frame undulating insistently beneath him. Ky couldn't stop looking at the guy's stomach muscles clench when he gasped, at the hard-on making a return appearance.

And the way the man appeared to have lost the ability to form words, his expression wrecked.

Noah's fingers dug deeper into his ass. "'M gonna—" His body tensed, back arching as he rocked his hard dick up through the hot, cum-slick skin between them.

Not only had Ky finally gotten to taste him, he was about to bring home the gold.

Right before the man finished, Ky leaned close and whispered, "First place goes to me again."

He watched with satisfaction as Noah tried to smile, argue, and groan out his orgasm, all at the same time.

~~~***~~~

Hours later, the sound of his cellular pulled Ky from a deep sleep. Given the time, the call likely forecasted a problem, but he struggled to open his eyes even as the phone went to voice mail.

Noah, naked and sprawled across his bed, slept partially beneath Ky, Ky's thigh slung across his legs, chest blanketing Noah's left shoulder. The skin-on-skin contact felt warm and *personal,* for lack of a better word.

Everything Ky might have been gasping for inside since...well, since forever.

Hunh.

All he wanted was to burrow closer and sink back into blissful oblivion. Achieving REM levels of sleep had always been a problem.

He'd spent years waking up to Savannah screaming, the nightmares starting after their mom died and lasting until his sister turned sixteen. Then there'd been the late-night study binges, dozing off between pages, and the learned habit of catching a few Zs during call, unconsciously braced for the next interruption.

The current interruption being a missed phone call.

He considered checking his message, but the bed was comfortable and the slow in and out of Noah's breaths were comforting. Not to mention, Ky's eyelids felt heavy...

A familiar tune started up somewhere in the living room, and he finally recognized the sound. He suspected whoever had called him had then dialed Noah's phone. Somewhere deep in Ky's muddled brain he knew this meant something significant. Regardless, while he had ignored his own call, Noah might feel differently.

"Hey," Ky said, gently poking him in the ribs.

The man snuffled against the pillow. "T'early..."

The sound of deep breathing returned.

"Noah."

"Go 'way. Your fault."

"What's my fault?"

"Broken." Face planted in the pillow, Noah blindly flailed an arm out to press his palm to Ky's forehead, gently pushing him back. "You broke me in a v'ry nice way."

Ky's lips quirked. "You don't sound broken."

"Well...'m takin' the day off anyway," he slurred sleepily.

"Your phone is ringing."

Noah rolled over and struggled to his elbow, hair mussed, and squinted at the bedside alarm clock. With a disgusted squawk, he flopped back against the mattress.

"None of my friends would dare call me before nine, much less *at four o'clock in the fucking morning*," he muttered.

"Not an early riser?"

"No," Noah said around a yawn, "and it's an unwritten social rule that four a.m. is reserved for booty calls and matters of life or death. We already covered the sex scenario, so unless someone is being whisked to the hospital—"

Ky blinked, the words slamming into him even as Noah bolted upright, eyes wide.

"The baby," Noah said.

~~~***~~~

If he'd been more awake, Noah would have recognized the disaster in the making sooner—the perfect storm of way-too-early morning afters. But when they parked at the hospital, sky still black as night, air frigid, his fuzzy brain was *still* protesting being forced to function at four a.m.

"Dylan's going to kill me if I miss the delivery. Do you think we missed the delivery?"

"Don't know," Ky said. "But we should hurry."

"I'm moving as fast as I can."

Noah was no less groggy now than when he'd stumbled out of the bedroom and scooped up the clothing littering his living room floor, tossing Ky's pants in his direction and tripping as he jammed his feet into a pair of jeans.

The double doors to the maternity ward *whooshed* open, and they stepped into a fake homey atmosphere with the scent of antiseptic. They rounded the corner, the long hallway ending at a waiting room filled with two people, Tyler and Memphis, who...would probably figure out what he and Ky had been up to.

Noah came to an abrupt halt. "Uhm, Ky?" He pulled his pea coat tighter. He felt exposed, tacky from dried sweat and cum, and sex rumpled. He also smelled, unsurprisingly, like he'd been used for a whiskey body shot. "How do you feel about everyone knowing we slept together?"

Ky's expression took a slow tumble through shock and concern before turning into outright alarm.

Alrighty then, question officially answered.

"Noah..."

"It's okay. You're not required to come out, *ever*, if you don't want to," Noah said in a serious tone. "Much like anal, this can't be forced."

"Jesus, Noah..."

"Okay, I get it," he said, rubbing his eyes. "Back to the problem at hand, right?" Think fast, *think fast*. They both needed a moment to mentally get themselves together before they could pull this off in front of his at times inconveniently observant friends. "Why don't you go grab everybody a coffee before joining us?"

"What are you gonna do?"

"I'll go talk to the guys."

"And say *what*?"

"Uh, I'll think of something."

Translation: *lie*.

Noah chewed on his lower lip, uneasy. But Ky had trusted him with private information, his deepest secret. Something he hadn't even shared with the people he loved the most, his sisters.

And after hearing the truth, after learning what *Noah* had done...

Christ, amazingly enough, Ky hadn't been disgusted. He hadn't looked at him in horror. In fact, there'd been no sign of judgment at all, just an easy understanding. Ky deserved Noah's best efforts.

So.

Time to stop looking like he'd been hit by an orgasmic freight train.

Combing fingers through his hair, Noah watched as Ky disappeared around the corner in search of coffee. Once alone, he headed for the waiting area with mauve carpet, fake flowers, and furniture arranged around two coffee tables.

"Sorry I'm late," he said as he approached his friends.

Tyler and Memphis sat on one of the couches—more accurately, Memphis sat while Tyler sprawled against him, looking content but barely awake. He'd been stretched across his boyfriend for so long he had a crease on his cheek from the seam on Memphis's shirt.

"How are the boys?" Noah asked.

"Just as you'd expect." Tyler sat up straighter, black hair flat on one side. "Alec can barely contain his excitement and Dylan looked on the verge of passing out," he said. "He kept trying to reach you, but you didn't answer. So he asked me to try you again."

Dylan.

Noah slowly sucked in a breath, guilt swamping him. His best friend had panicked and tried to call, but Noah had been too busy screwing the biological uncle of his about-to-be-born child.

Whoa, when had his life turned into a soap opera?

"I'll text him," Noah said, pulling out his phone, "and let him know I'm here."

Tyler ruffled a weary hand through his hair, gray eyes tired. "We've been trying to reach you for forever." He took in Noah's appearance with a look of suspicion. "Where have you been?"

Two awkward beats ticked by.

"*Nowhere,*" he answered and, God, what a stupid response.

"Really?" the man said dryly.

"I've—" Noah's mind spun.

Seriously, he needed coffee.

How could he be expected to produce a decent excuse so early in the morning minus caffeine? He took a moment to pace beside the coffee table before coming to a stop in the same place he'd started.

"Out dancing," he finally answered.

Tyler hiked a brow. "With a sander?"

"Huh?" Noah's hand flew to his neck, the skin stinging beneath.

He probably had more than a few marks from Ky's perfect stubble. Hoping to buy time to formulate an excuse, he slipped off his coat and hooked it over the back of a chair.

Memphis's hazel eyes crinkled as he smiled. "I can see you and Ky were busy."

"What...? No!" Noah stared at the two men looking up at him with varying degrees of amusement. "I just... We just..."

Jesus, he *sucked*. How had he managed to let Ky down so quickly? He inhaled through his nose, mentally gearing up for battle.

"Your call caught me mid-hookup with a delicious guy I met at Times of Crisis down on Castro Street. You know, my usual cruising ground. Loud music. Buff bodies." He knew he was babbling. "Unfortunately, my man du jour didn't get any closure 'cause I left to come here. I picked up Ky on the way," he lied.

"Yeah, right." Memphis leaned forward and tugged on the hem of Noah's shirt. "I guess this means you're turning over a new fashion leaf?"

Noah dropped his gaze to the T-shirt that, crap, was several sizes too big, an outline of Ky's home state on the front. And for the geographically challenged, the words *Everything's Bigger in Texas* printed in big, bold letters.

His brain hadn't appreciated being shoved from a sex-drugged sleep into adrenaline overdrive, and he'd tossed Ky his flannel button-up. Unfortunately, Noah had donned Ky's other shirt in the mad scramble to get out the door.

"Have you developed a new love for graphic tees?" Tyler asked.

"*God*, no."

"So...?"

"I can't wait to hear you explain this," the stuntman added.

Noah opened his mouth to say *me, either* but all that came out was a whimper of self-disgust.

"In case you weren't aware, wearing each other's clothes is the ultimate cutesy-couple statement," Tyler said. Noah recovered enough to shoot him a scandalized look, and the man laughed before continuing. "Oh, come on. Like you didn't mock me the entire time I dealt with Memphis's return."

"Lovingly," he replied with a finger raised, "I *lovingly* mocked you. That's what friends do."

"How long did you wait before you propositioned Ky?" Memphis asked, lips twitching in humor. "Five minutes? Ten?"

The unfairness of Memphis's words drove Noah's voice an octave higher. "Ohmygod," he said. "I didn't do *anything*."

Which wasn't exactly true, but... Ky had green-lighted the BJ. *Ky* had backed him against the bar and decimated his clothes, finally getting his frisky on.

And, good Lord, eventually they'd need to have a discussion about that amazing moment.

"It wasn't my fault," he insisted.

"Come on, Noah," Memphis said. "You? The one who refers to himself as the Blow Job Evangelist?"

"Uh—"

"I've only known you a few months," the guy went on, "and even I'm familiar with your endless search for the next guy to suck off."

Eyelids stretched wide, Noah considered how best to defend himself against the admittedly deserved accusation. He only had himself to blame—well, him and his big mouth. But long ago he'd learned being teased about his turbo slutty ways was far easier than being asked when he'd get over Rick's death.

When he would recover from the loss and move on.

He couldn't tell them that would never happen, because that would have invariably led to the question *why* and that...that was a question he could never answer.

Not if he wanted to keep the tenuous peace he'd carved out in his life. Not if he wanted to keep the friends that helped him remain sane. Dylan had loved Rick like a brother, and if he learned the truth about what Noah had done, he'd never forgive him...

Noah's airway threatened to collapse. Before he could formulate a defense, the *whoosh* of a second pair of automatic doors interrupted his thoughts.

Dylan, his sandy-colored hair a mess, appeared and headed in their direction. He looked stunned as he dropped onto the couch. "They kicked me out."

Halle-freaking-lujah. A distraction.

Noah assumed the comfortable pattern they'd established years ago, sitting beside the man and giving his knee a pat. "What did you do, handsome?"

The familiar nickname—and perhaps the reassuring gesture—appeared to help Dylan relax.

"Every time she had a contraction, she screamed and I cursed and started pacing." He looked slightly less pale than when he'd come through the doors. "And now the contractions are starting to come closer together, and the doctor started talking about a...a...*vacuum extraction*." He shuddered. "What the hell?"

"Sounds unpleasant."

Dylan shot him a sarcastic look. "No shit."

"So the staff decided the baby shouldn't be ushered into the world amidst hard-core profanity and booted you out?" Noah asked.

"Something like that." He looked around the waiting room, empty except for his friends. "What did I miss?"

"Noah seduced Ky," Tyler said.

"Dammit, I didn't seduce him," he said in protest, because there was no derailing this train wreck. "He seduced *me*."

Three sets of eyes blinked at him.

"Twice," he went on.

None of his friends looked convinced.

"The second time using a paring knife!" Noah said.

Seriously, he'd lived through the game-changing moment and he still couldn't believe it himself. Now the three men looked completely skeptical.

Why was the truth *always* stranger than fiction?

"Really, Noah?" Dylan said, green eyes squinting at him in doubt. "A paring knife?"

"I *know*, right?" Noah said. "It sounds creepy, doesn't it? But trust me, it was super hot. Like...like"—he made an explosion sound, fingers spreading from his temples— "mind-blowingly hot. I never stood a chance." When Dylan chuckled, Noah stood up. "I tried to resist, but then he pulled out the ice tongs and...and his tongue." Heat infusing his cheeks, he flicked an imaginary speck of lint from the T-shirt that reached his thighs and started pacing again.

Dylan sat there with a look that screamed *bullshit*.

All eyes followed Noah as he paced, the silence broken by the speaker overhead announcing for a patient to return to the ER. Finally he came to a stop and faced his friends.

"I tried to tell him no," he said.

Even to him, the words sounded weak.

Ugh.

"Don't," Noah went on, wearily rubbing a hand down his face. "Please don't say anything to Ky. Or *anyone*. He isn't officially out. No one is supposed to know. And if his family finds out..." The very least Noah could do was keep the man from worrying. "I need you to forget what you know."

"Already have," Dylan said at the same time Memphis said, "Consider it done."

Tyler nodded in agreement, and Noah sent them all a grateful smile. He knew he could trust them. His friends were the *best*.

"Man, I totally forgot to ask," Memphis said, turning to Dylan. "What are you guys naming the baby?"

"Maddie if it's a girl."

"And if it's a boy?" Noah asked.

Dylan looked up and met his gaze, the tension around his green eyes easing. "Rick, of course."

Christ.

Noah's legs gave out and he collapsed into a chair before the roller-coaster-like, gut-dropping sensation even registered. For a moment, he missed his boyfriend so much, the acute sense of loss was so profound, Noah felt ill.

Speaking of...

Huh. Noah glanced down at his skin, realizing he'd had no reaction after sleeping with Ky—no hives, no vomiting, *nothing*—most likely because there hadn't been a chance.

Apparently his body could only handle one freak out at a time.

A female voice interrupted his current baby-naming freak out. "Good news, gentlemen."

Noah turned and relief swept through him as he spied a smiling nurse.

"It's a boy. Eight pounds five ounces," she said. "Congratulations."

Everyone stood except Dylan, who had that stunned look again, fear and hope and joy—and a hell of a lot of *fear*—battling for dominance.

A full five seconds ticked by and nobody moved.

Ky appeared, setting a cardboard tray with four coffees down on the table. "We can see the baby from the nursery window," he said quietly, as though not to break the almost reverent tone in the room.

Man, he was beautiful.

Both inside and out.

Yet Noah had already outed Ky to his friends. Who did that? He was the *worst*. Less than ten minutes into his goal of protecting the guy and he'd failed. Why did he always fail the ones who mattered the most?

And, my God, when had the man begun to *matter*?

Suddenly Noah couldn't breathe, the atmosphere absent of air.

Ky jerked his head in the direction of a hallway that branched off to the left. "Follow me."

Pull yourself together, Noah.

The look on his best friend's face finally did the trick.

"Come on, Dad." Noah pulled Dylan to his feet and kept his hand on his arm as they all headed down the corridor.

The small group of men lined up along the bay of windows. Several babies slept in bassinets, and Alec stood next to a rocking chair, holding a bundle of what looked like blankets.

Blue eyes beaming, smiling like a besotted fool, Alec pulled the covers back and proudly displayed his pink, wrinkly looking son. Nobody said a thing until...

"Holy shit." The words slipped out before Noah could reconsider.

"He—" Dylan looked more stunned than before. "He has an alien cone head."

"It'll be okay," Noah breathed out, placing a comforting hand on Dylan's shoulder.

Clearly Tyler wasn't as good a friend as Noah because the guy looked completely unconcerned about the tragic turn of events.

"I'll buy him a hat," Noah went on. "Lots and lots of hats. One for every day of the month." He faced his best friend and sent what he hoped was an encouraging smile. "With any luck, hipster beanies will still be popular when he starts college."

"Guys, that's normal molding from the delivery," Ky said from behind. "It'll go away."

"Oh." Noah's shoulders slumped in relief. "What about the super premature male-pattern baldness thing he's got going?"

"Sierra had no hair when she was born."

Dylan looked at Ky as though seeing him for the first time, or maybe seeing the *real* him and not the surgeon or the super-protective older brother who had gone slightly apeshit when he'd learned about his sister's decision to donate her egg.

Balding and cone-head issues addressed, Dylan looked less like he was about to pass out. Another nurse came and took him into the nursery. Three minutes later, he sat in the empty rocking chair looking like the completely clueless Dad he was.

Dylan muttered something and Alec laughed, gently placing the bundle into his partner's arms. For a moment the mechanic looked as though he were awkwardly juggling a bag of spare motorcycle parts until he finally settled the infant into his lap. Carefully, he tugged a fold of blanket from the baby's face, and his son's tiny hand gripped his father's finger.

Dylan looked up at Noah with the most beautiful smile he'd ever seen.

And God, he just...

Noah couldn't...

"You okay?" Ky asked quietly.

An overwhelming pressure in Noah's chest left his brain fuzzy and his eyes burning. "I'm not crying," he said. Although he could understand the confusion. His lashes *were* a bit damp. "I'm just, uhm, over-hydrated." He cleared his throat and looked at Ky. "You?"

As Ky studied the baby, he appeared as though he had about ten different things he wanted to say. "I'm not sure."

Their eyes met and...shit. Heart pounding, Noah shifted his gaze back to the scene beyond the glass.

How could he be expected to hang out in the same room with Ky and pretend what had happened hadn't happened?

Every time he tried to say no to Ky, he failed.

Every time he vowed to keep it in his pants, he caved.

Evidently he couldn't restrain himself where Ky was concerned. Not only had Noah extended Rick's suffering, he was too selfish to deny himself sex with Ky. Worse, he sucked at keeping their activities on the down low, placing the man's secret at *risk*.

Shit.

Noah pressed a palm against the window. When he closed his eyes, all he could see was Ky's deeply disturbed expression at the idea of his friends learning the truth tonight, his fear that his sisters would be adversely affected if his family found out. And since the dude deserved better than being accidentally outed by a turbo slut extraordinaire—Noah's shoulders slumped in defeat—that led to one inevitable conclusion.

Now that his makeover duties were done, he'd just have to avoid the surgeon completely.

Chapter Nine

"Okay, hotshot," Noah said one month later. "Let's see what you've got."

The stuntman stood in Noah's kitchen staring down at the tofu and the two eggplants on the cutting board as though they were objects of complete mystery. Three seconds ticked by in silence.

"For chrissake, Memphis," he said, rounding the counter to stand beside him. "It's not a bomb about to detonate on your latest movie set."

"The soufflé from two weeks ago came close."

"Thanks to your impromptu baking-soda addition."

A disappointed frown crossed Memphis's face. "I thought I'd solved my deflation problem."

"I think my original Viagra suggestion was better."

"Maybe, but I still say we could've used Ky's help," he said with a loaded tone.

The subtle jab had Noah pressing his lips together. He knew there was something Memphis was itching to say. But he also knew what that subject would be, and he was *not* in the mood.

Besides, arguing was pointless. He'd told his friends four weeks ago he'd moved on to other things, things like preparations for the Bachelor Bid event itself—there were some arrangements Noah wanted to handle personally. He'd reiterated countless times that Ky's makeover was complete and there was nothing left to do.

Obviously, they knew this was about more than just clothes and haircuts.

The decision had left him restless and out of sorts. Fortunately, Memphis had been in his kitchen more often than usual. A welcome distraction, yes, but right now Noah could feel Memphis's gaze on him, vainly waiting for a response to his mention of Ky.

When none came, the man rolled his eyes. "Right, we're not talking about him," he finally said. "Here." He held out a second knife.

Noah stared down at it. "What's that for?"

"I heard you're partial to a good paring knife."

"*Cute*," he said with a tone that contradicted his response. He hopped up to sit on the counter. "I'm only here to provide moral support and sustenance."

"What kind of sustenance?" the stuntman asked dryly.

"The alcoholic kind."

Noah picked up his bloody Mary. Memphis finally got down to the business of cooking instead of passing judgment on Noah's life choices, and the next hour passed quickly. After a few false starts—including switching to a better utensil for peeling an eggplant—Memphis wrestled the ingredients into submission. Eventually the dish slid into the oven looking like his friend at least had a clue.

Memphis filled the sink with water. "I'll wash up."

"I'll dry," he offered, grabbing a dishtowel.

"Thanks." He shot him a grateful smile before setting about his task. "So...Ky's ready for the Bachelor Bid?"

Not this again.

Couldn't everyone see he was feeling conflicted about the whole situation?

Noah kept his eyes on the cutting board he was drying. "Yes, all set."

"You sure?"

"Totally sure."

"Maybe he could use some help putting together his bio? Make himself sound as attractive as possible?"

The dishtowel stilled in Noah's hands as he responded with a pointed look.

Memphis simply rinsed a few utensils and handed them over. "Careful of that paring knife," he murmured, humor in his tone.

"Really? Can we let that one go?"

Memphis opened his mouth, obviously about to say *no* when the sound of the front door closing interrupted them. Noah sighed in relief.

A few seconds later, Dylan entered, baby snuggled on his shoulder. His eyes had dark smudges beneath. His sandy-colored hair looked ruffled. "We have a parenting emergency."

"Thank God," Noah murmured.

Alec entered the kitchen carrying the car seat and shot him a confused look.

"Don't mind him," Memphis said to the new dads. "What's the emergency?"

"The last few weeks have been kinda rough," Dylan said, circling the center island. "As long as I keep moving, he doesn't cry." With the desperate expression of a sleep-deprived parent looking for answers, he eyed Alec. "Are you sure this isn't some sort of debilitating medical condition I should be aware of?"

"Yes," his equally fatigued-looking partner drawled wryly. "It's called colic. Ky said Sierra had it, too."

Every eye in the room landed on Noah, and he paused in the midst of drying the mixing bowl. Heat seeped up his face, and...damn.

How could he avoid the topic if everyone kept bringing up the man's name?

"When did Ky tell you Sierra had colic?" Noah asked.

"He stopped by for a visit," Dylan said.

"He's really good with him," Alec added.

Of course he was. He probably looked all cute and adorable as he cuddled his sort-of nephew, knowing just how to soothe him to sleep. And...dammit, that wasn't the point here.

Noah's smile felt strained. "I'm sure he is."

Okay, so saying his feelings were *conflicted* probably classified as an understatement. He missed his grumpy face. He missed his snarky comments. He missed...

Two seconds ticked by and Memphis looked as though he was about to bring the issue up again. Fortunately Noah's best friend had his back, changing the subject smoothly.

"Did I miss anything exciting?" Dylan asked as he walked.

"Other than a few predictable paring knife jokes?" the stuntman said. "Not much."

"Dude," Dylan said to Memphis, disappointment in his tone, "call me next time."

"What for?"

"I could've come up with some good stuff."

Noah frowned. So much for his best friend *sparing his conflicted feelings.*

As though trying not to disturb his son, Dylan used slow-motion-replay speed to carefully hitch his hip up over a barstool. Instantly, Rick started to cry and his father halted, mid-sit. The wailing grew louder and the exhausted dad began to slowly circle the room again, the infant snuggling deeper into the crook of his neck—an act that put a dopey grin on Dylan's face.

Or maybe that was the sleep deprivation.

"Is making him dizzy the game plan here?" Noah asked.

"Movement helps," he replied, gently bouncing his son. "Especially driving him in the car."

"Now that you two are parents, are you going to purchase the obligatory minivan?" Noah asked.

Dylan's horrified expression seemed answer enough, as though offended to his very core.

"Or in your family's case..." Noah went on because, hey, Dylan deserved some payback for being eager to participate in the paring knife ribbing, "a *man*ivan."

His best friend rolled his eyes. "I'm gonna go change his diaper."

"I'll help," Alec said, following him out of the kitchen.

A half hour later, Memphis pulled the lasagna from the oven, infusing the air with the smell of Italian herbs from the vodka sauce that Noah had insisted they substitute for the plain tomato one.

"Where did they go to change the baby?" Noah asked as he accepted a slice of the lasagna from Memphis. "Two states over?"

"Beats the hell out of me."

Noah took a bite; the herbs, sauce, and the texture of the eggplant combined for a satisfying taste. "Seriously, this..." He moaned, eyes closed as he savored the bite. "*This* is amazing." He lifted his lids and leveled a look at Memphis. "You'll definitely get in Tyler's pants with this one." He chewed and swallowed and cut another bite with his fork.

"Although that clearly never seemed to be a problem before."

"Still isn't." Memphis wiped some sauce from his mouth. "And this isn't about getting in his pants anyway."

"Well, then what—" The truth hit Noah, and his fork hit his plate with a *clink*. "Holy shit."

"What?"

"I've finally figured it out."

"Figured *what* out?"

"You're going to ask him to marry you."

Memphis's face grew a shade of red Noah had never seen before.

"You *are*," Noah said, pointing his fork in the man's direction, "aren't you? Why did it take me so long to clue into your plans?" Noah's mouth twisted into a fond smirk and he set his plate down. "After wooing Tyler with BASE jumps and high falls and explosions, I think a vegan lasagna is a rather, uhm, unique way to propose."

"I wanted to do something he wouldn't expect."

Noah cracked a grin. "Excellent choice."

"I'm going to find out what Alec and Dylan are up to," he replied with a frown, heading toward the guest room.

Whatever Alec and Dylan were up to, they were doing it together. And no matter how successful Memphis's birthday surprise would be, he and Tyler would be together, too. And here Noah stood in his kitchen...alone. Always alone. Which was his choice, really, but right now that did *nothing* to make him feel better.

A familiar ache built in his chest, and he rubbed his temples, concentrating on his breathing. One minute later Memphis returned with the car seat, Rick sleeping inside.

"Are they back there having sex?" Noah asked.

"Nope, they fell asleep. And I thought they could use a few extra minutes of rest." He set the baby carrier on the kitchen counter, well away from the edge. "I've got to get going. Thanks again for the use of your kitchen."

"But—" Noah stared at the sleeping baby strapped in his seat. "I can't— I don't..."

Memphis grinned. "Consider my delicious vegan lasagna payment for your babysitting services. Kids aren't your thing, I know. Word of warning, though"—he laid a hand on Noah's shoulder—"I think Dylan is working up to asking you to be a godfather."

And then he left.

He *left*.

Leaving Noah alone with a baby, for god's sake.

Noah stared down at the serene, sleeping face of his dead boyfriend's namesake...

Alcohol, Jesus, he needed *alcohol*.

Noah ignored his rapidly rising heart rate and began gathering the ingredients he needed, fingers fumbling as he set the bottle of Bacardi on the counter. It wasn't like he was planning on touching the little guy, after all.

A few moments later, Rick squirmed in his seat, making sounds like a bleating lamb. Oh, God. He was *waking up*. What the hell was he supposed to do?

Think, Noah. Think.

"The most important part of the mojito-making process," he began in his best documentary voice, "is muddling the mint." He dropped said herb into a glass. "This releases the essential oils responsible for the smooth flavor."

As he droned on about the very familiar process, explaining his every step, Rick stopped fussing.

Instead, the baby started sucking on his pacifier, eyes fixed on Noah.

All right, so talking seemed to help. Good thing he always had plenty of inane things to say.

"Your dad," he went on as he pushed on the tamper, pressing the mint leaves against the glass, "is going to ask me to be your godfather."

The vodka sauce rose in the back of his throat, and something went cold in his gut.

The idea was so absurd—so horrifically *wrong on so many levels*—that Noah set the glass down with a *clack* of crystal against marble. Chubby cheeks working, pacifier bobbing, Rick simply stared up at Noah.

"Does anything about my life qualify me as someone who should be allowed anywhere near your kind?" he asked the small person watching his every move. "The impressionable and the... innocent?"

'Cause he was anything *but*.

Five seconds crawled by without an answer, until Rick's face scrunched up again, as though working up for another cry.

Maybe that *was* his answer.

Noah grabbed his bottle-opener key chain from the counter and jiggled the keys in front of the baby's face. The infant stopped squirming and stared up at him as though offended anyone thought so little of his intellectual development, and a surprised laugh broke from Noah's throat. As he jangled the keys harder, wide blue eyes—the spitting image of Alec's—continued to blink up at him, clearly unimpressed. And maybe a little judgmental.

Yep, he could definitely sense the judgment. He'd just had his ass handed to him by a preverbal infant. An unfamiliar warmth filled Noah's chest.

God, he loved this kid already.

Watching Dylan and Alec during the predictable angst-filled teenage years was going to be wildly amusing, too. And what part would Noah play in his life?

Godfather?

Noah bit off a humorless laugh and resumed his cocktail task with less-than-steady hands, finishing the mojito that he'd definitely need before the afternoon was over. "Parenthood has warped both your fathers' minds."

Why else would they ask him to take part in their child's upbringing and personal development?

For the love of Jesus.

Noah's words came out tight. "Wasn't a godparent originally responsible for a baby's religious education? I mean, seriously, the only religious experiences I've had have been of the sexual kind." He stared down at the little guy, cheeks working overtime around the pacifier. "Oh, fuck, pretend you didn't hear that," he said. And then he frowned. "Or the four-letter word, either."

He hesitated.

"See," he said with a sigh, "I told you I wasn't safe for kids."

Task complete, he raised his drink in salute.

"So that..." He paused as a lump formed in his throat, unable to choke out the name *Rick*. "So that, my young Padawan—littlest of the little dudes—is how you make a mojito." He sipped the refreshing minty concoction, his muscles slowly relaxing. With his creative nicknaming skills, he could come up with a multitude of things to call the baby without stumbling over his dead boyfriend's name. The godfather idea was ridiculous, but the babysitting gig could work out if he learned to watch his tongue. No small task. "Would you like Uncle Noah to teach you the trick to the perfect margarita?"

"He's a little young for that lecture, don't you think?"

Noah whipped his head around, heat filling his cheeks. Grinning, Alec stood in the doorway.

"Can't start them too early," Noah said evenly. "Can I make you something?"

"No, thanks. I'm good."

"Where's Dylan?"

"Still sleeping in the guest room." He shifted the infant carrier to the center island, sat on a barstool, and rubbed the bottom of his son's foot as though he still couldn't believe his good fortune. He looked so happy and content.

Noah hadn't felt like that in forever.

Speaking of...

"Memphis said Dylan is going to ask me to be a godfather," Noah said.

Blue eyes met his. "That's true."

A loaded pause followed.

"Are you going to say yes?" his friend asked.

Noah bit his cheek and remained silent.

"It would mean a lot to Dylan," Alec went on quietly, and another toxic combo of guilt and shame burrowed deeper in Noah's gut. "We already asked Ky and Savannah and Sierra, for obvious reasons. And they said yes."

Oh, Geez.

Noah stared at Alec. Asking two men and two women to be co-godparents didn't seem too far outside the norm. And three of the four choices made sense. Savannah was as pure-hearted as they came. Sierra had given Rick life. Ky *saved* lives.

And Noah...

For chrissake, it was a like a tragic game of *which one doesn't belong?*

"I don't know," Noah answered, knowing full well he already did. "I'll have to think about the offer."

At the very least, a godfather needed to be someone a child could look up to. Someone with some semblance of wisdom. Which meant not only would Noah have to own his mistakes, something he excelled at, he'd have to find a way to move on. In short, he'd have to start seeing his past as something to be learned from. Did he have that in him?

Even his best friend would probably answer with a *no.*

The baby started to fuss again. Out of habit, Noah began to recite, in painstaking detail, the qualities of a good rum, and Rick settled down.

"I think he likes the sound of your voice," Alec said.

"Well, he'd be the first."

"Promise you'll think about the godfather thing. And"—Alec focused on his son, clearly avoiding Noah's gaze—"you should think about calling Ky." He cleared his throat. "It might make things easier in the long run."

Easier because Ky had agreed to play a permanent role in the baby's life, which meant the surgeon would be around more. Around them *all* more.

And what right did Noah have to muck everything up? Either Noah would have to be left out of the group gatherings or Ky would have to be left out—a thought that didn't sit well. Either that or every meet-up would be awkward as hell.

Noah chewed on his lower lip as he mentally worked through the problem. Alec never asked for much. In fact, his patience during the beginning of his and Dylan's relationship was legendary. And what right did Noah have to make things difficult for his...queer-heavy, motley group of friends?

His chosen family.

Noah massaged the bridge of his nose, gathering his fortitude. "I'll call him now."

He retreated to his bedroom, cell phone in hand, footsteps dragging. For a full minute, he stared at Ky's contact number—hunh, when had the man wound up in the favorites column?—before hitting speed dial.

"Hello," came the familiar deep voice.

Noah's tongue froze. Four weeks was a long time to go without contact. "Hi—uhm... It's me." Christ, he sounded like he was asking him to the junior prom. "I was hoping we could grab a cup of complicated coffee. Sometime. Whenever you're available."

A three-beat pause followed.

"My free time is kind of erratic," Ky said, sounding hesitant.

"Well, it just so happens I *don't* have a job. So our schedules will line up perfectly."

"Have you *ever* had a job?" There was no judgment in his tone, only curiosity.

Noah chuckled self-consciously. He appreciated the man's attempt at easing them back into conversation. "No," he said, muscles unclenching a bit. "And it took me five years to finish a four-year degree that I've never used." He rubbed his finger down the cool glass of his bedroom window overlooking the bay. "Ensuring Alec and Tyler's clinic remains well funded isn't a full-time gig, obviously. But it keeps me busy enough."

"A noble cause."

"And the Bachelor Bid has required an extra effort."

Ky's tone was bone-dry. "Yep, it sure has."

"And who else can claim that two a.m. cocktail-party chatter falls into the category of work?" Noah said, only half kidding.

The silence from the other end of the phone gave no indication what Ky was thinking.

Dammit, Noah, it's up to you to fix this.

"Look," Noah said, blowing out a long breath. "You and the girls are going to be a part of the baby's life. And I'm Dylan's best friend, so..." He paused. "We need to work something out."

"I understand," he said. "No more paring knives."

The sum of the words was obviously larger than their respective parts, and Noah's heart settled lower in his chest.

"So...friends?" the man asked.

Noah pressed his forehead against the cool windowpane, staring blindly down at the city and the bay beyond.

Friends.

Jesus, could he pull that off? He had plenty of friends. Good ones. The best, in fact. Better than he deserved, anyway.

But Noah had hoped he and the handsome doctor could come to some kind of agreement. A *truce* that would make the inevitable run-ins easier on everybody. More than that would probably be asking too mu—

"I could..." Ky cleared his throat. "I could use a few friends."

Oh, God.

Savannah's worries about her brother's lack of social life came back to haunt him. Not to mention the isolated look on the man's face as he'd frowned at the San Francisco skyline that eventful shopping day.

Noah rubbed his eyes.

If he couldn't get his act together, his friends wouldn't include Ky as often in an attempt to keep things from being uncomfortable. And that would leave Ky alone, an image Noah couldn't handle.

"Friends," Noah repeated. "Of course, no problem."

Dammit, he'd figure this out if it killed him.

~~~***~~~

Three weeks later, Noah flopped onto his comfy couch, feeling acutely out of sorts.

He'd been far too efficient taking care of his share of the details for the Bachelor Bid. He'd handled the printed programs and media relations— including the airing of Memphis's commercials for the event—while Savannah continued to do a bang-up job with online promotions. He'd had multiple meetings with the audiovisual vendor and had insisted on taste testing the signature cocktails the caterer was proposing. Now, the rest of the planning lay in Savannah's hands.

Leaving Noah with nothing immediate to do...a recipe for trouble.

Ky was on the tail end of a week-long marathon work session in which he'd had little free time. And the niggling sense of emptiness he'd left in his wake was concerning.

During the first two weeks of their friends-in-training experiment, Noah had gotten used to the big guy popping in unexpectedly. They'd spent a lot of time together. Numerous slightly awkward moments, sure. It hadn't been easy to ignore the *I've gasped your name while coming* thoughts while suppressing the urge to tackle the man to the ground and climb on top.

But they'd met multiple times for a cup of complicated coffee. They'd "discussed" Ky's wardrobe and looked at furniture while engaging in good-natured bickering without ever coming to an agreement. They'd watched several movies—the guy knew every spaghetti Western ever made and could quote a lot of the lines—while watching the baby last Sunday so Dylan and Alec could sleep or fuck uninterrupted. Or sleep *and* fuck uninterrupted.

Whatever.

And now? Twenty-one days into their trial run as friends, *twenty-one days*, and Ky's one-week absence had left a disturbingly large hole. And here Noah was on a Friday night, wallowing on his couch and wondering when Ky would have time to call.

Fuck. It was definitely past time for a drink.

Noah mixed himself a margarita on the rocks and returned to the couch, clutching his icy glass while staring up at his boring ceiling, the condo too quiet. Memphis had surprised Tyler with a weekend away, a bucket-list trip to a bed-and-breakfast up along the coast near a massive rock formation Tyler had been itching to climb. Around lunchtime, Alec and Dylan had brought their son by for a visit, which had been nice company. Curiously enough, Rick actually *did* like the sound of Noah's voice. Go figure.

Even better?

The horrified look on Dylan's face every time Noah referred to himself as The Baby Whisperer.

Noah found the timing of their visit today awfully convenient. He had a growing suspicion his friends were taking turns checking in on him. Which was nice, of course, but also made him feel like a loser-licious mess. Was he a loser-licious mess?

God, he was definitely a loser-licious mess.

His cellular belted out a country song from the playlist Noah had chosen for Ky's calls, and an electric surge of happiness lit his veins.

Hellz yeah.

Noah fumbled for the phone on the end table, so pathetically excited that the man was calling that he almost hit disconnect by mistake.

"So," Noah said, hoping he sounded breathless in a *just jerking off* kind of way and not a *flustered by a mere phone call from you* kind of way, "couldn't wait to talk to me, huh?"

The indecipherable grunt from the other end could have been a simple *hello* or a *what's up?* or a *you're being ridiculous.* Or any variation in between. It was just a freaking grunt, though, and Noah refused to go all gooey over a grunt. Absolutely refused. Besides, Ky had called.

He'd *called.*

"I just got a text message from Sierra," Ky said.

"What is your delightfully devious sister up to now?"

"She needs me to come down to Texas."

Noah's heart deflated a bit at the news.

"Ray's shoulder isn't any better, so he's scheduled for a rotator cuff repair this week," Ky went on. "But the lawyer in Seattle handling Sierra's and her fellow protestors' case had to move their meeting forward unexpectedly. Unfortunately, the meeting takes place at the same time as Ray's surgery."

"So she needs you to hold down the fort at the ranch while she goes to Seattle."

"Yep," Ky confirmed.

"How are you arranging that at work?"

"I just got done covering for one of my colleagues who wanted to visit his daughter. She delivered his first grandchild six weeks early. He owes me. Getting my shifts covered wasn't too hard."

Noah's heart deflated a bit more. And, dammit, a truly unselfish person would only feel happiness on Ky's behalf, the schedule working in his favor.

"Will I get to see you before you go?" Noah asked.

"Before she called, I was hoping I could swing by your place tonight, but now I need to pack to catch an early-morning flight and..." The brief pause ended when Ky said, "Goddamn."

"What's wrong now?"

"According to the weather report, it'll be ninety-five degrees in Oak Hollows for the next few weeks. Hotter than Hades."

Noah relaxed against the couch and smiled at the almost complaint. He'd been avoiding the thought that his former hookup and only single friend might decide to forgo the excitement of San Francisco—and Noah—and return to his Texas roots.

"If you have to fill in for her, I'm assuming she'll have to tell her dad about the arrest?" Noah asked.

There was no missing the small sigh from Ky. "She said she was going to anyway."

"That could cause some friction."

"You think?" he said dryly.

The attempt at humor fell short, and Noah's heart gave a sympathetic twist.

"Will she tell him about the baby?" Noah asked.

"Ha," he barked out without a trace of amusement. "I hope she's not planning on sharing that tidbit of information."

Noah could hear the concern in the man's voice.

"Maybe she'll keep her latest pet cause to herself," Noah said.

"Then you don't know my sister as well as I thought." He sounded...resigned. And troubled. "I have a bad feeling she's just waiting for the right moment to spring the news about Rick. All the more reason for me to go down there. So I can convince her otherwise."

Noah swiped at the condensation on his glass and tried to ignore the tug in his chest as he pictured Ky's expression. The overprotective, brother-bear one that left Noah itching to smooth the distressed furrows from the man's brow.

He also had an overwhelming urge to do something to put a smile on the man's face.

"Cheer up, cowboy. I'm sure she'll listen to her wise elder sibling. Before you know it, you'll be on your way back home." And then he reconsidered, his voice growing tight. "You will, won't you?"

Shit.

Instead of using a tone that encouraged a smile, he'd managed to sound...clingy.

Noah cleared his throat. "*Are* you coming back soon?"

"Well, I sure don't want to be there when Ray returns after his surgery." His tone spoke of his less-than-enthusiastic feelings on that possibility. "Fortunately, the VA hospital he's using is located about a hundred miles away. Until Ray's doctor declares he can drive again, he'll be staying with an old army buddy who lives closer to the facility. That'll take about three weeks after the procedure. Sierra will only be in Seattle a couple of days. But I managed to finagle a week off, so I'll probably stick around and help her out a bit after she gets back."

"I hope your sister appreciates her big brother."

"Maybe, but if I can't convince her to *not* tell her father about her cause..."

A bazillion questions raced through Noah's head, and he absently traced the leg of the coffee table with his foot as he considered asking a few. But his goal was to get the man to *smile*. Since the mention of Ray, Ky's muscles were probably cramping from the force of his scowl.

Time for a change in topic.

"Well, I'm sure it'll be nice to visit the ranch again. Returning to your fashion roots, so to speak," Noah said. "Won't your belt buckle be happy to be home?"

Ky produced one of those skeptical scoffs that did adorable things to his face. "My old neighbor used to wear one twice the size of mine."

"That's...amazing."

"It kinda was."

"Visible from outer space?"

"Maybe."

His tone didn't sound as tense, but no outright amusement yet.

"What will you do while you're there?" Noah asked.

"Make sure the cattle have food and water. Mend any fences that need fixing so they can't escape. And there's always a few mechanical issues that need taken care of."

Oh, God.

He closed his eyes, trying *not* to picture Ky in jeans and no shirt, sweating, muscles gleaming in the Texas sun as he mended fences or did mechanical things to various and sundry pieces of equipment that Noah couldn't begin to name.

"Will you visit old friends?" Noah asked.

The pause that followed felt heavy, even over the phone.

"In Oak Hollows, alone works out best for me," Ky said.

Noah opened his eyes. Although the man clearly loved his childhood home, no doubt the place held more than its share of bad memories.

"How do you feel about going back?" Noah asked.

The silence lasted longer than comfortable.

"It's complicated," Ky finally said.

Right now he was probably wearing a broody glower to beat all glowers. And his voice sounded brittle, as though applying pressure in just the right place would get him to crack.

Noah couldn't stand the thought of the man handling all the unhappiness alone. "You want me to come with you and keep you company?" The words were out before Noah'd had time to consider holding his tongue. "My calendar happens to be wide open."

Shit. Maybe that was taking their tentative friendship too far, too fast? But the thought of Ky, walking around with a heart-meltingly sad little frown...

"I could ride around in your truck and help you toss out bales of hay...or whatever it is you do to feed the cows." Noah rolled over onto his stomach and set his empty margarita glass on the coffee table.

The second pause was longer than the first.

"Pockets of Texas aren't safe," Ky said.

"You mean at the ranch?"

"Around Oak Hollows?" Ky said. "Nowhere is safe."

"Oh." Noah felt stupid for taking so long to figure the unspoken conversation out. The topic had as much to do with the residents of Ky's hometown as his stepfather. Clearly the man was worried about Noah's safety. "If it's only for a week, I wouldn't need to go to town anyway," he went on. By God, he didn't want his friend to face all this alone. "And who knows? I might surprise you." His lips quirked at the edges. "I'm quite capable of blending in."

The amused noise that broke from Ky's mouth warmed Noah's chest, leaving him pleased that the man sounded a little less...frowny.

Really, getting the man to smile shouldn't feel so death-defyingly important.

Ky sounded as though he were slowly...*reluctantly*...considering Noah's offer. "You'll probably change your mind when you learn the flight leaves tomorrow at six thirty a.m."

"Which means, after shopping for the appropriate clothes this afternoon, I'll have to get up early in the morning." Noah let out a fake sigh. "I wouldn't do this for just anyone, you know." His smile grew bigger in anticipation of his next words. "It would be worth the trip alone just to see your *tiara*..."

The snort that shot from Ky's mouth filled Noah's ear.

"Not gonna happen," Ky said.

"Please."

Ohmygod, was that a whine? That was definitely a whining tone. When Rick turned two, Noah would be able to out-toddler him.

"I'm not changing my mind," Ky said.

"Not even one little glimpse?"

"Not even in return for permission to wear my belt buckle."

"Funny," he deadpanned. He rolled over, wriggling until he was flat on his back and staring up at the ceiling again. He should be ashamed of the silly grin plastered across his face. "Nothing will tempt me into conceding the belt-buckle point."

Was that another amused sound he'd just heard from Ky? Or more of a *you're being ridiculous, as usual* huff?

The opportunity to see Ky in the place where he grew up, where the wearing of cowboy boots was the norm and not the exception, proved too much for Noah to pass on. He'd grovel if he had to. Too bad he couldn't bribe him with the promise of a blow job.

This friends-only thing really handicapped his power-of-persuasion techniques.

"Honestly, I don't mind coming down to Texas," Noah said, hoping he sounded as sincere as he felt. He crossed his ankles and the fingers of the hand not holding his phone. "That's what friends do, you know," he said, trying to convince himself as much as Ky. "Support each other through the difficult times. Like child-rearing and vegetable lasagna cooking and dealing with...uh"—Jesus, there were no words for Ky's upbringing—"with...cattle."

Neither mentioned the last part was a lie.

"Since when are you an expert on any of those things?" Ky asked.

"Since never," he replied. "But I *am* good company."

He chewed on his lower lip, waiting for a response and most definitely not holding his breath. Not at all.

"Why do you want to come with me so badly?"

"Well, Sierra has invited me down multiple times," Noah said truthfully. "And eventually I want to take her up on the offer. I can do it now, and keep you company at the same time. Or I can visit her later on my own."

A long pause ensued, as though Ky were considering the information further.

"Well, Ray would be gone by the time we got there," Ky said, still sounding worried. And far too reluctant. "As long as we stick to the ranch, I suppose it could go okay. So I guess you can tag along. "

"My, you're a real smooth talker," he said dryly, propping himself up on an elbow. "Is that a *please, Noah, come to Texas with me*?"

"I reckon it is," he drawled.

"You *reckon*?" he repeated, amused by the Texan phrase.

"I can probably get you booked on the flight with me tomorrow," Ky continued, ignoring the interruption.

"When we get there, will you at least let me see the *picture* of you in a tiara?"

The reply came back quick and decisive. "Nope."

"But you don't understand." He was so pleased to be going to Texas with Ky that the stupid grin on his face probably interfered with his persuasive tone. "It's on my bucket list."

Watching Memphis suffer through cancer treatment had brought a new appreciation for Noah compiling his *own* bucket list. Okay, so his was more of a sexual bucket list—lots of fetishes left to explore and all.

Sadly, Ky couldn't help him with those anymore.

"Seeing that photo is number one on my list of things to do before I die," Noah went on.

There was a two-beat pause before Ky responded. "Then you better hope you live forever."

This time, Noah was positive he heard a smile in the man's voice.

Chapter Ten

Their rental SUV rumbled across the cattle guard beneath the Davis Brothers Cattle Co. sign, gut-punching Ky with conflicting feelings—pleasure *and* pain. An intense sensation of well-being tainted with, unfortunately, an ominous weight crawling just beneath his skin.

From the passenger seat, Noah read the sign out loud with more than a trace of confusion. "Davis Brothers Cattle Co.?"

"My great grandfather and his brother started the place."

"I'm surprised your stepdad didn't change the name to Urban Cattle Company."

Ky gripped the steering wheel and forced himself to relax. Nurturing resentment took time and energy, neither of which he had to spare. More importantly, he'd decided long ago that places weren't important, *people* were. And if Sierra Urban eventually inherited the ranch that had been in the Davis family, *his* father's family for generations...well, he couldn't think of anyone more deserving.

Ky ignored the catch in his chest as he scanned the gently rolling pastureland. Crops of scrub oak broke the deep blue sky lining the horizon while cattle milled about, black dots clustered amidst a sea of green grass. Being in the house his mom and dad had built always left him feeling in touch with his parents.

Connected, if not in time, then by place.

Most nights in the city he'd ached to return home for a visit. The only reason he'd come today was because Ray wouldn't be there. The knowledge, however, did little to ease his nerves.

He couldn't shake a pesky sense of foreboding.

"So...why isn't this place called the Urban Cattle Co. now?" Noah asked.

"Changing the name of the LLC would require paying a fee," Ky said dryly. "And Ray never spends money unless forced—like hiring temporary help during calving season. Between my stepdad and Sierra, most months they do all the work themselves. I suspect that's why he's using the VA hospital for his surgery, 'cause it's cheaper for him, even though it's inconveniently located farther away."

"A penny pincher, huh?"

He shot Noah a look. "Fortunately for me, yes."

"Why specifically for you?"

"Because he's managed to keep this place in the black while some around here have gone broke."

Ray, if nothing else, excelled at managing the ranch. His people skills, on the other hand, sucked.

Ky forced an ever-so-casual shrug, trying to sound nonchalant as he went on. "And I suspect money is the *only* reason that, as a gay teen, I was allowed to stay. So I could help with the ranch work and take care of the girls." And he'd never regret his choice, ever, despite the prerequisite sacrifices. His lips twisted wryly. "As long as I met Ray's conditions, of course."

Which meant pretending to be something he wasn't.

"Of course," Noah said, gaze scanning his face.

And while Ky appreciated the empathetic concern and support in Noah's expression, the *only* reason he'd finally agreed to let him tag along was to keep the man from visiting Sierra at a later date, when Ky wouldn't be around to protect him. Jesus Christ, the thought of Noah dealing with his stepdad alone made Ky break out in a cold sweat, fear knotting in his stomach. There was no telling exactly how Ray would react, but if Ky's childhood was anything to go by...

Noah yawned, faint circles beneath his eyes.

"You really aren't a morning person," Ky said with amusement.

"Leaving the condo at four a.m. to make the flight was a particularly brutal form of torture." His words were followed by a tired groan. "Especially since I didn't start packing until midnight."

"Why so late?"

"Yesterday I found the boots I wanted on Mission Avenue, but I had to drive to their Palo Alto store to get the size I needed." He rubbed his temple. "Traffic was bad and it took me longer than I'd planned."

Ky still hadn't recovered from his first glimpse of Noah in cowboy boots. "By the way, nice look."

Noah perked up, appearing pleased with himself. "I thought I'd blend in well."

Ky bit back a smile. That Noah Tanner thought "fitting in" amounted to donning the right clothes would surprise exactly no one.

In his defense, Noah had managed to select a pair of sedate brown boots with simple stitching. Unfortunately, they were also buffed to a high sheen and suspiciously lacking in dust and cow shit. His white button-up shirt—Jesus, in this dusty countryside no one wore *white*—and Wrangler jeans looked tellingly crisp and brand-new. Paired with a vest and nothing appeared out of place. Except it was all too much and just not enough of any of the right qualities. He looked exactly like what he was: a city dweller attempting to go country casual.

Ky had to give him credit for trying. But Ray would have seen through the ruse before Noah opened his telltale sassy mouth.

"I can pull off being straight," Noah said with a serious expression. "And if you suddenly get the urge for us to return to Texas for another visit, just to piss off your stepdad"—a grin appeared—"I'd be honored to play the fake boyfriend."

What the ever-lovin' hell? Fake boyfriend? The phrase kicked Ky's libido into full gallop. But not only would that scenario never happen, Ky wasn't sure what all the idea entailed.

"I don't understand," Ky said, careful to keep his expression blank.

"When they first met, Dylan offered to pretend he was sleeping with Alec. The plan was to drive Tyler, the ex-boyfriend, crazy." At Ky's continued confused expression, Noah twisted in the passenger seat to face him before going on. "A long time ago Tyler and Alec used to be A Thing. Not a very well-matched one, mind you, but a thing nonetheless. Anyway, Dylan had a blast playing the role."

Ky blinked, trying to wrap his head around the crazy idea of a pretend relationship—and doggedly determined to ignore the thrum of *want* in his gut that was anything but a sham. "You were the one insisting we be friends only."

"I know."

"I'm assumin' you haven't changed your mind."

"You assumed correctly."

Ky ignored the flash of disappointment, still confused. "So why....?"

"Because pissing off your stepdad would feel good, don't you think?" Noah said as though explanations shouldn't be necessary. "And why should Dylan be the only one who gets the fun of playing the fake boyfriend?"

Ky mentally groaned and swiped a damp palm down his denim-covered thigh, his body still reacting to Noah's idea as though it included sex. It was like the dude had discovered a how-to-drive-Ky-crazy flow diagram and was meticulously following every pathway.

They rounded a curve, and the driveway opened to a large gravel area to the left of the two-story ranch-style home, his favorite massive oak tree still shading the front porch of wood and stone. He parked the Tahoe between Sierra's Chevy truck and the diesel flatbed loaded with hay, stepped out, and inhaled the scent of alfalfa and earth. Instantly, his muscles relaxed.

God, it was good to be home.

"You're here!" The screen door screeched open. Sierra, long blond hair hanging past her shoulders, lowered a carry-on suitcase to the porch before bounding down the steps. The door slapped shut behind her.

"I'm so glad you came," she said, beaming brighter than the morning sun as she jumped into Ky's arms.

He gave her a fierce hug, her happy demeanor easing his ever-present worries a bit. And then she turned to give Noah the same treatment.

"Hi, sweetie," Noah said, pure pleasure on his face as he returned Sierra's embrace. "I wish you weren't taking off so soon. We need to catch up."

"We can do that when I get back," she said, releasing Noah.

Ky pulled his bag from the Tahoe. "Need a ride to the airport?"

"Nah," she said with a wave of her hand. "Becky is gonna drive me." Her smirky smile, present since the mention of her high school friend, grew bigger. "Her car is in the garage again."

"Another fender bender?" Ky asked, amused.

"She pulled out in front of the mayor, of all people." Sierra gave an affectionate roll of her eyes. "Anyway, Becky's giving me a ride to and from the airport in exchange for the use of my truck while I'm gone. I offered her our gas hog of a diesel flatbed but she preferred my Chevy instead." She loped back up the porch steps, retrieved her carry-on bag, and descended the staircase again. "Daddy went into town for a new spark plug. He should be back soon."

Ky's whole body went cold.

For a moment he couldn't breathe.

"Ray is still here?" he finally managed.

"Yep," she said.

His stomach dropped another inch and got busy digging a hole the size of Texas as the blood pounded in his ears.

Jesus fucking Christ.

What the hell was he supposed to do now?

Ky stood, duffle bag in hand, suppressing the crushing urge to hustle Sierra and Noah somewhere else, *anywhere else*, in an attempt to evade the upcoming disaster. Bad enough dealing with Ray with Sierra around, now he had *two* people to protect. All the clothing in the world couldn't mask Noah's subtle mannerisms. Mannerisms that gave him away.

Dammit, he should have just forbidden Noah from coming.

Ever.

"Daddy's all packed up and ready to go. But he postponed leaving until this afternoon," Sierra went on, clearly oblivious to her brother's panicked thoughts. Her footsteps crunched on the gravel before she tossed her overnight bag into the bed of her small pickup. "The generator in the east field stopped working again, and he wanted to fix it today before he left."

She looked at him for a response. But the news had wrapped around Ky's throat and threatened to choke him.

Sierra sidled up next to him. "Just a word of warning..." She watched Noah pull his too-big-for-a-one-week-trip suitcase from the back of the Tahoe and leaned closer, lowering her voice. "Daddy's still ticked off at me," she went on. "News of my latest run-in with the law went over way worse than the previous one."

Ky knew her recent *cause*—reproductive rights for same sex couples—not the arrest, accounted for most of Ray's anger. Neither of his little sisters understood the full extent of their daddy's homo-hatin' ways.

And Ky would do his damnedest to ensure they never would.

"I take it you didn't tell him about the baby?" he said.

"No." She bit her lower lip. "The timing didn't feel right."

Thank God for small favors. Unfortunately, they were still headed for a collision of major proportions.

For God's sake, Ky. Do something.

Spurred into action, he tossed his duffle bag back into the Tahoe. "I'll take Noah on a tour of the property," he said. "We'll come back when Ray's done."

And *gone*.

"Don't be silly." Sierra looked at him as though he'd lost what little of his faculties he had left. "You both must be exhausted. Noah looks as though he's ready to fall asleep on his feet. So, come on"—she gently tugged him toward the front door and shot him her signature chastising look— "you and Daddy don't even need to talk. Y'all can mend some tightly strung fences just by existing in the same room."

Ky kept his feet firmly fixed on the walkway.

"It'll be good for you both," she went on.

"I doubt that."

"He's mad at me, Ky," Sierra said. "Not you."

"This isn't a good idea."

"I told you before, he's better now." Unlike their last conversation on this very topic, a sliver of doubt now rang in her voice. Despite that, she lifted her chin and firmly met his gaze. "And it would make me really happy if you two weren't so dead set against being around each other." She waited two beats before going on. "This is my home, Ky," she said softly. "I'd like my brother to visit me once in a while."

Oh, fuck. How could he argue with that?

"Sierra..." Ky closed his eyes, mind scrambling through a list of plausible explanations.

Yep, a part of him always ached for home, but coming here after Sierra had moved back proved too much of a gamble. He could maintain his cool around Ray—and had for *years*—but an adult Sierra was too observant to miss much. And pitting her against her father wouldn't go well.

For any of them.

All he knew was that he had to protect Noah from Ray and shield Sierra from the truth. He had to keep his sharp-eyed baby sister from learning too much. He could keep Noah busy showing him the property, enough to maintain a distance far from Ray until the man headed off.

"I'm not tired." Suitcase in hand, Noah gave Ky a knowing look. "After we drop off our bags inside, I'd love to take a tour now."

Relief surged. Noah's warm brown eyes, the steady, nonjudgmental gaze, and the accompanying sympathetic smile almost made Ky glad the man was here.

Almost.

"You can drive me around the property," Noah went on. "I'd like to get a feel for how big the ranch is."

At ten thousand acres, they could kill all the time they wanted.

"Good plan," Ky said.

He grabbed his bag again and closed the Tahoe door with a determined *thump*, and the three of them headed inside. Sierra took Noah toward the guest room on the other end of the house while Ky climbed the staircase and entered his old room, tossing the duffle bag onto the floor.

Nothing had been changed since he'd moved out. Same wrought iron headboard. Same blue quilt, the matching blue rug lining the floor between the bed and the oak dresser. The only light provided by the deer-antler chandelier, the one his father had made for his mom as a joke, hanging over the queen-sized bed.

Ky glanced around his room, happy to be back, before he loped down the staircase with a sense of urgency nipping at his heels. When he came to halt on the first floor, his stomach crawled up his throat.

Ray stood in the living room.

Dammit.

"You're here," his stepdad said with zero welcome in his tone and a frown on his face.

"I am."

Silence fell between them as Ky subdued the urge to bolt.

"You have a long drive ahead of you," Ky finally said. "I'll take care of the generator."

Ray's scowl grew deeper, as though leaving even that small task to Ky was distasteful.

"I s'pose," his stepfather said. He shifted on his feet and awkwardly jabbed a thumb in the general direction over his shoulder. "I'll go grab the new spark plug out in my truck, just in case the old one can't be—"

The sound of conversation came from the other end of the house as two sets of footsteps moved in the direction of the living room.

Damn. Damn. *Damn.*

"You know," Noah said as the two voices drifted closer, and Ky's every muscle tensed, preparing for the upcoming shit storm, "the stuffed animal heads on the walls are kind of creepy."

Sierra's laugh came next. "My dad likes to hunt. I reckon you probably don't."

"The only hunting I do is for the next pair of perfect skinny jeans," Noah said. "How can you stand so many dead eyes staring at you all the time..." Noah's words died out as the two rounded the corner.

Several seconds ticked by as Ray stared at their guest. Noah froze long enough to blink three times before sending Ray an overly bright smile—the gesture as forced as his outfit. Meanwhile, Ky forgot how to breathe.

"Who the hell is he?" Ray's question came out more as an accusation.

Sierra's face flushed blood red, her words harsh. "*Daddy*. Noah is a guest of Ky's." She shot Noah an apologetic look and looped her arm through his. "The flatbed is loaded with hay, so I need to park it in the barn before it rains. Why don't you tag along and I'll show you the horses?"

"Sounds fun," Noah said. "But I own a MINI Cooper, so don't make me drive that monstrous-sized truck. I'll take out half the poor horses' home." The guy shot Ky a *good luck* look before following Sierra toward the foyer.

Ky stood, stunned, his body hot as he waited during the sound of the front door closing and their footsteps clomping down the porch steps.

Ray pivoted to face him. "I can't believe you had the *nerve* to bring a man to the ranch."

For a moment, Ky was fifteen years old again, a doomed feeling swamping him as he got caught red-handed with man-on-man porn. And Ray's words...

Faggots aren't welcome here.

Headache blooming behind his eyes, Ky pushed away the memory and managed to maintain his cool. Because he wasn't that fifteen-year-old kid anymore.

"I came because someone needed to take care of things while you're both gone," Ky said.

"You think I don't know that?"

"Wouldn't from the way you're acting," he drawled. "I'd think you'd be grateful for the help."

"You can stay," Ray bit out. "But your boyfriend can't."

Anger surged, but Ky remained outwardly calm. "He's not my boyfriend."

"Then what is he?"

Ky pressed his lips together and counted to three before answering. "A friend."

Ray's tone turned caustic. "Bullcrap," he said as he stepped closer. "You're lucky I—"

"*I'm* lucky?" He stubbornly held his ground, refusing to give an inch even as he forced an even tone. "You should be grateful the girls don't know the truth about what you did."

And Lord, in a way, Ky was grateful his mama hadn't lived to witness how little her husband bought into her motto.

Family is everything, Ky. Everything.

He and Ray had never discussed that day. Not once. But Ky was having trouble keeping his mouth shut this time. Must be Noah's influence...

A defensive look came and went on Ray's face. "I allowed you to stay."

"Only because you wanted the free help."

"I gave you a *choice*."

"A choice?" Ky repeated slowly, his heart rate accelerating. "At fifteen, I was told to either give up my *faggoty ways*—"

"And that condition *still* applies—"

"—or get kicked off the ranch and never see my sisters again?" Ky finished, ignoring the interruption. "That's not a choice."

"No way in hell was I gonna allow a homo around *my daughters*—"

A small sound came from the direction of the hallway.

Sierra stood in the living room doorway, fingers clutched around the flatbed's keys, her face devoid of all color. "You threatened to kick him out of the house?"

Jesus God.

Heart thumping, Ky met his sister's gaze. Maybe he'd get lucky. Maybe she hadn't heard the most damning part. The horrified look on her face suggested otherwise.

"I thought you were moving the truck," Ray said.

"I forgot the keys," she said, her words stunned as she went on, her voice rising several octaves. "You threatened to never let him see us again?"

She ticked her eyes from Ky to her father and back to Ky again, as though asking them to say it wasn't true.

Ky strode toward her, reaching for her arm. "Sierra. I—"

"My God, Daddy." She sidestepped Ky and took two steps forward, slumping onto the couch. She stared up at her father. "You...you would have separated me and Savannah from our *brother*?"

Shit. Things were about to go all hell-in-a-handbasket like.

She still looked shell-shocked, gaze drifting to the coffee table. "He was only a kid."

"Homosexuals are not allowed here," Ray said.

Sierra's head jerked up. "You threatened a fifteen-year-old *child*."

"This is my house—"

Her expression grew hard. "You had no right—"

"I have *every* right," Ray said. "This is my house. I make the rules."

"You *emotionally blackmailed* a fifteen-year-old!" She shot to her feet. "You used me and Savannah as...as...tools to *manipulate* our brother."

Ray's expression turned defensive. "Your brother can stay, but"—he pointed in the direction of Noah, who currently hovered in the hallway— "his *boyfriend* isn't allowed."

Tears lined Sierra's lower lids—a mix of anger, betrayal, and devastating sadness—making Ky's heart hurt. Wherever his mother was, he hoped she couldn't see her daughter's face now.

True to form, his sister stubbornly crossed her arms. "If my brother isn't allowed to be himself, if he isn't allowed to bring a guest of his choosing, then this is no place I can call my home."

Fuck.

Ky briefly closed his eyes as everything he'd worked so hard to prevent seemed destined to come to fruition.

His stepdad's face slid through a round of emotions ranging from shock to anger and then to fear. Apparently the man had just begun to realize what his warped values would cost him. Finally, his expression closed down completely.

"I have some things to take care of before I get on the road," Ray said.

And with those vague words, he turned on his heel and left.

A heavy silence briefly settled around them as Ky's mind searched for a way to fix the situation. Unfortunately, he came up empty.

Sierra turned to Ky, fingers trembling as she rubbed her temple. "I'm sorry. I shouldn't have asked you to come." She shoved shaky hands through her hair. "But I didn't know. I didn't *know*."

"It's okay," he murmured, stepping closer.

"No, it's not okay. He emotionally *abused* you." Another horrified look swept across her face. "He didn't do anything else, did he?"

"No." He blurted out the lie as he pulled her into his arms, and she buried her head in his chest.

The occasional backhand across the face was one secret he'd take to his grave. His sisters would blame themselves, because they were the reason Ky had stuck around. And he couldn't do that to them.

He just *couldn't*.

"He never laid a hand on me," he lied again.

"I'm so sorry for what he did," she said, voice muffled against his torso.

"It's not your fault."

"I shouldn't have pushed the two of you together," she said. "I should have listened to you."

The devastated sound of her voice left him searching for a way to ease the tension.

"Listen to me?" he said, tightening his arms around his sister and inhaling her strawberry shampoo. "Why the heck would you start something you had no intention of continuing?"

"True." Her laugh sounded hoarse, followed by a faint sniffle before she tipped her chin to meet his gaze. "Wouldn't want to set up any unrealistic expectations, now would we?"

"Or lull me into a false sense of complacency."

"That either." Despite the wet lashes and the red-rimmed lids, the humor in her tone eased the painful catch in his chest.

"Becky should be here soon," he said, kissing her forehead. "You have a plane to catch."

Doubt clouded her eyes. "I should stay."

"You should *go*."

"I don't want to leave you alone..."

With Daddy, she didn't say.

"It's okay." He gave a long strand of her blond hair an affectionate tug. "I've been handling Ray for years. I'll be all right. Besides, he'll be leaving soon. If he hasn't already left."

Two seconds passed in silence.

"I don't care that you're gay," she said seriously.

"I never thought you would."

She wiped an impatient hand across her lashes. "But we still need to talk about you keeping something so important from me and Savannah." She shot him a look that was pure Sierra: sassy condemnation mixed with an extra dose of love.

Ky's smile felt lopsided. "We can do that when you get back."

She inhaled a breath and cleared her throat. "I meant what I said, Ky. I won't have you hiding anymore. If Daddy can't accept that, I guess I'll have to move." Her gaze slid to the right, and she shrugged.

"Come on, kiddo," he said softly. After everything they'd been through, his sister shouldn't have to sacrifice her dreams. Her *home.* Not on his account. "Don't decide to cut off your nose to spite your face just yet. We'll figure something out."

"Like what?"

"I'll think of something."

And as she gave him one last kiss on the cheek and headed out the door, he just wished he felt as confident as he'd sounded.

Chapter Eleven

Two hours later, the afternoon sun beat down on Ky's back. Overhead, the east-pasture windmill mocked him by not spinning—the occasional weak waft of wind mounting a half-assed attempt at getting the blades turning. The scent of warm earth and the sound of lowing cattle eased his taut nerves. With any luck, the worst of the drama was over.

Although Ky wasn't holding out much hope.

After the argument, Sierra had headed for the airport with Becky while Noah had retreated to the guest bedroom for a much-needed nap. Ky had spent the next forty-five minutes pacing the length of the house worried that Ray would come back and cause Noah trouble—until his guest had appeared and told him to quit hovering. And, yeah, the sound of Ky's footsteps probably made a nap impossible. But he couldn't shake the restless feeling, so he sought sanctuary out here.

God, he'd missed this.

While Ky craved the adrenaline and the excitement of a busy OR, he also loved peace and quiet and wide-open stretches. He loved slow sunsets, lightning bugs, and the sound of country music on his truck radio. But he'd forgotten how much he enjoyed the physical labor required on the ranch.

He'd already taken out his anger at Ray and worries about Sierra by tossing numerous bales of hay from the truck into the barn loft. He'd then hauled countless buckets of water to prime the pump. Now he needed to get the generator going or the cattle would run out of water.

Besides, the day had already gone to shit, and carving out a piece of success, no matter how small, felt vital to his sanity.

His shirt clung damply to his back, jeans stiff from the dust, as he pulled the old spark plug from the motor and began cleaning the oily gunk from between the electrodes with a rag. He reinserted the spark plug and gave the pull starter a tug. The ancient machine shuddered and coughed halfheartedly before dying out. He tried again with the same results, a *sputter-sputter-sputter-puh* and then fade to silence.

"Come on, baby," he murmured to the piece of equipment. "Come on."

Sweat dripped down his temple and plopped onto his beater plaid shirt.

He cleaned the spark plug some more, reinserted it, and then pulled the starter again. This time the generator roared to life, powering the pump. Water gurgled fitfully through the pipe in stops and starts until, finally, the spigot began to gush. Ky stepped back and watched the metal tank begin to fill.

Nicely done.

He took a break to admire his handiwork, his mind drifting to Noah, probably still napping while the air conditioner spit out cool air. Maybe he was dreaming, half-covered by sheets, his mouth twisted in that smile that drove Ky nuts and left him with a single-minded determination to *touchfeeltaste.* With Noah close, Ky couldn't stop thinking about climbing into his bed and finishing everything they'd started weeks ago.

Except for some reason the thought of doing that *here* felt...wrong.

But was that an emotion he owned? Or one he'd subconsciously bought into? Maybe the feeling was just a byproduct of years of conditioning by Ray Urban.

Jesus, if only he could lay the blame entirely at his stepdad's feet.

But Ky knew better.

He might have been born here, might have as much right to this land as Ray—morally and ethically, if not legally—but no matter how connected he felt to his parents' ranch, in truth he'd been raised in a world where he belonged in every way but one. 'Course, that *one* was a doozie.

Oak Hollows was homophobic country.

Growing up gay in this town meant learning to accept a part of himself he'd been repeatedly told was wrong/different/less than. Or outright evil. A teen left alone to deal with his stepfather's brutal words—and the random physical abuse—had made coming to terms with his orientation that much more of a struggle. Ky had been on this journey of self-acceptance for so long he couldn't tell if he'd reached the end yet.

Maybe he'd *never* fully reach the end.

But that would mean he'd been deluding himself all long. Maybe he hadn't achieved the healthy self-esteem as he'd been claiming. Maybe his self-doubt had played a bigger role in his decisions all along.

And if so, where did that leave him now?

Frustration flared as the dogs of doubt nipped at his heels.

The sense of frustration increased tenfold when a truck approached from down the road. The knocking of the engine sounded uncomfortably familiar.

Damn.

Ky sighed and leaned his arm against the roof of the small shed housing the generator as Ray's Ford F-150 dually bounced over the uneven ground, kicking up a cloud of dust that followed the truck ominously.

The vehicle came to a stop about twenty feet away, and the single occupant climbed out. Ky straightened his shoulders, actively ignoring all the thoughts currently at war inside his head.

Hold your tongue, Ky, he'll be gone soon interspersed with *how much longer do I have to put up with this bullshit?* This was followed by a *remember how the last argument only made things worse for Sierra.*

And long ago he'd sided with his mom. Places weren't important, people were. *Especially* family.

Ray slammed the door closed with a loud *thunk* that, like the dirt cloud slowly drifting toward them, put Ky even more on edge. His stepdad strode forward and hit the kill switch on the generator. The abrupt end to the thrumming engine left the silence vibrating in warning in its wake.

Yep, things were fixin' to get worse.

Ky forced himself to remain outwardly composed and began to gather his tools. "I thought you'd left."

"I had some errands to run in town first," Ray said. Mouth tight, he tossed a small package at Ky's feet. "Here's the new spark plug."

"Thanks." Ky turned back to the generator in an attempt to end the conversation. "I'll get back to filling the tank."

"We have a few things to get straight first."

"I thought you needed to get on the road."

"I can drive all night if I have to. I'm here to make sure you understand. Your boyfriend is *not* allowed to stay at the ranch."

Ky swallowed back a bitter laugh. This was the second time his stepdad had made the same assumption. Noah would be disappointed to hear he was playing the fake boyfriend but wasn't around to enjoy the ruse.

"I told you before, we're just friends," Ky drawled as calmly as he could.

Which, admittedly, wasn't too calm.

"Friends?" Ray said with a belittling tone.

"That's what I said."

"I don't believe you."

"That's your problem. Not mine," Ky said. "Besides, who I sleep with is none of your business."

"It is when you're sleeping in my home."

My home.

Motherfucker.

Ray Urban had been a destitute drifter cowboy without two cents to his name when Ky's father had died, leaving a widow with a one-year-old son and a ranch to run. Ky understood his mom's hasty decision to get married again. And he didn't blame Ray for marrying into half ownership of the operation. He'd worked tirelessly to keep this place afloat. He deserved credit for his hard work.

But, Jesus...

Ky had worked hard, too. He'd spent most of his life stacking and tossing out endless bales of hay, keeping the cattle fed and watered. He'd carted countless wheelbarrows full of horseshit from the barn. He'd practically single-handedly raised the girls.

If his mama had had the foresight to leave explicit instructions in her will, part of this operation would have been *his*.

Ky's jaw muscles clenched, grit between his teeth courtesy of the dust cloud slowly enveloping them.

"So when is he leaving?" Ray asked, anger in his tone.

"He's not."

Ray looked at him as though he were something he'd muck out of a horse stall using a pitchfork. "You are not allowed to bring a man into *my* house."

Something inside Ky broke loose. "Bullshit." He stood and tossed the wrench into the toolbox with a teeth-jarring *clang*. "Bullshit," he said again. "Part of this ranch should be *mine*. My mother would have insisted on that, and you know it."

Ray's expression turned belligerent, the truth in Ky's words clearly leaving him defensive. "You haven't even been around the last few years."

"I haven't been *welcome*."

"I've poured my blood and sweat and tears into keeping this place going. You left."

"Whose fault is that?"

"You made your choice."

"Goddammit, sexual orientation isn't a *choice*."

Ray carried on as though Ky hadn't spoken. "So you have no right to bring that *faggot*—"

"Don't." Anger flared, bright, hot, and all-consuming, propelling him a step closer. When Ky finally went on, the words came out raw. "You leave Noah out of this," he said. "He's ten times the man you'll ever be."

Ray's mouth twisted into a sneer.

Ky jammed his hands into his back pockets and fantasized about reaching out, gripping his stepdad by the collar, and tossing him against the side of the pump house.

Leastways, it couldn't hurt. The shed needed rebuilding anyway.

And Ky would certainly feel a helluva lot better.

"You have no right bringing him into *my* home," Ray repeated. "And you are not allowed to have sex with a man under my roof."

Enough of this bullshit.

"If I want to screw my boyfriend on the property that's been in my family for generations, *in the house my parents built*," Ky shot back, voice tight, hands fisted in his pockets, "I will." He mentally kicked himself for using the term *boyfriend* when it didn't apply, but he was too furious to care.

"Your mother would be ashamed."

"My mother wouldn't have *cared*."

The words shot from his mouth with a conviction that surprised even himself. And yet he knew the truth of his words with a certainty he could apply to little else in his life. He couldn't vouch for his dad, although by all accounts he'd been kind, but his mother he was absolutely sure of. And if she had not died so young, Ky's life would have turned out very different.

But this was about more than her acceptance.

Despite his stepdad's demeaning ways, Ky had still felt responsible for ensuring that the illusion of family harmony was preserved. To fix the broken parts of their family. The time had come to realize that this wasn't his to own, that his mother wouldn't expect that of him.

He deserved better.

And for the first time in his life, he felt certain his mother would've agreed.

"Mama wouldn't have cared," he repeated. "So what comes next is all on you."

Ray blinked, as though thrown by the statement. Several seconds ticked by before he said, "What are you talking about?"

"Because now you have a decision to make." Ky stared his stepfather down and paused so his words would have an impact. "Which is more important? Your love for your daughters?" he asked. "Or your hate for gays?"

A heavy silence followed.

Ray's face slowly turned an angry shade of red. "Ky—"

"We're done with this conversation." He turned on his heel, picked up his toolbox, and strode toward his vehicle. "We're *done*."

"You get your butt back here!" Ray called from behind.

Hell no.

Ky focused on the sun glinting off the beater flatbed truck, on the heat hitting his hat and the dust on the road. He absolutely refused to go back and give in to the urge to deck his stepdad.

The last thing Sierra needed was her brother and father coming to blows.

"Ky, don't you walk away from me!" his stepdad shouted.

Ray kept calling his name as Ky yanked on the driver-side handle, climbed inside, and closed the door. He fumbled with the key chain, surprised to find his hands shaking. He finally managed to turn on the flatbed, shift into gear, and press on the gas. The roar of the diesel engine kindly drowned out the rest of Ray's voice.

Mind churning, Ky pulled a sharp U-ey and headed back down the pock-marked dirt road toward the house. After twenty some odd years, he couldn't do this anymore.

He was tired, so *dog tired* of hiding who he was in his own home.

"Shit."

He reached for his cell phone and pushed Noah's number.

After three rings, a sleepy voice answered. "'Lo?" he said, the half word muffled by...a pillow, maybe?

The sound of his voice eased the churning in Ky's gut, and the image from before popped into his head. Except this time Noah was naked.

Naked.

Ky tightened his grip on his phone. "Where are you?"

"I didn't sleep very well. Too much on my mind. I was just lying here thinking about getting out of bed."

"Don't," Ky said, his voice rough.

He'd hoped the single-word command would get his intentions across. That for once he was taking a stand and doing what he wanted: sleeping with Noah at the ranch. In Ky's *childhood home*, Ray's and his own stupid doubts be damned. But the residual raw anger toward his stepdad was too prominent in his tone.

The mattress squeaked, as though Noah had rolled over, and his voice sounded concerned. "What happened?"

"I..." Nope. No need to go into gritty detail. Too depressing. "Ray showed up. We fought, as usual," he said. "And I told him I'd screw whoever I want whenever and wherever I want."

"Good for you," he said with a pleased tone.

"Probably not. I'm feeling a mite angry."

The understatement brought a wry twist to Ky's lips.

"You're in fuck-or-fight mode," Noah said.

"It's fight or *flight*," he said, voice bone-dry. Two seconds ticked by. "So"—Ky cleared his throat—"this fake boyfriend thing you mentioned before..." He gripped the steering wheel with one hand, the truck bouncing over a deep rut. "Is that still an option? And can it include having sex?"

Another long pause followed, and Ky imagined the look on Noah's face as he waded through the loaded question.

"Fake sex?" Noah asked. The timbre of his voice suggested interest. "Or real sex?"

Ky scrunched up his face. "How do you have fake sex?" he wondered out loud. Then again, this was Noah he was talking to. "Never mind, I don't want to know," he said. "I'm talking about live, in-person sex."

Seriously, was there any other way to fuck?

"Sweaty, loud—the whole works. With me," Ky added, which, stupid, stupid, stupid. Of course *with him*. "You interested?"

The three-beat pause that followed felt like an eternity.

"You want me to play the fake boyfriend and have real sex," Noah breathed out slowly, "and you're asking if I'm interested? It's like you don't know me at all!"

Ky stifled a chuckle.

"But we need to do this in *your* room, not mine," Noah went on. "So you can christen your childhood bed in the name of oppressed homosexuals everywhere by boning the bejesus out of me."

Sweet heaven above.

Ky's grip on his phone grew so tight he feared he'd crack the case in half. "You won't regret dropping the strictly friends decision?"

"It won't be for forever. Besides, you know me. When it comes to a worthy cause, I'm all in."

A small laugh escaped Ky. The inner workings of the man's mind must be a fascinating thing to be privy to.

"How much longer until you get here?" Noah asked.

"Unfortunately," he said, need taking on a life of its own, "about twenty very long"—*too long*—"minutes," he said, regretfully slowing the old truck as he maneuvered around another set of deep ruts. "But...I have an idea how we can kill the time."

The sound of rustling—the comforter, maybe?—came from the phone, followed by another squeak of the mattress, this time with an added scraping sound. Ky suspected Noah had just propped himself up against the headboard.

"I'm listening," Noah said, sounding breathless.

Ky's mouth opened but nothing came out. He blinked and tried again.

"I was hoping I'd be listening to you," Ky said.

"This was your idea, big guy," he said, the smile evident in his voice. "Your balls have the court."

"Shit," he muttered. "I'm not good with talk. I'm more of a doer."

"Yes, and you *do* just fine," he said. "But if you're not going to be here for another twenty minutes, not talking seems like a wasted opportunity." The break in the conversation ended when Noah went on with a helpful tone. "Maybe the words will come if you close your eyes and imagine you're holding a paring knife."

"I'm driving, remember?" he said dryly.

"Then, for god's sake, man, don't close your eyes."

There was another pause, this time longer than the one before.

"Just tell me what you want to do to me," Noah said.

Ky frowned. "I want to...fuck you hard until you come." Jesus, he'd just recited the most over-utilized porno line *ever*. He tried fixing his attempt by adding a, "Loudly."

Over the sudden thump of the tire hitting another pothole, he heard Noah's swift inhalation. Despite being the lamest dirty talk in the history of all dirty talk, the man didn't seem to care.

"Tell me more," Noah said.

More? Ugh, only thirty seconds into the twenty-minute trip and he'd already run out of words.

"We— I—" Ky's mind spun until he remembered the thrill of having Noah in his mouth. "I like how you say my name during an orgasm."

"How's that?"

"Like a prayer." He frowned, not quite satisfied with his answer. "Or maybe more like a swear."

"Funny how closely related the two are," he said. "Okay, my turn." A pause followed. "I love how your scowly eyebrows flatline during your O face." Noah waited a moment, as though gearing up to deliver the punch line. "I wanna make you look like that all night."

A surge of lust left Ky hard enough to drill through solid rock.

His heart thudded, his dick throbbed, and his body was already tensed and eager to *taketake*take. Dammit, at this rate he'd be too wound up to go slow, too worked up to give the man the attention he needed to get ready. And the *last* thing Ky wanted to do was hurt Noah.

Ky inhaled slowly through his nose, struggling to calm down before he crashed the truck. Or worse: lost control and wound up causing Noah pain.

"There won't be much time for prep," Ky said. "You bring a dildo with you?"

"Does the Pope dress funny?" he said in a *duh* tone of voice.

Ky's mouth quirked. "Yeah, I hear he's into Catholicism, too." His mind drifted back to Noah in bed. Naked. "I want you to use it."

"Catholicism?"

"The dildo," Ky said as he rolled his eyes with more fondness than he should for someone who only did fake relationships. "Use it. Now."

"*Oh.*"

The smoldering tone Noah had used during the one-word response kicked Ky's libido into high gear.

"I want you ready the moment I walk in the bedroom door." Ky let the heat in his veins show in his tone. "And I want to listen while you open yourself up."

A muffled, high-pitched noise came over the phone, like a dying frog, followed by the sound of silence. And maybe a little heavy breathing.

"Fuck." Ky pressed harder on the gas, the revving roar of the engine filling the cab. "Noah?" he said. "You still there?"

"Yeah," he whispered. "Yes." His voice came out thin and distracted. "Sorry, I was just... I couldn't..." A sigh came next. "Your dirty talk is improving exponentially. My understanding of English briefly disappeared."

A self-satisfied grin spread across Ky's face. "Better now?"

"Totally turned on now."

"And you weren't before?"

"Are you kidding?" Noah said. "With you around, I practically live with one nut in go-mode at all times. Which has made this friendship-only thing-y extra specially difficult, you evil manly bastard, you." The words held zero heat. The sound of a suitcase being unzipped came from the phone followed by the slap of bare feet over hardwood floors. "No dildo is as wonderful as your fantastic cock, of course. But I brought along my glittery, pink silicon boyfriend to remind me of my gay roots while gallivanting across the Texas countryside."

"You're an idiot." Jesus, Ky's grin was definitely too fond.

"Maybe, but I bet my newly purchased sex toy would go perfectly with *your* tiara." The sound of a door opening was followed by a sharp intake of breath. "Your childhood bedroom is appropriately masculine. Which reminds me," the man went on as a mattress gave a small squeak in the background, "when *do* I get to see that picture of Princess Ky?"

"Never."

Noah used his come-hither tone. "Do I get to voice any of my sexual-bucket-list requests?"

Ky's libido punched him in the solar plexus again, because the dude probably had a million of 'em. "Tell me."

On the other end of the line, Noah hummed out a *hmm* as if preparing to recite a long list of wishes. Ky wasn't gonna complain.

"Your boots," Noah said. "Ever since the first time I saw you in those Stetsons I...I've wanted you to fuck me while wearing them."

"You want me to fuck you while you wear my cowboy boots?" he said, feigning confusion.

"What? No. Are you...? *No*," he said firmly. "Now you're just messing with me. You're supposed to wear the boots while *I'm* naked."

As Ky waited for the guy to go on, he slowed to turn onto the county road—paved, not dirt, *thank you, Jesus*, so now he could drive faster. Then a low groan sounded over the phone. A squelching noise, likely the lube, and Ky knew that Noah was getting himself ready.

Lust, pure and undiluted, jolted him like a defibrillator to the testicles. He pressed the phone between his shoulder and chin and his free hand to his crotch. The pathetic attempt relieved little of the discomfort, his hard-on straining beneath his jeans.

Unfortunately, the friction felt too good, and he moaned out an, "Any other requests?"

"Requests. Right." Noah's voice shifted lower. "Anything remotely cowboy-ish. Ropes. Jeans. Hat," he listed out. "Dirt. Sweat."

Ky looked down at the dusty denim covering his legs. "Not gonna be a problem."

"No farm animals or manure, though," he went on as though Ky hadn't spoken. "Everything else is on the table." A pause followed. "Except the belt buckle," he added. "I have to insist you lose the bloody belt buckle. I might get distracted."

"You're telling me you'd interrupt a good screwin' to offer fashion advice?"

"Let's just say it's a risk you shouldn't take."

Ky laughed, the sound rumbling up from the bottom of his stomach for what felt like forever. Something inside his chest shifted, and he suspected it was permanent.

"Yeah," he said, not surprised by Noah's advice, "I can picture that happening." And then his voice dropped a hundred octaves and went serious. "But I promise I can fuck that thought right outta your head."

An oncoming truck passed, honking its horn in warning.

"Dammit." Ky swerved to correct the course of his drifting vehicle. "I'm hanging up before I get killed."

Noah's response sounded more pornographic than confirmatory, and Ky whined, tossed the phone onto the passenger seat, and stepped on the gas.

Chapter Twelve

Naked, Noah had a hand on his cock and the dildo up his ass, muscles clenching in pleasure, when he heard the front door slam on the first floor below.

"*Ky*." Already breathless, Noah pushed against the adult toy, feet pressing against the mattress.

His bent legs trembled, his neck damp with sweat. Anticipation, hot and heavy and so damn distracting, had fisted in his chest the moment Ky had suggested this. The memory made focusing on the task of self-prepping difficult.

In fact, the minute he'd left the guest room for Ky's, the last of his concentration abilities had evaporated.

But Noah had another not-job to do. An *important* one. Namely, help Ky baptize his bed in the name of all that was unholy. Replace teenage memories of angst, alienation, and condemnation with some sexy times.

Some *seriously* sexy times.

And how had Noah's firm hands-off vow morphed so easily into *fuck the conflicted expression from Ky's face*?

The answer was easy enough.

In the presence of Ray, a new flavor of Ky's frown had been born: a fifteen-year-old boy's misery evident in his thirty-four-year-old face. Of course the misery was about way more than just sex. But no one deserved any of it, least of all Ky. And Noah would do anything, *anything*, Ky asked to make the miserable look go away.

If their dicks got to participate, too, so much the better

Footsteps thudded on the staircase and up the hall, growing closer, and Noah moaned, the *snick, snick, snick* of his palm working his cock coming faster.

When the bedroom door was flung open, Manly Ranch Hand Ky appeared. Noah stared down between his bent knees, hand stripping his dick, naked thighs framing the vision in the threshold like a pornographic picture frame.

An embarrassing need-filled, keening sound leaked from Noah's throat. But he refused to call it a whimper.

Frozen in the doorway, Ky stared at him. "Jesus, Mary, and Joseph."

"They're not here, thank God."

"I know, but..."

The gawking continued as the self-loving action ticked up a notch.

"Yes?" Noah said.

"You're..."

When Ky didn't—or *couldn't*—finish, Noah tried to help. "I'm what? A consummate self-prepper? A professional masturbationist?"

No response.

Noah swallowed, refusing to blush. So what if he looked like the beginning of a raunchy porno flick with the dildo up his ass? The exposed feeling was totally worth it, because he loved putting that brain-just-melted expression on the man's face.

Noah's every fantasy come to life.

With broad shoulders strong enough to carry Drunk Noah to his condo, Ky looked hot and dirty, chest damp with sweat beneath the already unbuttoned shirt.

Noah grew short of breath.

Because somewhere en route, the man had unfastened, well, *everything*. Along with his shirt, his belt hung open. Even his sleeves were rolled to the elbows, exposing the muscles and sinew of his forearms. The first snap of his jeans had been undone, the happy trail exposed.

Oh, God.

Unfortunately, he could only deal with *one libido-revving crisis at a time.*

And when Ky kicked the door shut behind him, the scuffed leather beneath the hem of his jeans came into view...

"Thank God," Noah whined, his desire now in crisis mother-freaking overload. And, yeah, that was definitely a whimper. "The *boots*."

Seriously, he was so weak.

Helpless in the face of footwear.

"What's with the fixation on a pair of old Stetsons?" Ky asked.

"Not sure. You can spank me for it later," he said, the words strained from exertion. "For chrissake, I thought you'd never get here."

"Me, either." He finally moved, tossing his cellular onto the dresser, phone clattering across the top. "Almost wrecked twice on the way."

"I'm so glad you didn't."

"Me, too. We need—"

"Lube and condom are already on the bed."

"Good thinking."

"Clothes."

Ky crossed the floor in Noah's direction and jerked his belt off. The buckle hit the wood floor with a loud *clunk*, probably leaving a divot the size of Texas. He stopped at the end of the mattress, near Noah's feet, yanking open the rest of his fly and—

sweet *Jesus*—shoving his jeans and boxer briefs partway down his thighs.

Panic swelled even as the lust surged.

"Stop," Noah managed to pant out, and the man halted mid-strip. "Don't forget to leave the boots *on*." His ass cheeks gave an anticipatory clench around the dildo, his palm jerking his dick faster. "And if you take any longer, I'll finish without—"

"Come here," Ky whispered hoarsely. He tugged on Noah's hips until his butt reached the end of the bed. After rolling on a condom and slicking himself with lube, Ky dropped his gaze to Noah's ass and froze. "What the ever-lovin' hell?"

But Noah couldn't respond, blinded by the beautiful sight of Ky in all his hot-'n-dusty Texas glory, pants around his thighs. Hard cock exposed and primed for action. The man was a freaking fantasy come to life.

Except for the *staring at him like he was crazy* part.

"What is that?" Ky asked.

"Surely you've seen a sex toy before."

"Of course, it's just...you weren't kidding. It's *pink*."

"Hot-pink, actually. What, you don't approve?"

With a groan, Ky pulled out the dildo—leaving Noah briefly empty—chucked it aside, and, without missing a beat, buried his dick deep.

Hot sparks flared, and Noah arched his back, toes curling. "Ohmygod," he gasped out, the stretch in his ass just this side of too much. "Everything *is* bigger in Texas."

Two seconds of adjustment occurred, Ky's hips flush against Noah's ass.

"As good as your dildo?" Ky rasped out.

"Better."

Heaven help him, *so much better.*

Ky pulled back and began to fuck into him, every third thrust hitting his prostate, pleasure bursting like internal fireworks. Noah's hard cock bounced off his belly, leaving a slick trail of precum across his abdomen.

And Ky? His blissed-out, *things are about to reach fourth level of transcendent* look?

"So much better," Noah said in reference to both the fucking and Ky's expression.

The forceful snap of Ky's hips left him sounding winded. "Even though it's not pink and sparkly?"

"*Yes,*" Noah said, both in answer and in encouragement. He reached up and clutched the man's shoulders, providing better leverage. "But give me a marker and some glitter, and I can fix that problem for you."

"Screw that."

"No, screw *me.*"

Ky proceeded to pound into him as though he had something to prove. Like twenty years of hiding who he was needed to be exorcised from his memory. Every thrust seemed to drive him closer to some unseen goal, sending a repeated hallelujah chorus singing in Noah's head.

Pleasure zapped him like a cattle prod, and Noah bowed his back. "Harder." Currents of hot electricity coursed along his every nerve.

With broad, sweeping strokes of his hips, more force now and less speed, the surgeon repeated the process with the same results, shoving Noah a little higher on the bed.

"Christ." Noah threw his arms out, fisting the comforter again, fingers tight as he tried to hold on. "That's good... O*h.*"

Ky ducked his head and caught the tail end of Noah's groan with his lips. A few biting kisses later and, with a hot swipe of his tongue, Ky had him opening his mouth and panting out needy sounds.

Shameless sounds, really.

But Noah had come to terms with his greedy bottom ways a long time ago. He loved tongues, fingers, and cocks. He liked them in his mouth, liked them up his ass in various and assorted combinations.

The headboard hit the wall with a sturdy *thump*, and a swinging motion above the bed caught Noah's eye. "Wait!"

"Dammit."

The man closed his eyes and pressed his forehead against Noah's, his thighs trembling as though trying to hold himself back.

Noah whimpered again, his body craving more of that deliciously frenzied motion.

But fear briefly overruled.

"Uh...Ky?" Despite the danger, his hips had a mind of their own and they arched higher, taking more of the man inside.

Ky groaned and gripped his ass, halting further movement. "Yeah?"

"Am I at risk here?"

"From what?" he gritted out, obviously struggling to hold still.

Noah eyed the light fixture on the ceiling, sharp prongs pointed downward. "The antler chandelier impaling us."

"It's fake, really lightweight." Ky shifted a fraction, the motion sending all Noah's nerves impatiently screaming to continue. "Wouldn't hurt too much."

"In that case, fuck me harder," he gasped. "Because, seriously, I shouldn't be this coherent."

"No," he said with a growl. "You shouldn't."

And, yee-freaking-haw, the man took those words as a rallying cry. Soon every pound of Ky's cock hit pay dirt, until pornographic sounds began escaping Noah with each thrust.

The slapping sound of damp flesh hitting damp flesh mixed with the wrought iron headboard thumping against the wall. A warm breeze drifted through the open window, doing little to cool the sweat building on Noah's skin or quiet the ridiculous noises coming from his mouth.

But, uh, *open window*...

"I— Guh." Okay, the coherency issue had definitely been addressed. "What if someone drives up...?"

"I don't care," Ky said, gaze burning and body glistening with sweat. "*I don't care.*"

Noah gave up all pretense of trying to be quiet. Bedcovers still clutched in his grasp, he did his best to meet every forceful arch of Ky's hips.

The pleasure twisted higher.

Dug deeper.

Until Noah came with a loud shout and supplication to a deity that probably didn't exist. His vision briefly went gray, his muscles overcome with shocky little spasms of joy. He was vaguely aware of Ky continuing until, with three thrusts that threatened to reach undiscovered parts, Ky's O face made an appearance.

The most satisfying expression of all.

Ky collapsed on top of Noah, the silence filled with panting sounds as they both fought to catch their breath.

"Iz official," Noah eventually slurred, tongue too drunk on endorphins for a proper singsong voice. "Your comin'-out story just became my fav'rite."

All Ky managed was an amused-sounding *huh*.

Noah gave the man a lethargic pat on the shoulder and yawned, eyelids growing heavy as the previous night's sketchy sleep, the rousing round of fucking, and the effects of bone-sapping pleasure began to catch up with him.

Some unknown minutes later, without warning, Ky rolled off, leaving Noah feeling disconcertingly weightless and cold.

"Where're ya goin'?" Noah valiantly fought his too-heavy lids.

"To get something to clean you up with," he said as he padded toward the bathroom.

"'Kay."

When Ky returned, Noah lay there, limp and useless, while the man wiped a warm, damp washrag up his inner thighs, the action way too gentle to be considered sexy—which likely had more to do with the good doctor's penchant for taking care of others than anything else. But then Ky's free hand brushed back the damp hair stuck to Noah's forehead, an oddly tender gesture.

Holy shit...

Noah's pulse picked up speed, and he was only half-aware as the warm, wet rag reached his belly, Ky scrubbing away the mess Noah's cock had left.

Now that the guy was officially out to those who mattered most in his life, would he start wanting more from a man than just sex? He seemed the sort who would.

He seemed the sort who *should*.

Noah closed his eyes, mind too sluggish to give the idea the panicky response it probably deserved.

Eventually they'd need to talk about what just happened, but as far as Noah was concerned, that was *tomorrow's* problem. And tomorrow was still hours and hours away.

Fortunately, when Ky settled next to him, a delicious postcoital buzz and the insistent pull of sleep finally did Noah in.

~~~***~~~

Ky woke to the warmth of bright sunshine on his chest and realized he was alone in the bedroom. He sat up, squinting against the light, the sun too high in the sky to still classify as morning. He checked his phone on the nightstand to determine the time, but the battery had died. And why did his face feel so...weird?

Confused, he touched his brow. "What the—?"

His hand landed on a piece of paper stuck to his forehead. He pulled the yellow Post-it note from his skin and read Noah's slanted writing.

Off to ransack the kitchen in search of breakfast.
P.S. Yay! The antlers didn't impale us.

A pair of scowly eyebrows scribbled along the bottom of the paper had been perfectly placed on Ky's face given the position of the note, and he had to chuckle.

After the momentous events in bed yesterday, Noah had drifted off and slept straight through until this morning. No wonder the man had left in search for food. As for himself, Ky had eventually gotten out of bed to muck out the barn, check the water level in the stock tanks, and take a shower before scarfing down a sandwich. Afterward, he'd collapsed in an exhausted heap next to Noah's still-passed-out form.

Ky stretched his arms over his head with a small, self-satisfied grin. Every muscle felt wrung out and sore, like he'd spent yesterday running a marathon at sprint-like speed. Which, well...

His gaze landed on the deep dent dug in the wall behind the headboard, and the smile slowly died on his face. He'd burned off his frustration by doing exactly what he'd wanted: screwing the hell out of Noah, in particular *here in this house*. Taking one more step on that continuing journey of self-acceptance. Taking a stand against Ray and an adolescence that had declared him less than, different, and wrong.

Yep, he'd taken a stand, all right. But he also couldn't put too noble a label on his actions. In a way, he'd used Noah.

He'd *used* him.

Ky closed his eyes. "Shit."

'Course, there was no one more likely to encourage the sexual exploitation of his body than Noah Tanner. Taken alone, the event was hardly worth getting worked up about. Unfortunately, it was just one more item on a slowly growing stack of concerns. Ky frowned, remembering their interaction as he'd removed Noah's clothes with a paring knife.

"You're saying the destruction of clothing should've automatically been considered a no-go—?"

"Yes," Noah said.

"—but bodily injury needed to be clarified up front?" Ky asked, his concerns growing deeper. "What kinda people have you been sleepin' with?"

The two-second pause felt longer than it should have before the answer came.

"The wrong types, apparently."

The conflicted, embarrassed look on Noah's face at the time had given Ky pause. Clearly some of the man's "sexcapades" had involved letting himself be used to the point of abuse. And the thought of doing the same, no matter how marginally, left Ky feeling nauseous. The facts also supported one inescapable conclusion.

Noah was bold and beautiful and more than a little bit broken.

But exactly how deep did the damage go? How big were the scars? And, more importantly, were they permanent?

"Shit," Ky muttered again as he scrubbed a hand down his face.

Pushing the disturbing thoughts aside—he was home, Noah was here, and by God, Ky was gonna enjoy himself—he plugged his phone into the charger on the nightstand. He pressed Noah's contact number, and the man answered on the second ring.

"Scowly eyebrows?" Ky said, tone desert dry. "Really?"

"I woke up feeling inspired."

"And I woke up *alone*." His lips twitched. "I feel so cheap."

"Don't," Noah said without pause, a tease in his tone. "I'm a man who grew up with expensive tastes. Granted, I had a few questionable years, but now I only sleep with quality."

Ky let himself smile again and relaxed against the pillow, staring up at the antlers interlocked into a pendant light above the bed, points aiming directly at the center of the mattress. From this angle, he could appreciate Noah's concern from yesterday.

"Well, big guy?" Noah asked. "How does it feel?"

"How does what feel?"

Noah laughed. "I wasn't referring to your fantastic cock, if that's what you were thinking."

"If I *had* assumed that," he drawled, "you'd only have yourself to blame."

Another laugh drifted over the phone. "True," he said. "But what I really want to know is how you feel after publicly acknowledging to your sister that you're gay?"

"Oh. That."

"Yeah," Noah said with a droll tone. "*That.*"

Ky rubbed the sleep from his eyes.

While mucking out the barn last evening, he'd pondered that very question. All he'd ever really wanted was his sisters' well-being. He knew his mother would have wanted the same thing.

But there would be no fairy-tale ending. That had never been possible. The hard part had been recognizing that fact and finding the courage to move on. He'd never completely recover from the devastated look on Sierra's face after learning about her father's actions, but what was done was done. There was no going back. Sierra knew the truth, and if she didn't already, soon so would Savannah.

"It feels..." Ky slowly took in a breath, searching for the right words.

He and his sisters had survived the loss of their mother. His mom had been right, family *was* everything. And as long as the three of them stuck together, they'd survive this, too—and maybe be stronger than before.

And honesty was surprisingly...freeing.

"It feels good," Ky finally decided.

"Good?" he echoed. "A *back rub* feels good, Ky. This feels...this feels..." Apparently even Noah had trouble finding the right expression. "Epic," he finally finished.

"Okay." He grinned. "Not exactly a word I normally use, but epic it is."

"Thank you. And you totally owe me for the interaction I had with your stepfather earlier."

"Fuck." He sat up, heart thudding. Ray hadn't shown up at the house last night, so Ky had assumed the man had left town.

Goddammit.

Noah being on the receiving end of any more of Ray's asshattery was unacceptable.

"Are you all right?" Ky launched himself from the bed, his sleep-clumsy movements nearly landing him on his ass, the phone's charge wire stretched to the max. "Where are you?"

"Downstairs on the front porch—"

"Stay there." He struggled to clamp the phone between his ear and his shoulder while reaching for his jeans. Heaven help him, if Ray had so much as made Noah feel bad about his choice of *breakfast*—

"It's okay, Ky. Ray just—"

"I'm on my way." Ky tossed his phone onto the bed and hiked his jeans over his hips, not bothering with a shirt.

His mind spun on all the possibilities, Ray and his judgmental faces and his sharp tongue and his angry eyes directed at Noah. And all the while, Ky had slept like the dead.

Jesus.

He hustled down the staircase and out the front door, unprepared for the tranquil scene. Noah, one leg folded beneath him on the porch swing, gazed at the cattle grazing in the distance. The screen door slipped from Ky's fingers, slapping shut behind him with a loud *clap.*

"It was just a phone call." Noah's mouth quirked. "He's not here."

Ky's shoulders sagged in relief. "What did he say?" He crossed the porch and sank onto the bench next to Noah, the seat groaning noisily in response.

"Not much. Just that he wanted to speak with you," Noah said.

"That's everything he said?"

"He told me he tried to reach you on your cell phone first. And, uhm"—Noah appeared reluctant to go on—"he did mention that I'd better be gone when he got back."

"Dammit, he had *no right*—"

"He had every right," he said easily. "He is the sole owner of this place. Which, by the way, I think is incredibly unfair."

Well...at least Noah didn't look damaged. Then again, he never did.

But by now Ky knew better.

"To hell with the ranch," Ky said firmly, because *people* always came first. Especially Noah. "Sierra and I will figure something out," he went on.

The need to protect still thrummed through his system, both for his sisters and the guy sitting beside him. Noah being subjected to anything less than total respect was unacceptable. Ky inhaled the scent of grass, concentrating on the warm breeze in an attempt to lower his heart rate.

The porch swing swayed back and forth, the rhythmic *squeak, squeak, squeak* filling the air.

"You sure you're okay?" Ky asked.

"Please," he said with a blasé wave of his hand. "You think I can't handle an amateur homo hater like Ray?" A genuine glint of amusement shone in his eyes. "Remember, I've been tossed into a dumpster before. After that, there's nowhere to go but up."

A small laugh escaped Ky, relief following in its wake.

"Right after the lovely interaction with your stepfather," Noah went on with a dry tone, "Sierra called."

"Sierra?" Christ, he shouldn't have let his phone die. "Is there a problem?"

"Nope, no problem. She just wanted to, and this is a direct quote, 'check up on the two of you.'" Noah sent him a wry look. "I think she knows we've slept together. Why else would she choose that moment to casually inform me she knows how to castrate a bull." His lips twitched at the edges. "Translation? My manhood is in danger should I hurt you in any way."

"She's..." Ky's head spun as he tried to keep up with the whiplash turn of events in his life. "That's..."

"What a loving, concerned sister *should* do," Noah finished for him. "But family drama aside, how are we going to commemorate your coming out? This definitely requires serious celebration."

Ky rolled his eyes.

"I'm going to interpret your sarcastic eye roll as an *I don't have a clue, so please help me with my tragic lack of imagination*," Noah said.

"I assume you have somethin' particular in mind?" Although, by now he should know better than to ask.

"A little line dancing at the local dive bar?"

The horrified look on Ky's face probably constituted answer enough.

"Yeah, probably a bad plan, huh?" Noah went on. "Here at Homophobic Central we might get a shiv in the liver for our efforts. But never fear. I am, as always, full of ideas. So"—he straddled Ky's lap, a surprised grunt escaping Ky even as the pit in his stomach filled with heat—"Dr. Davis, let's talk about your fantasies."

Ky's groan in response held more heat than judgment.

"Do these fantasies include big, buff cowboys pinning you down and having their wicked way with you?" Noah went on.

Ky managed a skeptical look even as he clasped the man's thighs in welcome.

"Maybe you masturbated to the thoughts of some threesome action?" Noah winked suggestively.

"Not really."

"No lusting after smutty double penetration?"

"Nope."

"Little golden showers?"

"No," Ky said, letting out an amused scoff.

"Remember, there is no kink shaming here."

Noah shifted his hips—and, oh God, the friction felt good—and linked his fingers behind Ky's neck.

"So what *was* your number one fantasy, cowboy?"

The only response Ky could mount was an embarrassing flush of heat to his cheeks.

"Come on," the man went on with a smirky smile. "Fess up. It can't be that bad. Unless..." He narrowed his eyes. "It doesn't involve livestock, does it?"

"For cryin' out loud, Noah."

"Okay, I'll tell you my ultimate fantasy if you'll tell me yours."

"I'm not sure I'm prepared to hear yours," Ky said, tone dryer than week-old toast. "Not without a shot of alcohol and a bottle of brain bleach for afterward."

"The shot of tequila is a given, but brain bleach sounds like a definite mood killer. Perhaps you should share your ultimate sex-pectations first, before I share mine."

"Okay," Ky said with a frown. He stared across the pasture and cleared his throat, ignoring the gut-churning *you're gonna sound ridiculous* words repeating in his head. "My, uh, biggest fantasy as a teenager was having a boyfriend..."

A horse whinnied out in the barn, the call answered by another.

Noah stared at him, waiting for him to go on. "And?"

A soft sigh escaped Ky's lips. *Fuck.* "I fantasized about having a boyfriend. Period," he added, knowing how lame he sounded. He turned to meet Noah's gaze. "As in, that is the end of that sentence."

Yep, definitely lame. And the expression on Noah's face was a mood killer for sure.

Chapter Thirteen

A boyfriend. Period. The beginning and end of Ky's fantasy.

"Oh." Noah blinked and swore he heard his heart crack.

Damn.

He rubbed his eyes, refusing to let the mushy parts of him take over. Not while straddling Ky's lap, and not when they should be celebrating. Yes, some *serious* celebrating should be happening.

Like right the hell now.

Ky's grin looked halfhearted. "I do believe you mentioned something about a tragic lack of imagination."

"Are you kidding me? Your cocktail utensil maneuver is one for the history books," he said with a meaningful look. Ky's cute, self-satisfied look did another twisty number on Noah's heart, but he ignored that, too. "In thanks, I'm offering you an exclusive deal: twenty-four hours to slake your slutty-boyfriend fantasies—"

"Slutty? Who said he'd have been slutty?"

"That's my very helpful imagination helping you out."

"Sure," Ky drawled, lips twitching in amusement. He sounded less than convinced. "You're only thinking of me, right?"

"Of course." Noah hiked his chin with feigned modesty. "Just one more philanthropic service that I offer," he said. He waited two beats before going on. "And in return, I'd like one of my fantasies addressed as well."

"Which one?"

"A tie and tease." Just the thought set his body humming, and he squirmed, the libido-accelerating contact of budding hard-on against budding hard-on leaving Noah short of breath and Ky's eyes dark. "You put me in restraints and do all sorts of wicked things to me while giving me a critical case of blue balls before letting me come."

"Seriously?" His tone suddenly doubtful, he tipped his head back, as though trying to discourage the idea with his gaze. "Orgasm denial?"

Noah tried to shrug nonchalantly, failing miserably. "I'm in a subby state of mind." He shifted his hips again, heat flaring, and nearly groaned. "I want you to hold me down and make me—"

"Noah—"

"Yes," he said, hips rolling in search of more, *better*, contact. "You should make me do all sorts of—"

"Wait." His fingertips dug into Noah's ass, putting a stop to his needy squirming, and his voice dropped low. A concerned look settled on Ky's face. "I...I don't want to hurt you like those bastards did."

Noah's heart stopped. "Oh."

Nothing cured those emerging boner issues like being kneecapped by reality.

In this case, reality being the memory of Ky asking *what kinda people have you been sleepin' with?* And Noah's idiotically truthful response: the wrong types.

Jesus, one throw-away comment about bad decisions and a little bloodshed during a sexual encounter and Ky went all protective bear at the thought of tying him up...

Frustrated, Noah squeezed his eyes shut.

Fortunately, after the surprise sadomasochistic encounter, he'd gotten smarter. Noah had learned to be very selective about his choice of men—those questioning their sexual orientation had proven to be reassuringly predictable. He'd also been careful to restrict all encounters to a relatively safe place. And he'd never, *ever* entered another man's home for sex again.

Current situation excepted, of course. Including yesterday's momentous fucking.

And...wait. Why hadn't he noticed that until now?

Why was he just figuring this out?

He trusted Ky. Somehow, somewhere along the way, he'd grown to trust Ky. So much so Noah hadn't given his long-held personal rules a second thought. Or even a *first* thought. Actually, there'd been no thinking at all, which would normally be a bad thing but—

He heard Ky's voice as if from a distance.

Noah refocused on the guy whose lap he currently occupied. "What did you say?"

"I said, are you *okay*?"

A slow smile spread up Noah's face, the sense of freedom thrilling. And arousing. "I am better than okay," he said. "I've got the World's Hottest Surgeon right where I want him. Between my legs." His grin grew bigger. "A doctor who's been specially trained in the perfect knot. A Texan who's been taught how to hog-tie...." He paused. "I assume you have, anyway."

"In youth rodeo events, not on the ranch." Ky's lips quirked. "But yep, I'm accomplished in the art of roping."

"Oh, God, you are... That is... I am so..."

Freaking turned on.

"Are you sure about this?" the man asked.

Long-dormant fantasies suddenly became possible again because this was *Ky*. And Noah had plenty of evidence attesting to the man's trustworthiness.

"Absolutely sure."

~~~***~~~

"Orgasm denial," Ky said, finally giving the request his full attention.

Except he had Noah pinned face forward against the kitchen counter and was feeling a mite distracted. The sight of the man's bare ass and Ky's cock thrusting between the guy's thighs were hardly conducive to rational thought, either.

The heat, the skin...Jesus, the *friction*.

"Remember," Noah said. "No kink shaming."

"'Course not."

"And that includes my costume."

Butt naked took on new meaning when a bib apron used for barbequing was involved—Noah had insisted the prop set the appropriate subservient mood. Ky would have rolled his eyes a second time except...God.

The "costume" displayed the man's ass to full advantage. Intentionally, no doubt.

Heaven help him.

Ky thrust his hips harder. The tight heat provided by Noah's closed legs was *so close* to enough that the sensation was torture.

Ky gritted his teeth. "I assume this deal doesn't include depriving your cock of stimulation in the name of denial."

Noah whipped his head around, and the brief flair of his lids—the sudden spark of interest in his eyes—should have come as a surprise.

But didn't.

Ky let out an amused huff. "I guess I assumed wrong."

"That wasn't in my original plan, no. But that's a fabulous idea and I... *Oh.*"

Sparks flared in Ky's cock, and he moaned in unison with the man as Ky repeated the exact angle of thrust again, the head of his cock jabbing lightly at Noah's balls a second time.

Leaving them both breathless.

"And, holy shit," Noah groaned out. "Which idiot suggested you had a tragic lack of imagination?"

"Uh, that would be you."

"You shouldn't listen to me. I clearly don't know what I'm talking about. And now that you suggested deprivation..." Noah's eyes took on a glazed look that communicated his interest.

Ky pumped his hips faster, ramping up the toe-curling sensation between his naked cock and the coarse hair covering Noah's perineum.

The pleasure definitely appeared to be mutual, if the whimpering sounds were anything to go by.

But the question still needed to be definitively answered.

"So..." Ky paused his hips briefly so his tongue could function, "I'm assuming you *like* my cock deprivation suggestion."

"I do." The reply sounded hoarse.

Ky's hips resumed their pumping action at a faster pace. "Is all stimulus off-limits, or are you the only one who isn't allowed to touch your dick?"

"*Yes—*"

Which, again, didn't answer the question. Ky slid a fingertip across the man's hole, perfectly timed with an ever harder jab to his balls.

"Sweet mother, *yes*," Noah gasped out. "A wholehearted unqualified *yes* to the ass play only." Knuckles white, he gripped the counter and tilted said ass higher, pressing closer to Ky's finger. "And here's to fewer assumptions and more awesomeness all around."

Ky's insides twist into an aroused knot. How had they wound up here?

His track record somewhat sparse to date, he liked sex, any kind of sex—ordinary blow jobs were fine by him. He liked vanilla ice cream, plain pepperoni pizza, and whatever sex he could have. Well, as long as it was with Noah.

Which...sounded a lot like a relationship.

Shit.

His heart and hips stuttered briefly.

Still mindlessly thrusting, seeking *more*, Ky closed his eyes and resumed his rhythm, the idea of a relationship a revelation. And one Noah wasn't likely to go along with.

One dilemma at a time, Ky. One dilemma at a time.

And right now he had a whole twenty-four hours before Sierra came back home. Plenty of time to do exactly what he'd fantasized about: screw Noah on every piece of furniture in this house. Not only that, so far all their sexual encounters had been mostly about Ky getting what he wanted. And, sweet Jesus, he wanted to give something back.

Now was his chance.

~~~***~~~

By the time Ky had him bent over the rawhide-covered couch, opening him with his fingers, Noah was convinced his cock was hard enough to dig through concrete.

"So good," Noah rasped out. In search of relief, he reached for his very needy cock, but Ky gently—too gently, really—steered his hand away. Noah gripped the back of the couch. "So *good*. Except..."

"Except?" Ky said.

"I'm your slutty boyfriend, remember? I should be punished." Heat snaked up his spine and he hummed out a filthy *hmmm*. "*Definitely* punished."

"For what?"

"For..."

As he mentally sifted through the possible scenarios, he felt Ky's smile, lips pressed against his back.

"For being slutty?" Ky suggested.

"No, absolutely not," he said. The fingers opening him up brushed against his happy spot, lighting him up—electrifying him—and he produced another pornographic noise. "No...wait, yes. Absolutely, *yes*." His mind spun, trying to function in the midst of the burning stretch, the *pleasure*. Always sensational, but not enough to get him off. "Not for cheating, because that would have brought a sad little frown to teenager Ky's face and that isn't allowed." An amused breath hit his skin. "I've got it," Noah went on. He turned his head to look over his shoulder, meeting Ky's gaze. "You caught me in my masturbatorium—"

No expression of comprehension followed.

"My bedroom," Noah clarified distractedly, now warming up to the fantasy. "You called to say you were coming over to my house to fuck me senseless. But I, turbo slut extraordinaire, couldn't wait and got started without you." He sent Ky a huge smile as the scenario raced through his head. "And now you're making me pay."

Another groan slipped from Noah's lips.

Two beats passed before Ky responded. "I'm making you pay for..." He tilted his head in disbelief. "For jerking off?"

"Yep," he said, enthusiastically popping the "p" on the word.

Ky frowned. "I don't sound so nice in this scenario."

"Oh"—fingers brushed Noah's prostate again, spreading the electric current deeper, fire carving out a space for another finger—"*fuck*." His brain briefly imploded, and he bowed his head. "You," he panted out. "Nice. So very, very *nice*." He pushed back with his hips, trying to match those fabulous rhythmic fingers and take *more*.

For a moment, his groin tightened in anticipation of coming.

"Stop." Ky clamped down on Noah's back, pinning him firmly to the couch and stilling his efforts. "You're not allowed to move."

Noah whimpered.

Loudly.

Because, yeah, now the man was starting to catch on.

~~~***~~~

Noah writhed against the stable wall, the wood, thank fuck, smooth against his bare back.

"I'll admit," he gritted out, "standing here naked with a butt plug up my ass, watching you feed the horses, was a definite turn-on."

He got a distracted *mmhmm* in response.

"But I thought you brought me along to fuck me afterward," Noah said.

Ky, disappointingly still dressed and on his knees, dragged his teeth across Noah's abdomen before sucking a bruise on his hip. A shiver ghosted up Noah's spine as, damn, every hair stood on end, his body covered in tiny little erections.

Which paled in comparison to the massive one straining between his legs. But still, a hickey on his hip wasn't the kind of bruising he'd been hoping for.

"You're supposed to be punishing me," Noah said.

The grin on Ky's face was downright diabolical. His mouth moved up Noah's happy trail toward his belly button.

Holy shit, wrong direction.

Wrong direction.

"Punish me," Noah groaned out. Sweat trickled down his neck. He wanted to be restrained. He wanted pounding and fingertip marks and—

"I am," Ky said.

The man stood and nipped at a nipple.

Noah sucked in a breath, cock throbbing harder. "Better."

"But not good enough?"

"You could have bitten me harder."

"That's the whole point."

"Huh?" He blinked, trying to focus as the man brushed a rough knuckle along his balls—an encouraging whine slipped from Noah—but ignored his straining cock.

Ky's grin grew bigger. "Because giving you what you ask for, but *not quite*, only makes you want it more." He gripped Noah's hair—*Jesus*—and his gaze grew darker. "You'll get what you want. Eventually."

Directed by the sharp tug on his hair, Noah sank to his knees with a happy sigh.

At least some part of him was gonna get fucked.

~~~***~~~

Ky was surprised that the first orgasm of the day—his, of course, because he never backed out on a deal—would take place in the shower.

How had he managed to last until now?

"This time," Ky gasped out, the building momentum in his cock refusing to be ignored any longer, "I'm not stopping."

"Hmm?" Noah murmured in return, tongue curling around Ky's dick, lapping at the sensitive head before swallowing him to the root.

"*Jesus Christ.*" Muscles tensed and ready to spring, Ky couldn't breathe.

The man loved giving head. He *excelled* at giving head. And Ky adored being on the receiving end. Steam rose, water pounding his back. Ky's heart set a frantic pace as his senses sang.

The tight, wet suction of Noah's mouth drove him insane—as though Ky's cock contained treasures inside and Noah was determined to suck out the largest one.

"Fuck, not stopping," Ky managed again, "because..."

Noah managed to hike a questioning eyebrow.

"'Cause the next event involves my cock in your ass, and I'm gonna make it last a long time." Ky gripped Noah's wrists and pinned them against the wall above the man's head, eliciting an encouraging moan. "A very long time."

If the man's mouth hadn't been full, he probably would have murmured a *hell yeah* that matched the expression on his face. As it was, his plead-y little whimpers only stopped when it was time to swallow.

~~~***~~~

Somewhere around five p.m., when Ky began to fuck Noah against the dining room table, the man leaked so much precum Ky wondered out loud if it qualified as coming.

Noah told him no.

~~~***~~~

The sun had set, and Noah lay with his legs spread on the bed, heart thudding, butt plug in place, cock straining in anticipation.

The scene resembled the prelude to yesterday's sexual event.

Except...

Noah wiggled the single hand bound directly above his head. "This needs to be tighter."

Biting his lip in concentration, Ky worked to secure Noah's wrist to the wrought iron headboard, the rope *still* a touch too loose. The moment his partner in sexy crime finished the knot, doubt crept across the man's face.

"Look." Ky sat back on his knees. "I'm—"

Thank God the dude was finally *naked,* all hard, rippling muscle with an amazing, bone-him-until-he-screamed erection that was—

"—not convinced this is a good idea," the man finished.

Noah stared up at him, briefly stunned, before a wry smile twisted his lips. "By now my balls are so blue they're purple." His body glowed with a sheen of sweat courtesy of their earlier activities. "So let's remember that orgasm *denial*, in this particular case, should really be labeled orgasm *delay*."

Ky had brought him close to the brink several times, never once touching his dick. As a result, Noah's cock throbbed so insistently he wondered if it hated him or loved him for suggesting this scenario.

Probably both.

"And we have delayed. My God, how we've delayed," Noah went on. "So now it's past time for...*not* denial."

"I think this is more about orgasm control."

"Whatever."

"And screwing you ain't the problem," Ky said, wincing as he went on. "The potential for hurting you is."

Noah blinked.

Oh.

His mind briefly shifted gears. "You couldn't hurt me if you tried, Ky."

A skeptical sound shot from the man's lips.

"Jesus," Noah muttered, arching his hips in invitation as his body temperature spiked to an unbearable degree, "your fear that you're gonna hurt me shouldn't be such a turn-on."

Ky squeezed his eyes closed. "Noah..."

The conflicted word reeked of apprehension.

Shit.

Clearly, the time had come for Noah's rarely used sincere tone.

"Hey," Noah said softly. He reached up with his free hand and cupped the stubbly jaw. "Don't worry about me, big guy," he went on quietly. "I felt safer with a knife-wielding Ky than I ever felt with any weaponless, one-and-done dude."

Somehow the statement only made Ky frown harder. "I don't want to do anything that triggers bad memories."

"Ky," he said seriously. "I want this."

No, he *needed* this.

His submissive fantasies had been tainted and trashed. One stupid decision and his favorite kinks had been *stolen* from him. Now he was taking them *back*, goddammit.

He wanted to be controlled and commanded—Bossy Ky had fascinated Noah from the moment they first met.

He wanted to be *consumed.*

He wanted to feel *powerless*—he wriggled his wrist and fuck, that was hot—*powerless and helpless.*

But not really, of course.

"In fact," Noah went on, "I wouldn't mind a few bruises in the shape of your fingertips—"

Ky's hand tightened around his wrist, biting into Noah's skin and bringing an encouraging smile to Noah's lips.

"Exactly, cowboy..." he said, raising his second hand next to the first, "just like that."

Ky fastened the wrists together, binding them both to the center rail.

"Finally," Noah groaned, spreading his legs in a *fuck me now* gesture.

"Not exactly." Amusement lit his eyes as he lowered his mouth to Noah's inner thigh.

The thigh?

He'd screwed him on the dining room table and now they were back to *thighs*?

"Are you kidding me?" Noah arched his hips trying to will the man to focus on his ass. "I think I hate you," he lied.

He got a chuckle in return.

Over the next...well, God only knew how long, Noah lost track of time and became one giant nerve ending. On hands and knees, hovering, Ky used deliberate touches to drive him crazy—or crazier, depending on the perspective.

Bound, Noah squeezed his eyes closed anticipating the next contact. The next brush of skin against skin. Teeth nipped a nipple. Stubble scraped the sensitive flesh of his belly.

Warm breath ghosted over his bursting-at-the-seams cock, but not touching—Jesus, he wasn't gonna survive this newly recovered kink—and every hair on his body prickled in response.

Noah trembled and tugged on the ropes. He'd never felt so safe and frustrated and *aroused* in his life. Seriously, the blue balls just might kill him.

But he loved being dominated, being *conquered*. For his brain and breath and body to be controlled by the deliberate movements of a pair of lips, teeth and tongue, or the well-placed rasp of stubble.

Because conquering something meant it had value.

Worth.

Noah squeezed his ass against the butt plug and wriggled, the tip pressing against his prostate.

"Ohmygod, *Ky*," he keened out. Sweat slicked his chest as he rocked his hips, drops of precum smearing against his belly. Just a hint of friction and he'd come.

Just a hint...

With a diabolical smile, Ky leaned over and breathed against the head of Noah's dick, breath fanning the invisible flame, which, dammit, wasn't enough.

Never quite *enough*.

"For chrissake," Noah gasped, vainly thrusting against air. "I've created a monster. A monster-hot freak in the sack."

Ky chuckled and pressed Noah's hips to the bed, staying the movement. He then proceeded to drag his tongue closer and closer to his dick. When he was close enough to take him in his mouth, he licked the precum on his abdomen, never touching his cock.

"Jesus-mother-freaking-Christ," Noah whispered hoarsely, ass cheeks clenching harder around the butt plug.

The need to touch his cock, to offer it some sort of relief, left him twisting his wrists in an attempt to pull them free.

Ky froze. "Alcohol."

"Huh?" He stopped fighting the rope, need leaving his limbs buzzing, and forced himself to focus. "You want a drink *now*?"

Ky rolled his eyes. "Your safe word," he said dryly. His expression turned serious. "Unless I hear the word *alcohol*, I'll...keep going."

The words sounded as though they cost him. Apparently Noah trying to free himself worried the man. Despite that, he seemed determined to follow through on his promise.

"Alcohol?" Noah said, grateful for this beautiful, beautiful—if somewhat overly protective—human being. "You know me so well."

"Know you?" He looked amused. "I've had my tongue and dick inside your every orifice at this point."

"Well..." Noah sent him a mock glare. "Not *exactly*."

Ky, deities be praised, got the hint. He removed the butt plug—Noah hissing at the sudden loss—and spread his cheeks, pressing his mouth to Noah's hole.

Sparks burst behind Noah's lids and in his balls, and he bowed his back, pulling on the restraints. "Exactly!"

He fought for breath. He wanted to reach down and spread himself wider; he wanted to grip Ky's hair and keep that talented, talented tongue pressed against the furl of muscle until...

Laving little kitten licks at his entrance, Ky slid his thumbs into his hole, tongue reaching higher.

"Ngh. Djuh." Noah attempted words of praise but failed. "Guh." Thighs shaky, Noah writhed on the bed while high-pitched whines ripped from the back of his throat.

Ky sounded far too articulate. "Be still."

Jesus, that bossy *voice*.

A second wave of heat rushed through Noah's veins and filled his dick, and he made an almost pained sound. He did as instructed, his cock now hard as steel.

Christ, if Ky would allow him just a smidgen of friction...

Ky's thumbs slid farther inside, his tongue mimicking the very action Noah's ass, at this point, craved beyond anything.

Every stab of warm tongue exquisitely electrocuting his spine.

Noah gripped the headboard and spread his bent legs wider. "Please."

Suddenly, Ky sat back on his knees, the loss of his tongue a physical ache.

"Oh, God," Noah whined. He refused to say the word *alcohol*. Refused. Because that would be throwing in the towel. "Ky, please." He wasn't above begging, though. "Fuck me... Fuck me or suck me off. I don't care which, just...*please*."

Ky adjusted the rope and flipped Noah onto his stomach, arms extended, wrists now crossed and fastened above his head. When Ky thrust inside— exactly like yesterday, except totally *not*—a celebratory shout ripped from Noah's throat.

Already close to coming, Noah lost what little coordination he'd had left. But Ky, fortunately, appeared to have coordination enough for them both. His fingers dug into Noah's shoulders, blunt nails digging deep and holding him still as he began to fuck him senseless.

Steam built in Noah's veins.

Liquid lightning pooled in his balls.

His ass cheered at finally being the focus of Ky's single-minded intent, the man clearly determined to go out in an epic frenzy.

A meltdown at an atomic fucking level.

Noah's body shook, the repeated hits to his prostate a visceral punch in the libido. "Ky, I can't—"

Think anymore.
"Ungh, I need—"
To come.
"'M gonna—"
Explode.

Every thrust shoved Noah up the mattress. His super-sensitive cock rubbed against the damp spot his precum left on the sheets. Legs spread, ass tilted in supplication, Noah lost all vocal coordination as Ky pounded into him.

The pleasure grew so intense every muscle clenched. Noah's face felt wet—fuck, why were his cheeks wet?—his voice raw.

And when he finally came, heat shooting up his spine, ass clenching around Ky's hard cock, his scream came out as a hoarse whisper.

~~~***~~~

What felt like an hour later, Noah lay draped across Ky's chest.

"Holy shit," Noah whispered, the words weak. "I blanked out at the end. I hope you managed to finish."

In response, he received an affirmative hum.

"Good," Noah went on, "because you've totally made a convert out of me."

Ky snorted, his chest rising and falling beneath Noah's cheek, and smoothed his palm down Noah's sweat-slicked shoulder blades.

"A convert?" Ky's sex-slurred voice meant a heavier Texas drawl. "Was there a secret second fantasy I didn't know about? One where I fuck you so hard I turn you gay?"

For the second time that day, Noah's heart stopped.

Oh, my God. That's hot.

Despite its exhausted state, Noah's cock attempted to fire a few cylinders. "Guh— That's— Your imagination needs no help at all," he said. "Definitely save that idea for later. Right now I'm talking about a higher being."

Ky lifted his head and stared down at him. "Religion?"

"Don't sound so surprised, Dr. Delicious. Because thanks to you"—Noah propped his chin on Ky's chest—"I have just seen the face of God."

The rumble of laughter from below tickled Noah's throat. Ky adjusted his arms, pulling him closer. But Noah had no issues with getting his cuddle on.

In fact, as of today, he fucking loved cuddles.

"So," Ky eventually said, "which belief would you sign on for? Buddhism? Hinduism?"

"Why are you assuming an *Eastern* religion?"

"Your love for Indian cuisine."

"Ah, the perfect criteria for making such a life-changing decision."

"In your world, I'm sure it is."

"Well, I've developed my own belief system." Noah dropped his chin back to Ky's chest. When he went on, the words came out mumbled, his bottom lip partially smooshed against Ky's skin. "I now worship the ground your cock jizzes upon."

The resulting roll of Ky's eyes came paired with a smile that could light the world.

"You're completely twisted," Ky said.

"Ha!" He rubbed his chin against coarse chest hair, his tone teasing. "You love me and you know it."

"Love, huh?" he murmured sleepily, his tone too serious for the smutty-slash-snarky atmosphere. A thoughtful look flitted across the man's face as he yawned just before his lids drifted close. "That's probably true."

Every cell in Noah's body clenched tight as he listened to Ky drift off, small snuffling breaths too adorable for words, and his brain replayed the last few seconds.

Love.

Noah blinked twice, his pulse striving to reach a record rate.

The momentous trip to Texas had changed everything, and since his big mouth now posed less of a threat to Ky, maybe Noah should rethink the impossibility of giving another relationship a try. He'd sucked at love, and he still had his doubts he even deserved it. But surely he'd grown as a person since Rick? God knows he'd tried—he'd just had so far to go. Maybe he now qualified as boyfriend material. What were the odds this time would go as badly as the first?

And maybe, just maybe, this time around it wouldn't *hurt so goddamn much*...

Jesus.

His stomach executed a sickening roll that left his mouth watering in warning. Five thumping heartbeats later, his skin developed a familiar itch. If he didn't do something, he knew what would come next: hives and an unpleasant tossing of his cookies.

As he fought to control his breathing, the prickling sensation crept up his chest and spread higher.

"Shit," he breathed out.

He slipped clumsily out of bed, careful not to wake Ky, and went in search of the only thing that would help.

Chapter Fourteen

Five hours after the best sex of his life, Ky parked the old diesel flatbed next to the rental SUV in front of the unfamiliar bar. Thank God he'd found Noah.

But what in the hell had possessed the man to come to this particular establishment?

Ky squinted down at his phone, the sky pitch-black at one a.m., and rubbed his eyes. Completely spent and dead to the world, he hadn't woken up until the fourth text—increasingly tipsy texts, going by the deteriorating spelling.

9:05 p.m. *Why didn't you tell me Ray was a teetotaler? No alcohol at your house, so went in search of bar. Celebrating to be done!*

10:26 p.m. *Now drinkin shots and line dancing.*

11:22 p.m. *Don't worry, they dn't know u here.*

11:38 p.m. *PS Teh little snuffly sounds u make while sleeping r cute.*

11: 46 p.m. *Uh oh. Not everyne at Hlls Watering Hol thinks im charmin.*

Fuck. The last text from over an hour ago still had Ky worried. Wandering in to a Texas bar with Noah's special brand of charm could be dangerous.

Ky glanced up at the sign *Hell's Watering Hole.* Google's magic ability to unscramble the name had helped him locate the honky-tonk two counties over from Oak Hollows. The relatively safe distance from home didn't ease the tension in his shoulders as he climbed out of his truck and braced for the worst: glares and insults, fists flying.

Maybe even a little blood on the floor.

Noah's blood.

The thought made breathing tough. Ky jerked the front door open, stepped inside, and—

What the ever-lovin' hell?

Ky came to a halt. Of all the horrendous possibilities relentlessly circulating through his head, he certainly hadn't prepared for the scene in front of him. In the dim light of the old establishment, country music playing, a few couples danced. A smattering of people sat at the tables lining the floor.

And Noah...?

Hand towel slung over his light pink Polo-covered shoulder, Noah stood behind the oak bar, a cluster of customers watching. The middle-aged bartender was leaning against the counter observing his self-appointed employee at work.

Looking decidedly more sober than his texts had suggested, Noah strained the buttery-yellow contents of a cocktail shaker into a glass. "Here you go, Caleb." He slid the concoction in front of a gray-haired man seated at the bar. "A drink guaranteed to put a smile on your face."

"What's this?"

"A spicy grapefruit margarita," Noah said. "Tart with a nice little kick."

The handful of customers gathered developed varying degrees of doubtful expressions as Caleb squinted down at the glass. The man's leathery face spoke of a lifetime of manual labor and too many years in the sun. Smilin' didn't look likely.

"What's the white, crusty stuff on the rim?" Caleb asked.

Noah braced an arm against the bar. "Crushed Viagra."

Jesus.

Ky stifled a groan, the bartender looked shock, and the tiny audience shifted closer, as though to get a better look.

"Ohmygod," Noah said, patting the bartender on the back. "Gary, I'm just kidding."

"Sure wouldn't hurt business none," the man said.

"Beats that shit you call food," a customer added.

"Shut up, Ted," the bartender replied amicably.

"The crusty stuff is chili pepper and salt." Noah downed the contents of his own shot glass—tequila, from the looks of it. "But the muddled jalapeno in the drink gives it the kick."

Caleb took a sip, a delighted grin creasing his weathered face. Several observers immediately asked Noah to make them one, too.

Huh. Perhaps not the disaster in the making Ky had envisioned. Had he panicked for nothing? Or was the worst yet to come? Trying to decide, he took a seat at the end of the bar, Noah's back to him as the impromptu employee cheerfully began to fill their orders.

The real bartender crossed over to Ky.

"What happened there?" Ky asked, nodding at the animal heads overlooking the bar.

Hell's Watering Hole bandannas covered their eyes, as though lined up in front of a firing squad.

"His idea." Gary nodded in Noah's direction. "He said their judgmental eyes would stifle his creativity."

Ky's lips quirked. "Why am I not surprised?"

He should have recognized the work—less firing squad, apparently, and more S and M meets Field & Stream.

Gary swept his thinning hair from his forehead. "What can I get you?"

"Beer."

"Preferences?"

"Whatever's on tap."

Without a word, the bartender filled an icy mug and set it in front of Ky. "Here ya go."

"Thanks."

They spent a few companionable minutes watching Noah serve the group of customers while Ky sipped his drink—the frosty bitter taste working wonders against the muggy, half-assed air conditioning inside—still trying to decide if the current situation was a problem that needed fixing.

The answer came two minutes later.

Gary nodded in Noah's direction again. "Friend of yours, I take it?"

Ky's mouth twisted wryly. "Of sorts."

Noah appeared engrossed in conversation with the men gathered at the bar. If the laugh that just belted from Caleb was any indication, Noah had them eating out of his manicured hand.

With a lopsided grin, Gary studied Noah's back. "He's a character."

Ky hummed in agreement and met the bartender's gaze.

Gary's smile grew rueful. "This ain't much more than a beer-and-whiskey joint. And he's charmed a few of my older regulars with his froufrou cocktails. But..."

The beer grew colder in Ky's gut. "But?"

"Them dipshits over there?" Gary nodded toward three twentysomething guys in the far corner who were glaring at Noah from a distance. "They haven't taken a shinin' to him like the others," he said. "You might want to warn your...friend to be careful."

Ky gripped his mug tight, the implication in the loaded pause before the word *friend* couldn't be any clearer. But the man's expression was easygoing enough.

"Back-ass backwards, all three of 'em. And mean, to boot," Gary went on, his concerned gaze meeting Ky's again. "The only kind of diplomacy they understand involves fists."

"Yep." He sighed and pushed up from the bar. "I understand."

Convincing Noah to leave wasn't gonna happen quietly.

Eyes glittering too brightly, Noah spotted him the moment he rounded the corner of the counter. "You're here!"

"You're drunk," Ky said dryly.

Noah threw out his arms in *voila!* fashion. "Why, yes, I am," he said cheerfully. "I spent an hour out on the dance floor and sobered up briefly. Long enough to make a few fabulous cocktails, anyway. However"—he swayed a little on his feet and tossed back another generous shot glass—"several rounds of tequila in a short period of time took care of that sobriety problem."

"Since when is sobriety a problem?"

"Since now."

A concerned frown crept up Ky's face. "We should go home."

"Feel free. I'm going to stick around here with my new friends."

"Noah..." He groaned and ran a hand down his face. "It's late. You're trashed."

And this won't end well, he didn't say.

The smile that lit the man's face didn't come close to reaching his eyes—hell, they weren't even in the same room. The vague warning humming in the back of Ky's mind grew more pronounced.

"You say that like being trashed is a bad thing," Noah said. "Though it does make the line dancing more challenging."

He winked at Ky, turned on his heel, and headed toward the dance floor. And damn if he wasn't wearing an old pair of Ky's cowboy boots. Apparently Noah had learned several of the basic steps earlier. Because two minutes later he was in the middle of a group of women, plus two men, shuffling those boots across the scuffed wood.

Despite his concerns, Ky grinned. He leaned against the wall and hooked his thumbs through the belt loops of his jeans, contemplating his next move. The loud music left his head thumping, but he definitely enjoyed the view.

Noah shook his hips more than the other men, not to mention a few of the women. If Ky didn't know better, he'd think the guy was having a good time. But the too-bright-eyed look, the frenetic energy left Ky feeling like he should do something.

He'd slept with Noah several times—*Jesus*, today's marathon session alone should count as five—but Ky still had trouble understanding the man. Or how to handle him. Clearly, two choices existed.

He could wait him out and drive him home after *last call.* Or he could drag him away sooner against his will, before things turned ugly.

Or maybe that would *make* things ugly.

Damn.

Ky pursed his lips, trying to decide, while eying the three men along the wall still glaring at Noah. They looked toasted and itching for a fight.

After one more minute of deliberation, Ky pulled out his phone and filmed Noah, surrounded by another set of new friends, shaking his ass to "Country Girl (Shake it for Me)." He sent a text with a link to the video to Memphis, the man listed in his contacts since the first vegan lasagna discussion.

Ky: *He's trashed. Do I intervene? Or leave him be?*

Memphis: *No clue. I'll check.*

Check? Ky frowned down at his screen. Check how? Five more minutes passed before Ky's phone started buzzing with rapid fire responses from several different people.

A group text had been sent out—Dylan, Alec, and Tyler included—linked to Ky's question and the video clip.

Alec: *Dylan's driving Rick around. He'll have to pull over to respond. I don't have any advice, but I'll send you the hangover recipe I make him.*

Tyler: *Could be bad. Not sure. Rec waiting on D's input. In the meantime...plz get a close-up of the boots he's wearing.*

None of which was particularly helpful. And Ky wasn't sure how he felt about providing blackmail fodder for Noah's friends to give him shit about. Then again, Noah seemed to dish out a fair amount of shit himself. Perhaps he had some payback coming his way, hence Tyler's request.

Three more minutes ticked by before the deciding vote arrived.

Dylan: *Fuck. Not again.*

Wait... what?

What did he mean by *again*?

Dylan: *Definitely drag his ass out of there.*

The worry gnawing in Ky's gut didn't seem over the top now.

Ky: *Is there a precedent here?*

A pause followed, all eyes likely studying cell phones while waiting for Dylan's response. With every second that passed, the delay in his reply added more weight to Ky's suspicions.

Dylan: *Same thing happened on 1st anniver of Rick's death.*

Great.

Ky rubbed his temple as his breath snagged on something uncomfortable in his chest, disappointment dousing the last of his sex-induced afterglow. How did an afternoon of fabulous sex rate a similar response to the anniversary of a boyfriend's death? He kept his gaze on the screen, wondering if Dylan would share a few details and half hoping he would. Yet dreading the answer just the same.

Dylan: *Biker bar, heavy booze, spoiling for fight, night in jail.*

Shit.

Memphis: *Noah got into a fistfight?*

Ky let out a scoff, not at all surprised that the biker bar, heavy booze, and the night in jail *hadn't* generated much of a reaction. But spoiling for a fight? And *participating* in one? Yeah, he could imagine the disaster.

Dylan: *Didn't end well.*

Double fuck.

Decision made, Ky shoved his phone in his back pocket and headed toward Noah. Threading through the side-stepping bodies turned out to be more problematic than he'd planned. He finally made his way to the front, where Noah had been adopted as tonight's mascot of Hell's Watering Hole.

Unfortunately, not everyone approved.

The three back-ass backwards locals now stood in front of the group, tossing insults back and forth with Noah. True to form, the more insulting the words the sassier Noah's smile.

"Fuckin' fairy," one of them called.

"Beats being a knuckle dragger," Noah said.

"Beats taking it up the ass," called another.

"Oh, and I do." Noah's smile grew bigger. "Every chance I get."

"Jesus," Ky muttered, gently pushing Noah back and stepping between him and the men. "What do you hope to accomplish here?"

"Uhm, nothing?"

"And how do you expect this to end?"

Noah gave a sloppy shrug. "Probably with them dragging me out back and bashing me in the head for being gay," he said casually. "Maybe tossing my body in the dumpster?"

Sweat broke out across Ky's forehead, his palms cold and clammy. He couldn't decide which scared him more: Noah's prediction? Or the nonchalant view he took of the scenario?

"Jesus *Christ,* Noah." He instinctively stepped closer, fear making his voice harsh enough to be heard over the twangy music. "Are you *trying* to get yourself killed?"

The pause in the conversation filled with the sound of a new song and the line of bodies shifting in unison around them.

"Well?" Ky prompted.

Noah blinked up at him for a moment. "I'm *trying* to *dance.*"

Trying, at this point in the evening, being the key word. The recent shots of tequila had caught up with him, his footwork clumsy, and he stumbled through a few more moves.

"You've had enough," Ky said. "It's time to go home."

One of the three men called out, "You heard the man. Go home, queen."

Shit. For a moment, Ky had blissfully forgotten about the three idiots behind them.

"Butt pirate," the second one said just as the third called out, "fagotty pink-wearing cocksucker."

White-hot anger blazed through Ky, and he clenched his hand, preparing to plant a fist in the asshole behind him if need be.

"There's a suspicious amount of protesting going on here." Noah gracelessly shuffled the dance steps while smirking at the men. "Must mean you want my mouth on your—"

Enough.

Ky leaned forward and hoisted Noah over his shoulder, turning the rest of the bound-to-be-poorly-received statement into an *oof.*

With the man now draped in a fireman's carry position, Ky adjusted his load and made a beeline for the door. One of the dancers called out Noah's name and whistled. Noah cheerfully called back *good night* to each and every one of the customers who waved as they went by. Ky ignored the catcalls and well-wishers—and not-so-well-wishers—boots thumping on the floor, Noah dangling loosely down his back. He sensed a commotion behind him and got the feeling the three assholes were trying to follow but got cut off by the crowd. He picked up his pace.

They exited the bar, the door slapping shut behind them with a *thwack,* and the headache-inducing level of country music was instantly muted.

Thank God.

Ky blew out a relieved breath and headed across the parking lot.

"I have a question," Noah slurred out as he patted Ky on the butt. "Is this supposed to be a punishment or a reward?"

Ky's lips twisted into a reluctant grin, but he didn't have time to be turned on. Especially if the unhappy trio inside decided to follow them into the parking lot.

"This is definitely a reward." Noah clumsily poked him in the ass again. "'Cause the view is *fabulous*. Hellamazing."

"I'm glad you're enjoying the show," he said dryly.

Boots crunched against the gravel as they approached his truck.

"Wha—*hey*," Noah said, the words stumbling out. "You passed the Tahoe!"

"Did you really think I was gonna let you drive?"

At his truck, Ky hefted the man into the vehicle, ignoring the ass wiggle and the sloppy laugh as he got him situated. Once inside himself, Ky closed the driver side door.

"I should suck you off right here, right now," Noah said, eyes bright, hair mussed. "As a final *fuck you* to the trio of idiots inside."

Ky's lips quirked. "You're drunk."

"I prefer the term Beyond Buzzed. And, FYI"— Noah draped himself against Ky's shoulder, limp as a newborn kitten—"we should add the manhandling caveman carry to our list of future fantasies to be fulfilled."

Hunh.

Ky pursed his lips, his heart rate shifting several notches higher. After all the back-and-forth, all the ups and downs, the casual mention of a future, *any* kind of future that included sex, felt like progress.

In fact, those words were the most encouraging ones Ky had heard to date.

Something unclenched inside, that same something that had seized up when he'd realized he wasn't interested in sleeping with anyone else anymore.

Right now, though, he just needed to get the man buckled in. But Noah snuggled closer, limiting Ky's efforts, and rubbed his cheek against his chest.

"And just look at that belt buckle," Noah murmured, patting the offending fashion piece affectionately before his fingers drifted lower with intent. "Fate must be laughing her ass off that I've fallen for a man who—"

Instantly, Noah's back stiffened, and every oxygen molecule got sucked out the open window.

Son of a...

"Ohmygod," Noah whispered as he fumbled back to his side of the cab. Breathing heavy, he stared at Ky. The guy looked as though he'd been hit by a Mack truck and left for roadkill.

Ky knew how he felt.

Noah scratched at his neck, red blotches visible in the dim light. "I think—" He slid farther away from Ky. "I think I need to get out."

"Dammit, wait—" Ky reached for him, but Noah dodged his hand. The alarm bells clanging in Ky's head intensified a hundredfold as the blotches spread to the man's face.

His short, choppy breaths weren't reassuring, either.

What the hell was happening?

"Noah, are you—?"

But Noah opened the passenger door, clumsily exited the truck, and promptly threw up.

~~~***~~~

After a fitful night's sleep, Ky felt no closer to figuring out what to do about Noah than before the paraphrased words *I've fallen for you* had made the man vomit.

Sweet mother Mary.

Ky rubbed his eyes, gritty from a lack of sleep, and leaned a hip against his dresser. Heat from the late-morning sun pressed in through the window he'd opened to air out the bedroom. The smell of puke from the clothes on the floor mixed with the scent of cedar from the junipers outside. Industrious cicadas buzzed in the trees, the sound mirroring the ominous hum of apprehension in Ky's body as he studied Noah's form, still passed out cold in the bed.

He looked peaceful.

But every time Ky closed his eyes, he saw the look on Noah's blotchy face just before he'd vomited, all the result of a simple confession of affection. Ky's lips twisted grimly. He'd never felt so close to having a boyfriend...

...and yet so miserably far away.

His gaze caught in the dresser mirror, eyes drawn to the faint purple mark on his neck from yesterday's marathon sex extravaganza, and he let out a wry huff. He really needed to figure out what the heck to do about this relationship.

More than likely Noah expected Ky to slap on a smile and pretend yesterday—the fucking and the bar fighting and the puking, essentially *all of it*— hadn't happened. A week ago, Ky probably would have. Today he wasn't so sure.

At this point all Ky knew was that somethin' had to give.

But standing here wasn't fixing anything. Besides, Sierra was due home any moment.

Ky made his way downstairs, brewed a much-needed pot of coffee, and spent the following hour sitting on the front porch swing pondering his next move in this crazy relationship. He was no closer to an answer when the sound of tires crunching on gravel interrupted his pessimistic thoughts.

He silently watched Sierra pull her bag from the passenger side of the Toyota and close the door. When her friend pulled a U-ey and drove the vehicle back out the driveway, Ky lifted a brow in surprise.

"How much longer is Becky keeping your truck?" he asked.

"Her car is supposed to be ready Monday."

"How did your trip go?"

"Good, I guess." She frowned as she made her way up the porch steps, dropped her bag, and then collapsed onto the porch swing beside him. "Our lawyer thinks he'll be able to get the charges against us dropped."

Relief surged, and his lips twitched. "Try not to look so happy."

Her frown grew bigger. "I was looking forward to my day in court."

"Of course you were," he drawled dryly.

Sierra twisted on the bench to face him and eyed his neck, a grin appearing on her face—the kind of grin his sister always got right before she gave him a hard time.

"I see you and Noah have been having fun while I was away," she said.

Good grief.

He slowly inhaled a breath and scanned the cattle in the pasture in search of a peaceful scene to quiet his heart rate. He wasn't sure how to handle this topic with his sister. Sierra gave a small push with her legs to set the swing in motion, the chain creaking overhead.

"Yeah...well." Ky struggled for something appropriate to say. "I shouldn't have—"

"Shut up." She knocked an affectionate shoulder against his. "Yes, you should have. You should have been doing things like this all along." Her eyes grew soft, the smirk falling away and leaving a serious expression behind. "It makes me really happy. I want this for you."

He asked the safest question he could think of. "How long have you known I was gay?"

"Do you remember Jesse?" she said, and Ky pursed his lips, trying to match a face with the name as she went on. "He's the guy who used to fix our old tractor before Daddy finally broke down and bought the new one."

"Oh." Ky stared at his sister and knew he was about to be served a healthy dose of humiliation.

"Yeah, *oh.*" The teasing look returned to her eyes. "Every time Jesse came to the house, you used to watch him a tad too closely," she said, and when Ky felt the blood crowding his cheeks, she laughed. "One time, I saw you spying on him through the kitchen window. It was a particularly hot day, and when Jesse took off his shirt, you did a fist pump in excitement."

Ky scrubbed a hand down his face, hoping to wipe away the embarrassment. Sierra patted him on the shoulder, both in consolation and amusement.

"I was twelve, Ky." Sierra inched her chin higher. "*Twelve.*" She lifted a hand to wave away a lazy fly. "Before I truly understood what the term gay meant, I knew you were attracted to men, not women. I didn't care then and I don't care now."

"And Savannah? Does she know?"

"We've discussed it. She...wasn't as convinced as I was."

Ky tipped his head. "Why didn't you say anything?"

"I was waiting for you to *tell me*," she said with a gently chastising tone of voice. Sierra sent him a side-eyed look. "I mean, it would be kind of rude for me to assume, don't you think?"

The relaxed smile on her face eased some of his residual tension, and Ky shifted on the bench, setting the porch swing rocking again.

They spent a few minutes in comfortable silence, and Ky watched a calf wander close to the fence and gave a high-pitched *mmaaww* for his mama. The calf's mother lumbered toward her offspring, and the sound of the cows' reunion filled the air.

"I'm sorry I was so wrong," Sierra said quietly, breaking the pause in conversation. "I didn't think Daddy could be so hateful."

Fuck.

She turned her gaze to Ky, unshed tears glistening in the sun.

"Sierra—"

"No." She made an impatient sound and swiped a frustrated hand across her eyes, the tears reduced to a streak across her skin. "I've decided I'm done crying about this."

"Good, because it's not worth crying over," he said with conviction. "And I hope that means you won't be giving up on the ranch, either." He sent his sister a firm look. "You love this place. You deserve to stay."

"Oh, I'm not leaving."

The words were reassuring. The tone of her voice, on the other hand? Ky stared at his sister.

What was she planning now?

"I'm going to convince Daddy to let me buy out his half of the ranch now, instead of later," she went on. "The plan was for him to retire in a couple of years anyway. He wants to move to his hunting cabin in Kentucky. I think the problem with his shoulder has shortened his time frame."

Hunh. That was a solution Ky hadn't considered. And a little part of him wondered if the "shortened time frame" was something that Ray had mentioned? Or something his daughter would convince him he wanted.

Ky bit back a laugh, because if things were reduced to a battle of wills between Sierra and her dad? Well, Ky would bet good money on his too-stubborn sister.

"Will you keep working on turning the place into a grass-fed operation?" he asked.

"It's a work in progress, but yes. Absolutely. No feedlots," she said firmly. "No hormones or antibiotics. It's more humane and the beef is healthier."

"That's going to take cash, too."

She shrugged. "I'll just have to convince the bank to loan me money."

It wouldn't be easy. But once Sierra set her mind on something, God help anything that got in her way.

Ky smiled. "You want a financial partner?"

Her surprised look slowly morphed into a grin. "If it's you?" she said with a second affectionate knock of her shoulder against his. "Of course."

The porch swing continued creaking back and forth as Sierra turned her gaze to the horizon. And if she convinced her father to go along with her plan...

For the first time since Ky had realized he was a gay teen living in a too-straight world, he imagined a future that wasn't so fractured. Unfortunately, his newfound sense of peace was soon disrupted.

"So," Sierra said, "about you and Noah."

A pit opened beneath Ky's stomach, and he sighed. "What about us?"

"I just want you to know I'm happy y'all are together, that's all."

"We're not really together."

Jesus, what exactly were they? He could hear Noah's gleeful voice in his head, offering a suggestion. More than likely something along the lines of *fist-bump buddies with benefits*.

He could feel his sister's gaze burning a hole in the side of his face.

"Okay," she said easily. "Then the question is: do you want to be?"

He swallowed, his mind churning through the many thoughts currently parading through his head.

Do you want to be together?

"I do," he said.

Problem was, he was pretty sure Noah didn't. Not in any meaningful sense.

Sierra laid a hand on his shoulder in a gesture presumably meant to be encouraging, but given what they both knew about Noah, it came across more like sympathy.

Apparently even his baby sister knew, as far as Noah was concerned, Ky was screwed.

"Were not..." He studied his bare feet beyond his jeans. "We're just—"

Ky cleared his throat and gave up trying to explain something he didn't understand himself.

"Look," she said. "Just because you two are sleepin' together doesn't mean you owe me, *or anyone else*, for that matter, an explanation."

His lips twisted, and he couldn't hold back the frown.

"You deserve to be happy, Ky," she said softly. "And more than anyone else I know, outside of Savannah, I want you happy."

He gathered the courage to ask another question. He just wasn't sure he was ready to hear the answer.

"When you donated your eggs," Ky said as he turned to look down at his sister, "did you do it for me?"

The *squeak, squeak, squeak* of the porch swing filled the brief pause.

"I did it for a lot of reasons," she said. "First, I love Dylan and Alec. I wanted them to have the family they deserve."

She looked at him with the same green gaze as their mother's.

"Second," she went on, "I knew I never wanted to have kids of my own—"

"You can't know that," he said. "You might change your mind one day."

"Maybe," she said. "Maybe not." She shrugged as if the point was irrelevant. "And third—"

Ky shot her an amused look. "How many reasons did you have?"

She tipped her chin in mock defiance. "And *third*," she said, ignoring his teasing tone, "I did it because I love you and I wanted you to know that you deserve to have everything you want. *Everything*."

Well...damn.

His heart suffered a serious tug as her words washed over him.

"Just like anybody else, Ky," she said softly. "You deserve love. A family and kids, too—just like Dylan and Alec—if that's what you decide you want. I won't have you thinking you have to settle for less."

The words were a punch to the stomach, but his brain refused to acknowledge the feeling.

Instead, he slowly shook his head and smiled down at his sister. "How did you get to be so wise?"

A huge grin slipped up her face. "I owe everything I am to my big brother."

He rolled his eyes in disagreement.

"Oh, come on," she said in rebuttal. "As a teen, you stuck around when you had every reason to leave. And as a result, my life turned out very different than it could have. As far as I'm concerned, technically half of this should be yours," she said with a gesture in the general direction of the surrounding land. "Have you ever thought of moving back to Texas? Or do you want to stay in San Francisco?"

Ky paused. What did he want?

Just last week he would have responded with a hell no, he wasn't coming back.

Savannah didn't need him as much now, but San Francisco had grown on him. He'd made some real friends. And he liked the idea of living his life out in the open—no suffering through rude stares when he finally went out on a *real* date. Around here, that would always be his reality. At least for now.

But he missed Texas. He missed muddy boots, porch swings, and a nighttime sky filled with stars. He missed slow sunsets, lightning bugs, and folks who remembered his parents.

He'd gone online this morning and discovered his old job at Dallas Surgeon Associates still hadn't been filled, and the one-hour commute would mean he could be here as much as he wanted.

If Sierra convinced Ray to retire early and the guy moved away... Well, that was a real game changer.

"If you *did* decide to move back," Sierra went on, "what would happen between you and Noah?"

Ky puffed out a breath, the sound as much in angst as amusement. "I don't know."

But after years and years of "making do" with nothing remotely resembling a relationship, Ky had finally reached a place where he could do more, *be* more to someone worth being more to. Right now all he and Noah shared was a possibility.

A *potential.*

And Ky was tired, so dog tired of wasting his.

Hell, two men who enjoyed each other's company and shared some powerful chemistry in bed should be able to form some sort of doable relationship.

Probably.

Maybe.

But Ky didn't think Noah was gonna like his ultimatum.

Chapter Fifteen

Ah, dammit. Being sober sucked.

Step by step, Noah cautiously exited the house and squinted into the sun, a bright, hot, malicious ball of fire that probably rose today purely to punish him for drinking too much last night.

The screen door squeaked, the noise adding to the hammer pounding inside his skull, and he carefully kept the door from slapping shut behind. Proud of this small but vitally important accomplishment, he stepped forward and slumped against the porch column, pressing his cheek against the scratchy wood and silently praising the house for holding him up.

Spicy tomato-juice concoction clutched in his hand—bless Ky for preparing the hangover recipe and leaving the pitcher in the fridge—Noah assessed his current, yuck-filled state. His stomach rolled, his head ached, and his legs felt shaky. But the fatigue? The fatigue was the *worst*.

A lilting *chirp, chirp, chirp* split the air, and Noah frowned, squinting up at the massive oak tree shading the house. A tiny bird darted happily from branch to branch.

Cheerful little fucker.

But that was just the lingering effects of too much alcohol talking. Or maybe his ridiculous behavior last night had left him grumpy. Noah inhaled the fresh air and took in the stillness of the admittedly beautiful green countryside.

But he missed the hustle and bustle of San Francisco. The activity and the endless opportunities. The constant stream of cars and concrete and crowds.

Because here there wasn't enough noise to drown out the loud memories—memories he couldn't seem to shake. The most recent in his ever-growing pile being those of dancing like a fool, heckling a trio of homo haters, and words that roughly translated into *I've fallen for you.* He mentally pushed that one aside in favor of his embarrassing actions that had turned his blow-job-in-a-truck fantasy into a vomit fest.

Holy shit, he'd probably killed Ky's sexual interest in him for good. In fact, he might have killed the poor man's sexual appetite for the next thirty years.

Amazing.

How *did* he manage day-to-day life with all the crap he piled upon himself?

Noah took a gulp of the icy drink laced with Tabasco, hoping to chase away the lingering dregs of a hangover the likes of which he hadn't had since his boyfriend died.

A clinking sound in the distance captured his attention. With effort, Noah rolled his head against the porch column and spied Ky in the driveway.

Ky.

Noah pushed up from the railing and fought the swell of emotion. The man was tinkering beneath the hood of a tractor, probably because that was what manly men did when they needed to ponder how to break up with their not-boyfriend who only held not-jobs. Ky had left the bed this morning without waking him first. But what was the poor guy supposed to say?

Thanks for not following through on the blow job?

Love the throw-up smell in my truck?

Props to you for forever killing my sex drive?

Noah inhaled an unsteady breath and set his glass on the porch rail, searching for the right lie to fortify himself prior to apologizing for last night. If he waited too long, he'd talk himself out of facing this problem now in favor of later.

Or never, preferably.

He forced himself down the steps and crossed the yard in Ky's direction, unconcerned about his lack of shoes, the lawn crinkling beneath his feet. And never let it be said that Noah Tanner didn't know how to appreciate the little things in life— carpe diem and all that jazz.

Tension creeping higher, he took solace in the scent of earth and oak. He welcomed the warm grass tickling his toes. He stared at his onetime pretend boyfriend, appreciating the way Ky's T-shirt rode up his back as he stretched over the engine trying to reach a bolt, and then—

Oh. A strip of skin peeked from between the hem of Ky's shirt and his jeans and...

Noah quickly shut down the unhelpful direction of his thoughts. Best way to get past his idiotic actions from the previous evening? Toss out a quick apology and then proceed as though nothing eventful had happened. Like stripping away wax during unwanted hair removal, it was best done quickly.

"Thanks for making the hangover recipe. And sorry about last night," Noah said, the words careful and even. *There*, thank God that was over. He wet his lips and pushed on as he stepped closer to the tractor. "This scene isn't quite right, though."

Ky slowly straightened and his gaze landed on Noah.

Damn.

The guarded look on the man's face felt far from encouraging. Not quite the scowl he'd run into that first night at the Humane Society Gala, and certainly not the reluctant look he'd initially received during the beginning of their makeover endeavors. No, this held a certain amount of reserve that, even at Ky's grumpiest, had never been directed at Noah.

Until now.

Obviously the man didn't subscribe to the *ignore the issue until it went away* method of dealing with problems. Or the *so sorry, now can we pretend that never happened?* form of apology.

"Exactly how is this scene wrong?" Ky asked.

Noah shifted on his feet, feeling exposed. The only way past the predicament he'd created was straight through. Too late to adopt a different course of action now.

Feeling the pending collision, heart rate shifting higher, he began to babble, gesturing a touch too wildly. "In my fantasies—which are very detailed, I'll have you know—you're fixing machinery out in a pasture or tossing hay into the back of a truck. While wearing the boots, of course." Noah reined in his flailing hands and shaded his eyes from the evil rays of the relentless sun, squinting up at Ky. "Anyway, some task that requires more muscle. And"—might as well go for broke—"you weren't wearing a shirt."

Ky exhaled sharply and tossed his wrench toward a decrepit toolbox that had probably been in existence longer than Noah, landing with a bone-jarring *clang*.

The expression on his face, more so than the headache-enhancing sound, made Noah's skull pound and his insides clench.

"God forbid we discuss anything other than sex," the man said.

Noah pressed his lips together as his pulse ticked up several more notches. Maybe tossing out a quick apology hadn't been the right thing to do. But something told him keeping his mouth shut and waiting for Ky to go on was incredibly important.

He just wasn't prepared for what the man said.

"I spent a lot of years wondering what it'd be like to do the things that dating couples do," Ky began slowly, not meeting his eyes. He gave a small shrug. "Have a drink at a bar. See a movie at the movie theater. Hold my boyfriend's hand in public."

Noah's pulse skipped a beat at the visual, and he swallowed, his throat as dry as a dusty country road.

"Or even something as simple as grocery shopping." Ky stared across the vast expanse of green pasture that surrounded the house. "With someone just like you," he said, ticking his gaze back to Noah's again. "Because I've never met someone who made me smile harder."

Oh, God.

Noah blinked, his eyes burning.

That was just...that was just...

The most heartbreaking and heartwarming thing he'd ever heard.

"Unfortunately," Ky said, cocking his head thoughtfully, "I'm just startin' to figure out that those who make you smile the hardest are the ones best at bringing the misery. Something you learned the hard way, I suppose."

"Ky," he said, his voice shaking as he took a step closer. "I'm sorry I—"

Ky slammed the hood closed and turned to lean against the tractor. The way he crossed his arms across his chest looked disturbingly final, as though he'd come to a decision.

One Noah wouldn't like.

"I waited a long time to get to a point where I could have a real relationship," Ky went on. "I never wanted to fall for someone who hated himself because of his orientation, though I know there are plenty of those around to choose from." He studied Noah's face. "I sure didn't expect to fall for a guy who hated himself for something else."

The words sat on Noah's chest with the weight of the monster-sized flatbed truck parked in the driveway, crushing the breath from his lungs.

"At first I thought maybe you just loved Rick so much you couldn't picture yourself with someone else. But everything that's happened left you more fucked up than I thought."

A humorless laugh rumbled out of Noah, smarting as it came out. "I could have told you that myself."

His attempt at easing the moment failed.

Miserably.

"You said you'd fallen for me," the surgeon said.

Noah's throat grew tight.

Ky tipped his head. "And then you threw up."

"I...I'd been drinking."

"I don't think that's why you vomited. Your face and neck got blotchy as well. "

Noah's eyes grew wide. So that was *real?* He rubbed the area beneath his collarbone, remembering the need to claw at his skin. "So the itching wasn't my imagination?"

"Cholinergic urticaria."

Noah blinked hard, even though his vision was fine. It was just his brain that was cloudy. "Um...what?"

"Hives," Ky supplied helpfully.

"Huh. Everyone kept telling me I was making it up." Noah slowly turned the unexpected news over in his head, grateful for the easier topic. "So...what does that mean?" He did his best to smile, lips faltering at the ends. "Being with you requires an antihistamine?"

Unfortunately, Ky's arms remained crossed, his expression stuck in serious mode.

Noah tried harder to make his smile appear less forced. "Sounds like a bad country-western song."

"No antihistamines. But it *is* gonna require treatment."

"Drugs?" he asked hopefully.

"Counseling."

Noah's sharp inhalation came too fast, fine dust particles burning his nose and making him cough, his eyes watering. Ky kept his steady gaze on Noah, and for a moment, he felt trapped. The hot, dry air constricting his lungs.

"How does counseling help with hives?" Noah knew his tone was riddled with doubt and a hint of sarcasm.

"There's a well-known association between anxiety and cholinergic urticaria. In your case I suspect it's PTSD related. Not to mention the negative coping skills you've developed along the way."

Wait...what? A bubble of self-deprecating laughter rose from his chest.

PTSD?

All this time he'd halfway joked about being allergic to monogamy, as though the reaction was hilarious and the kind of emotional baggage he could carry with pride. Or just simply being the screwed-up drama queen he'd facetiously claimed to be all along.

But ;PTSD? That sounded awful and entirely too prosaic and...really, really plausible, actually.

He'd hate the man for being so smart and a doctor and all, except for the fact that he couldn't.

He *couldn't*.

"I'll admit I had a few questionable years, but I think I'm coping much better now," Noah said, voice strained. "I've—"

"Just because you've sucked a lot of guys off, Noah," he said dryly, "doesn't mean you've recovered from your boyfriend's death." Ky paused before going on. "Or from being sexually assaulted."

Noah's chest burned.

Fuck.

The behavior he'd embraced several years ago— and yeah, he supposed they could be labeled "negative coping skills," for sure—had forever changed his life. Ky excelled at calling a spade a spade, no matter how painful. And perhaps it was past time for Noah to admit the encounter in the masochistic man's apartment amounted to sexual assault.

Good God, between Rick's last days and Noah's questionable life choices, the tangle of so many memories continued to fly at him like sharp knives...

"And honestly," Ky continued, spearing his fingers through his hair, "I think we need to cool things off until you figure out exactly what you want."

A chill ran through Noah, leaving his body shaking and curing him of his hangover fatigue more effectively than if he'd been doused in icy water. Anger he could handle. Ky's disappointment in Noah hurt, too. But calling things off? Going back to being just friends? Now that he'd experienced this...time with Ky, he didn't know how he was supposed to be satisfied when it ended.

He pushed shaky fingers into his front pockets, hoping to protect himself with a defensive statement of his own. "You knew from the beginning I wasn't into monogamy—"

"Don't," Ky said softly but with no less of an edge to his voice. "If I really thought you were just living out your lifestyle choices, I would be moving on without saying a word. So, just..." He looked down at his boots for a moment before meeting Noah's eyes again. "Spare the words for someone who believes your bullshit."

"Bullshit?"

"Wanting to spend your life fucking around is perfectly fine," Ky went on. "Breaking out in hives and puking when you develop more than a casual one-and-done acquaintance *isn't*."

A small breeze kicked up but didn't block the sun beating down on Noah's head or overcome the cheerful sound of the *chirp, chirp, chirp* behind him. He needed his sunglasses. He needed ibuprofen for his pounding head.

He needed for that stupid fucking bird to stop being so *happy*.

Ky shrugged as though he'd given up. "Either way it doesn't matter. And I understand why you do the things you do. But that's not the biggest problem here." The words that followed hit hard. "Self-loathing is self-loathing, no matter the cause."

"I don't—" Noah fisted his hands in his pockets, hoping to ease the rapid-fire beating of his heart. "What's done is done. I don't want to talk about the assault." Jesus, speaking the word out loud left his voice hoarse. He didn't want to discuss his motivations. The counseling issue seemed safer. "And I *refuse* to spend another second of my life discussing Rick's death. Especially with a stranger, someone who couldn't understand." He went on with what little air he managed to suck into his lungs. "I can't."

He'd meant to say he wouldn't but *can't* would just have to do.

"Noah, you need to talk to someone. Maybe start with Dylan—"

"Dylan doesn't know the truth about Rick!"

The whole world went still, Ky scanning Noah's face, and a full minute passed before the man went on.

"You should tell him," Ky said.

Noah briefly flicked his gaze to the ground, trying not to picture his friend's reaction—his *best* friend—and pressed his lips together. He couldn't take that risk.

"Difficult choices suck," Ky went on. "And you've had to make one of the most difficult ones out there. You need to learn better ways to manage the baggage from your past, and that should start with being honest with your friend." He exhaled slowly and wearily massaged his temple. "Either way, I can't watch you do this to yourself anymore."

Can't watch this anymore.

What did he mean by that? Noah braced his hand against the John Deere tractor. "Listen, Ky," he said, rubbing eyes that felt as though they'd been filled with sand. He just needed to do some damage control. "I know last night didn't end well."

The Brow of Judgment finally made an appearance at Noah's understatement.

The tension in the air didn't dissipate.

"I'm beginning to suspect the orgasm-denial kink was just another form of self-torture," Ky said. "Because you can't have sex with me unless it's for a good 'cause,' like my coming out. Or baptizing my bed for some lame-ass reason or another. You won't allow yourself to have sex with me just because you *want* to." His forehead developed several more furrows before slowly adding the Sad Eyes. "That's seriously messed up."

God, no. Not the Sad Eyes.

Bone-deep exhaustion hit, and Noah dragged the back of his hand across his sweaty face.

His chest ached. His whole damn world ached. He missed the man's scruffier stubble. He missed the teasing look in Ky's gaze and, more than anything, the smile on the man's face. Even the occasional scowl had been easier to bear.

Worse, Noah hated being the sole cause of the man's current expression of sorrow.

"Unfortunately, your actions don't just effect you," Ky said. "They have an effect on everyone around you. The people who care about you. Your friends." Another second passed. "And me."

"You don't qualify as my friend?"

Ah...hell. As soon as the words left his mouth, Noah knew they'd been a horrendous choice.

Ky sucked in a slow breath, shifting his focus to the horizon. "It's painful watching you do this to yourself, the negative coping mechanisms." His beautiful eyes, the central browns and yellows fading to blues and greens in the periphery, landed back on Noah with a resignation that *hurt*. "After last night, I sure don't want to stick around and watch you flirt with death again because you don't think you deserve to live."

Oh...hell.

Mouthing off to the homo-hating trio at the bar had been a stupidly risky thing to do, just like Noah's week of imbibing following Rick's death—in retrospect, likely a wussy, halfhearted attempt to completely kill his liver.

A warm flush of shame filled Noah's face, and he tried to deflect the feeling with a weak smile. "Don't want to stick around for my negative coping mechanisms, huh? Thinking about leaving San Francisco?"

"Might be easier that way," he said far too seriously.

Wait, *what*? Noah had only been joking.

Obviously, Ky wasn't. Was he really thinking about moving back to Texas? Leaving San Francisco for good?

"In fact, I know it would be," Ky went on.

Noah's mind spun, trying to gather all the threads of this conversation and weave them into a happier truth. But clearly the man loved the ranch and missed home. That had been evident in all the unpacked boxes in his living room. And now that Savannah was better and Ky had come out, there wasn't much keeping him in San Francisco, especially if all Noah brought out in Ky was the Sad Eyes.

Noah's panic escalated to truly alarming proportions. "Ky—"

"I can love you as hard as I know how, but it won't make a difference." He pushed up from the tractor as though done with the conversation, as though the words weren't tearing huge holes in Noah's carefully constructed reality. "Not until you learn to love yourself again first."

Fuck, he needed air.

His heart throbbed and his lungs couldn't get enough oxygen as the prickles crept across his chest.

Noah rubbed the itching skin.

He should say something, do something. He needed to fix this, fix *himself*. He'd been prepared to live without Ky sleeping in his bed—it would suck, sure, but he could have totally survived as long as they could remain friends. Noah just needed to see him. He was still learning how to live without Rick—so far he'd done a piss-poor job.

Giving up Ky's presence completely felt like asking too much.

But when Ky turned and headed into the barn, Noah—the guy who rarely stopped talking—couldn't think of a thing to say.

~~~***~~~

Forty-eight hours later, after leaving Texas early, Noah vaguely took note of the knocking outside his condo as he lay sprawled on his couch, mouth tasting of tequila, head swimming as he stared at the ceiling.

"Noah," Dylan called through the front door.

Oh, God...

"Open up," his friend went on, voice filled with concern.

The heart-pounding fear and dread—and too much tequila—congealed in his gut, leaving his stomach sour, the hefty weight of his past effectively pinning him to the couch.

Through the difficult years, he'd clung to Dylan's friendship like a lifeline. Later, he'd thrown himself into keeping the Front Street Clinic well funded, trying to paper over the great, happiness-sucking black hole in his heart. Mostly, though, he'd relied on Dylan.

The last thing Noah wanted was to disappoint him, *too*.

But Ky had been right about one thing—well, he'd been right about *most* things, actually, minus the god-awful choice of a belt buckle. More importantly, he was right about Noah needing to tell the truth.

Unfortunately, he'd been living with the secret for so long it had become a habit. Dylan would hate him, for sure. If Noah came clean about what happened all those years ago, he might lose his best friend.

The last little piece of Rick he had left.

"Come on, man," Dylan said, voice muffled by the door. "We know you're in there."

Noah considered trying to stand, but he didn't think he could, his legs too loose and wobbly. His head certainly wouldn't tolerate any more shouting through the door, though. Then again, the loud knocks really had to stop, too.

The pounding outside his door and inside Noah's head grew louder, and he groaned, pressing his hands to his temples. The lights spun viciously overhead. The alcohol in his system had left numb behind hours ago and now seemed intent on taking him for a merry-go-round ride, right here in his living room.

No entrance fee required, aside from complete heartbreak, of course.

"Open up!" Dylan called again. "I've been trying to reach you all day."

He had? Blinking hard, Noah tried to focus on his cell phone. He had twenty-five—or fifty-five? He didn't trust his vision right now—missed calls and texts, half from Dylan and the rest evenly split between Tyler, Alec, and Memphis. Three more had been left by Julissa, Memphis's ex-wife and Noah's favorite shopping buddy.

Not a single message from Ky.

A few seconds later he heard a key turning in the lock, and Noah sighed in relief. Thank God he didn't have to try and assume a vertical position. The sounds of multiple footsteps, the door closing, and banter-y conversation came from his front entryway.

Dylan's voice drifted in from the foyer. "Why do you have a key to Noah's condo, anyway?"

Memphis's voice came next. "He gave it to me so I could practice making Tyler's birthday dinner here."

"You practiced?" Tyler asked, sounding surprised.

"A little, yeah," came his boyfriend's answer.

The three men entered the living room, and Noah resisted the urge to cover his eyes with his hand, both relieved and horrified they were here. His friends settled into various seats around the room, Dylan on the other end of the couch. Right at Noah's feet.

Several tense seconds ticked by as three sets of eyes bored into his skin.

"Where the hell have you been?" Dylan asked.

"I've been here." How could he move? His muscles lax and loose and warm from the alcohol, his limbs had become anchors. Kind of like after mind-blowing, life-altering sex with Ky but not nearly as nice. "Here in the condo contemplating the meaning of life."

Or the fact that he didn't have one.

"Dude," Dylan said, the word strained with worried doubt. "Are you okay?"

"I'm fine."

"Fine," his friend repeated, voice flat and unbelieving.

"Of course," Noah said, attempting a smile. "As long as you define *fine* as Fucked-up, Insecure, Neurotic, and Emotional."

The awkward pause that followed stretched on forever. In their band of dysfunctional friends, when one of them went off the deep end, Noah usually took the lead in these little brotherly interventions. Clearly he needed to train a successor, because no one else appeared capable of filling the role that normally fell to him. Another not-job to add to his rather impressive nonexistent resume.

Clearly the boys were searching for the right thing to say.

Noah took pity on them and provided them with a reprieve. "Your boyfriend was in my kitchen every week for six weeks, practicing your birthday dinner."

"Really?" Tyler shifted on the love seat, twisting to face Memphis.

Noah would rather let this particular discussion take place around him than address why he was currently holed up in his home, wallowing on his couch. Hiding from the world.

Like the big freaking indecisive coward he was.

Two beats passed without a response before Tyler went on. "Memphis," he said slowly.

"Yeah?"

"You know you don't have to work so hard to make me happy."

"I want to." The stuntman leaned forward and tossed his key onto the coffee table with a faint *tinkle* of metal on glass. "After all you went through, you deserve it."

"Look..." Tyler swiped a frustrated hand through his black hair. "I definitely wouldn't choose to relive the first year after you left, because college sucked after that. But I don't have—" He frowned and rested his arm along the back of the love seat, a thoughtful look on his face. "As painful as it sometimes was, I wouldn't change a thing. Ultimately, everything I went through brought me to this point in my life." He waved a hand that encompassed the room but obviously meant so much more. "Led to my choice of occupation, my current job. Even my friends."

"Who were worth the suffering alone," Noah said, cringing at the wrecked quality of his voice.

But Tyler, bless him, didn't comment on his horrible attempt at changing the subject or lightening the tension. Or how raspy and thin his words had come out.

Instead the man's mouth curled into an easy smile. "Exactly." Tyler turned his gaze back to his boyfriend. "I like where I ended up." He sent Memphis a level look and linked their fingers together. "I don't regret a thing. So, please, do nice things for me if you want. But don't do them because you think you owe me."

Memphis blinked, his expression easing. "Okay," he said with a small grin.

Which Noah could stomach just fine, until the stuntman leaned forward to give Tyler a kiss.

A groan escaped Noah's mouth. "Oh, my God," he said, and he wasn't too proud to admit the words came out a whimper. "You all suck at interventions. And you two, Christamighty, you're so fuck-eyed for each other. Can you please take your smoochy faces somewhere else?"

Guilt washed over the two men's expressions.

Tyler was the one who spoke first. "I'm sorry," he said. "I shouldn't have—"

"No," Noah said, feeling like crap. What kind of terrible friend was he? "You should have." He covered his eyes with his hand again, because the darkness helped with his thudding headache, even if the spinning got worse. "It's okay."

But they didn't understand. How could they understand? They were just so...so...happy. And he was glad that all his friends were happy. Seriously, he definitely *wanted* them to be happy. But being around so much happy when he was so *un*happy...well, that just made everything worse.

Because he desperately wanted to be happy, too, dammit. But he wasn't sure he knew how anymore.

Fuck, all of this silent rambling was making his head hurt worse.

"We've been trying to reach you for the last twenty-four hours," Dylan said. "You scared the shit out of everybody. I called Ky and he said you two had had a bit of a falling-out." The man stared at Noah with concern. "What the hell happened?"

Two beats passed before he could give an answer. The *real* answer that it was well past time to share. "It's my fault."

"Noah," Dylan groaned with a wince. "Did you blow one of his ranch hands or something?"

"They don't have any ranch hands."

"Did you purposely try to offend the locals?"

"No." And then he remembered the three assholes in the dive bar. "At least, not all of them."

"Well, whatever you did in Texas can be fixed."

"I'm not talking about that." Noah swallowed and forced himself to go on. "It's my fault that Rick died."

The silence in the room became oppressive, the air in the condo thick. Memphis's and Tyler's expressions froze, as if they sensed an impending storm and wanted to flee but were too good of a friend to bolt and leave Noah to his well-deserved fate.

Good men, both. Even if they were fuck-eyed for each other.

Noah ignored them, studying his oldest friend instead. His *best* friend...but not for long.

Dylan's face screwed up into a look of confusion. "He died of a complication from his HIV infection. How is that your fault?"

"He hated that county hospital." Noah felt a pressing need to explain. To justify his actions. "He was miserable."

A painful pause followed.

"Jesus, this isn't news," Dylan finally mumbled, his voice pinched. He slumped forward to rest his elbows on his knees, looking tired. "I was there, too. Remember?"

"Those last few weeks were *torture* for him—"

"I know," Dylan said with a faint frown.

"And we wanted to help—"

"I *know*."

"No, you *don't* know." Noah's tongue felt thick and the words sharp, desperate. He couldn't look at his friend as he plowed on. "All I wanted to do was make things better for him, and, *Christ*, I would have given anything to make it better. But neither one of us could do shit about anything, and he was in so much pain"—he pressed his palms to his eyes as words started tumbling out too fast—"and they had him on that stupid, stupid morphine pump. But it wasn't enough. The doctor knew he'd been hooking for a living. And everyone who hooks for a living must be a drug seeker, right?" His laugh sounded bitter, and he shifted his gaze to the wall, wiping a sweaty hand down his jeans. "They wouldn't give him any more... It wasn't enough. It wasn't *enough*. And so he..."

The wall of silence felt too big to climb.

For the first time, Dylan's tone sounded guarded. "He what?"

Noah forced himself to meet his gaze. "He asked me to bring him the pain pills he had left at home," he said. "The bottle they'd prescribed just before they'd admitted him."

Dylan's breathing hitched. It was easy to pinpoint the exact moment he put the words together into a coherent whole.

And then Dylan blinked, the words rough. "He took them?" he asked, his voice growing hoarse. "All of them? On *purpose*?"

"Yes." Noah closed his eyes, and the dizziness increased, his head swirling from a mix of pain and tequila and memories that haunted him every night of his life. He could almost smell the fire and brimstone from here and...

Jesus, he deserved the nickname Mr. Melodramatic.

"You couldn't have known—" Tyler began, only to be stopped by the sound that escaped Noah.

It started out as a bitter snort and ended on an embarrassingly dismal noise resembling a laughing sob. A sobbing laugh?

Maybe more like a horrible squeak.

"I knew," Noah said, staring up at the ceiling. "He never said anything specific, but deep down a part of me knew."

And if Rick had clearly articulated his intentions out loud, would Noah have told him no? Or would he have made the same choice? Or would he have pushed for a better alternative?

Shit, he was tired. So goddamn tired.

"Why are you just getting around to telling me this now?" Dylan said, his face pale.

Tyler and Memphis exchanged a look, the kind that communicated whole conversations without any words, and Noah...

Seriously, Noah wanted that with someone, too. He'd had it with Rick. He'd had it with Ky as well, almost from the get-go. Like the *just do as I say* and the *fine, fine, you big ridiculously handsome guy* he'd given in answer during their friendly showdown at the Humane Society Gala. Although, later Ky had admitted he'd thought Noah had been making a sexually suggestive gesture.

Couldn't fault the guy for the assumption.

Ugh. He was mentally rambling again.

He closed his eyes and ignored the alcohol-induced spinning sensation for a moment, the odd feeling of being too light and too heavy at the same time, until he felt the couch shift. When Noah lifted his lids, Tyler now stood, looking down at him with understanding in his gaze as he tugged Dylan up by his arm.

"Come on, let's call it a night," Tyler said to the mechanic. "Everyone's tired. This isn't the time for this particular discussion. I'll take you home, Dylan." His gray gaze landed back on Memphis, eyes purposefully wide with a silent request, and the man sent him a nod in return.

"I'll stay here," the stuntman said.

Noah sighed and tried to give a flippant wave that came out less than convincing. "I don't need a babysitter, boys."

A muzzle maybe but not a babysitter.

Noah leaned his head back against the couch and focused on the footsteps and the murmuring voices of the two men as they left. At least his friend hadn't yelled at him. But the stunned look on Dylan's face wouldn't last long. Eventually he'd process the news, and he would either forgive Noah or never speak to him ever again.

By the end of all this, Noah might lose both a sort-of boyfriend *and* a best friend.

Damn.

Impressive job, self. Impressive job. Imagine all you could have accomplished if you'd actually intended to fuck things up.

Memphis had disappeared into the kitchen. Noah listened to the man's movements—a cabinet door opening and closing, the whir of the burr grinder—grateful for the brief break from having to put on an *I'm a functional human being* face.

Several minutes later the rich smell of freshly brewed coffee drifted into the living room. His friend returned and crossed the carpet, setting a mug on the side table with the muted *clink* of ceramic on glass.

"This will help," Memphis said.

"Hunh," he murmured, struggling to assume a sitting position. "Thanks. But while I appreciate the gesture, I don't think caffeine is going to fix my problems, hotshot." Noah reached for the coffee and sent him a weak smile. "I screwed up, more so than usual."

On so many levels.

He sipped the strong brew, and the hazelnut reminded him of almonds. Which reminded him of Ky. Which probably brought a woeful expression to his face, if the wobbly feel of his facial muscles were anything to go by.

This lovesick, preteen girly phase was really unpleasant.

Memphis hummed in sympathy. "I royally effed things up with Tyler," he said, ruffling his sandy-colored hair. "And then let ten years pass before I did anything about it. And promptly screwed them up *again* before they got fixed."

Noah let out another snort. "I don't want to get into a Who's The Bigger Dick contest with you. I'm too afraid I'll win. Besides, you and Tyler are so sickeningly happy you should come with your own anti-nausea medication dispenser."

"Yeah, well," he said as he collapsed into the seat beside Noah. "It took us two forevers and a day to get to this point."

Noah contemplated the words. Tyler hadn't seemed to care how things had gone down. Having Memphis back made him happy. Obviously the man had decided that letting the past go and embracing today, letting Memphis back in, was well worth the effort.

And then some.

Avoiding the conversation they needed to have, Noah asked, "How did the vegan lasagna turn out, anyway?"

A grin crept up the stuntman's face. "I got the process down pat." He shifted, nestling into the far corner of the couch and facing Noah. "It almost tasted like real food."

"So the birthday surprise was a success." A smile tugged at Noah's mouth. "Is there an engagement on the horizon?"

"Maybe."

"Will your lovely ex-wife stand up as best wo-man at the wedding?"

"Possibly," he said, grin growing bigger.

And then the words fell out of Noah's mouth, unchecked. "He's not going to forgive me."

To his credit, Memphis didn't even blink at the abrupt change in topic to Dylan. Instead he sent him an appraising look and remained silent for a moment.

"I think he will," Memphis finally said.

"Well..." He dropped his gaze to his mug of coffee. "Many people wouldn't."

A loud scoff broke from the stuntman's throat. "One thing you can be guaranteed of in life, people will have opinions." He leaned forward, and the earnest expression on his face almost hurt. "Listen, I've been through three cancer diagnoses. I've fought the fight. I've faced death a time or two." His lips twisted into a wry smirk. "Or three."

"You face death every time you go to work," Noah said dryly.

"Being a stuntman is nothing." A quirky grin briefly flickered across his mouth. But the smile slowly faded as his expression grew serious. "I've literally died on a hospital bed and come back, Noah. And one thing I've learned, those who haven't experienced what you've suffered through? All those people who think they know what they'd do if they'd been in your shoes?" His hazel eyes glowed with the kind of conviction only years of up-close-and-personal time with the grim reaper could bring. "They don't know shit. They don't have a *clue*."

Memphis set his coffee on the table with a careful movement as Noah considered the man's words. He'd never wish those kinds of experiences on anyone. But right now he was grateful for the newest friend in his life.

"No one knows what they'll do in any given situation," Memphis said in a subdued voice, eyes unfocused, as if watching something from a great distance. "They'd like to think that they do, but that's bullshit. Because it's easy to pass judgment on a hypothetical. It's hard to actually be faced with the reality. To be forced to make the difficult decisions. Everyone else?" He shook his head as though he'd been through this kind of conversation a thousand times before—given his history, Noah wouldn't doubt it—and met his gaze again. "Everyone else is just passing judgment, man."

Noah eased deeper into the cushions and stared back up at the ceiling—at this rate, he really should get a fresco painted up there. Maybe a naked portrait of a man. Preferably of Ky.

Ky...

"What would you have done?" Noah asked.

He kept his gaze firmly on the ceiling and waited for the answer, fear and hope dueling for the right to reign supreme.

"I don't have a clue," Memphis said with a certainty that Noah didn't doubt.

As much as he craved to hear a different answer, he appreciated the honesty, because so far he hadn't had the decency to be honest with himself.

Memphis reached out and laid a hand on Noah's foot. "But after going three rounds in the ring with the big CA, let me tell you what I *do* know," he said. "I know what it's like to be too weak to lift a glass to your lips. I know about being sick and in pain, every breath an agony." His voice grew rough and raw. "And I sure as hell know how it feels to want it all to end. But here's the thing." He cocked his head. "I also know with one hundred percent certainty that you did what Rick wanted with the best of intentions. And if that doesn't define love, I don't know what does."

Noah's eyes burned.

"In the end, that's all anyone can ask of themselves," his friend said with a shrug. "Give Dylan time to adjust to the news." The stuntman gave one last squeeze of Noah's foot before letting go. "Have some faith in your friends and"—Memphis sent him a side-eyed look—"the people who are more than friends."

Noah groaned and leaned his head back against the couch, the remains of the alcohol and the coffee warming his veins. He could only tolerate so much torture in one day. Worrying about Dylan's reaction, although difficult, seemed easier than worrying about Ky.

So what now?

He'd learned to survive and thrive, of a sort, but only in the shallowest of worlds. And there was so much he needed to do to make things right. Noah had a sneaking suspicion he knew how he had to start. The first step he needed to take.

But it wasn't going to be easy.

Chapter Sixteen

"A bloody Mary, please," Noah said, raising his voice to be heard over the music. "*Without* the vodka."

Toby, the blond waiter, narrowed his kohl-lined eyes in a *WTF?* expression while the loud *thump, thump, thump* of a dance-music mashup song filled the night club. Times of Crisis should have been named Cliché, what with its dark leather furniture, LED-lit dance floor flashing in time with the beat, and the half-naked—or might-as-well-be naked, in some cases—sweating, gyrating bodies of mostly gay men.

This used to be all Noah needed, used to feel like a second home. Which made the establishment the perfect place to test his new resolve. Unfortunately, without a good buzz, all he could focus on was the surprisingly tacky leather bench seat beneath his ass while amusing himself with images of the place redone in cowhide.

"No alcohol at all?" Toby said. "Sugar, you sure you don't want the real thing?"

"No vodka," he forced himself to repeat.

"But...that's just spicy tomato juice."

"No," he said stubbornly, "I want a virgin bloody Mary."

Toby squinted down at him in doubt. "What's the difference?"

Noah frowned, briefly stumped by the question. "One is a breakfast drink and the other is..." for pathetic people who'd spent far too much time using alcohol as a crutch—or a motorized wheelchair, in

Noah's case. "The other is a festive nonalcoholic celebration of life."

Or something like that.

The bleached-blond twink shrugged in a *whatever* gesture and headed off to fill the order. Noah should have known that Step One in addressing his heinous problems was gonna be a doozy. Facing his issues, sans alcohol, had to be his most ridiculous idea yet. Which was pretty impressive seeing how he once thought line dancing at a country-western bar would be the answer.

Surprisingly fun, yes. A method for solving his problems?

Uh...that would be a big fat no.

The waiter returned and set the glass on the table in front of Noah. "Let me know if you change your mind. You look like you need the real deal. Whatever your man problems are," Toby went on, smoothing long fingers down pants so tight he looked as though he'd been dipped in denim paint, "vodka can make it better."

Yes, but using a good buzz to dull the pain hadn't been helping him heal. Ky hadn't said a thing, and neither had any of Noah's friends. This was one realization he'd come to all by himself. Instead of medicating himself, the only way to get past the pain was to plow through it.

To *feel* it.

So....no more alcohol until he declared himself better. Which, unfortunately, could take a very long time. He wasn't holding out hope that Ky would be waiting around as a reward for doing what he should have done ages ago.

Ohmygod, my life is going to suck from here on out.

Noah took a sip of his soulless bloody Mary. The spicy tomato drink looked bright and colorful and deceptively real but failed to provide the necessary dulling of the senses needed as he pictured Ky's face.

Someone dropped into the seat next to him, and Noah turned to tell the newcomer he wasn't interested in hooking up—

He spied sandy-colored hair and green eyes studying him seriously, and Noah's stomach hit the floor.

Dylan.

"I shouldn't have mentioned to Alec where I was going tonight," Noah groaned.

He hadn't spoken to Dylan since the little confession to end all confessions several days ago. Noah needed...he needed so many things, one of which was to avoid hearing how his best friend felt about him now. Especially tonight. Tonight was all about testing his new resolve to forgo the Dutch courage—wait, that sounded awfully offensive, almost racist—forgoing the *liquid* courage. Facing Dylan at the same time would require more than Noah could stand.

Did he hate him now? Was he gonna give him a piece of his mind? Or a warm and fuzzy healing hug? Not likely.

Little information was forthcoming.

Full beer mug clutched in one hand, Dylan reached over to fix the collar of Noah's shirt. "You look like hell," he said with a frown.

The tension in Noah's gut ratcheted up several degrees. "What a surprise. I feel like hell, too," he said with a smile that constituted a total fail. "Must be the lack of alcohol."

Seriously, there had to be an easier way to earn back some Jesus points.

"Yeah, well," his friend went on, his gaze drifting to the dance floor, "we need to talk..."

Shit.

Alec appeared beside the booth, and his obvious attempt at a reassuring look didn't bode well for fun times ahead.

Noah groaned. "Seriously, guys? I can't do this sober." He tried to frown at his friends but probably just wound up looking desperate. "And why are you crashing my night out? I thought you had a child to raise. Shouldn't you two be somewhere else?"

Can't we discuss the reasons to hate me later?

Can't we tour the devastating remains of my not-love life another time?

Alec slid into the booth next to Dylan. His friends had learned Noah's total disregard for proper boundaries so he was forced to shift to accommodate them in the semi-circular booth.

"Yes, we have a child to raise. But tonight," Alec said with a smile, "is date night." He twisted in his seat to lean back against Dylan's chest and link their fingers together in a blatant portrayal of monogamous bliss.

Great. Spending the evening proving he could abstain from alcohol was only proving that alcohol might have become a necessary component of his personality.

And his ability to function.

"Is that it?" Noah asked as they stared at him in confusion. "Is that your plan to talk some sense in to me?"

Alec shrugged. "Maybe we've decided to lead by example."

"Well, you've wasted the babysitting fee, then." He glared at the red mixture in his glass as though his steely stare could magically instill it with numbing powers if not necessarily the vodka itself.

Because Dylan still looked far too serious and Alec appeared to be working too hard to ease the tension.

"No fee paying required," Alec said. "Savannah begged to babysit Rick for the night. She takes her auntie duties seriously."

The little bit of news about Ky's family felt inadequate. "And Sierra?"

And her brother? a voice inside his head asked. *How is her brother?*

"Sierra will be in town for a visit next month," Alec said. "And she Skypes about once a week to read Rick a story."

"Isn't he a little young for that?"

"Maybe," Alec said. "But her skill with animal noises while reading *Where The Wild Things Are* is pretty impressive."

"That doesn't surprise me at all." Noah rolled his eyes. "If your son inherited even a tenth of Sierra's willfulness, you two realize the teenage years are going to be hell, right?"

Alec simply laughed at the statement. "The good news?" He glanced at his partner. "We'll outnumber him."

The two men shared a warm smile, and Noah stopped pretending to be functional friend for a moment, suddenly too tired for the effort. He listlessly stirred his virgin bloody Mary that was about as exciting as...well, as a breakfast drink.

Tyler appeared, leading Memphis by the hand, and Noah groaned even louder. The two sat at the other end of the round booth, the men shifting to the left to make room, until Noah was firmly sandwiched between the two couples.

Trapped, Noah felt his insides crumple a little. There wasn't enough tomato juice in the world for this.

"Is this a surprise party?" he asked.

"A stealth intervention," Memphis said.

"Another one?" Noah moaned. He slowly lowered his head until his forehead rested against the table, where the lingering smell of alcohol was strong—so close and yet so far.... "I hope you guys have improved your technique."

"Remember back when I had my stubborn head firmly fixed up my ass?" Dylan asked.

Noah's breath stalled in his throat. It was the first time the man had spoken since the ominous *we need to talk* statement.

"Head up your ass?" Tyler asked with a grin for the mechanic. "Which time would that be?"

Dylan shot him a middle finger with an amused smirk that spoke of a friendship that had taken a long time and several frank conversations for the two men to achieve. The kind of amused smirk he used to send Noah all the time.

Maybe Tyler had taken Noah's place as BFF?

"Actually," Alec said, his voice turning serious, "we came tonight to discuss the godfather thing."

Godfather...to Rick's namesake.

Silence fell across the group, which only made the techno music feel louder. Alec's gaze flitted over to Dylan's, and they engaged in a conversation using only their eyes. Alec looked like he wanted his partner to say something, but the man turned his uncomfortable glare down at his beer.

Shit.

"I didn't think... I figured you..." Noah studied his half-finished tomato juice and rubbed the condensation on the glass before downing the rest.

He closed his eyes and willed his muscles to relax, if only for a bit.

Someone coughed and shifted in the booth, and Noah lifted his gaze.

Now standing, Alec picked up his mostly full mug of beer. "I'm going to get a refill." He nodded at Memphis and Tyler before taking off for the bar, the two men following dutifully behind.

The unhappy look on Dylan's face after being abandoned didn't ease any of the tension in Noah's body. As the three guys wandered away, they left the best friends alone and a stilted atmosphere in their wake.

"I know you're—" Noah cleared his throat, hoping he'd sound less hoarse when he tried to speak again. "I don't blame you for being mad at me for what I did."

"Nope," he said with a shake of his head. "No. I'm mad that I was kept out of the loop." An uncomfortable pause followed. "Dammit, Noah." Dylan dropped his fist to the table with a determined thump that made his mug jump slightly on the table, sloshing beer over the top. Ignoring the mess, he leaned forward, green eyes intense. "You should have told me what was going on."

"It didn't seem important at the time."

"That's bullshit and you know it."

"Rick asked me to protect you."

"I don't understand *why*."

The words tumbled forcefully from Noah's mouth. "Because he didn't think you could handle it!"

Dylan blinked several times, the rest of his body frozen, before coming back to life, an arm flailing out to his side in a frustrated gesture. "Who the hell can handle shit like that?" he asked. "No one should ever *have* to." He dropped his hand back to the table and waited a moment before going on. "Do you think you've handled it?"

Techno dance music thumped around them as Noah felt obligated to reply, and the only response possible slipped from his mouth. "Fuck."

He planted his elbows on the sticky table, ignoring the risk to his button-down shirt and the urge to desperately lick the traces of alcohol from the Formica. Even a little might ease a fraction of the tension in his muscles.

"'Cause I don't know, man," Dylan went on with an unhappy twist of his lips, "but I think you're almost as miserable now as when Rick died. So how the hell does this"—he gestured down Noah's slumped body, clearly indicating his miserable state—"qualify as handling it?"

After examining the situation from every angle, Noah still didn't have any answer.

Dylan reached across the table and gripped Noah's sleeve, as if his life depended on holding on. "Dude," he said, his voice rough. "You know I love you, right?"

The tightness in Noah's heart eased, and he gave a relieved nod.

"Damn straight." His friend slowly relaxed his grip, releasing the shirt now pulled off center. "And I'm telling you that you *have* to let what happened with Rick go," Dylan said, adjusting Noah's collar again. "If you can't do it for yourself, then do it for me. Because I gotta tell you, it hurts like a bitch to see you like this."

Noah stared down at the tabletop and blinked until his vision cleared. His friend didn't hate him. He was *worried*. Suddenly, breathing got a little easier.

Despite the reprieve, he kept torturing himself by asking the same question.

"Back then," Noah said, "what would you have done?"

"I honestly don't know what the fuck I would have told Rick if he'd asked me first."

Oh, for the love of God, more honesty. Why did none of his friends have the decency to lie?

Dylan's gaze landed back on him. "But I *should* have been given the option to know what the hell was going on. If only to keep you from going through this alone."

Originally, Noah had thought time would take care of the problem. But ignoring his issues had led him to make bad decisions, which in turn had led to an assault. He knew he'd feel the weight of those choices every day for the rest of his life. Those moments would never go away, would always be a lodestone around his neck. The question now was, was he going to let them continue to drown him or finally learn how to be a stronger swimmer?

"What now?" Noah asked.

"Well," he said, leaning back against the bench. Three heartbeats later, he went on. "I'd like to start with you saying yes to being Rick's godfather."

Noah briefly dropped his gaze, picking at the seam in the leather seat. "Maybe that shouldn't be an option anymore."

"Come on, man." He braced his forearms on the table, his eyes burning with intent. "Of course it is."

The pause grew unbearable. Dylan pursed his lips as though considering what to say next.

"Remember our conversation after I fell for Alec?" Dylan asked.

"I believe you accused me of being a walking, talking, lying sack of shit."

"Yeah, because you insisted your hookup habits weren't a sign of a larger problem," he said dryly. Two loaded moments passed before he went on. "And then you said...?" He cocked his head with a *go on* expression, like Noah was intentionally being obtuse.

"I know. I *know.*" Noah's lips quirked into a bittersweet grin. "I told you if I ever fell in love again, you could rub the news in my face."

"And this is me," he said, leaning closer with a tiny smirk on his lips, understanding and affection in his gaze, "rubbing the news in your face."

Noah rolled his eyes, and then his sarcastic expression kind of fell apart. Suddenly he couldn't pretend to not miss Ky or to ignore the profound ache that now lived just beneath his breastbone. The hollow feeling that gnawed at him and left him too sad to pull off a breezy attitude for extended periods of time.

He was definitely losing his touch.

"Ky thinks I need help. *Professional* help. " He buried his fingers in his hair, ignoring the way his sticky fingers stuck to the strands, the sharp pull as he massaged his scalp. "But I don't even know where to start."

"My suggestion? Realize Rick would have wanted you to be happy," he said. Noah refused to look up, and his friend gently gripped Noah's arm as he went on. "You know I hate talking about feelings and shit, but I think Ky is right. You should see a counselor like he suggested."

The thought of opening all that up again, of sharing everything with a *stranger...*

"Dude." His friend squeezed Noah's wrist in a reassuring gesture before letting go. "I'll take you there. I'll even go to the session with you if that will make things easier." He let go and licked spilt beer from the back of his hand. "Or just wait in the waiting room with you and make faces behind the secretary's back."

Noah's laugh sounded weak. "You'd do that for me?"

"Of course," he said with a smile. And then his face lost all trace of teasing humor, his voice firm. "Whatever you want, man," Dylan said. "Whatever it takes."

Noah closed his eyes, feeling hopeless and hopeful at the same time.

~~~***~~~

Three long, lonely weeks after his ultimatum to Noah, Ky stood behind the small makeshift bar in the rapidly filling aquarium hall and stared down at the Bachelor Bid program, where *Dr. Kyland Davis* had been listed under the "Gloriously Gay" column.

A small smile crossed his lips. Clearly someone had lost their mind and allowed Noah to name the categories. Ky was most definitely gay. Glorious? Heck no. Nervous as fuck?

Absolutely.

The sight of his name next to his orientation left him feeling fiercely proud, profoundly liberated, and scared as shit, all at the same time. Coming out wasn't something he'd devoted too much thought to. Dwelling on the "maybe someday" would've only left him frustrated—he'd accepted the event would take place in the future, when the truth wouldn't be such a divisive issue between Sierra and her father, protecting his family as he'd been taught. And maybe Ky would've celebrated the momentous occasion by hitting a club. Or joining a dating website.

But, Jesus, something less high-profile than tonight would have been easier.

All of which probably meant he wasn't quite as self-actualized as he thought. Yep, it always seemed as though, just when he believed his travels were done, he had one more step to take on this journey of self-acceptance.

Integrating his public life with his private felt like a formidable task.

In cocktail-party apparel, people continued to file into the nearly packed room, and Ky's lips twitched, straining at the edges. No matter what happened, he vowed to keep, at minimum, a hint of a confident smile firmly fixed on his face. Even if at times he had to fake one. After everything he'd gone through to get to this moment, even if the moment was *vastly* different than he'd envisioned, anything less would be...well, would be letting his fifteen-year-old self down.

Which meant pulling tonight off with dignity.

Then again, dignity seemed a lofty goal while participating in a *bachelor bid*, the very name calling to mind a not-so-serious air.

Christ.

Ky rolled his shoulders, trying to relax, but the unfamiliar feel of a jacket didn't help. At the last minute, he'd decided to purchase the gray suit Noah had drooled over in the store. A rush tailoring job and...here Ky was. He felt like a fucking idiot. He still couldn't decide whether the decision was an inspired idea.

Or not.

A familiar female voice came from behind. "There you are."

Ky spun around, met Savannah's gaze over the bar, and his heart stalled.

She tugged on the tiny lacy jacket of her black cocktail dress. "How are you holding up?"

"As well as can be expected."

Which meant puking felt like a definite possibility.

"Especially given the size of the crowd," he went on.

Hardly the place for a frank conversation.

Between her schedule leading up to tonight and his insane work hours, they'd only had time for *one* heart-to-heart chat since his return from Texas. A chat that had consisted of her concerns about Sierra's dreams going up in smoke and Savannah's guilt over Ray's treatment of Ky, which was seriously misplaced.

Watching his sisters struggle with their misguided obligation toward their brother only highlighted how counterproductive his own actions had been.

He suspected the twins had privately discussed his relationship with Noah, but so far Savannah's opinions about her brother's orientation hadn't come up. And Ky hadn't pushed the issue because that discussion would inevitably lead to one about Noah.

And Ky's heart still ached too much for a calm conversation.

"I know how you feel," she said with a nervous glance around. "This place is packed,"

Damn, how could he be so dense? He wasn't the only one worried about tonight.

The life-long need to protect had him reaching across the bar to touch her arm. "Well done, kiddo." He sent his baby sister a smile he didn't have to force. "Not only is the room packed"—which was great, really, except for the mother-frickin' size of the crowd—"I saw the mayor."

Savannah's cheeks flushed. "Memphis Haines's very successful ad campaign made this the place to be."

"Maybe." He took in the meticulously decorated aquarium as a wave of pride warmed his chest. "But *you* did a spectacular job."

"You think so?"

"I *know* so."

His sister's hard work showed in every detail. White lights lit the potted palms placed between the portable bars lining the walls. White tablecloths covered the tables. On the far end of the room, the shark tank, with its deep blues and greens of a simulated coral reef, provided a striking backdrop for the raised stage and—

"Fuck, a catwalk." Ky stared at the long strip of well-lit platform jutting into the sea of tables. He'd been too preoccupied to notice it before. He glanced at his sister. "No one mentioned I'd have to walk down a runway," he said dryly.

"We didn't tell anyone."

"Afraid participants would drop out?"

"We decided we couldn't risk the bottom line," she said with a tiny grin.

We, as in Savannah and *Noah*. And, yeah, eventually Ky would run into his former fake boyfriend for the first time since he'd told the man to get psychiatric help.

Damn, that almost sounded as bad in his head as living through the reality.

Ky's stomach gave a less-than-dignified roll, but he pushed the worries aside. "I don't think the bottom line is gonna suffer, Savannah." He dropped his gaze back to the program. "Y'all convinced some pretty impressive bachelors to participate."

A local TV celebrity was up for bid, listed under the "Strictly Straight" category, and a city council member, too—a self-proclaimed bisexual if his "Sold, to the Highest Bidder!" designation was anything to go by. Three of the participants were among the area's most prominent businessmen.

Toes feeling pinched, he shifted on his feet and frowned. Maybe he should have nixed the new boots and gone with more traditional footwear.

"Ky?" Savannah said, and he forced himself to focus on her face. "Are you sure you don't want to change into the other outfit? I brought it along in my car, just in case."

He felt like an idiot. But the last time he'd seen Noah, the man had looked gutted by the insistence he needed counseling. The suit Noah had lobbied hard for was worth a little suffering, if nothing else just so Ky could see him smile again.

And sweet heaven above, when had he gotten so pathetic?

"The suit is fabulous," she said. "But something needs to give, because your expression—"

She winced and stared up at him with growing concern.

Hoping to breathe easier, he tugged at his collar, already open at the neck and minus a tie. "I feel stupid," he muttered. Stupid and exposed and woefully not up to tonight's task. "But..." he finished with a lame shrug.

Savannah shot him a smile. "If it's any consolation, you look amazing." Her eyes briefly dropped to the brochure in his hand. "Definitely *glorious*."

The program crinkled a little under his grip.

When she cleared her throat, he braced himself. No denying where this conversation was headed.

She reached out to smooth a hand down his two-button jacket. "Noah is going to suffer a nuclear meltdown when he sees you in this thing."

"Maybe."

"You really like him, don't you?"

"Yeah," he drawled, although the description didn't come close.

Not that it mattered. Ky was beginning to accept the man might be too broken to fix in the ways that really counted.

He pushed the depressing thought away before meeting his sister's gaze. "Is me, uhm, liking him a problem for you?"

The tiny pause felt like a lifetime.

"Are you serious?" She punched him lightly on the arm. "Of course not, you big goof."

"Ow," he said lightly, the sick feeling in his stomach easing a bit. "Seriously, though, I'm sorry I didn't tell you and Sierra sooner."

"You should be. At least I can give Lisa a reason for your pathetic 'it's not you, it's me' speech after the blind date. And I should have listened to Sierra's warnings about setting you up," Savannah said with a sigh. "She and I have been arguing about this subject for years."

"She told me."

"Yeah? Well, I didn't think we needed to ask because I *assumed* my brother would tell me something so important." She crossed her arms in silent reprimand.

Her short, blond hair was growing out, and her dress showed way more cleavage than he preferred. And while he'd always have the urge to throw a coat over his sisters' shoulders, to keep them from looking like the grown women they'd become, he'd never been happier she was more like her old, confident self.

Even though she still had a ways to go.

Maybe *everyone's* life was just one journey step after another toward self-actualization, no matter their issues.

Ky pressed his lips together. "Dealing with you two as adults has been, well—" Hoping to decrease the amount of exposed skin, he pulled the front of her slinky jacket farther over the spaghetti straps of a dress that, ugh, almost looked like a nightgown. "I'd say *an adjustment*, but that sounds a mite too optimistic."

Her sage-green eyes twinkled. "How about we call it a work in progress?"

"Sounds about right."

"I have faith in my big brother."

He exhaled sharply through his nose, the sound more in amusement than disagreement. "I'm afraid your faith might be misplaced. But how 'bout this? I'll agree to stop being too protective if you agree to stop letting your lousy ex-boyfriend keep you from living a full life." He glanced at her dress. "And I mean more than just your wardrobe."

Savannah's gaze drifted to his left as she seemed to give his words some consideration.

"You having the courage to come out, despite all that Daddy did—" She pressed her lips together before going on. "Well...suffice it to say you've inspired me to *not* let past fears ruin my future."

"*Good.*"

Although the relief surging through him came riddled with worries about his sister dating again, he'd learn to adjust. Best just to focus on a logistical question he had about tonight's event. "Did you make the changes like I asked?"

"I can't believe you're really going through with this, Ky."

"Me, either."

"But, yes," she said with an amused smirk, "I made the changes."

A strange mix of dread and anticipation curled beneath his sternum, the pressure on his heart making each beat painful.

Which wasn't the suit's fault. Mostly.

But maybe he should reconsider his *second* last-minute decision about tonight—

"Time for the meet-and-greet," Savannah said.

Oh, shit.

"Good luck." A teasing smile full of affection lit her face. "You'll charm every man within a twenty-mile radius."

Savannah leaned over the bar to kiss his cheek. The steadfast fondness in the familiar gesture almost hurt, and he blew out the last breath he'd been holding since he'd realized he was gay. He watched her walk away, proud and a little bit humbled. Until he realized she'd abandoned him to the first part of the evening's festivities.

God save him.

Ky was positive the bartender meet-and-greet idea belonged to Noah and Noah alone. Who else would request that their contestants choose a signature drink to prepare for potential bidders? As far as icebreakers went, the idea was inspired. Too bad Ky sucked at small talk.

Even more difficult, he'd spent his entire life pretending *not* to be attracted to men. And, fuck, breaking free of old habits was gonna be harder than he'd originally thought.

Ky's palms began to sweat when his first "customer" arrived.

He spent the next thirty minutes using his Leatherman multi-tool keychain to pry the caps off bottles of beer—his version of mixing a drink—and handing out his choice of beverage. All the while answering a million and one questions from the guests. But every time he opened his mouth, Ky's words felt wooden. Getting his flirting mojo on wasn't happening.

In fact, the confident smile got harder and harder to maintain.

A brief lull in the line finally arrived, and Ky blew out a breath, discreetly checking his watch and praying the end would come soon. Then again, his next job would entail strolling down a catwalk...

He grabbed another beer from the refrigerator and was contemplating downing one himself when he heard a delicate cough from behind. Bracing himself for the next encounter, he turned.

From across the bar counter, a tall blond greeted him. "Logan Chase," he said as he held out his hand.

"Nice to meet you." Ky returned the shake, opened the bottle with a hissing *pop*, and passed him the drink, hoping his nerves didn't show.

"A beer guy, huh?" A charming set of dimples appeared as the man nodded at the contestant manning the bar next to the eel tank. "The line for the city council guy looks long, but choosing the Ramos Gin Fizz as his signature drink? Way too complicated. That cocktail shaker is really getting a workout."

"Yep, his elbow is gonna hate him tomorrow."

The man lifted his bottle in a toast before taking a swig. "You're definitely my kind of date."

Hunh, hard not to feel flattered, especially from such an attractive guy.

This is where you're supposed participate with your words, Ky.

He cleared his throat, mind sifting through potential conversation starters. "What do you do?" he asked. "When you're not bidding on dates, that is."

An amused smile lit Logan's face. "I make films, documentaries mostly."

"Cool," he replied, the word out before he had a chance to think too hard about his response. "Anything I would have seen?"

"Maybe." He took another sip of his beer. "Ever heard of *Heroin and HIV: An Epidemic Comes to the Heartland*?"

Ky's eyebrows rose. "The one that won several awards and has been nominated for an Oscar?" he asked. When the man nodded, he added, "That's impressive."

Logan shrugged off the praise. "Not as impressive as saving a life with a scalpel."

"It has its moments." He studied the man's blue eyes, the wholesome good looks seemingly straight from an ad for the Heartland—although the expensive suit and the confident way he wore it suggested otherwise. "I suppose your documentary led to you getting involved tonight."

"Not really," he said, the corner of his eyes crinkling in amusement. "I used to date Tyler."

"Memphis Haines's boyfriend?"

Well, damn. Mentioning the ex's new partner probably didn't qualify as acceptable conversation. Forget flirty mojo, his potential dating skills sucked worse than he'd thought.

"Yes, the very one." Logan casually leaned his elbow on the bar counter. He didn't appear disturbed by the mention of the association. "Tyler's the one who got me interested in doing my latest documentary. So if any more acceptance speeches are in my future, it will require a thank you to my ex," he said with a chuckle.

For the first time since the meet-and-greet began, a genuine smile crept up Ky's face. "Would've been the perfect plan if he'd been out for revenge."

Logan laughed. "That's what I said." He set his empty bottle on the bar and looked as though he'd settled in for a longer chat. "I wasn't interested in any of the other signature drinks. Think I could snag another beer?"

"Coming right up."

Ky turned to open the small refrigerator behind the bar. He should feel pleased Logan wanted to stick around. And he *did*...mostly. Unfortunately, the easygoing interaction with an attractive, phenomenally successful man combined with Ky's total lack of desire for more only served as a reminder of how much he missed Noah.

Heart sinking lower, he grabbed a beer and set the bottle on the counter, another hissing *pop* courtesy of his Leatherman.

"The rugged, manly bottle opener provides the perfect touch," a familiar voice said. "I wanted to—"

Ky looked up to meet Noah's gaze, heart contracting hard, and whatever the guy had been set to say next died, his mouth slightly open. Ky's world narrowed down to a single set of dark brown eyes.

God, he'd missed him. His smile and his quirky ways. His irreverent mouth and the way he made Ky feel inside. He should say something. But what?

Met any good therapists lately?

Have you missed me?

Or maybe: *Have you blown anyone else lately?*

Fuck. What a disheartening thought.

Noah's Adam's apple rose and fell in a hard swallow. "Logan," he said, turning to the filmmaker. "Good to see you, as always." He clapped the blond on the shoulder, his smile strained. "Although I think the bidding is about to start?"

An uncomfortable pause followed during which Logan looked as though he were about to argue the need to leave.

"All right," the man finally replied. "Good luck with the bidding." He accepted the new beer from Ky and shot him a wink. "I'm sure you'll fetch a hefty price."

The blond headed back into the crowd, and the lull in the conversation left Ky dying to knock back a six-pack of beer. But getting down that catwalk without throwing up was going to be difficult enough.

At this point smilin' might be asking too much.

"The suit looks...the suit looks incredible," Noah said. "You look good, too." Along with the playful tone and the awkward, stilted smile, his eyes were achingly sincere. "Having a good time?"

Ky bit back a scoff and rubbed the tight muscles along the back of his neck, attempting a light tone. Apparently serious talk wasn't on the table. "I suppose I have you to thank for the category names?"

"Mostly," he said. "Dylan provided the perfect bi designation."

"Yeah, well..." He dropped his arm to his side, rapidly running out of ideas for conversation. "I'm pretty sure the runway idea belongs to you and you alone."

"Of course."

He narrowed his eyes at Noah, burying his want and his longing and the hopelessness in a show of humor. "It's like you were trying to make tonight as difficult as possible." He paused and then realized how that might sound, his words tumbling out. "For the contestants, I mean."

"Your lack of confidence hurts."

"Exactly how am I supposed to walk naturally on that narrow strip of stage?" he asked.

"Uhm." Noah bit his lip and shot him a weak smile. "By channeling your inner vixen?"

Ky raised an eyebrow dryly and ignored the memories of the man's mouth on him, the surge of heat infiltrating his veins, and the pointless longing. Noah held his gaze for two ticks, during which Ky waffled between railing at the guy to get his act together—to get help *healing*—and saying to hell with it all and jerking him closer for a kiss.

'Cause Ky could do that now. In public. During daylight hours. In part, thanks to the encouragement and support from the man standing on the other side of the bar. The thought left Ky's mouth dry, dying to tell Noah he loved him too hard to let him go.

But the ball—or *balls*, to borrow a phrase from a certain sex-obsessed individual—were now firmly in Noah's court.

"Logan's right." Noah's gaze held his. "I'm sure you'll fetch a nice price," he said with a halfhearted wave at the room around them. "So thanks for your help."

Several seconds passed in silence.

Was that it? Was that all he'd come to say?

Ky's chest grew tight, his accent thicker. "No problem."

The last of his strained grin faded away, and three more awkward beats passed. He'd failed at his task of keeping a confident smile on his face, but with Noah around, always *just* out of emotional reach, the goal had been unrealistic.

Noah frowned. "I just wanted to—" A beeping sound from his watch interrupted, and he briefly glared down at the timer. "Shit. Time to get ready." For a moment he looked as though he were about to tell Ky something important, but then he said, "I'll see you out on stage?"

"Sure."

Ky watched the man head off, his heart a fist in his chest.

He missed Noah and he missed Texas, but he missed Noah *more*. And that would never change. Seeing him again crushed too many vital parts. Clearly there'd be no moving on if Ky stayed in San Francisco. Yep, he definitely needed to get the hell out of town.

Just as soon as he survived the rest of this night.

Chapter Seventeen

Waiting behind the stage's side curtain, Noah stared down at the disappointing text he'd just received. Great, another one of tonight's plans in ruins. First he'd botched his prepared speech to Ky and now this.

Somehow, the evening had managed to go from bad to worse. He'd been mentally picturing himself handling the interaction with Ky with grace and flair.

But, Jesus, who could blame him for flubbing his well-rehearsed lines?

Because Ky, bless his little insane Texas heart, had forgone the dress jeans for a black dress shirt, open at the throat, paired with the slim, two-button gray Versace suit. The one he'd tried on the first time Noah had gone down on him. A gorgeous suit that hugged his broad shoulders, tapered to his narrow waist, and showcased powerful legs that went on forever and ended in a pair of brand new beautiful black Stetsons.

Swear to God those fucking boots...

Noah would happily spend the rest of his life with those boots—and any others the man might decide to wear, muddied or otherwise—parked in his closet or beneath his bed. As long as the owner came with the deal. Unfortunately, the prospect of convincing the man to stay in San Francisco felt further out of reach now than when he'd walked away.

Noah's heart shifted closer to his throat, leaving him feeling short of breath. A hand touched his elbow, startling him out of his chaotic thoughts.

"You ready?" Alec asked.

"Uhh, I..." Fingers tight around his phone and its depressing message, Noah slowly shook his head, his mind swimming and barely breaching the surface for air.

"Noah?" Alec said, blue eyes concerned.

"No," he said. "I'm not ready."

"You've been looking forward to MC'ing this event for over a year."

Had he? Really? He'd laugh at himself if he wasn't so busy trying not to panic.

Noah held up the message for Alec to read. "I just got a text from Destiny's Bitch." And, wow, wasn't her stage name fitting in this scenario? He slid the phone back into his pocket. "She twisted her ankle while performing in a pair of six-inch heels. She isn't coming tonight."

Alec stared at him as though trying to find a link between the drag queen's current mobility troubles and what probably amounted to a pretty distressed look on Noah's face. But Alec didn't know about the plan.

Step one had been to have a meaningful interaction with Ky, and Noah had totally botched that up. And now step two...

"She was supposed to show up and bid on Ky," Noah said.

"Why?"

"For me. As MC, I can't do it myself."

And right now winning a date with the world's hottest surgeon—knowing workaholic Ky, probably the guy's *first* real date as a gay man—felt like Noah's last hope.

"Ah," his friend said, eyes crinkling in understanding. "You remember this is just a fundraiser, right?" He touched Noah's arm in a gesture of comfort as he went on. "The top bidder doesn't actually own the bachelor they win."

"Last year's top bidder is now living with the very guy he took on a date." The sentence ended an octave too high.

"Noah," Alec said in a soothing tone. "You yourself said tonight was all about having fun."

"Fun?" How the hell was he supposed to be having fun? "That was before I'd fallen in love with one of the contestants!"

"Christ," Dylan murmured as he approached, gazing at him as though he were about to explode. "Alec, man, I think you were wrong. He doesn't look okay," he said to his partner before turning to Noah, forehead furrowed in concern. "Are you gonna be okay?"

"Tonight?" Noah asked, the pounding in his chest escalating. "Or for the rest of my life?"

For God's sake, he really needed to pull his big-boy panties on. How else could he convince Ky that he was willing to put in the pain to get better?

Because he had.

He'd spent every Monday, Wednesday, and Friday of the last three miserable weeks cracking open his chest and spewing all his shit at the beyond-patient therapist, who, seriously, was gonna deserve a medal by their one month-versary. Noah was supposed to be working on becoming a capable adult who could handle adult feelings, but the Bachelor Bid—with the now out-of-the-closet, freaking fucking beautiful Ky with his freaking fucking adorable face smiling at another freaking man by the name of Logan—was too much to take.

Thing was, Ky totally deserved the attention and more. He deserved men like documentary makers who lugged around movie cameras that changed the world instead of horrible baggage that made them a pain in the ass to love.

Oh, God.

"Let's just focus on getting through the evening," Dylan said.

"I spoke with Savannah," Alec said. "Apparently the ticket sales were so good that we've already met our housing financial goals. After two years of hard work, you finally did it, Noah. Congratulations."

Congratulations...

Noah blinked and tried to muster some enthusiasm. At one time, getting funding for the temporary housing had meant everything—a service that could have changed Rick's life. Noah was still proud of the accomplishment. But it was no longer everything.

Shit. He briefly rubbed his eyes. Life had been so much simpler in the shallow end.

"Jesus Christ, Noah." Dylan lightly punched him on the shoulder—the mechanic's version of a warm, fuzzy hug. "Now is not the time to fall apart. You're about to go on stage before a huge friggin' crowd," he said, and his partner shot him a *that wasn't helpful* look.

Noah flailed his hand toward the now-empty bar where he'd flubbed his apology earlier. "I was doing okay until...until..."

"Until you saw Ky," Dylan finished for him.

"Exactly."

"I told you the suit would be the end of him," Dylan said to his boyfriend.

"It's just a suit," Alec said dryly.

"Yeah, but this is Noah we're talking about."

"Fair point."

"Boys," Noah interjected. "Can we please focus on averting a potential disaster?" The word ended in an embarrassing half squawk, half squeak—neither of which would sound attractive blaring over the sound system.

His two friends watched him with a growing air of concern.

"Dude, what's the worst that can happen?" Dylan asked.

"What if I look at the cue cards and forget how to read?" he replied, because right now that was feeling like a real possibility. "What if I choke on my own tongue?"

What if I throw myself at Ky on stage and beg him to stay with me in San Francisco forever and he says no?

The Big Declaration always worked in rom-coms, but Ky probably wasn't familiar with that particular rule.

"It's gonna be all right," Dylan said. "I'll stick close by, okay?" He pointed at the podium set up to the far left of the stage. The portable platform included curtains at either end, the perfect place for someone to wait and step in if things went to hell. "I can take over the microphone if need be."

"You'd do that?"

"Abso-fucking-lutely. I've got your back," he said, his voice serious. "I'll always have your back."

Noah's throat burned and his chest felt too tight. "Thanks," he said, sending him a relieved smile.

Thank God for his friends—

"So when you fuck up," Dylan went on, "I'll be right behind you." At Noah's now wide-eyed look, the guy hurried on. "Not that you're going to. Fuck up, that is."

Several seconds passed, the air thick with tension.

Dylan cleared his throat. "I'll go take my place," he said, green gaze steady on his as he adjusted Noah's jacket. "Now...pull yourself together, man." He gave his shoulder one last squeeze before shoving the microphone into his hand. "You're gonna be fine."

Despite the reassuring words, his voice still sounded concerned. Noah watched as his friend left and made his way over to the other side of the stage. Unfortunately, his brain couldn't get beyond the task of fixing his thwarted-by-a-bitchy-universe plans.

Alec turned to face him. "Looks like you're up."

Noah's throat began to close completely.

But his friend continued talking. "Good luck—"

"You have to bid on Ky for me," he blurted out.

Alec looked at him like he'd gone off the deep end. "You want me to what?"

"Historically, the highest bid went to five thousand," he plowed on, the idea now firmly taking hold. "I'm authorizing you to spend fifteen."

"That's not necessary, Noah. We—"

"I need you to." With his free hand, he gripped his friend's coat.

"But I'm not even single—"

"Alec." His fingers dug into the man's defenseless jacket, no doubt wrinkling the lapel. "Either you bid on Ky for me or"—he shoved the microphone at his friend—"you take over as MC."

"Okay, okay," he said soothingly. "I'll bid on him." He handed the mic back before giving him a gentle shove toward the stage, another less-than-convincing smile plastered on his face. "You're going to do great."

Shit, this was going to be a disaster.

~~~***~~~

"Sold, to the persistent hell-on-heels lady for six thousand!" Noah said, managing a smile.

Holy Christballs, the local celebrity had really fetched a fantastic price.

At the last minute, Noah had changed the order of contestants. Initially he'd wanted the TV personality dude to end the night. But putting Ky last meant that, right after he'd been bought, Noah could fall apart.

Genius move.

Another genius idea? Opening the event to bisexuals. The bidding had turned particularly rabid when women were pitted against the men to bid for the right for a dinner date—a friendly, funny, yet fierce bout of one-upmanship, or one-upwo/manship, that had the audience laughing and the money flowing to ridiculously obscene amounts.

Even better, Noah hadn't taken a verbal tumble. Yet. Perhaps tonight wouldn't end as badly as he thought?

A personal disaster probably, but not a public one.

He had five seconds to cling to that belief before Ky stepped on stage and speaking became more difficult.

Noah swallowed. "Last but most definitely not least, Dr. Kyland Davis."

How am I going to get through this?

"A surgeon from Texas, guys," he said, forcing his gaze away from Ky. "He saves lives. He rescues kittens from trees...no, wait. That was the fireman four bachelors ago." Watching the easily amused audience laugh—hooray for alcohol—made the words come easier. "This local hottie is as comfortable in the operating room as he is on the back of a horse."

As the huge projector lit the screen behind him and began to flick through the pictures of Ky, Noah kept his eyes firmly fixed on the crowd. He couldn't stand to see Ky in his scrubs. Or the one of him in the OR. And, whatever happened, Noah absolutely could not look at the picture of the man sitting on the front porch swing in Texas, legs crossed, booted feet propped on the railing.

And...

What was he supposed to be doing? Right, reading. He stared down at the card Ky had put together describing himself—clearly without his sister's help, if the lackluster description meant anything.

"He prefers watching movies at home to going out..."

His voice died out. But, seriously, the man's self-description did him a huge disservice.

Right before Ky turned to take a trip down the catwalk, their gazes met. Ky sent him a reassuring smile, as though sensing his difficulty—because *of course* he would—and Noah made a decision.

He tucked the card into his suit pocket, the notes unnecessary in this instance. "He likes the feeling at the end of a hard day's work," Noah said into the microphone. "He likes slow sunsets, lightning bugs"—a grin crept up Noah's face—"bubble baths...and an honest, no-nonsense life."

And Noah was nothing *but* nonsense. Who wouldn't grow tired of him?

Focus, Noah. Focus.

"I have it on good authority he is a man of integrity," he went on, "as well as—and I'm quoting his sister here—'a loyal, kick-ass older brother.'" Smile growing bigger, he felt like he'd finally hit his stride during this bitch of an endeavor. "Those boots aren't just for show, either—"

A burst of laughter from the crowd cut Noah off. He turned to look up at the huge screen, and the vision hit him like a body slam to the solar plexus.

A picture of a much younger Ky sandwiched between his two laughing sisters, a frown on his face and a sparkly, audacious-to-the-max tiara on his head. The girls couldn't have been more than six or seven years old. In jeans and a T-shirt and, of all things, a laughably too-small purple tutu tied around his waist, Ky looked ridiculous and uncomfortable and adorably perfect all at the same time.

"Okay..." Noah's voice briefly gave out. A mangled mess of emotions fought for superiority as he cleared his throat. "Okay, ladies and gentlemen," he said, refusing to be embarrassed by the husky tone. "If that amazing photo doesn't set every pair of underwear in the audience on fire, nothing will. That was worth the price of admission alone. Don't you think?"

Thank *God* the audience responded with applause, giving him a brief break from the need to speak.

Noah stared as Ky turned at the end of the runway and strode back toward the stage, gaze meeting his again. Despite everything they'd been through, despite all the sex and the life-changing, brutal honesty and their parting of ways—and, holy crap, all the *sex*—Noah sent Ky a *what the hell, big guy?* expression.

Why post the picture here of all places?

Ky responded with a half smile and a sheepish shrug that was the most endearing thing Noah had ever seen.

He gripped the podium and fought back the urge to tackle-hug the man on stage before tying him up and branding him with a big, bold *property of Noah Tanner* mark. Unfortunately, he still had to get through the process of auctioning him off.

"All right, friends," Noah said. "Let's start the bidding at five hundred."

Ky stopped at the midway point of the catwalk, clearly trying to hide his discomfort at being on display.

Three tables back, Alec raised his hand. "Two thousand dollars."

Noah grinned at his friend. Starting high ought to limit the competition—

"Three thousand dollars!" someone called from the left side of the room.

Well...shit, Noah hadn't even had a chance to egg the participants on yet.

"Three thousand," he repeated into the microphone as he searched for the latest bidder in the dim light, his chest tight. When the elusive new guy couldn't be spotted, Noah glanced at his friend. "Do I hear—?"

"Thirty-five hundred," Alec called.

The surge of relief didn't have time to take hold before Noah heard, "Four thousand!"

Fuck.

A third bidder had entered the mix, a twenty-something black-haired guy in the back who looked...super-cute, dammit.

Noah began to sweat.

"Four thousand," he repeated into the mic even as his mind spun. Too fast. The bidding was going *too fast.* "The vision of Dr. Davis in a tiara is worth way more than that." Noah stared hard at Alec. "Do I hear forty-five hundred?"

"Five thousand," Alec responded.

Noah didn't have time to smile at his friend before a "Fifty-five hundred!" came from the black-haired fellow. This was followed immediately from the left by a firm, "Eight thousand!"

What the hell?

That got the audience buzzing, buying Noah some time again. His gaze finally found the second bidder standing off to the side, arms crossed and a determined look on his face: Logan, Tyler's ex.

The smiling blond that had flirted with Ky at the meet-and-greet and had the audacity to be gorgeous and successful, the maker of Oscar-nominated documentaries about Very Important Things.

And very tastefully dressed, damn him.

Noah never should have affectionately dubbed him the boomerang boyfriend back in the day. Because now the affection had *completely* evaporated.

Alec sent Noah a shrug, but he didn't look near enough concerned. "Eleven thousand," his friend called.

Good, Noah was completely on board with—

"Thirty thousand dollars!"

The collective gasps filled the cavernous room, and nearly every person froze mid whatever-the-hell-they-were-doing to stare at the crazy bidder— Logan, the handsome son of a bitch wearing a lopsided grin and a gorgeous black Hugo Boss suit. Someone, somewhere, knocked their glass over onto their plate, the shocked-into-silence room briefly filling with a *clang.*

Thirty thousand dollars?

The man clearly intended to outbid everyone.

Noah managed to stutter out a few words. "That's... That's..."

Despicable.

Evil.

And who the hell did this guy think he was? And what all did he *want* from Ky for that much money? Alec looked as shell-shocked as the rest of the crowd. When he turned his gaze to Noah, he raised his hands, palms up, in a gesture of defeat.

But—

"Sold!" Dylan called as he appeared from behind. He then leaned down to speak into the microphone still clutched in Noah's bloodless fingers. "Sold, for thirty thousand dollars."

The words jump-started Noah's heart again and triggered a thunderous wave of applause dwarfed only by the pounding in Noah's chest.

"Thanks for coming, folks," Dylan continued in the mic, voice loud and clear over the continued clapping. He gently pried Noah's fingers free from the microphone before going on. "Plenty of food and drinks left, so...enjoy. And have a good night."

The applause increased in intensity just before the guests began to stir, standing and milling about, the clapping slowly replaced by the buzz of a hundred different conversations. Noah couldn't move. He'd just failed again.

Plan B had gone down like a flaming house of cards.

"Hey," Dylan said, lightly nudging him with an elbow, "just go talk to the dude."

Yes, because there were so many things Noah wanted to know, like why Ky had let Savannah put up that picture and why he'd chosen the suit and was there any hope for them at all or had Noah screwed things up beyond repair?

He wasn't sure he wanted to know the answer to the last.

"Go get 'em, tiger," Dylan repeated as he gently pushed him in the direction of Ky, who'd just left the stage.

The sight of Ky heading off finally spurred Noah into action. He hopped off the platform and began to weave his way through the throng of people. Unfortunately, Ky was getting farther away instead of closer.

Do something, Noah.

"Even I've never donned a tutu," Noah called out, and the man stopped ten feet away and turned to face him, his beautiful eyes guarded. Oh, God. Noah felt stripped bare, people streaming around them. "Savannah was right. Purple is definitely your color."

Ky huffed out a breath, and his forehead developed furrows that looked part embarrassed and part fond. For Noah? Or Ky's sister? Or maybe that was just relief the night was over and he could leave.

Leave.

The panic building all evening finally crested, washing over him like a tsunami and leaving him floundering.

Because, my God, he wanted those frowny fond looks directed at him every day for the rest of his life.

"Sooo..." Feigning a casualness he didn't feel, Noah brushed his hair back, fingers less than steady, and stepped closer. "Apparently someone who knows me pretty well thinks I need to stop drifting aimlessly through life."

"I never said those words."

"True, but you could have. I"—he was forced to step to the right, letting a group of women pass, gawking curiously as they went— "I decided to put my up-to-this-point useless college degree to good use working as a freelance grant writer." Pride swelled, a strangely unfamiliar feeling he'd just now begun to identify. "I wrote a proposal and actually went for an interview."

Ky stared at him, his mouth gaping slightly before lifting in the corner. "Good for you."

"Even more unbelievable, they hired me."

"Not hard to believe at all."

A pleasurable heat filled his face, and Noah tried to shrug it off as he went on. "It's not the glamorous life of a scrub-wearing hottie surgeon. And the salary is dismal, not that I care. But the only difference between what I used to do and what I do now will be utilizing my skills with the written word, not just the oral persuasion kind."

Ky's mouth gave a wry twist. "You do have a talented tongue."

Noah tried to smile. People kept streaming past, chattering, some ignoring them completely, others eying them curiously, and good God, a less public place to fillet his heart open would have been nice.

And perhaps the filleting was taking too long.

"I have to talk to Logan, I guess. To make arrangements." Ky rubbed the back of his neck, his gaze shifting away. "And then, well, I should probably get going."

"Wait." Noah's arm shot forward of its own volition. And the next thing he knew, he was clutching Ky's sleeve. "I...I started seeing a therapist."

"You did?"

"I did."

Five seconds ticked by.

"And?" Ky asked.

"And she told me it was time to stop focusing on fixing the world and fix myself instead."

Ky didn't move for several seconds. Sadly, now that Noah wasn't struggling on stage, the man's expression seemed to have reverted back to a vague, hard-to-interpret frown.

The pressure in Noah's chest increased, and he blurted out the first thing that popped into his head. "The therapist is actually quite pleasant. Although some days it's difficult concentrating in her presence," he said. "Her business attire... Well, let's just say your belt buckle is an iconic fashion piece in comparison—" He stopped babbling and forced himself to start discussing the Important Things. "I paid her good money for the same advice you gave me for free." He sent Ky a self-deprecating smile. "She told me I need to stop denying myself the things I want."

He'd spent years doing exactly that, and so far, the guilt and shame hadn't eased one bit. So why shouldn't he try?

For Ky, he could.

"Denying yourself the things you want, huh?" Ky said.

"I know, right?" he said. "Obviously she's never seen my overflowing closets."

Ky's grin looked strained, but, hey, it wasn't a frown. "She sounds like a smart lady."

"She is," he said, swiping a damp palm down his jacket. "Except for those god-awful, boxy gray suits and—dammit, why did you let Savannah put up that photo?"

Ky stared at him for a moment before focusing his gaze on the masses filtering around them and out the exit. When he turned his gaze back to Noah, the guarded expression on his face set him on edge. "Because I wanted to help you achieve your bucket list."

His bucket list.

As a gift to make Noah happy? Or something to use as a good-bye?

The thought left his chest with an ache too big to hold.

"Do I get a copy?" Noah asked.

"Hell no."

"Not even as a negotiating tactic?"

The pause lasted long enough for Noah to feel as though he'd made a mistake.

"Depends." Ky slipped his hands into his pant pockets. "What are we negotiating for?"

For the first time, Ky appeared ready for a real discussion.

"Well..." Noah coughed, trying to clear his heart from his throat. Time to go big or go home. "The rest of my life?"

A wall of silence shot up between them, and Ky looked too stunned to move.

For Heaven's sake, don't stop talking now, Noah.

"I've spent so many years hating myself that I couldn't..." Noah closed his eyes hoping he didn't look as raw as he felt. "I just couldn't understand that you didn't feel the same way. After finding out, you know, about what I'd done...and what I'd let happen to me." He pressed both palms to his eyes, pushing the memories of the assault aside. "I still can't wrap my head around the fact you don't, really." He dropped his hands, and if Ky so much as blinked, Noah knew he'd collapse in a dramatic heap. "It's hard for me to imagine you looking at me and seeing something worthwhile. Worth loving. I'm working on it, though."

Ky frowned. "Noah—"

"Wait." He held up a hand and plowed ahead. He needed Ky to *understand*. "I'll probably always be three different brands of fucked up—"

"Excuse me," a masculine voice interrupted.

Logan.

Evil, blond-headed, thirty-thousand-dollar Logan handed an envelope to Ky. "Here."

"What's this?"

"A gift," Logan said, his cheeky grin growing bigger. "From your friends."

"A gift?" Ky slid his finger under the envelope and broke the seal.

"The card is an invitation, authorizing the holder to one date. With you." Logan jerked his head in the direction of the exit where Dylan, Alec, Tyler, and Memphis stood in a group, every one of them laughing. "They pooled their money and told me to keep bidding on you until I won."

Noah blinked against the sudden rush of gratitude. Although, seriously, couldn't Alec have told him about the plans before they'd started instead of letting him sweat?

Up on stage, of all places?

Those wonderful bastards.

"They argued about who to give it to, you or Noah." Logan gave a shrug. "Eventually they decided you needed to choose your date yourself."

"They're...uh..." Ky swallowed, Adam's apple rising and falling. "They're generous friends."

"Yes, they are," Logan said with a smile, and then he turned and walked away.

Ky continued to stare at the printed card as though unsure what to do next. And, heaven help him, Noah had too many suggestions to share: take him to dinner, seduce him with a paring knife and then fuck him senseless, and, most importantly, hold on to him for keeps.

Ky adopted a thoughtful frown. "I didn't really wanna go on a dinner date with someone I don't know," he said, holding out the card in Noah's direction. "Probably wouldn't have ended well."

Heart pounding, Noah sucked in a breath, feeling the first rush of hope. "You *do* have a pretty scary grumpy face," he said, accepting the gift. He looked up at Ky's furrowed forehead of concentration with an expression he knew reeked of affection and every other little positive emotion the man brought out. Fingers clumsy, Noah gently pushed up on Ky's right temple in an attempt to ease the man's expression. "And those Eyebrows of Impending Doom are—"

Ky clasped the back of Noah's neck and dragged him closer with such surprising force that Noah tripped over his own feet, face-planting against Ky's solid chest with an *oof.*

All in all, not a particularly smooth move on Noah's part but definitely the right one.

Thank *God.*

He pressed his nose against the hard plane of muscle and wrapped his arms around Ky's middle, loving, as usual, how the man's size made him feel. A constant that could get Noah through the tough road ahead with his therapist. He knew the hard times weren't completely behind him, but he was headed in the right direction now.

For Ky, he'd gladly take every painful step.

"Now that you're out, I assumed you'd move back to Texas," Noah managed to mumble, lips smooshed against Ky. "Like I was saying before, I'll always be three different brands of fucked up. Are you sure you wouldn't rather go back to Oak Hollows?"

For chrissake, Noah. What the hell are you saying?

Apparently, letting the self-torture thing go was a work in progress. His heart pumped too hard, and he pressed his mouth harder to Ky's chest, hoping to stifle any more ridiculously self-sabotaging suggestions.

"With you is the only place I've ever one hundred percent belonged," Ky said.

Oh.

That's just...

Christ.

Noah blinked to clear his vision. "I think my eyelids are sweating."

Ky chuckled, the sound vibrating beneath Noah's face.

"Or maybe I'm just over-hydrated," he said as he leaned more of his weight against Ky. This sentimental stuff was exhausting. But he inhaled a rejuvenating breath, enjoying the scent of mahogany tinged with almonds and vanilla. "Thirty thousand dollars for our first date," he mused. He rose on his tiptoes to press his face against the warm skin of Ky's neck. "Apparently I have very expensive taste."

"Yeah, well, our friends are on their way over," Ky murmured.

"They all wanted to go out for a drink after."

Noah pulled back to look up at Ky, keeping his arms around his waist.

Ky's tiny frown looked adorable. "Think they'd mind if we rescheduled?"

"You have something else in mind for tonight?" He struggled to maintain a serious expression, a sense of joy and peace sinking deep. "A bubble bath, maybe? Shopping for a new tiara?" His mouth slanted sideways into a suggestive grin. "Searching for the perfect pair of handcuffs?"

"Are you always going to be this needy?" he asked with a smile.

"I'm not needy, I'm *want-y*. Which reminds me, you were right about a lot of things but totally wrong about the whole orgasm-denial accusation." Ignoring Ky's eye roll, Noah stepped back and poked the guy in the chest. "That was all about self-*indulgence*, not self-torture. Which means more of those mind-blowing moments should definitely be on the table for the future. And next time? I get to—"

Ky leaned forward, planting his shoulder against Noah's belly, and Noah let out another *oof*. The next thing he knew, the world tilted forward and his upper half was left dangling down the man's back.

Noah stared at Ky's ass. "Holy shit," he wheezed out, breathless from the solid body pressing on his lower abdomen. "I guess 'next time' is going to happen sooner than I thought."

Ky headed for the exit, the *clunk* of brand new boots ringing against the floor, the pretty leather moving at a determined clip.

"In a hurry?" Tyler said, amusement in his voice.

Short of breath, Noah wheezed out a laugh as he was carried through a group consisting of...well, it was hard to see from upside down. He thought he saw Savannah with his friends, in addition to Julissa, Memphis's ex-wife, who was smiling and holding hands with Logan.

Seriously? How had Noah missed that bit of hookup news? He must have been more distracted lately than he thought. And imagine how amusing it would be if Memphis's ex-wife wound up marrying Tyler's former boyfriend.

"Helluva a first-date gift card," Ky said to the group as he carried Noah past. "Thanks."

"Memphis kicked in ninety-five percent of the cost," Dylan said.

"Most entertaining donation *ever,*" Memphis replied, and then jabbed his thumb in the mechanic's direction. "But it was his idea."

"You're welcome," his best friend said with amusement. As the distance between them grew, the guy raised his voice to be heard. "I assume this means you two wanna take a rain check on drinks with the rest of us?"

"Dinner," Ky called out without glancing back. "My place tomorrow night at six."

As Noah continued to dangle from a very broad shoulder, he sent his friends a goofy grin and a wave. Dinner sounded like fun, except...

"Wait," Noah said with a finger poke to Ky's delectably tight ass. "I guess this means we need to go shopping for furniture. People will need a place to sit. And your plastic-tote coffee table has got to be replaced."

"I'll freely admit I'm crazy kinds of in love with you..." came the reply.

Sweet Jesus.

Eyes burning, Noah blinked hard, concentrating on the ass cheeks of glorious proportions as his boyfriend—fuck yeah, *boyfriend*—went on.

"But I draw the line at another shopping expedition," Ky went on dryly.

"Not even if I promise to go down on you in a dressing room again?"

The brand new Stetsons stumbled briefly before picking up their pace, and Noah's heart surged in satisfaction. The man's voice was gruff, but Noah could hear the smile in his tone when he replied.

"I could be persuaded."

Epilogue

One Year Later.

Noah stood on the sidewalk outside the newly christened four-story Rick Adams House while bright sunshine tempered the cool air smelling of freshly cut grass. The ribbon-cutting ceremony had just ended. After years of hard work, transitional housing was now available to the clinic's neediest patients. He'd expected the fierce sense of pride and accomplishment. The lack of melancholy, however, was a surprise.

One lifetime goal achieved, one more to go. Speaking of...

Noah's stomach gave a nervous ping as his boyfriend approached.

In jeans, boots, and a black leather jacket, Ky hooked an arm around Noah and stared up at the red brick building. "You done good."

"Thanks." He snuggled closer, seeking out the warmth, hard muscle, and broad shoulders that had seen him through some pretty shitty times—a year's worth of counseling that, amazingly enough, had actually helped. "I'm not going to lie, though. A lot of hard work went into getting here."

And he wasn't just referring to the opening. Now was the perfect time to address his next very important goal. Or maybe he'd waited too long, his chance long gone.

Please don't let it be too late.

"Well," Ky said, interrupting the disturbing thought, "you definitely deserved a prize for a job well done."

"I know, right?"

"Except your choice of reward was unexpected."

"How so?"

Ky's lips quirked. "I figured you'd request something sexual."

Heat shot up Noah's limbs. "That does sound like something I'd do. But I can't get *too* predictable. That would be boring. Anyway"—he glanced at the two motorcycles, Ky's gift, parked on the street directly behind them—"I think I'll enjoy riding my prize almost as much as I enjoy riding you." He sent him a smirky smile. "*Almost.*"

Ky rolled his eyes and then tightened the arm around his shoulders, dragging him closer for a kiss. And not one of those PG, public-approved kind. Firm lips slid across Noah's, as though seeking the heat from his mouth. All he could do was hang on and give in. A sharp nip of his lower lip, and a shocky thrum of pleasure joined the fire in his veins.

God, even after a year together, his boyfriend still lit him up like the fucking sun.

When Ky pulled back, eyes burning bright, Noah fisted the man's shirt, savoring the lingering buzz and feeling torn: torn between dragging him back to his mouth or using said mouth to share his next brilliant plan. The idea was risky, sure...

Say something. Say something now, you coward.

"I'm gonna see if Sierra needs any help with Rick," Ky said. He gave the top of Noah's head a good-bye kiss and then headed across the green grass of the front lawn.

Noah's euphoric bubble popped.

Shit. Another missed opportunity.

Then again, procrastination had provided him the perfect opportunity to ogle his hot boyfriend's very hot ass. An excellent consolation prize dipped in the perfect coating of adorable. He watched little Rick patting down Memphis and Tyler's pockets for organic gummy bears—the little guy had made a game of searching them for the ever-present prize—before joyfully giving Ky's knees a toddler-sized bear hug. Savannah laughed as the one-year-old squealed in delight as he was lifted by his uncle and plopped onto his shoulders.

The godfather gig definitely had its perks: all the fun of raising kids with zero responsibilities—well, except for their Wednesday night babysitting commitment. Not to mention the ridiculously melty things Noah's heart did at the sight of Ky with Rick. But where were his parents? As chairman of today's festivities, Alec was finishing up his duties inside. Dylan, however, was nowhere to be seen.

A familiar male voice from behind answered the question.

"Those are some kick-ass bikes."

Noah turned and spied Dylan, who was busy staring at the two motorcycles. "Thank you," he said with a grin, knowing his best friend's next move would be to have a coronary.

Dylan didn't disappoint, green eyes wide, his expression apoplectic.

"One of these is yours?" Dylan sounded skeptical.

"Yep. Ky bought himself the red one. He bought me the black." Pride seeped into his voice as he gazed at his bike, clean, stylish, and beautifully finished. "An Indian, like yours. Except it's brand new while yours is decrepit—"

"No, a classic. The word is *classic*."

"—and old," he continued without pause. "This baby has a 111 cubic inch engine, six-speed transmission, and—even more importantly—a super comfy seat," he finished with a smile.

"Dude," Dylan whispered in awe. "She's sweet." The man ran a reverent hand across the shiny chrome handlebar and up the plush leather seat. "After all these years of refusing to ride along with me, why'd you finally buy one?"

Noah rubbed his neck and decided to share reason number two because reason number one was too embarrassing.

"In celebration of today's accomplishment," Noah said. "And because I got tired of being left behind when Ky borrowed one of yours and went riding with you and Alec. Besides," Noah said, crossing his arms and deciding to share reason number three, "I want to come along on your charity poker run this year. Memphis and Tyler are participating this time, and I refuse to be left behind like I'm some annoying little kid."

His friend, bless him, only sent an *I'm gonna let that one slide without comment* look in response.

"Pretty ambitious for a dude who can't even drive a stick shift," Dylan said. "I'm surprised your safety-obsessed boyfriend, otherwise known as Dr. Let-me-install-the-car-seat-'cause-you'll-do-it-wrong-and-kill-my-nephew, went along with your idea."

"Uhm..." Noah rubbed his jaw. "I might have let him assume I'm a more accomplished rider than I am. Being your best friend helped make the assumption plausible. But I think he's starting to get suspicious."

"How so?"

"My shifting isn't exactly...smooth." He tried not to flush at the understatement.

Dylan's lips twitched, as though holding back a chuckle. Years ago the man had laughed himself silly at Noah's fumbling attempts as Rick had valiantly taught him the basics of driving a motorcycle. The memory seemed to descend upon them both at the same time.

"Yeah, well"—his friend grinned as he stared at the plaque on the door of the brick building, the words *Dedicated to the Memory of Rick Adams* etched in the brass—"Rick would be really happy for you. About Ky, I mean."

Would he? Noah felt certain the answer was *yes*. Emotion warmed his chest, and he smiled, grateful for the hard-won ability to focus on the happy memories that, for a while, had been lost to him.

In a way, therapy had given him his old boyfriend back. The ability to remember all the good, without being overwhelmed by the bad, was a gift he'd never take for granted.

During the companionable pause that followed, they watched Alec emerge from the building. The delighted squeal from his son came with some serious wiggling, and, with a laugh, Ky set him down. The toddler tackle-hugged Alec, who pretended to lose his balance and fell to the ground. The loud smacking kiss the toddler gave his dad could be heard from ten feet away.

"Hunh," Noah murmured. "I think he'd be happy for both of us."

Dylan stared at his family with a fond expression. "I think he would, too."

"Anyway," Noah went on, "I might need you to give me a few riding lessons on the sly."

"No problem." He glanced at Noah and cocked his head in that stubborn way of his. "As long as you tell me the real reason you decided to get a bike."

Dammit, Observant Dylan always appeared at the most inconvenient times.

"I gave you the real reason," Noah lied.

All he got in response was a skeptical eye roll.

"Fine." Noah sighed, realizing resistance was a wasted effort. "Ky wanted to buy one but didn't have anywhere to keep it. So I told him he could have my extra parking spot at the condo."

"And?"

Heat filled Noah's face, despite the crisp air. "I thought two motorcycles parked in a single parking spot would be a good way to ease him into the idea of moving in with me."

Dylan stared at him, ratcheting up Noah's self-conscious feeling by a hundred degrees, before finally speaking. "That's a big fucking deal, Noah," he said, expression serious. "Congratulations, dude."

"Yeah?" A nervous laugh escaped. "Except I have to ask him first. And then he has to say yes."

"He'll say yes."

"I'm not so sure." Dammit, verbalizing his fears out loud, like his therapist had advised, didn't always make them easier. Sometimes words just lent them credence. "He mentioned moving in together eleven months ago, but I told him no." He rubbed his chest in a defensive gesture. "I mean, a man shouldn't come out of the closet one day and then move in with his boyfriend the next."

"And he's had a year to think it over. So what's the problem now?"

Noah frowned at the memory. "Back then, he wasn't upset with me for saying no."

"So?"

"So he hasn't mentioned it again since!"

"Maybe he's waiting on you."

Noah closed his eyes and inhaled a breath. "What if he says no?"

"He's not gonna say no." But his hesitant tone suggested he had some doubts as well.

Maybe Ky had grown tired of Noah's shenanigans. Maybe that explained why Ky hadn't revisited the idea of living together. And if the man turned him down, everything would change. And Noah had been so happy this last year, seriously happy, not just a *lying to everyone including himself* kind of happy. And he wasn't sure if he could go back.

To before.

Dylan's voice broke through the depressing thoughts. "Your boyfriend's headed this way."

The words set Noah's heart pounding in that sickening way he got when he drank too much tequila. Which, admittedly, he didn't do much anymore. Except for when they'd celebrated obtaining the accompanying grant that would keep the Rick Adams House serving the community for years to come. Noah had done that in his official capacity as grant writer—which he fucking excelled at, if he did say so himself. But now he had to ask his boyfriend if he wanted to—

Dylan gave his shoulder a squeeze. "Just ask him already." His friend pivoted to join the group on the lawn.

Oh, God.

Noah's stomach lurched, and he reached for his friend's sleeve. "Wait—"

Dylan dodged his hand. "Hey, Doc," he said to Ky as he approached. "Your boyfriend has something he wants to ask you." He sent Noah a *don't friggin weasel out now* look. "Something *important*."

Ky tipped his head. "Now I'm intrigued."

"Me, too." The glare Noah sent his best friend lacked any heat, but, Jesus, Dylan was now walking away, deserting him in his hour of need. "I try never to say anything important."

Unfortunately, the inane statement was met with silence, his boyfriend patiently waiting with an expectant expression. Which meant it was still Noah's turn to speak.

Christ.

Noah watched Sierra and Savannah—and Savannah's fiancé, an adorable guy too sweet and sincere for their worldly wise crowd—referee as Tyler and Memphis argued which was the best flavor of gummy bear. Alec and Dylan passed their son between them while making smart-alecky observations about the debate. And heaven help him, Noah wanted that domestic bliss, too. Well, the adult part anyway, like coming home from work to Ky in the kitchen. Or kissing his boyfriend good-bye when he left for his shift at the hospital. He just needed to summon the courage to ask.

No risk, no reward.

Noah cleared his throat, his pulse picking up its pace. "I was thinking maybe...sometime..." Good God, a heart attack felt like a real possibility. "I was hoping that you would park more than your motorcycle in my garage."

Ky stared at him with the frown that represented confusion. "Is that a sexual innuendo?"

Noah groaned in frustration. His mouth and his slutty ways were his own worst enemy. "No," he said. "This isn't a sex-pectation on my part." He rubbed his chin, feeling like an idiot. "Move in. With me."

Every breath felt like trying to suck in oxygen through wet concrete. "Please."

Ky sent him a small smile. "Okay."

The simple answer didn't register, and Noah waited for the conditional-use clause. "That's it?" he finally asked. "That's all you have to say?"

"Yep," Ky said. "I reckon it is."

"Christ," Noah muttered. He stepped forward and wrapped his arms around the chest that made the world's most perfect pillow, his heart rate easing. "I got myself all worked up for nothing."

Ky's grin was evident in his voice. "You were the one who insisted I needed to be free to 'sow some wild oats' after I came out."

"I didn't want you to feel like you missed out."

"And I appreciate the sentiment. But"—Ky shrugged, arms steady around Noah—"I already had everything I needed."

"Well...damn," he said. "If I'd known that, I would have selfishly asked you to move in ages ago."

"That's okay." Ky kissed the top of his head and pulled him closer, and Noah could hear the sincerity in his boyfriend's tone as the man went on. "You were worth the wait."

~~~ The End ~~~

About the Author

By day, River works as a (mostly) mild mannered physician in a remote Alaskan town and has accumulated the wacky stories that come with the job. At night, her inner badass comes out to play. River likes to read and write edgy books that contain varying levels of humor and plenty of hot, steamy sex between two hunky men.

Word-of-mouth is important for any author to succeed. If you enjoyed the book, please consider leaving a review where you purchased it, or on Goodreads, even if it's only a line or two; it would make all the difference and would be very much appreciated.

Coming up next from River Jaymes:
Bad Mood Rising
Men of Alaska - Book 1

Lunar, Alaska has a deadly secret.
Five years ago, Jacob Tyler's boyfriend was murdered and the residents of the quirky town of Lunar, Alaska—with its even quirkier inhabitants—are convinced he's guilty. All the investigation definitively proves is that his boyfriend had been a cheating dirtbag, and Jacob refuses to be driven from the only home he's ever known. These days he trusts no one, so he's fine with his isolated life in the